About the author

JEAN STUBBS, the daughter of a
university lecturer, was born in Lancashire
and educated at Manchester High School
and Manchester College of Art. She now
lives in Wimbledon and claims that she
wrote her first novel on the Underground
on the way to work. She is the successful
author of several novels and of some
non-fiction works.

Editorial adviser: Julia Watson

An Unknown Welshman

JEAN STUBBS

A novel based on the early life of
Henry Tudor, Earl of Richmond,
later King Henry VII of England,
from 1457 to 1486

SPHERE BOOKS LIMITED
30/32 Gray's Inn Road, London WC1X 8JL

First published in Great Britain in 1972 by Macmillan London Ltd
© Jean Stubbs 1972
First Sphere Books edition 1973

To the memory of my father
JOSEPH HIGHAM (1889 - 1956)
with my love

TRADE
MARK

Set in Intertype Baskerville

Printed in Great Britain by
Hazell Watson & Viney Ltd
Aylesbury, Bucks

ISBN 0 7221 8211 2

ACKNOWLEDGEMENTS

My thanks go first to Major Kenneth Adams for saying 'Now Henry Tudor had a very interesting early life!' and so beginning the whole venture. The Borough Librarian of Merton, Mr E. J. Adsett, F.L.A., Mr Gordon Richards of the Wimbledon Park Branch, and their staff, surpassed even former efforts by producing a legion of books from all over the country for my research. The British Museum has filled inevitable gaps, and given me hours of opportunity for quiet study. Mr Laurence Nobes of Anglesey appointed himself researcher for much of the Welsh background, both giving and lending books. Miss Josephine Pullein-Thompson enlightened my ignorance on medieval horses. Wyatt Rawson produced information on a number of subjects, from Welsh myths to medieval costume. Miss Audrey Williamson not only lent but personally annotated books on medieval music, and offered her own treatise on Richard III for my interest. And no doubt I owe some gratitude to chance, for being Lancastrian born and bred and having a grandmother whose maiden name was Alice Maud Owen, which made sure whose side *I* was on.

The Houses of Lancaster and York

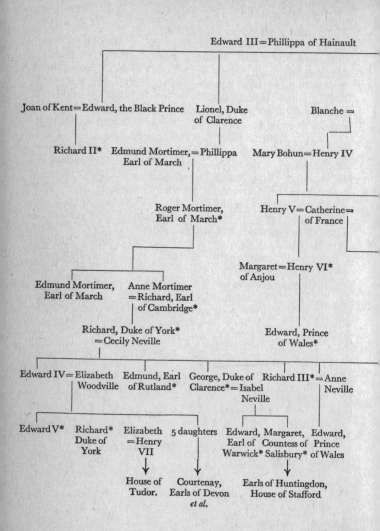

Edward III = Phillippa of Hainault

Joan of Kent = Edward, the Black Prince   Lionel, Duke of Clarence   Blanche =

Richard II*   Edmund Mortimer, Earl of March = Phillippa   Mary Bohun = Henry IV

Roger Mortimer, Earl of March*   Henry V = Catherine = of France

Margaret = Henry VI* of Anjou

Edmund Mortimer, Earl of March   Anne Mortimer = Richard, Earl of Cambridge*

Edward, Prince of Wales*

Richard, Duke of York* = Cecily Neville

Edward IV = Elizabeth Woodville   Edmund, Earl of Rutland*   George, Duke of Clarence* = Isabel Neville   Richard III* = Anne Neville

Edward V*   Richard* Duke of York   Elizabeth = Henry VII   5 daughters   Edward, Earl of Warwick*   Margaret, Countess of Salisbury*   Edward, Prince of Wales

House of Tudor.   Courtenay, Earls of Devon *et al.*   Earls of Huntingdon, House of Stafford

Killed in battle, executed or murdered.

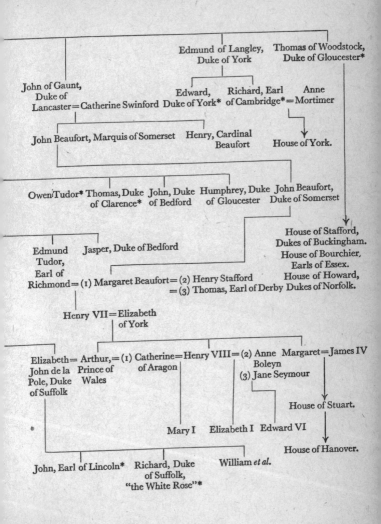

An unknown Welshman, whose father I never knew,
nor hym personally sawe!

King Richard III
speaking of the Earl of Richmond

FOREWORD

Catherine of Valois, the young widow of King Henry V, fell in love with and secretly married her courtier, Owen Tudor of Anglesey, descendant of the Welsh King Cadwaladr. Of that union came four children, Edmund of Richmond, Jasper of Pembroke, Owen, and Margaret who lived but a brief time.

After Catherine's death, the English summoned Owen Tudor and imprisoned him. His only fault was to have won the heart of a queen of England.

But King Henry VI, son of Queen Catherine's first marriage, pardoned Owen Tudor and gave him money from his privy purse, watching over his children and saying that these were his half brothers. And he put them in the charge of discreet persons to be raised according to their rank.

CONTENTS

PART ONE

THE STAR OF OWEN

1457–71

Beware of Walys, Criste Jhesu must us kepe
That it make not oure childeis childe to wepe

> The Libell of English Policye
> c. 1436

CHAPTER ONE

A fire has been kindled in the land from Cynan,
a yellow-tipped flickering flame to Owen
of the blood of the South.
Under a cloak comes a leader,
And he that we name is the second Harry . . .
Secure for us is the star of Owen.

The Patrick Ode
Dafydd Llwyd, fifteenth century

They had built the walls of Pembroke Castle to a mighty
thickness so that they could not be battered down; and set
them on forty feet of sheer rock that could not be scaled.
They had used the sea as their defender, to compass three
sides of the fortress at high water and protect it with a marsh
of slime and ooze at the ebb. On the fourth side they had
dug a dry ditch and planted it with stakes. They had set
three iron gates in the walls and flanked them with six pro-
jecting towers, in one of which ran a spring of fresh water.
They had stretched two bridges, like frail arms, from the
promontory to the land, where they could be watched. And
this watching was built into the castle and the town, so that
they were as one great eye from which nothing on sea or
land was hidden for many miles. And within the embracing
walls the gatehouse stood on a fair green sward between its
drum-towers, and guarded the inner ward. And within this
ward the cylindrical keep reared its seventy-five foot column
of limestone, which even in the weakest part was seven feet
thick and in other parts up to twenty feet thick, and had
four storeys – and each storey full of eyes – and a domed
roof of stone.

So Arnolfe of Montgomery, second son of the first Earl of
Shropshire and Arundell, had begun its building in the reign
of William Rufus, when the Christian world was almost
eleven hundred years old. Here had the valiant Strongbow
ruled as Earl of Pembroke for over three decades, and others
after him. Earls in name and deed, answerable to no man
but themselves in their own territory, sprigs of royalty,
mighty lords. And the castle stood through blasts of tem-

pest and sudden lightning and storm, and the weathercock turns of fate and state : impregnable upon the rock's back. Cold and grey and steadfast as the sea that broke upon the wild coast. Barbarous as the country that surrounded it. Wild and desolate as the gulls that cried and wheeled above its walls. Stood in the mailed grip of the Normans, in the flowering revival of Wales, through the dream of Llewelyn the Great and its shattering, through the rise of Owain Glyndŵr and the destruction that followed it; and three and a half centuries old still stood in readiness, on the Eve of St Agnes. The twenty-eighth day of January, 1457.

Wind whipped across the creek of Pennar, clawing and buffeting the battlements, sending icy shafts whistling through every aperture, and howling like a thousand warriors. It rattled the drawbridge chains, tore out the flames of torches, and brought the blood to the watchmen's cheeks so that they muttered 'Jesu have mercy on an honest soldier this winter night!' and were not answered. While within the walls of a little room in the outer ward another siege of nature neared its conclusion, for good or ill, as Margaret Tudor, Countess of Richmond, laboured over her first child.

Jasper Tudor, Earl of Pembroke, sat in his high carved chair on one side of the hearth, and the Welsh bard Robin Ddu sat on a stool on the other side. The one had ceased to sing and the other to listen, as the feast of St Agnes dragged on and they awaited the birth. The soldiers were as silent as they could be, and the servants as noiseless, but the logs in the brazier crackled and spat as the tempest reached long fingers down the chimney and harried the flames into curious shapes.

'Strange portents, my lord,' said Robin Ddu, seeing people struggle and form in the fire.

He bent his thin dark face over the strings of his harp and sang softly to himself, trying out words. He was older by many years than the young earl opposite, and versed in misfortune. A true Welshman, he forgot and forgave nothing, neither an insult to himself nor an injury to his country. And having the gift of prophecy, a certain wild courage – though he was no fighting man – and the ability to reach the hearts of his audience, he was welcomed by the great lords in their halls from Anglesey to Pembroke. There he sang of old glories and the coming of the new Arthur foretold by Merlin. Gifted and tender, fanciful and proud, scholarly, bitter, and inclined to finger his hurts lest they be forgotten or overlooked.

'Hard times, my lord,' he said suddenly, as a log cascaded into the hearth and diverted his thoughts. 'Hard times when a Welsh bard is served by his patron as I was served by Griffith ap Nicholas. For when I sang to him scarce a year ago, and prophesied that a scion of the house of Owen would wear the crown of England, he gave me a jewel from his cap. For your elder brother, Edmund Earl of Richmond, had taken a fair and goodly maid to wife. And I foresaw the time when the red dragon should triumph over the Saxons, and the red rose rule in splendour.

'But your brother was captured three short months after, in the castle of Carmarthen, and he at war until then so that his wife's arms offered him brief solace. Then spake the great Griffith from a proud stomach. "Why, Robin, dark Robin," he quoth, "you are a flickering fellow and over-busy with your tongue! What is your prophecy worth now? For Owen Tudor has but three sons, and the third that bears his name embraces the Holy Church, Jasper of Pembroke is wedded to his sword and shield, and now Edmund of Richmond is taken."

' "Mercy, my lord,' says I. "Perchance the Lady Margaret is yet with child."

'But he cast me into his dungeon, which, my lord, stinks worse than any sty and lodges more rats than straw — and the straw is damp!

' "Christ keep me," says I, for no man says other, and for a time I languished.

'And then, my lord, my patron came to me smiling and saying, "Why, good Robin, now is the Countess of Richmond indeed heavy with child, and she may yet bear a son that shall be scion of the house of Owen, and mayhap *he* shall one day rule upon the throne of England!" "God save you, my good lord," quoth I, taking leave of the rats. "Get you to Pembroke!" says he. "And sing to the lady that she may give safe birth in right goodwill, upheld by the vision that has been vouchsafed you, Robin." And so, my lord, I came. Only, one matter puzzles me,' and he grinned up at the earl.

'And what may that be, good Robin?'

'If the lady bear a daughter must I be cast in prison for that offence also?'

'Nay, Robin. For I am a soldier, and a plain man that

17

knows nothing of prophecy. If the child be a son then I shall spend my life in his service, for love of that brother who is slain. And if it shall be a daughter then shall I find a husband for her. And if the child be not born alive – which God forbear,' and they crossed themselves, 'why then, Robin, you shall comfort us as best you can and sing of another that shall release Wales from her bondage.'

A child herself, not yet fourteen years old, Lady Margaret Beaufort – now Countess of Richmond – had been wedded and widowed in a few short months. Hardly had she become accustomed to her married dignity before she entered the twin contests of bereavement and birth. Her women shook their heads privately over her narrow hips, held up their hands and looked meaningfully across the big bed, and whispered as they made a posset. Their efforts to assist the girl redoubled. They poured hot milk on ale, flavoured it with sugar, thickened it with eggs and grated biscuit, to tempt her and keep up her strength. They kept a fire raging up the throat of the chimney, and the tempest raged down to meet it. They rubbed her swollen belly with sweet oils, and as fast as she brought up the posset they persuaded her to another spoonful, to keep the bowels open and free the body of poisons. So what with their ministrations, and their prayers to a Christian God, and their incantations to older deities, the lady and the child had to tussle as best they could and hope for a good end.

She had been born a Beaufort : great-grand-daughter of John of Gaunt and Lancaster and his paramour Katharine Swynford, whose line was legitimized by King Richard II : a representative of the senior line of her house. All these things she repeated feverishly to uphold her against the pain, and the midwife – seeing her uncertain between living and dying – wondered whether they should send for the chaplain.

But the phantom of a king's son stood in the shadows of the room to sustain her. She saw Gaunt's long face beneath the helm and his long hands folded on the sword's hilt, and remembered that the soothsayers had said that though he should never rule England his descendants would. She remembered the joy on the face of her brother-in-law, Jasper of Pembroke, when he heard she was with child. The bard had sung that evening of how the red dragon should swallow the white. So though she was only a girl she gathered strength from Gaunt's obstinacy and would not die; bearing this child in whose veins ran the blood of King Edward III. Fire, wind and sword became as one. With a final shriek she gave birth to a son and lay still.

Her ladies hastened to bathe and dry him, raising her in their arms as they made her easy, so that she should see him and take heart. His objections did not cease until they had swaddled him and wrapped him in a velvet robe, lined with fur against the cold, and laid him beside her. Tears of weakness and joy ran down her cheeks as she cradled him, but she recollected the courtesy that was due from her and asked if the Earl of Pembroke had been told of the birth.

When they assured her that this had been done, and even now he was waiting on both mother and child, she bent over the baby and held him closer, whispering for his red crumpled ears alone. Then her ladies smiled and began to chatter quietly among themselves as they set the chamber right, and thanked God for a safe arrival. And they hung fresh sprigs of rosemary to ward off the evil spirits.

'Be glad and rejoice!' ran like flame through Pembroke. 'A son is born to the house of Owen!'

January, held in a fist of ice, became as summer. Oxen were roasted whole and the poor came forward to warm their bodies and claim their strip of flesh; while the children crawled surreptitiously round the legs of their elders, and soaked their bits of rough bread in the beasts' drippings of fat and blood. Bonfires blazed into the bitter air, throwing up soft flakes of ash, melting the snow. And in the castle, Robin Ddu poured forth a paean of praise that transported his listeners into a golden age when Wales should be one nation. He sang of the God of battle, of a mighty host clad in armour without price, mounted upon princely steeds, of pennants and standards and ten thousand marching men. He sang of one who should lead them, of the mark of wisdom on his brow and the words of justice in his mouth, of the healing in his hands and the paths of truth where his feet trod. Until the men of Pembroke, from the earl the meanest servitor, felt themselves for a brief time to be members of a race with a noble destiny.

CHAPTER TWO

*Let not the feminine pity of your wives destroy
your children; pomp them not at home in furred coats,
and their shirts to be warmed against their uprising,
and suffer them not to lie in their beds till ten of
the clock, and then a warm breakfast ere their hands
be washed. Dandle them not too dearly, lest folly
fasten upon them, for oftentimes all that you leave
they spend in an unthrifty manner.*

Dudley's *Tree of the Commonwealth*

Henry Tudor passed quickly through the stages of his infancy, hushed with lullabies, smothered in kisses and praises : his cries a summons of alarm, his laughter a cause for rejoicing. And the girl, his mother, played with him and cradled him in her arms as often as they would let her. For a noble widow should not be too concerned in her baby's upbringing, but be looking about her for another husband. So the Lady Margaret bound her childish breasts with bands of linen, to curb the rise of milk, and watched her son's mouth fasten on the big nipples of Joan Howell the wet-nurse.

On the day of thanksgiving she was dressed richly and taken to church with her friends and company; and later sat doll-like at the feast in the great hall and heard the minstrels sing praises. Her natural high spirits had not yet recovered from the shock of birth. She ate little and was seen to smile only once, when a dwarf imported from France pretended to stumble at the sight of her beauty. Jasper, noting her involuntary pleasure at the compliment and the foolery, bestowed the dwarf on her as a gift. And he, hump-backed and ugly, made his obeisance with some devotion and then tripped up a servitor who was carrying out dirty plates. Had he been so unwise as to humiliate the butler, or to cause good wine or food to fall, a stripping and whipping would have rewarded him. But the churl was clumsy and the dwarf malicious, capering and whooping about him; and the company rocked with delight at the muddle of fallen pewter and gnawed bones. The Lady Margaret laughed out loud, showing small white teeth, and spoke to the dwarf prettily in his own tongue, so that he stood by her for the rest of the supper, and would let no one serve her but himself : his eyes, above the hideous hump, were unused to kindness.

Henry Tudor was three years old when the Lady Margaret underlined a Lancastrian tie by marrying the younger son of the Duke of Buckingham : a descendant of Gaunt's youngest brother, Thomas of Woodstock. She was seventeen and ripe for matrimony. And though the match had not been made for love – which could only be a peasant's portion – the Lord Stafford was well-favoured and a gallant soldier, and the connection seemed good. Since Jasper's claim on the boy was greater than hers she left Henry in his keeping. But she parted from her son with bitter tears, because this was the only love she had known : an orphan at one year old, a valuable ward in the hands of successive guardians, and an important piece in the game of politics.

Henry wept as hard as she did. It was the end of his brief security, the beginning of what he was to know as his life – which he said, years later, became that of either a prisoner or a fugitive. It was the first change and the first parting, and none would be as poignant ever again.

From the battlements of Pembroke Castle, held in the vice of Joan Howell's arms, the child watched Lady Margaret ride away : very small and fine in her scarlet velvet mantle, lined and trimmed with grey squirrel fur.

'Your lady mother has a thousand pearls embroidered on the collar and sleeves of her gown,' Joan whispered for his comfort, 'and jewelled rings on every finger, and silver gilt upon her girdle.'

'Who is he?' Henry Tudor asked, of the gentleman who rode at her side.

'That is my lord Stafford, your lady mother's husband. See how fine, in green and white and gold, and his hand doubled on his hip, and the other reining in his horse so that he does not ride too fast for the lady. What a goodly gentleman! And his sword so long and keen that no robbers dare come nigh.'

The little company picked its way into the wild stretches of heather and moorland, and were lost to sight.

The boy woke and cried and would not be comforted, and though the thick candle was lit by the side of his pallet he could not sleep, until at last Joan Howell sent a message to the earl who sat late over the fire in the great hall. Jasper stood by his nephew's bed and called to the sorry lump beneath its fustian blankets.

'Why, Harry, Harry! What? Weeping like a girl? Then must I take this wolfskin from you and give you velvet in its stead. For no warrior wets his cheeks with tears.'

'I am – no – warrior, uncle.'

'Not yet awhile, but shall be,' said Jasper gently. 'Come sit by the fire, lad, and I'll tell you tales of war and dark Robin shall sing to us. And we shall bide like two soldiers together before the eve of battle.'

The child's face was smeared and swollen as he came from under the bedclothes, but he looked hopeful and rubbed his eyes with his fists.

'Put on his shirt, Mistress Howell,' Jasper commanded, and when this was done he wrapped the boy in the wolfskin and carried him downstairs.

Safe in his grasp, Henry stared at the flaming torches in their iron holders as they passed them, and made wild pictures from wild shadows. He heard the echo of his uncle's footsteps follow; and greeted the dogs that rose from their places by the hearth and snuffled his bare feet with friendly noses.

'More logs, boy!' Jasper ordered, and watched them hoisted on the dying fire, and signalled Robin Ddu to draw his foot-stool closer and fetch his harp. 'Now, Harry, open your heart,' he said, 'for tears wash clean but words heal faster, lad. And dark Robin here, and your uncle, are your good friends, Harry. And good friends listen and speak not of what they have heard.'

Then he rested in the high chair and cradled the child, and though he was not soft and stout like Joan Howell, but hard and muscular, the strength of his arms was comforting. He listened to the long, disjointed recital of childish woes, punctuated by hiccups, with as much patience as any woman.

'Now are you not the first, nor yet the last, to lose his mother,' he said at length, and Robin nodded. 'And the greater the lady the sooner her son loses her. My mother was a queen, Harry, and wedded my father secretly. I was but a little older than you when King Henry placed me in the care of Catherine de la Pole, that was the Abbess of Barking and sister to the Earl of Suffolk. And though she was a goodly woman, chaste and pious and well-learned, your father and I had a hard time of it. Yet here am I, in my thirtieth year, as hale as any man, and as ready to serve the king with my sword as to spit another wolf on my spear. I was this fellow's hunter, Harry!' And he ruffled the grey pelt with his fingers.

The child's eyes were round above the coarse fur.

'Aye, the hunt is a fine thing, lad. With the forester and his men to see that all is ready – the people kept away, and trysts of green boughs so interlaced that all might rest in their shade, and the grooms watching that the game is not disturbed. And the mists of early morning, and the sound of horns, and the chase, and at last the quarry breaking cover. This was an old wolf, Harry, that had run wild and grown great in cunning, and he defied me with his eyes even as he died upon the steel. He lies gently on you now, Harry, but he had given you cause to weep three years since!'

'Shall I hunt wolves, uncle?'

'Not yet awhile, lad. We'll begin with small beasts first, beasts of the chase and beasts of sweet flight. The buck, the doe, the fox, the hare. And those that afford great disport such as the badger, the otter and the wildcat. But you must be seasoned, Harry, to hunt the wolf and the boar, for these may kill a man and it is best that the hunter be not the hunted.'

'But you were not the hunted, uncle?'

'Not yet, my lord Henry,' Robin broke in, 'and yet, if York pleases, he may be. Then shall he be chased as cruelly as any beast, and Wales herself lie torn and bleeding.'

Henry struggled into sitting position, looking from Jasper's frown to Robin's bitter smile.

'What say you, dark Robin?' the boy demanded imperiously, and both men were amused at the tone.

'Why, my lord Henry, the earl must go forth to fight the king's enemies, and leave Pembroke in your keeping,' said Robin briskly, as though this were a normal statement. 'And so it brooks you not to weep like a woman but to care for us like a man.'

The child took the news with perfect seriousness, mulling it over like some old soldier who is quite prepared to shoulder the responsibility but doubts his strength to do so. They had not expected more than a boyish shout of pleasure, and watched his gravity with amazement.

'How shall I order them, uncle?' he asked finally.

'Why, Harry, I'll leave a captain with you, that shall order for you.'

'I had best see to the weapons first, and tell Joan Howell not to fear for aught, since I am here.'

'Captain Roberts will show you the armoury tomorrow,' said Jasper solemnly, and Robin shook his head from side to side in astonishment.

'Is it the king your brother that you fight for?' Henry asked, the tears dry on his cheeks.

'Aye, the king my half-brother. King Henry VI, whose mother was my mother, but whose father was the great warrior that brought France to heel.'

'Is he a warrior also, uncle?'

Jasper hesitated, and Robin was silent.

'Nay, Harry, he is not, but he is king annointed and no Duke of York shall uncrown him. He is a goodly man that would have England at peace, but York has a proud stomach and a mighty following and he seeks to take his place.'

'His queen is a better warrior,' said Robin savagely.

'Aye, but not so wise in counsel,' cried Jasper, forgetful of the child on his knee, 'though my sword is hers and her son's as long as the house of Lancaster commands it. She is proud and self-willed and thinks of nothing but Prince Edward. How else would she leave the king in London at the mercy of his enemies while she raises men in North Wales?'

'Nay, my lord,' said Robin, 'the king is even now upon his knees, I swear it, with a hair shirt grazing his royal flesh, praying that all shall be well. But Queen Margaret knows all is not well and flees accordingly, to call loyal men to her standard. What princely heart and stomach has the king shown that would barter his son's inheritance for a poor peace in his lifetime – and leave York and York's sons to divide England between them?'

'Uncle,' said Henry, tugging at his sleeve for attention, 'where is England, I pray you?'

So they drew him a map in the ashes with a stick, and showed him that Wales – which he had thought was all the world – was a part of a larger country, capped by a wilder country called Scotland and shouldered by Ireland, and all of them struggling for an independence, and yet all linked: like warring brothers under one roof.

'Which while I live shall be the roof of Lancaster!' cried Jasper, throwing down the stick.

But Robin said that his allegiance was to the house of

24

Owen, and he cared not a fig for England except that they ceased to meddle with Wales, and his own loyalties lay further back than Henry Lancaster.

'For what is it that the Holy Book says, my lord?' he persisted. *'Woe to thee, O land, when thy king is a child, and thy princes eat in the morning.* And so it has been since King Henry came to the throne, when he was only nine months old, and his nurse Dame Alice Butler had the ruling of him. He has been ruled always by one great lord and another. By his uncle, Humphrey of Gloucester. By the Duke of Suffolk. By the Lady Margaret's kinsman, Edmund Beaufort, Duke of Somerset – and, save your lordship's presence – there are those that say Prince Edward was no son of the king, but of Beaufort which is another Lancaster. For did not the king, when he had recovered his senses after many months, say that the child must have been conceived by the Holy Spirit, for he knew of nothing he had done . . .'

'Beware, dark Robin!' Jasper counselled. 'Speak no treason here. Tongues clatter at court to an ill purpose. King Henry is a holy man.'

'Aye, and more like a monk than a king. He confuses policy with friendship. He counsels the boys at Eton not to come to court, since it is full of bad men that will corrupt them! He grants the same office to two rivals, and writes letters of high commendation for two enemies, and then sits by while others make his errors right again. He thinks velvet and satin and fur and jewels are sinful, and one time gave his royal robes to a mendicant abbot. Would he could cast off the crown so easily. It should save all of us a bloody reckoning.'

'Go you to York, Robin Ddu!' cried Jasper wrathfully. 'He welcomes such as you. For you speak with the tongue of York himself.'

'I'll not to England for any lord on earth,' growled Robin, unsubdued. 'I said my loyalties lay deeper than an English quarrel. England has milked us, and shall do, until a Welshborn king sits on the English throne. Welshmen have died in France for her, and now die upon her soil also. Aye, and on this soil too, my lord. Their damned wars divide one Welshman from another, even one bard from another. I know my enemy, my lord, and it is not York nor Lancaster but all England that will not let us rule ourselves.'

The great candle, almost as thick as a man's arm, ate steadily into the second hour after midnight, and still Jasper and Robin talked, hot and fierce, back and forth over the issue. Yet far below the present argument lay a common ground of consent. As they spoke, images rose before the child's closing eyes. The meek King Henry with a hair shirt beneath his royal robes. The Lancastrian Queen Margaret clasping the Duke of York's hand in seeming amity, as they trod in a love-day procession. The first clash at St Alban's, five years earlier, when young Neville, Earl of Warwick began his rise to power. And the king upon his war-horse, tutting with horror as the hacking and hewing started, making no effort either to fight or to defend himself, so that he was grazed on the neck by a flying arrow. Afterwards he sat in the cottage of a poor tanner, to have his little wound dressed, and could only say 'Forsooth and forsooth!', troubled in his weak mind. The French, mindful of former wrongs, sallying across the Channel and burning and sacking Fowey before they were driven off. Then he felt himself lifted, and cried out, 'Nay, uncle – your sword!'

'He cares not a goat for your sword, my lord,' said Robin, smiling, 'but, like the child he is, seeks to put away the time when he must go to bed!'

'What of my sword, Harry?'

'I wish to – see it drawn.'

So Jasper set him in the carved chair and reached for the weapon. But Henry cried that he must buckle it on first, and then shout as he did in battle. Then Jasper, standing well away, changed from gentle kinsman to dark warrior, flourishing the bright blade so that Henry winked with sympathy. And through the great hall rang his battle-cry. 'A Tudor! A Tudor!' So that the child shuddered pleasurably and opened his eyes wide, and drew his breath sharply, and dug his fingers into the wolf's grey rough pelt.

'Let me see it!' he demanded. 'Tell me what those words say!'

Engraved upon the blade was *pro vincere inimicus meus.* To conquer my enemy. Henry touched the words tenderly and fearfully, marvelling.

'Now is that enough, my lord!' cried Joan Howell from the stairs, outraged. 'A child play with a keen edge! Why, what way is this to deal with him?'

She hurried across the flags in her bare feet, and swept Henry up. The two men stood abashed, and Jasper sheathed the sword.

'My uncle is to go to war, good Mistress Howell,' said

Henry, patting her red face. 'But fear not, for I am in charge of Pembroke, and no hurt shall come to you.'

'Such moonshine. Come to bed, Lord Henry. I bid your lordship a very good night – nay a good morning, for such is the hour!' And she swept Jasper a curtsey that held some venom.

'I crave your pardon, Mistress Howell,' said Jasper. 'But the boy will sleep now.'

'And tomorrow I see the – the . . .'

'Armoury,' Jasper promised.

The two men smiled shamefacedly as woman and boy mounted into the shadows.

'I would we could send the women's tongues to war, my lord,' said Robin. 'Then should we have peace both at home and abroad.'

The Christmas of 1460 found Queen Margaret of England and her son Prince Edward hiding in Wales. The Duke of York, Salisbury and their forces roistered at Sandal Castle in Yorkshire. Close by, at Pontefract, the Lancastrian Duke of Somerset and Lord Percy of Northumberland, kept a watchful festival. In the House of Friars at Shrewsbury, York's eldest son, Edward of March, waited with his own army. And in London, under the vigilant eyes of the Earl of Warwick, King Henry VI gave thanks for the birth of Christ and prayed for peace, which showed no signs of forthcoming.

The Duke of York, though no more altruistic than the next man, had first of all sought national stability, when he landed from Ireland six years before. By birth, dowry and inheritance he was the richest magnate in the kingdom; by soldierly training and temperament he was fitted for power, and able to wield it. And he believed that as long as Henry VI sat upon the throne of England there would be disorder, for thirty-eight years of weak monarchy had produced an over-mighty nobility. Each lord was paramount in his own castle, with a private host of retainers who wore his livery and fed and lodged and were armed at his expense. Lesser men, those of both gentle and common blood, relied upon the patronage of a noble to keep them from harm. Justice could be bought and sold, and was. The House of Commons swayed to and fro under the command of the Upper House. No honest citizen walked or rode abroad, by day or night, without constant fear of robbery and violence. Lords picked private quarrels, solved them with private armies, and were

27

not punished. From the highest to the lowest in the land came sounds of grievance. And John Paston, merchant of Norfolk, seeking redress for an injury was told, 'Go, get you a lord, for thereby hang the law and the prophets!'

So York had struggled for England and himself, and was now in the position of Protector and Heir to the realm, and his sons would rule after him. Only, just as this moment, he had a little matter of Lancastrians making local pillagings to settle; and Somerset and Northumberland had the advantage of numbers. His first decision was to send a message to his son Edward to march from Shrewsbury to his aid. But York was old in war, more used to riding than walking, and had survived campaigns of great magnitude and gained great honour by them. Irritated by the Lancastrian forces at his gates, he donned his helm and decided to cut them down himself.

'Advance the standards!' he shouted, and galloped out at the head of his men.

His sense of destiny had clouded his judgement, for Somerset and Northumberland were drawn up to the north of Sandal Castle. To engage with them he had to wheel sharply at the foot of the hill below the main gate, and they were on his flank before he could attack.

They put his severed head upon a pole, set it on the walls of York, and crowned him with paper and straw, who had hoped to be crowned with gold.

Henry would not allow Joan Howell to hold him as he watched Jasper ride out, late in the January of 1461. Instead he held the hand of Captain Roberts, and felt himself to be lord of Pembroke indeed. Nor did he wave as a child would, but returned Jasper's final salute with a raised hand as resolute as Jasper's own. His uncle, with the Earl of Wiltshire, their own men augmented by troops from France and Brittany and Ireland, were to conquer young Edward of March on their way to London; and there meet Queen Margaret, who had raised an army in Scotland. And joining them was young Henry's grandfather, Owen Tudor of the one-yellow hair and gallant bearing, who had wooed and won a queen and been punished for it until Henry VI treated him kindly and granted him a little pension.

The news reached Pembroke ten days later, at night. From his room Henry heard the chains rattle as the draw-bridge was let down, and then the clatter of hooves over the wood, and crept from his bed. He was not yet able to dress himself, and tugged on a curious assortment of clothes, getting them back to front and being quite unable to tie his laces. But he judged it incumbent upon him to know what was afoot, and made his way down to the great hall, where it seemed to him every man in Pembroke had gathered. From the shelter of the stairs he surveyed the messenger.

The hand that accepted a tankard of mulled wine was white and wet with cold. There was an air of defeat about him. He had been wounded in the arm, and the bandage reddened afresh as he moved. One man who knew him better than the others came forward, and began to unwind the dirty strip of cloth and staunch the flow, while he told his tale.

'We were following hard on the heels of Earl Edward, and thought to overtake him, but he wheeled and fell upon us instead. Five thousand of them had come up. Christ knows how fast they must have marched to meet us at Mortimer's Cross. And there was a strange sign in the sky that first day of February. Three suns. A fearful omen – or so it was for us. From the highest to the lowest each man knelt and crossed himself and thought on his sins. And the three suns shone like the Holy Trinity.' He bowed his head in recollection, and crossed himself again. 'Sir William Herbert of Raglan was at his side. We fought bravely, but to no avail. Jasper, the Earl of Pembroke is fled . . .'

Mishearing him Henry rose from his perch on the stairs, crying, 'Dead, sir? My uncle dead?'

They turned, astonished at the terrified child in his jumble of clothes.

'Nay, my lord,' cried the messenger, recognizing him, 'the earl is not dead. He has escaped and shall fight another day. Escaped with no more than a scratch! But not so his father,' he added in a lower tone. 'Owen Tudor is slain.'

Captain Roberts lifted Henry up, and would have taken him back to his bed, but the boy struggled hysterically.

'It is not meet that you should hear this, my lord,' said Roberts sternly.

'Nay, let him hear!' cried Robin Ddu, savage with sorrow. 'The sire of the House of Owen is dead. Aye, *Owen*, sirs, not *Tudor* as the English call it. This noble boy is all that is left in Pembroke of their blood, and must avenge it in his time. So let him hear, Captain Roberts, an he will. But one tear from you, my lord Henry, and back to the women with you!'

Trembling, the boy stood before the messenger and looked up into his exhausted face.

'Your news, sir, if you please,' he said with dignity. 'And as you would tell it to my uncle were he here.'

'My lord, among the many that were taken was your grandsire, Owen Tudor. They cut off his head, my lord, and stood it on the top step of the market cross. But when the people had done staring and murmuring, a poor silly woman came up and combed the tangled hair and washed the blood and dust from off the face, so that he was seemly. And she set a great circle of candles about his head and lit them for the good of his soul.'

Henry knotted his hands together and compressed his lips. Robin Ddu gave a wild cry that brought the hounds to their feet, and the others spoke softly and fearfully to each other.

'And the Earl of Pembroke, sir? What of him?' Henry asked.

'My lord, the earl gave good account of himself. But seeing all was lost he slipped away, and whither he has gone no man knows. Some say he seeks the Queen's army, and others that he returns here by devious routes. I know not.'

'And what of the Earl Edward of March? What of York's son?' demanded Captain Roberts.

'Sir, the earl is not yet nineteen summers old, and his father that led him is dead. And yet, sir, he makes a mighty warrior. Fearless and cunning, swift and fell of purpose. And men love him, for he is comely and rides among them, and his smile is like the sun. Queen Margaret marches south for London with her Scottish forces. The Earl of March may strive to intercept her, or to join the Earl of Warwick who has King Henry in his keeping,. But what they do, or where they are now, or what the outcome will be I cannot say. I did but bring you news from Mortimer's Cross. And now I ask you leave, sir, for I am faint and my poor beast is ridden to its knees.'

'Aye, man, and look to that wound which bleeds. Who gave it you?'

'One that I know not, and now he is dead.'

'Then that is well done. Come, my lord Henry, to bed. Griffith, set a double watch upon the walls. Hughes, give this man meat and ale. Everyone to his post, and hasten. If the Earl of March wins through to London it shall be Pembroke's turn soon after.'

CHAPTER THREE

See you not the way of the wind and the rain?
See you not oaktrees buffet together?
See you not the sea stinging the land?
See you not truth in travail?

Lament, Gruffudd Ab Yr Ynad Coch, 1282,
translated by Anthony Conran

Jasper did not return, though Henry prayed night and
morning for his safety and his homecoming. Each time a
messenger galloped into the courtyard he escaped Joan
Howell, slipping like a fish from her fingers, and begged for
news. But the tide ran strongly for York, and throughout a
cold spring and a wet summer the figure of Edward, Earl
of March, rode in triumph to the crown; and by his side
fought Richard Neville, Earl of Warwick, making his first
king.

The cause of Lancaster fell piece by piece, though the
clash at St Alban's went to Queen Margaret and her wild
Scots, and King Henry was rescued. London lay ahead of
her, but the quality of her army was against her. Tales of
looting and burning, the prodigal stealing of food and provisions, reports of soldiery as pitiless as beasts, had reached the
capital before the queen could. The citizens took matters
into their own hands, barred their gates, and thanked God
for a wide ditch round their walls. Queen Margaret turned
again, with her helpless king and eight-year-old prince, and
sought refuge in the north from whence she had come. So
London received defeated Warwick and victorious Edward,
and proclaimed Edward king.

In the March of 1461 the house of Lancaster and the
house of York met at Towton, a few miles outside York,
and fought in a blinding snowstorm for upwards of eight
hours until the queen's forces were routed and slain in their
hundreds, and she slipped into Scotland with her husband
and son and a handful of the faithful.

Wales and winter delayed each message miserably, and
for all his quickness and tenacity young Henry gleaned only

snaps and scraps of news, which jumbled in his mind and haunted his dreams.

'Now God be merciful,' said Joan Howell, rocking him, 'but I have not had one good night in the last month, Lord Henry. This is worse than when your lady mother went! You should not talk of war with the guards, for never a man among them has been further than Pembroke, so they tell monstrous lies to make them seem the braver.'

'Captain Roberts,' Henry sobbed, 'Captain Roberts has, Mistress Howell.'

'Ah, well, he has served with the earl your uncle, but he would not tell you of such things. So do not talk with the guards!'

She lit the candle by his pallet, and ordered a sullen servant to fetch her bed into the chamber.

'Now I am here, Lord Henry, and should a hobgoblin so much as show his snout I'll snip it off! And it was you, my lord,' she grumbled, heaving herself on to the hard bed, 'that said I should not fear, for you ruled Pembroke! Fine words!'

The child lay white and exhausted on his pillow, watching her.

'But what shall I do, Mistress Howell, when King Henry comes to me in my dreams, and laughs and smiles?'

'Tell him to go about his business,' said Joan Howell roundly. 'If he had looked to it earlier we should not have King Edward now!'

She did not close her eyes until the child slept soundly, and was troubled in her own mind; for here they were upon the rocky coast, and nothing before them but siege or surrender. So she said her prayers, with a special one for the boy's safety, and another for her own. The thought of rape troubled her dignity.

King Edward IV, having conquered England – though it heaved here and there with trouble – sent his faithful Welsh warrior to conquer Wales. In a dank November at the end of the troubled year, Sir William Herbert of Raglan laid siege to Pembroke by land and sea.

They had expected his coming and were as ready as a garrison could be with its best men gone to war and scattered. Barrels of gunpowder stood dry and compact in waiting; reserve stocks of silk and hempen bowstrings, well-waxed, promised the bowmen several months' supply;

eight sizes of single-barrelled heavy guns reared their blind muzzles from walls and towers. The fruits of a poor harvest were garnered; biscuit baked; stockfish, ling, salmon and herring salted; bacon preserved in bran; pipes of wine laid down; barrels of ale stored; weys of cheese stacked in coarse net; and the winter's meat penned until it should be slaughtered.

But from the first they had known Pembroke to be a lost cause, however bravely Captain Roberts answered Sir William from the battlements. For he was no stranger upon foreign soil but a neighbouring Welshman, with supplies to hand, and the treasury of the new king behind him. The garrison looked stoutly upon the invaders, but their hearts misgave them. Sir William had in one stroke prevented help being brought by water up the Haven, and threatened them with boats of soldiery well out of reach of their largest artillery. The practical way in which pavilioners were setting up tents, the carts of scaling ladders, the wagons of ammunition and baggage and artillery, the teams of horses drawing four types of cannon, made them uneasy. Disturbed, they counted both long- and short-range guns, to batter the fortifications. Pot-guns which could lob fused bombs into the stronghold, destroying people and buildings. Field-guns, to fire grape-shot, some of them many-barrelled to spread the damage.

A heavy mist rolled in from the sea, laying a dripping mantle on both men and stones, obscuring both parties. When it had lifted Pembroke found a canvas settlement at its back, and a host of infantry silently scaling its walls at the front. They sent the latter clawing and falling back into the water with cauldrons of hot pitch, and then were distracted by cannonade from the former. Between the two they strove to survive, and as they conquered one advance the other prospered. Sir William Herbert ran at leisure through the main courses of action. He bombarded sections of the wall, to make a wide breach for his assault forces. He bombarded the inside of the stronghold. He was quite prepared to stay there until they were starved out. And at length, though this was a risky operation, he mined a wall while his sea troops diverted attention, and two hundred men-at-arms poured in over the rubble.

In the keep the boy and his nurse held each other, and shrieked in unison. But outside its walls Captain Roberts ordered his men to throw down their arms, and proffered his sword to the conqueror. For they had fought gallantly, and he hoped by this gesture to spare the lives of common folk whose only fault was one of being there. Nor was Sir William Herbert a mean enemy with a thirst for bloodshed, but a practical knight who saw no sense in destruction for destruction's sake; moreover his king was young and merciful, and sought the people's favour. So he accepted the sword, gave orders that any man who was guilty of rape, theft or further killing would be hanged forthwith, and brought in a little troop of pioneers to mend the damaged fortifications. Then in the smoke and confusion he cried that King Edward wished ill to no man that would espouse the cause of York, and all could return peaceably to their former occupations. Hearing that the young Earl of Richmond was with the defenders, he commanded him to be brought forth, and sat in Jasper's carved chair with the air of a victor.

Joan Howell curtseyed so low, and trembled so much, that Henry thought she might, with luck, fall on her backside; and he watched her narrowly. Sir William he regarded with terror, clad in his armour which was dented and scratched and from which the smell of gunpowder still issued. But he stood as tall as he could in his stained blue velvet doublet, and resolved not to cry.

'Here is a goodly lordling!' cried Sir William benevolently, of the small body and yellow head. 'Why we shall have him upon a charger ere Christmas!'

He bent to swing the boy up in his steel arms, and Henry stared fearfully into the hard merry face, and hoped he would not let him fall since the stone floor was a good way off.

'I have a son but two years older than this sprig. Do you play draughts or backgammon yet, my lord Henry? Or chess? He has lost his tongue. Perchance my bombard shook it out!'

And he laughed so long that his arms quivered, and Henry quivered in them.

'He is but a child, noble lord,' Joan Howell ventured to say fearfully, 'and much afraid.'

So Sir William set him gently down again, and felt the boy's limbs and pronounced them not as sturdy as he could wish. Then he called the nurse forward to report on his health, which she did to such length and to so little purpose that presently Sir William dismissed them both. But later he came to their quarters, while Henry was saying his prayers into Joan's skirts, and told them kindly that they had nothing to fear from himself or the king.

'We do not make war on women and children, Mistress Howell, so do not fill the child's head with bloody tales. He shall be cared for since he has no guardian. Meanwhile, Lord Henry, you shall be as safe with me as with your uncle Pembroke. Sleep sound, lad, and grow great.'

Sir William Herbert had stood on King Edward's right hand that February morning when three suns burst upon the heavens, and his services were being well rewarded. For the successful capture of Pembroke the king elevated him to the title of Lord Herbert. He gave him Pembroke too, but not the earldom, and he listened with interest to the proposal that Lord Herbert should buy the wardship of Henry, Earl of Richmond. One thousand pounds was the price for this noble puppy and his marriage prospects, but the boy's own care was considered, and he remained at Pembroke with Joan Howell to become a part of the Herbert family.

Though holding reservations about young William, the child took instantly to Herbert's wife, Lady Ann, for she reminded him a little of his mother with her gentle voice and fine clothes. So he ascended cautiously to her lap, and listened round-eyed as she told her sturdy son this was his brother; counselling the frowning lad to treat Lord Henry tenderly, since he was weaker; saying they were one family and should be loving with each other. Then she made them join childish hands and swear friendship, which they did: Henry timidly and William reluctantly. And she kissed them both and bade them run away and play.

Lord Herbert's approach was somewhat different from his wife's. On the following day he lifted Henry on to the smallest horse in the stables and personally walked him over the green sward, leaving instructions with his retainer Hugh Jenkins to give the boy riding lessons daily. And in the afternoon, since it was too wet and foggy for sport, he sent for Henry and ordered out Jasper's massive ivory chess-board, with pieces and pawns so huge that the child could scarcely close his hands about them.

'This is a lord's game, Harry, for it teaches both wit and guile, and should you wish to rise in the world you must know something of each. They tell me you begin to play a little, so shall we play together – and I shall not be hard on you, Harry.'

The child's grey eyes watched his, fascinated, between the massive pieces, each so intricately carved that their faces bore distinct characteristics of their own.

'There is a new king on the throne of England, Harry, Edward IV is his name. He is young and well-favoured, bold and hardy in the field, a goodly personage. He should reign long, and he wishes you no ill, Harry – though your uncle Jasper Tudor fought him, and has lost his title and his lands in consequence.

'So learn to sit a horse and wield a sword, and then you shall defend King Edward when you are a man. And learn your lessons, Harry, that you might be wise enough to serve him. Why, God knows, with a strong king and a long peace you may yet be Treasurer of England – and a good Yorkist to boot, for all your inheritance.'

Still the child's eyes stared and he remained silent, torn between awe and incomprehension.

'Play, Harry,' said Lord William, moving his pawn to king's third, and smiling as the child copied him. 'Play and fear not!' Moving to king's fourth.

They boy bent such an old look on the board that Lord William laughed outright, and shook his head as he drank his wine. For a minute or so Henry considered the possibility of doing likewise, then changed his mind and summoned Robin Ddu from the hearth, pointing imperiously to his king's knight. Gravely the bard bowed, placing the carved warrior under the direction of that lordly little finger to threaten Herbert's pawn.

'What, Harry? Do you challenge me at the outset, lad?'

The child ducked his yellow head up and down and laughed suddenly, showing small white teeth.

'We have a man of valour here, dark Robin!'

'Aye, my lord,' said Robin, smiling thinly, 'for though he has not the knowledge to win yet will he try full well. And when his wit is grown to manhood some shall find him worth a reckoning.'

Lord Herbert looked stern, since the bard had been warned that his visit might be suddenly curtailed unless he changed his Lancastrian tune.

'It is well for you, Robin, that I am as good a Welshman as I am a Yorkist, else should your impudence earn you a whipping! Now, Harry, is your bard to play for you?'

'Nay, my lord,' said Henry, his chin lengthening. 'I play

36

for myself. Yet must he lift the knights, for though I can push the others the knights jump.'

Lord Herbert slapped his knees and declared this was a witty earl indeed.

'Give the lad a piece of green ginger, Robin,' he cried in high good humour, 'for he has a stout heart. And say nothing of the ginger to the women, Harry, else they will cry out upon me that I spoiled your stomach!'

CHAPTER FOUR

As I lay, skilled in hiding,
Sleeping in a secret place,
I saw as day was breaking
A dream on the brow of dawn.

> *The Dream*, Dafydd ap Gwilym,
> translated by Joseph P. Clancy,
> fourteenth century.

There could be none more different, Henry thought, than
Lord Herbert and his Lady Ann : the one war-like and
hard-headed, the other soft-spoken and loving. And yet they
needed one another, for his harsh world protected her gentle
one, and her mild counsel soothed his ruffling spirit. He
treated her like a queen, lowering his great voice and making his stride shorter as he visited her in the solar, surrounded
by her women. And she, sweet-toned, with a little flush upon
her cheeks, would ask him how he did and whether she
should mull a cup of wine with her own hands. And he
would bend a bewildered gaze upon the tapestry that
flowered beneath her fingers, for this was a cushion for his
chair and she had made a manly hunting scene.

'Now is this a very hawk !' he cried, his blunt head shaking from side to side in admiration. 'A proper hawk, my
lady.' And he surveyed the worsted bird with pride.

The women fluttered in his presence, drawing apart that
husband and wife should enjoy a private conversation, whispering and smiling among themselves. But Henry stayed by
her skirts, squatting on the carpet and pretending to master
his alphabet, for she would not let him go to his tutors in
ignorance. And he marvelled how Lord Herbert minimized
an approaching campaign or retailed a past one; careful of
a woman's sensibilities, so that one thought war was men's
play, rich in colour, noble with fine names, and bloodless
withal. And Lady Ann, who had nursed her husband's soldiers and bound wounds almost as terrible to see as to bear,
inclined to his courtesy and accepted his reports. Only,
when he had gone far afield, she sat for hours at her window,

the sewing in her lap, and watched and prayed for his return.

Henry crept closer to her than to any except his girl mother, and she told him what the shape of a cloud meant on a winter's day, and the meaning of a bee-swarm on the branch of a dead tree, and that one crow foretold a perilous journey but that two brought good luck. She was wise in healing, too : counselling sheep's dung flavoured with nutmeg as a medicine for the measles and the smallpox, both of which were great scourges. When Henry had the toothache she personally drove an iron nail into an oak tree, on which was engraved *Alga-Sabaoth-Anthanatos*, so that the ache should not return. He did not like to tell her that it plagued him until Joan Howell drew out the tooth with a silk thread and let the new one grow in its place. And when her baby daughter, Maud, wept at night she dropped a hot cinder into a little water to quieten her; and brought the seventh son of a forester in to lay his hands on young William when he suffered from the whooping cough, and the boy got better.

At Christmas time they placed holly in the castle, to bring success and security in the coming year : a relic of the druids' gift of evergreens. At Twelfth Night a vast cake was baked and divided into portions for the Virgin Mary and her Son. And they celebrated each festival with music, from the rippling harp with its ninety-eight strings, to the tabrwydd – that little drum which gave timing and percussion to the others. There were bagpipes, too, and the reed-type pibgorn with seven holes : the one wailing sorrowfully, the other pure and thin as a bird's song; and the corn buelin fashioned from the horn of an ox, on which the man blew bravely; and the plaintive viol, which had displaced the pear-shaped rebec with its three clamorous strings.

Best of all the boy loved carols, both religious and secular, and listened with his yellow head slightly on one side to '*I sing of a maid that is makeless*' and '*Lully, lulley, lully, lulley, the falcon hath borne my mate away.*' And Lady Ann, endeavouring to teach Yorkist sympathy to Henry, told him that King Edward had given both gold an encouragement to the musicians in his realm, and hoped to establish a fine royal choir.

So the boy grew seven years old, protected by the might of the man who had adopted him, nourished by the grace and beauty of the lady who mothered him, and in the early spring of 1464 began his formal education. Joan Howell was relegated to the background, the Lady Ann to her solar and the upbringing of little Maud; while Lord William concentrated on Henry's military prowess, Haseley, Dean of Warwick, on his soul, and Andreas Scotus on his learning and manners.

'Trust in God, Henry,' said the dean devoutly, 'since He alone will never desert those who love Him.'

'Trust in your sword, lad!' cried Lord William, slapping the hilt of his own. 'A god-fearing man is a good thing, but a bright blade is even better, for prayers alone cannot save you. No villain alive shall stay his hand for the sake of a paternoster!'

'The child had better not have been born,' said Andreas Scotus, 'if he do not acquire learning.'

The boy prayed devoutly, for his mother and for these his guardians and for the king that sat upon the throne. And just as assiduously he applied himself to the arts of war and to his books.

Upon his birthday, each year, Hugh Jenkins measured him against the wall and selected a new bow.

'No man shoots well unless he is brought up to it,' said Jenkins, who had bent his bow in his master's service all his adult life. 'And a bowman has twice the wages of a labourer and honour beside. Now, my lord, I pray you try this one which is something larger than the last, now you are older. And keep your left hand steady and draw with your right, but press the weight of your body into the horns of the bow – for that is how we shoot, as the French learned to their cost!'

The boy aimed and shot, and another retainer removed the arrow from its target.

'Fair, my lord, very fair. We term this method "bending the bow" whereas the French say "drawing the bow". But who won at Agincourt, my lord? And who at Harfleur? Is not bending finer than drawing?'

'Aye, Master Jenkins, and I like it full well.'

And he lingered long at the earth butts, preferring this to the rougher games of singlestick, lance-practice and quintain. Yet he tried hard with all of them, and thanked God that Joan Howell did not see his bruises. Quintain was difficult, though at first it seemed easy to charge the sandbag upon its post with a lance. But it swivelled wildly under his onslaught and clouted him from his horse. Under the eyes and laughter of the retainers he mounted again, trembling, and cantered back for another try: again and again, for weeks, until the puppet enemy fell and he drew rein victorious. But the quickness of eye and skill of hand required in fencing appealed to him, and he promised to become a fair swordsman.

'Truly, my lord,' said Hugh Jenkins, making his report to Lord Herbert, 'your lordship's ward is not lacking in valour, but there is no fire in him for such matters. He will do what he must and no more.' Then seeing Lord Herbert's disappointment he added, 'Yet that he does with a good heart.'

But Andreas Scotus had nothing but praise, saying that this was the aptest pupil he had ever taught. Henry stared for hours at the plan of the universe. The earth was surrounded by water and then by air and then by ether; with Sun, Moon, Mercury, Venus, Mars, Jupiter and Saturn circling round it. In the centre of the earth, forked with flames, lay Hell – which must be avoided. But outside these planets sparkled the firmament and the aqueous and immaterial heavens, and finally the Heaven of Heavens. And these he loved, for the nine choirs of angels rested there eternally and sang their praises to God. He learned astronomy, astrology, Latin and French. He read the Bible closely, preferring stories of miracles and prophecies to those of battle. He studied history, and revelled in the heroes of Greece, and he particularly liked the wooden horse of Troy and went back to it again and again.

'For, Master Scotus,' he said gravely, 'though it had been braver to fight in the open, yet was it wiser to ride in the belly of the horse and so surprise them. For thus they took a city with less cost to themselves.'

'Aye, my lord,' said Scotus, 'and so will you find in other matters also. For this,' tapping his head, 'has often conquered that!' And he pointed to Henry's little jewelled sword.

'My lady Ann counsels me to be good. Lord William counsels me to be brave. And you, Master Scotus, counsel me to be wise. Now which is best?'

'Nay, my lord, what think you?' Scotus replied, interested in the boy's reaching mind.

'I think it best that I be good and brave and wise, all three. But that is no easy matter, for as the one comes to my hand the others slip from it.'

'And so always, my lord, for all your days. But strive for

all three, and though you fall short yet you shall live well.'

He was a silent boy, speaking little, thinking much, watching and judging and listening, and he learned the arts of diplomacy early. In company he played his part, sometimes in a manner old for his years, as though he knew he must be gracious whether he would or not. But when he was happy his manner warmed, his eyes lit, and he threw back his head and laughed so that others laughed with him.

He observed and obeyed so well that he passed for a good child who could be led, whereas he merely bided his time. Each morning he rose with a smile for his tutor, and remembered God. Then he stretched his limbs and rubbed his body with warm linen, saw that his breeches were well brushed within and without and set them near the fire in winter for his comfort. He combed his hair with an ivory comb, coughed and spat to rid his lungs of poison, and went to his stool to void his bowels of infirmities. He washed his face, paying particular attention to its orifices, and cleaned his teeth with a bit of cloth and cold water. Then he walked in the air before mass and gave thanks to God, before breaking his fast with ale and bread and herrings.

In custom with other boys of his years he waited on his elders at table and wished them joy of their repast, standing by Lord William with a silver basin of warm water and a towel of clean white linen, seeing that his bread was newly baked and cut fairly and that he had the choicest portion of meat. And afterwards he sat upright with the younger members of the household on his bench, and did not venture to move until his food was brought from the kitchen.

There they ate, children and wards together, breaking off only as much bread as was needful, a little at a time, and taking care not to stuff their cheeks like apes. They wiped their mouths before drinking, and did not speak until food or drink had been swallowed, lest they sprayed drops or crumbs into each other's faces. And though he often longed to scratch or stroke the dogs and cats that crept lovingly round his short legs and begged for morsels, he knew he must not for this was a dirty habit. Nor did he wipe his eyes or teeth on the table-cloth, knowing that the napkin was provided for this purpose. And when he had washed his hands he never spat in the bowl.

'And do not lean your elbow upon the table,' cried Andreas Scotus, a martinet for fine manners, 'and do not dip your food in the salt cellar but take a little on your trencher and so dip. And do not sup your pottage with a loud sound.'

The admonitions seemed endless, but he mastered them all. Within himself he was waiting for something, what he did not know, and this apparently was the road to it.

There were five Knappan days in Pembrokeshire: the first at Burysands on Shrove Tuesday, the second at Pont Gynon on Easter Monday, the third at Llanfihangel, Penbedw, on Low Easter Day, and the fourth and fifth at St Meygans in Kemes on Ascension Day and Corpus Christi. These latter two being the most important events, Henry had been conveyed to see one of them.

He knew, from the way his tutor had handed him over to Hugh Jenkins, that this would be a rough game. But he also knew that Hugh would let no harm come to him, so he stood by the retainer on a little knoll and held himself carelessly so that the people might think he had watched Knappan before.

Merchants, mercers, pedlars, taking advantage of a good crowd, had set up their stalls and booths before daybreak, and were shouting and crying their wares the moment the first onlookers appeared. And the Welsh, noted for their fairs, came prepared to drink themselves silly on wine and ale, to endanger their digestions with mutton pies, salted herrings and fritters, and to cheer their side on.

'There are the men of Kemes, my lord,' said Hugh Jenkins, pointing to a great body of men, who laughed and shouted and knotted their hands above their heads as the crowd applauded. 'And there the men of Cardigan. Stalwart fellows, all.'

'How many, Master Jenkins?'

'Nay, my lord, I know not. Close on a thousand and a half, all told. There are the keepers that watch their clothes in heaps, for, look you, they must strip to the waist and take off their shoes. And they would not lose their clothes.'

'Why do they strip, Master Jenkins?'

'Their shirts would be in fragments, else, my lord. It is a wild game and an old one.'

'Master Scotus said it was descended from the Trojans, but that he much misliked it.'

'Aye. Well.' He did not wish to appear disrespectful to a scholar. 'Master Scotus is a learned man,' he said.

The boy looked sharply up into his face, reading what he had not said, and smiled to himself.

'Think you that *I* shall mislike it, Master Jenkins?'

'Nay, my lord, I know not. I pray not. For living is a rough business and you will have your fortune to seek. What is a broken head or a lame leg to a soldier? Master Scotus has nought to fight but his Latin!'

'You do him wrong,' said Henry courteously, but coolly enough to remind him that they should not discuss his tutor behind his back. 'To conquer Latin is no little matter. Tell me, Master Jenkins, where is the Knappan ball?'

'In the hands of that gentleman who is calling the sides together, my lord. Yonder.'

'Is it of wood or metal, Master Jenkins?'

'Of yew, my lord, and made small enough that a man might hold it easily in his palm. And yet he does not hold it easily for it is boiled in tallow so that it slips. Mark how he takes it tenderly in his palms, like a trapped bird. Now he speaks, and when he has done speaking he will throw it into the air.'

A hush had descended on the early afternoon as the people, standing well away from the contestants, waited for the game to begin.

'Why are those horsemen bearing cudgels, Master Jenkins?' whispered Henry, tugging at his sleeve.

'To belabour those on foot who hold the Knappan ball, that they might deliver it up, my lord.'

The cudgels, carved from holly tree wood, were three and a half feet long, cruelly knobbed, and thick in proportion. Henry looked at the bare heads and bodies of the men who were to play on foot, and winced out of sympathy.

'Nay, my lord,' said Jenkins, noticing that he shrank, and deploring the fact, 'this is fair play. For if the man delivers up the Knappan and holds his hands above his head and cries *Heddwch*! *Heddwch*! – meaning *Peace*! *Peace*! – then they forbear.'

'And if he does not cry *Peace*! Master Jenkins, what then?'

'Then has he a broken pate for his pains, my lord.'

The little dark shining Knappan flew into the air, accompanied by a great shout from the crowd. And in an instant it was lost as six or seven hundred men surged forward in an effort to find it. A Kemes man, on foot, caught and threw it in the direction of St Meygans. As he straightened up, a Cardigan horseman swung at him with the cudgel and sent him, streaming blood, to the ground.

'Master Jenkins,' said Henry uncertainly, 'that gentleman

44

had thrown the ball *before* he was cudgelled, so did not have time or cause to cry *Heddwch* !'

'No, my lord. Well, that is the way of it,' said Jenkins, unperturbed. 'Perchance his cudgellor had a private grudge against him.'

'And now I do not see the gentleman that was hurt so grievously.'

Jenkins would have preferred to keep his eye on the Knappan ball, the possession of which was wreaking havoc on all who momentarily held it. But out of deference he glanced at the side lines, and saw that the man had jostled his way to safety and was even now, head roughly bound with a strip of cloth, jostling his way back into the fray.

'There, my lord. It was but a scratch.'

Horses whinnied and stamped, naked bodies wrestled and fought. Cries of *Cadw Ôl* – support the back of the game – rose above the yells of laughter, the crack of cudgels, the thud of hooves. From time to time the Knappan spurted towards the Kemes or Cardigan side, and the mob swayed and struggled after it. Then the pace grew faster, and the Cardigan men were away.

'Come, my lord, we must follow them,' cried Jenkins, and he swung the boy up on his shoulders and trotted forward.

'How far – must we – go – Master Jenkins ?'

'Why – two miles or more – either side of the – starting point – my lord. Until it is safe – with the Kemes men – or the Cardigan men.'

'And how long – will that – be, Master Jenkins ?'

'Three or four – hours, my lord. Until – one side can – go no further.'

Henry saw bloody heads, swollen eyes, broken noses, bruised chests and backs, but few of the men withdrew – except for a breathing space or a bandage.

'*Llyw! Llyw!*'

'They call for the man to throw, my lord !'

'I know,' said Henry. 'My nurse used to speak to me in Welsh.'

Jenkins hands tightened momentarily on the boy's legs, and Henry knew that he was pleased.

'And others cry *Câd* ! *Câd* ! my lord.'

'It means *Fight* ! *Fight* !'

'Aye, my lord. Aye, my good lord. You do not mislike Knappan, my lord ?'

'No-o,' said Henry slowly, 'though when I am a man I shall not play unless I must. But they laugh and make merry for the most part. And yet I dislike foul play and I see something of that.'

Jenkins lifted him down, since the contestants were in a solid scrum and the Knappan somewhere beneath them.

'But that is the way of it, my lord,' he said, accepting good and evil alike in the interests of the game.

The boy thought for a while, frowning, and then nodded.

'I would go a little way further, if it please you, Master Jenkins,' said Henry wistfully, reining in his horse. 'To the top of Cwm Cerwyn, if it please you, These gentlemen will wait a little for us.'

'We must lodge before dark, my lord, and this is a wild place.' He saw the look on the boy's face and capitulated, for the lad had watched the Knappan game through to the end and murmured at nothing. 'Come then, my lord. The company will doubtless wait a while. To the top of Cwm Cerwyn! And there shall you see the seven fairest cantreds in Wales.'

The boy slipped from his horse and stared all about him.

On one side, on this evening, lay the coast of North Devon, and on the other the pudding-purple strongholds of North Wales. He saw the twin rivers of East and West Cleddau meet in the port of Haverford West. He saw the river Teifi surging past the dark rocks of Cilgerran, and the modest streams of Gwaun and Syvynvy glide shyly. He saw Pen Cemmaes Head, pitted like a sponge with caverns, hammered into fantasy by the Atlantic rollers. And each river was sheltered by a wooded valley, and above each valley a castle rose like a watcher over warm hills and gentle dales, over rough heather and bleak moorland.

'It is not the same colour up here as it seems from below, Master Jenkins.'

'No, my lord. For when we look a long way off all seems grey and blue in the distance. And yet it is brown and green and gold at close hand.'

The wind blew suddenly and whipped Henry's cap off, and the boy laughed and clapped his hands, watching it circle smaller and smaller with its brave feather acting as a wing.

'I am king of Cwm Cerwyn!' he shouted, liberated.

'Aye, my lord. We are all kings for a moment in such

46

places. And yet, down there, where we must presently seek your cap, we shall be but men again. Come, my lord, else will it be Thursday before we reach Pembroke, and the Countess will fear for your safety and Lord Herbert sauce my supper with hard words.'

The boy turned as they began to lead the horses down, and said, 'Today we are Welshmen, Master Jenkins.'

He had meant the words simply as a courtesy and was astonished at the change in the man's face. Suddenly the air was fire between them. Then Jenkins put on his common mien again and said they must hasten; but they had shared something in that moment that neither would forget.

'Well, Harry,' said Lord Herbert, over their game of chess that Friday, 'It seems that Master Jenkins reports well on your prowess – though he says you do not relish bloody heads. Tell me, what should I give you? What should best please you?'

The boy had grown well for his ten years, though he was slender still and his health had yet to be watched, but he was long past needing help in moving his knights. Lips tightly compressed as he surveyed the board, he gave the impression of an old mind in a young body. No one in Pembroke had ever slighted him, and Lord Herbert seriously contemplated a marriage between Henry and his daughter Maud, but the boy felt his position keenly. King Edward had granted the county, honour and lordship of Richmond first to his younger brother Richard of Gloucester in the summer after the fall of Pembroke – and then one month later transferred the gift to the older George of Clarence. Whichever royal duke possessed it mattered not, only that Henry knew he was but Henry Tudor, Earl of Nowhere, and beholden to Lord Herbert. His mother, silenced by her Lancastrian inheritance and her Lancastrian husband, in a Yorkist realm, dared lay no claim on him. His uncle Jasper was an exile without voice or possessions. And yet within him, nourished by his nurse and the prophecies of Robin Ddu, lay a sense of destiny. But the dream was vague and reality hard, so between the two of them he had learned to watch and listen and hold his tongue.

'Why, sir, what would you have me say?' he parried, and warmed the evasion with a smile.

'You are a saucy rogue, Harry. As one honest gentleman

to another I bid you tell me what would please you best. So fear not and speak out.'

The boy's eyes strayed to the night outside.

'Why, sir, I wish for nothing but a horse, two hounds and a goshawk.'

'A goshawk, sirrah! You speak like a yeoman. The adage says *an eagle for a king, a falcon for an earl, a goshawk for a yeoman*!'

The boy eyed him but said gently, 'I think I cannot claim a falcon, my lord, since I am not an earl.'

'Do you bandy words with me, Harry?'

'I spoke but as you bade me, my lord. I have no title that warrants a falcon. A goshawk will suit me very well.'

He had hoped that his first reply, aimed at the masculine heart of Lord Herbert, would have pleased his guardian. He was dismayed to find himself drawn into political argument. Lord Herbert made a judicious move and noted the boy's flushed face.

'You shall have your falcon, Harry, in a few more years. Tell me, lad, do you like a hound or a falcon better?'

This was becoming more difficult than the chess, but the boy endeavoured to marshal his arguments as Master Scotus had taught him.

'My lord, I have no favourite, for the hound loves his master and obeys his commands from the heart. The falcon is moulded to his master's will and so cannot love him – and yet the one will love the other.' He drew a deep breath and tried to remember how he had intended to trap Lord Herbert's queen. 'So, my lord, the beast appeals to the heart and the bird to the head. Your move, my lord.'

'Why, Harry, you speak like a lawyer. Shall we send you to Oxford or to Cambridge? Nay, to Cambridge, for Oxford is a nest of heretics.'

'An' it please your lordship.'

He watched his little scheme thrown over, and sighed, but his losses put Lord Herbert in a good humour.

'Master Scotus tells me you have a clever head for figures, Harry.'

'Figures are orderly, my lord,' said the boy automatically, 'and that I like very well. And they remain the same, and that I like also.'

Lord Herbert was astounded that life should seem so small and mean.

'But what of chance, Harry? What of the eternal wheel

of fortune that now dips down low and now swings up high again? Greatness and good position come not from keeping your head in a book of sums. They must be sought out like a woman, and subdued like a woman. A pox on order!'

'Perchance I am not meant for greatness, sir, and had best hold to my learning.'

'So war and glory on the field are not to your liking, Harry?'

'Not in themselves, my lord, and yet I love tales of chivalry and the noble wars of old.'

'Aye? Aye?' said Lord Herbert good-naturedly, demolishing Henry's little battle-line and setting his king finally at hazard. 'What tales?'

'About the host in Rhosfair, my lord, of which the bards sing. And the Lord Llewelyn and his warriors in white and green. Now could I die with them, for Wales my lord, and never count the cost.'

His evening and his game were over. He could no longer recollect the poignancy of the words, only that they had once moved him deeply. So he waited to be released and hoped he might dream of the Lord Llewelyn – and his dreams be undisturbed by memories of Knappan.

There was a silence between them and then Lord Herbert said, 'I judged you harshly, Harry, and too soon. There are two kinds of warriors. The one man fights because he can think of no finer work, the other for something greater than himself. Should it please God to give you a noble cause, Harry, you will fight as valiantly as any. Overturn your ivory king, lad, for he is lost tonight. But he shall fight another day. Summon Guto'r Glyn for me and get you to bed. God bless you, Harry.'

He saw defeat in the obedient shoulders and his conscience smote him. The Lady Ann would have looked on him with gentle rebuke, for he had pitted his wits against those of a boy who could not answer him.

'Harry!' he shouted, as the small figure reached the chamber door, 'Master Jones, the forester is training a falcon for the Lady Ann. Two days and two nights has he stayed sleepless, for the bird must close its eyes before he shuts his own. Tomorrow you may go to him from me, and ask him courteously is the bird's will subdued.'

'Why, thank you, my lord. Oh thank you, sir.'

Lingering on the stairs, smiling at the thought of the falcon, Henry heard the bard's voice uplifted from Lord

Herbert's chamber. Clear and sweet and unearthly came the song he had fumbled to explain.

> *There is a host in Rhosfair, there is drinking, there are golden bells,*
> *There is my Lord Llewelyn, and tall warriors follow him;*
> *A thousand, a host in green and white . . .*

Andreas Scotus, approaching from the gallery to see him safely to bed, stopped at the sight of the boy's face. He did not know what images surged in that yellow head, what visions rose before those grey eyes, but he had enough perception not to disturb the boy with his presence.

Henry Tudor, twice-great grandson of Gaunt and grandson of a queen, was experiencing something he had not known. He heard the rumble of carts and wagons, laden with arms and provisions, the heavy hooves of war-horses carrying Welsh knights into battle on Saxon soil. He felt the heat and smelled the dust of a long yellow summer. And at the head of this phantom army, so far away that he could not see his face, rode the king who would release Wales from an old bondage. As the bard's song died away so did the images, until only one banner could be seen in the distance : its white and green bearing the red dragon of Cadwaladr.

CHAPTER FIVE

What better fort against siege,
Now Pembroke's wall is broken?
You hurled, shook till it tumbled,
Carreg Gennen to the glen.
The trenches above Harlech
Held no better than a pen.
No house stays you, no tower,
No white fort, no conqueror.

> *Wiliam Herbart*, by Guto'r Glyn,
> fifteenth century,
> translated by Joseph P. Clancy

Though well known in France and Brittany, Jasper Tudor was an exile and a fugitive. He owned no possessions richer than his horse and armour, and he rode and battled tirelessly : a grey-headed warrior in his middle thirties, half-brother to a dethroned king. He nourished no deep personal affection but for the nephew, Henry, that was lost to him, and the image of the boy stayed fresh in his memory though it was seven years since he had seen him. Occasional reports filtered through to him : Henry was still delicate, and moved from place to Yorkist place in Wales to benefit by the change of air and surroundings. Jasper noted these regular movements with a thought of future meeting. He heard that the young Lancastrian was intelligent and showed promise with bow and sword, that he had been well-cared for, but seemed thoughtful and grave beyond his years. And he knew that his nephew was most vigilantly held in the charge of a man whose power expanded as he climbed the ladder of Yorkist honours, and would not easily be recaptured.

To Lord Herbert's peerage had been added the office of Chief Justice and Chamberlain of South Wales, and a host of minor offices and lordships. He had been made a Knight of the Garter, and in 1467 Chief Justice of North Wales. His son William was married, at the age of eleven, to a sister of King Edward's queen. He had subdued the south of Wales, and now promised to bring his considerable military prowess to bear on those little Lancastrian pockets of the north. His followers and friends were many, his lands and connections vast.

On a spring afternoon in 1468, a combination of fine planning and considerable daring came to fruition. Henry's retainer drew aside from the hunting party in a forest glade and begged to look to his horse.

'She seems well enough to me, Master Powys,' said Henry, puzzled.

'Nay, my lord, she has a stone in her hoof that I shall fetch out presently. Leave us, and we shall meet again. Else will the mare be lamed,' he added, turning to his companions.

'The Lord Herbert commanded that we stay with Lord Henry always.'

Powys reddened and bent over the horse's hoof, and Henry smelled fear on the man and saw the sweat rise.

'What harm can come to him in the Lord Herbert's territory?' Powys grumbled, very busy with the hoof.

'You know well enough, Powys, that men may be bought – aye, and sold – in any part of Wales. So hasten, and we shall wait together. Be speedy, man, else shall the forester beat out the game and we not there to see it.'

Powys lifted his shaggy head and looked meaningfully at Henry, and all the colour fled the boy's face. He stared from retainer to retainer, perplexed, his hand straying to his dagger. Suspicion had been his shadow since Pembroke fell, though he could find no reason why a man should kill him. He looked closely at the mare's hoof and saw that Powys merely played with his knife and no stone was visible. Suspicion grew, and even as he struggled against it his judgement clouded.

'Stay with me, I pray you,' he implored the retainers, fearing treachery, and suddenly Powys leaped to his feet and ran.

The man who brought him down, with an arrow between his shoulders, flung out his own arms, and toppled from his horse. And suddenly the glade was full of armed men. Backing against a tree, shaking, Henry drew out his dagger and held it before him. So Jasper saw him, after all the years: a long slim lad with fear in his face and a blade in his hand.

'Do you not know me, Harry?' he asked. 'Come, mount your horse and quickly, lad. We must be gone.'

His soldiers were cutting down the servants, as he spoke.

Horrified, Henry saw men fall whom he had known as friendly jailors. Jehu and Hughes and Gittings, all with wives and children, spitting their blood on the trampled grass. He felt himself swung into Jasper's saddle, and twisted to see the hard face above him. It held no answer to the slaughter. The smiles and joy could come later when they were safe in the Nant-Conway. And Henry knew before even he asked that Jasper would tell him this was the price of his freedom, and those who were not for him were against him. But he regretted the bloodshed, and Powys lying in the forest with a Herbert arrow in his back and Tudor money in his pouch.

Harlech reared four strong and shapely towers from a precipitous cliff, above the marshes that stretched out to the sea. Edward I had built it, but upon the site of an older stronghold. Men said it could not be conquered by force, protected as it was by the rock itself, then by a middle ward below the walls – from which assailants would suffer rivers of boiling pitch and molten lead, and a hailstorm of arrows. Snugly within its stout defences, Harlech armed and fed the bodies and souls of its garrison, from granary and bakehouse and kitchen and chapel and the great hall where they gathered together. To this echoing fortress, this last Lancastrian foothold in North Wales, Jasper brought Henry Tudor.

The boy's wardship had been close, but his temporary freedom was closer, for once inside those grey walls he stayed there. A little world lay all about him, but it was a man's world of war and the bard's songs were bitter.

In Lord William Herbert's care Henry had lived like a gentleman, now he lived like a soldier. Though the military world was not greatly to his liking he adapted himself yet again to new demands and old loyalties, and re-discovered his uncle. He had forgotten how he loved the man, even at those points where they most differed. Intuitively, he sensed that Jasper was more familiar with weapons than books, so he kept his learning to himself and strove to master the arts of war. His Latin was slipping away but his French improved, since Jasper could speak it as fluently as English and Welsh. Nephew and uncle enjoyed each other's company for only a short space of time, since Jasper must again be about King Henry's business. So the boy remained at Harlech and watched him ride away again, to take assizes in the name of Lancaster and to elude Lancaster's enemies. And spring became summer, and still the castle loomed above a Yorkist Wales and seemed to have a power of its own, for none came near it.

They had been twice as watchful since Lord Herbert was promoted to Chief Justice of North Wales the year before, for they knew that neither his pride nor his prowess would let them be. And now this last rock of Lancaster must beckon him twice as persuasively, since it contained his ward. They had held their breaths when Jasper Tudor rode in with the boy, and crossed themselves in thanksgiving that Lord Herbert did not come upon them straightway, for they needed the fruits of a good harvest to hold them through the coming winter. The last apples, wrinkled and sweet, had been eaten. The granary was low, and fuel too green to gather and stack. Still, there was fish and meat salted, and flitches of bacon smoked and hung, and they could at least replenish the ammunition. If he would but give them a respite until autumn they could face him.

So men-at-arms strode the battlements with pride, looking across Tremadoc Bay to the ranges of Caernarvonshire on the west and north, and the Cambrian mountains on the east, and down to the south where Cader Idris flung a long dark arm of defence. And each week that passed brought the harvest nearer.

He came when fruit was green and small on the trees, and the grain green-gold in the fields, but he approached them as a nobleman should, with courtesy and a triple summons from his herald – who rode ahead of the long columns and demanded a peaceful surrender. And most courteously did the governor of Harlech decline his invitation.

From a watchtower, Henry saw the herald canter gently back with his message. Lord Herbert was observing all the rules of chivalry. For a second time the messenger invited the governor to surrender, and this time the request was more insistent. Threats of no quarter, of hangings, of ruin, hurtled across like so many arrows. Dafydd ap Einion answered in kind.

'I held a tower in France until all the old women in Wales had heard of it; And now all the old women in France shall hear how I defend this castle!'

A great cheer drowned the noise of hooves as the messenger returned again, so that Henry saw him moving, dream-like, silently in the summer landscape.

'Sir,' Henry whispered, touching ap Einion's arm, 'sir, I have been besieged at Pembroke by Lord Herbert.'

The governor did not turn his head, watching the leisurely movements of an invading force settling down for a long wait. The pavilioners were marking out their canvas town, a simple affair built on a cross-plan, while the wagons un-loaded tents and guy-ropes and iron pins. They had some difficulty in finding sufficient level ground, free of trees but near enough to them to give boughs for the common soldiers' shelter and fuel for camp fires. The day was warm and clear. Harlech itself was ready. So its inmates had nothing to do but watch their enemy's activity.

'Sir,' Henry said, tugging ap Einion's arm, 'Lord Herbert besieged us by land and water. I was there, sir, with my nurse Joan Howell and Captain Roberts.'

The tents were going up, bellied by a wind from the sea. Here a marquee for Lord Herbert and another for his brother Sir Richard Herbert, connected by a gallery of canvas. There a group of soldiers erected their own humble houses: simple huts of branches covered by sheets. More carts drew up, and their contents were unloaded: two wooden chamber-stools for the two noblemen, chests and chairs and tables; barrels of gunpowder, barrels of beer, barrels of wheat flour, of beef, of wine; hay, oats and horse-bread for the animals; and as an afterthought, tin basins for the chamber-stools which had been packed elsewhere. Round tents for physicians and surgeons and their assistants, for trumpeters and harbingers and heralds, for secretaries. Square tents with pyramid-shaped roofs to form the bake-house, pantry, scullery, buttery – and another for the laundry. And as each cart was emptied the carters drove it into place in the great ring surrounding the camp, and a sentry of the standwatch went with it.

'Sir,' said Henry desperately, 'Lord Herbert mined Pembroke while his soldiers scaled the wall from the sea.'

Dafydd ap Einion stirred and gave him his attention.

'He shall not threaten us from the sea this time, Lord Henry, for we have iron chains stretched across, and trunks of trees driven into the sea-bed which would be a hazard to his boats.'

Teams of horses were drawing the heavy guns, which joined the carts and wagons like a shield about the camp. Numbed with terror Henry counted them: two horses to a

55

falconet, which fired two-inch balls; ten horses for a demi-culverin.

'He had a bombard,' Henry cried. 'He had a bombard, sir, at Pembroke.'

They were leading the sweating animals away to drink at the stream. And then Henry recognized the deep chests and shoulders of the Flanders mares, toiling, toiling : muscles heaving, great legs plodding, heads down as they hauled Lord Herbert's centre-piece of artillery. Fearfully Henry counted this team, too.

'Twenty-four, sir. Twenty-four Flanders mares. Sir, it is Lord Herbert's bombard! And they call it "The Messenger".'

'I have seen a bombard,' said ap Einion, expressionless.

'Sir, the noise is like a thousand devils mocking souls in hell.'

'You are descended from the royal blood of Wales, France and England,' said the governor, but kindly enough, tempering the rebuke with passion. 'I shall look to you to act as your uncle Pembroke would, that withstood the siege of Bamburgh and kept his wits about him, Lord Henry.'

'I shall not play the coward, sir, but I mislike the noise exceedingly.'

'Your ears shall not be troubled yet awhile, lad. They must construct emplacements for these great gunnys of theirs, and we shall harry them I swear on it! For every stake and every hinge and every plank a soldier shall fall. Get you below, Lord Henry, and see what the cooks prepare for us. This will be a quiet night, the last for many a day.'

He stayed on the battlements a long time, watching Lord Herbert's men entrenching themselves, digging ordure pits, penning their horses, until the evening came and he could only see the lights of their fires and the dim white shapes of their tents.

They were at work again as soon as dawn broke, and the trumpeters on both sides sounded the end of the night-watch. This was the signal for danger. A troop of men-at-arms formed in the castle yard. The drawbridge was lowered and the Harlech bowmen picked off out-riders from the camp, and gave covering fire as ap Einion's soldiers ran out. Throughout the day Lord Herbert's carpenters and labourers had a perilous time of it, struggling to erect the vast wooden screens that would protect them while they mounted the cannons. Again and again the Harlech defenders shot and cut down those who sweated over rope and lever, and their toll was small compared to that of their enemy. They even sought to penetrate the camp and take one of the Herberts prisoner, but both men were old campaigners and well-guarded. And at the last they had to retreat as the multiple-barrelled 'organ' was wheeled into position, and christened them with a burst of grape-shot. So they made their way back, leaving their dead and carrying their wounded, and shut themselves into their stronghold.

The first roar of the bombard tumbled Henry from his bed and sent him to peer from a slit in the wall, wrapped in his blanket.

'Dress yourself, Lord Henry,' said the soldier who stood nearest him, not looking at the boy, keeping his eyes always on the camp. 'And do not take off your clothes now until the siege is over, for you shall have need of them.'

Shivering, Henry moved closer until he could feel the warmth of the man's body through his leathern jacket.

'They have not yet got their aim, my lord,' said the man easily. 'The ball splintered the rock. Now must they wait five hours before they can fire again, and cool the barrel with vinegar, and their other guns menace us less than this.'

The smoke was clearing enough for the boy to see the bombard rearing its eye : twelve feet of iron with a thirty-inch muzzle, cast by a master gunsmith. A monster weapon with a perilous recoil, red-hot from its charge of eighty pounds of gunpowder. Two men had handled the iron ball into place, and it weighed almost as much as one of them : scattered into fragments, and fragmenting rock as it scattered. The other guns opened up now, and Henry crouched by the soldier's feet and clapped his hands over his numbed ears.

But the man stood at his post, surveying the attack, and again said in a calm voice, 'They have not yet got their aim, my lord !'

Henry took courage, scrambled to his feet, and went down for his breakfast of bread and ale and herring. He brought the soldier's own food and drink back with him : and both munched and drank, and watched Lord Herbert's men and horses fall in the hails of arrows as they strove to move the artillery nearer.

Throughout a long day the Yorkists blasted holes in Harlech, and though every movement of the guns and every pause in the attack cost them lives they grew more accurate.

At noon the bombard was fired again, and this time damaged the earthwork. And now they had the pot-guns close enough to lob over the walls, so that the inside of the fortress became a well of missiles; and they were pouring tar-dipped coarse hemp over the gun stones, and lighting them before the muzzle was rammed, so that they brought flames as well as death and the men were hard put to keep the fires out.

Ap Einion organized a counter-assault. Harlech's own heavy guns, charged again and again, put the front line of Lord Herbert's culverins out of action. The bowmen wrapped tow about their arrows and soaked them in resin and lit them, aiming at the gun screens. And he looked to their own damage constantly, so that the smiths piled coal high on their fires and forged the shattered iron anew, working in shifts so that all might be ready again – as fast as a man could sweat. By night they repaired the walls with sandbags, though no party of pioneers ever returned with the same number that went out.

Buckets of seething oil, buckets of burning lime and sulphur, were poured in scalding streams through the machicolations on to the first daring troops who attempted to scale the rock. As men fell, ap Einion spread them thinner about the walls, but spread them so that every part was guarded. He seemed neither to eat nor sleep, and they were content to emulate him. They were not to be starved into submission, but battered until each defender died.

At first Henry stayed below, out of danger, and made himself as useful as he could. He ran innumerable errands for the armourer, the cooks, the physician and the chaplain. To batten down his fears he worked until sleep came to him even as he crouched over his food. But later, when men were scarce, he carried sheaves of arrows to the battlements, crawling between the gapped teeth of stone, and bread and meat and ale to the watchers in the towers. He ran to the chaplain with news of those who desired their souls to be eased into heaven, as they laboured out of their burned bodies, and held water and strips of linen for the physician. The blockade did not cease either by night or by day, and every five hours the bombard hurled its millstone at the earthwork. Lord Herbert timed its firing so that they might expect it at dawn and noon, at five o'clock and at the close of evening, and once terribly in the night when it lit the countryside. They clenched their teeth and waited at those hours, knowing what would come.

58

As the end drew closer so did the defenders. And Henry, who had been 'my lord' to all of them, became simply 'lad' or 'Harry'. They patted his slim shoulders and winked in comradeship, they gave him a cuff or a grim joke. And he was courteous with each, for who knew whether men whose teeth tore at a crust in the morning might not set those same teeth in death before evening? Sometimes, afraid to go below, where the fortress seemed to press upon him and threaten to engulf him in a dark fall of stone, he would crouch on the battlements : his arms about his knees, pressed against the rough wet blocks that shielded them all.

They no longer had sufficient men to repel Lord Herbert's miners, and on a fine October morning in 1468 – even as they strove to put out a great fire in the woodwork of the barbican – an explosion tore Harlech open. Yorkists ran in out of the smoke, leaping the fallen rubble. Yorkists threw bundles of sticks into the smouldering breach and trod over them. As the barbican roared and the men fell back before the heat, Sir Richard Herbert called his forces to heel and shouted to ap Einion to surrender.

The governor of Harlech stood before him and proffered his sword. He was unsteady on his feet, blackened with smoke, and the sweat made little runnels down his face. He raised his voice so that all his men could hear him.

'You have cost us fire and blood, Sir Richard, but so have we cost you. It shall not be said that Harlech fell lightly, and I say this day that those who conquered Harlech are lesser men than those that did defend it.'

The knight surveyed him without rancour.

'So shall I tell King Edward, sir, and crave a pardon for you. For in my judgement no man could have resisted better or more bravely, and I shall not be silent in your praise.'

Fifty men and one boy had survived the blockade, but King Edward was to prove less merciful than his servant.

Lord Herbert, arriving when his pioneers were already at work on the castle, glimpsed a familiar yellow head shrinking back in the shadows of the great hall.

'Well, Harry!' he called good-naturedly, 'this is the longest siege that you and I have endured, lad! Did my bombard rattle your pate? Come, speak with me and tell me what you think of war. They tell me you have played the soldier well, and am I glad of it.'

Slowly Henry knelt before him, head bent.

'What, what a way is this to treat your guardian!' Lord Herbert continued in the same bantering tone. 'Do you not know that even as you hid from me I made my will? You shall have my daughter Maud – your little playfellow – in marriage by and by.'

'You honour me, my lord. I like Maud very well,' said Henry wanly.

Then he remembered her, a little girl with a mind of her own, and the siege faded for a moment. He would have tales to tell her when they met. They would want to hear of his exploits.

'How is my lady Ann, and how is Maud?' he asked more easily.

'They are well, very well. Get off your knees, lad, and I'll give you news of them. But you shall not see them yet awhile. I'll leave you here in safe-keeping, and when Wales is less troublesome you'll to Pembroke. And seeing you have tasted war, Harry, I'll take you with me on my next campaign. For the king's enemies are in every place – aye, even in the bosom of his family – and I am a king's man, Harry. And so shall you be also.'

CHAPTER SIX

If the land's been, brave Herbart,
Faithless, so once was Saint Paul:
Wrath's to blame for what has been;
When that ends, they'll be christened.

Wiliam Herbart, by Guto'r Glyn,
fifteenth century,
translated by Joseph P. Clancy

A submissiveness about the boy, that was not acceptance, struck even Lord Herbert at last. To the loud enquiries of what ailed him Henry answered with a start and a mechanical courtesy, and relapsed into pallor and silence.

'Is he sick, brother?' Lord Herbert asked Sir Richard, puzzled.

'With a sickness that the country breeds in him, for he is torn this way and that.'

'No man tears me,' said Lord Herbert sincerely. 'I fight for the king and his house, ever have done and shall ever. Why, Dick, the lad has been as a son in my keeping for twice as long as Jasper Tudor had him. True, he has suffered, but I bore the lad benevolence in my heart even as I besieged this fortress. At every burst of fire, brother, I crossed myself and begged sweet Christ to spare him. He knows I love him, Dick, and would keep him safe by me.'

'Then keep him not in Harlech for the ruin hurts him. These were his comrades, Will, and he loved them even as we love those who fight with us. He is torn between York and Lancaster. Take him to Pembroke, or to Raglan, and bid the Lady Ann attend to him.'

'What? Nursemaid him? Cosset him? You will ask me for a wet-nurse yet, brother, and say that woman's milk serves him better than ale!'

'I have seen you, Will, after a battle, go into your wife's chamber as a man seeks air, and take comfort from her presence. He is a boy, and has borne as much as a man might. Let him to home and the Lady Ann. Let Maud plague the terror out of him, and fat Joan Howell spoil him with comfits. We shall see Harry before summer.'

'Well, well, be it as you say, but I am not for spoiling!'

But he sat down that evening in his tent and dictated a letter to his wife, bidding her meet him at Raglan where they would celebrate the Twelve Days of Christmas together, and explaining as best he could why the boy languished.

'And give my loving greetings,' he ended, 'and say – nay, fellow, give the paper to me, for your pen splutters like a turkey-cock and I cannot think!'

Then, modestly, he wrote in his own hand : *And I would see you, wife, for it is long since you lay in my arms.*

They set out in the middle of December with the cap of Snowdon already white, and the north wind promising more snow. Stoically, the Herberts rode, wrapped in their fur mantles with their hoods pulled down to their eyes. Stoically, their army rode or plodded behind them, and the massive horses pulled their iron loads. And between the two brothers rode Henry Tudor.

At any other time he would have gasped and pointed as a rabbit broke from cover and fled across the frozen bracken; or looked with curiosity at the way a man's beard was covered with drops of rime and his eyebrows frosted; or gazed upon the trees floured with snow. Now he saw everything and valued nothing as though the ice congealed him. He rode like a Lazarus, with the mark of the tomb on him. To all enquiries he replied that he was very well. They placed the best titbits on his plate and bade him eat and be hearty, and he thanked them and sat with the untouched food awhile, and then gave it to one of the soldiers. Once when Lord Herbert cuffed him the tears rolled down his cheeks, but he made no sound, standing there until he was told, gruffly and shamefacedly, to take himself hence.

There were cases of dysentery among the troops and one or two men died of weakness coupled with cold. His face was expressionless when they stopped to bury them. He had wept for Harlech, he could not weep for those who had besieged her, though they were humble men with wives and children, doing as they were ordered. Sir Richard told him he must not grieve.

'What? Grieve, sir?' he said bitterly. 'I have been taught better than that, for they are at peace so who should grieve for them?' Andreas Scotus had trained his pupil well. With the garrulousness of one who has been long silent Henry mounted his arguments. 'The priests tell us that the other world is better even than the best of this one. So how fine shall it seem to two poor men-at-arms that have spent their days eating hard bread and lying under a hedge on a winter's night? Why, it will be a very palace to them, a marvel of light and music, so that they wonder why they did not die before – even why they were ever born.'

'What is the boy at now?' Lord Herbert grumbled. 'Mount, lad. We must to Raglan, and speedily, or die in a drift.'

'There are worse deaths, my lord,' said Henry slowly, 'and I have seen them. I have heard that when a man dies in the snow he feels nothing, but thinks himself warm at home in his bed, and so sleeps.'

'The snow has got in his brain!' Lord Herbert muttered. 'First he will say nothing but *yea* or *nay* or *I thank you*, and now he chatters like dice in a box! Get on your horse, Harry.'

'Come, Harry,' said Sir Richard gently.

Mutely the boy pulled himself into his saddle, his little flow of talk dammed up.

That night Lord Herbert stood over him and demanded that he should eat his meat, which he did, and vomited it neatly ten minutes later. So they left him to himself and prayed that he would survive till Raglan. He showed one flash of his former self as they approached the castle. Seeing a holly tree blanketed in snow he rode near and broke off a sprig and rubbed the scarlet berries on his sleeve.

'For the Lady Ann,' he said in explanation, and Lord Herbert shook his head in quiet amazement.

She was waiting for them in the great hall, smiling to greet them as they stamped and clattered into the warmth, with the wine ready-mulled by the hearth. First she embraced her lord and welcomed his brother, and then turned to the boy who waited with his green and scarlet gift, and held out her arms. For a moment he clung, his face in her shoulder, his hands clasped round her waist.

'Come, Harry,' she said softly. 'I have a gift for you.'

He held himself proudly until they were in the privacy of her solar.

Sir Richard's advice was sound, though nothing would erase Harlech, for by Christmas Eve Henry had already slapped Maud for pulling his hair.

'And you whip me, my lord, I will not have her plague me!' he cried, and the honest anger in his voice lifted Lord Herbert's spirits. 'Yet, she may ride on my back,' Henry added, out of good nature. 'Come, dry your eyes, Maud.'

'What?' Lord Herbert shouted, glad to see the boy reviving, 'shall she mount you now, Harry? That is very fair, lad, for you shall mount her later!'

And he laughed so much over his joke that the wine went down the wrong way.

The Christmas festivities were long and boisterous, punctuated by more food and wine than was needful, and broad humour became sharp and sarcastic as Twelfth Night approached. Lord Herbert's fool, a quick dark fellow by the name of Jack Morgan, had been the prime mover in all the horse-play, sitting apart and poking fun even at the fun he had created. He was a solitary man, a fierce Welsh nationalist, more subtle than his master, so that Lord Herbert often roared at his jests when others perceived a keener edge. Now he sat at his lord's feet and commanded silence for the players.

'Why, Jack you are a very *knave*,' cried Lord Herbert, stressing the pun, at which everyone laughed except the fool who shook his head and grimaced.

'What, Jack? Do you like no jokes but your own?' Herbert shouted.

'My lord, you must think me a greater fool than I am, to say that a lord is a fool!' Jack countered. 'You must be more foolish than you are before you wear this!' And he stuck his belled cap on Lord Herbert's head, whereat they all roared again, and even Henry smiled at the martial face beneath the motley.

'I say you are a knave to command silence,' said Herbert, snatching off the cap and throwing it at him. 'For it is I who should command that the players begin.'

'They cannot begin while you speak, my lord, and so I command you to be silent!'

'What, would you silence me, you Jack-sauce?'

'Aye, my lord, else you take the bread from their mouths, and they would eat, being poor players.'

'Let them come on, you saucy fellow. And hold your tongue lest I have it out,' Lord Herbert growled, bested yet again.

Jack clapped his hands and the chief player strode forward, tawdry fine, and bowed low.

'Have you comedy or tragedy for us?' Herbert asked.

'Both, my lord,' the man intoned, 'and a play to suit the season. For it is a tale of good and evil, and yet merry!'

'Is it brief?' Lord Herbert asked, in no mood for morality.

'Aye, brief as a woman's codpiece!' said Jack Morgan, and raised a laugh of his own.

'Have you a fool in it?' Lord Herbert enquired.

'A foolish monk, my lord, that rides upon an ass, and he begins the play.'

'Then let him come, for we have had trouble enough, and would laugh at Christmastide.'

The player dressed as a monk was a great success, for he told them that he was an abbot both rich and wise that ruled a vast monastery. But even as he assured them of his status someone came behind him and pushed him from the ass, which brayed and started at the commotion. As solemnly as though nothing had happened, the monk scrambled on again and resumed his oration; while a few paces away the real abbot gathered his retinue about him, including a woman who winked at the audience and said she was his wife. Lord Herbert's fancy was tickled and he slapped his knees and cried, 'This is a goodly abbot, for he lives like a prince of both spiritual and temporal power!'

The players had judged their spectators shrewdly for the piece was never allowed to flag, and as the abbot unfolded his ambition to make the monastery both wealthy and strong the monk kept riding in on the ass, with his pathetic insistences. And each time he either fell from his mount or was pushed, and his incredible meekness and solemnity made them hold their sides, for he would be heard – though they chased him right from the hall at one point, and still he rode back, talking incessantly. And at every lull in the proceedings the boy painted like a whore cried, 'I am the abbot's wife!' which set them off again.

He was a worldly abbot indeed, surrounded by relatives, and he had a huge chest of gold and jewels beside him in which he placed the tributes to the monastery. But whenever someone knelt and presented a bag of money or a bauble, and the abbot put it in the chest, the wife took it out again with a wink and either gave it to someone near her or kept it for herself. Another diversion was caused by the abbot's friend, and his drunken companion, who also attempted to dip their hands in the treasure and were chased off by the wife.

The hall was in an uproar.

'Why, this is a very play!' Lord Herbert kept shouting, wiping his eyes, 'For one knows not where to look, with every fool snatching for himself!'

'It is a mirror to life itself, my lord,' said Jack Morgan slyly, and Henry looked at him, suddenly afraid.

The monk was back again, greeted with shouts, and this time the abbot's friend took counsel with the drunkard, who reeled to and fro and could not concentrate, to their intense delight. It seemed they thought they might snatch the treasure by befriending the mad monk, and they attempted to mount the ass and all fell off. The abbot now noticed them for the first time and flew into a fine passion, and his retinue ran forward and set the monk firmly on his donkey and urged them from the hall. But at every step the monk swayed so dangerously that they finally tied his feet beneath the animal's belly, to its terror and the audience's shaking merriment, and he blessing them meekly.

Only Henry remained white and mute in his seat so that Lady Ann leaned forward and asked him if he was sick.

'Madam,' he said, almost inaudibly, 'I like not that they mock a king.'

She stared from him to the players and then whispered to her husband, who could hardly hear her, watching the antics of the monk and laughing. Then he, too, stopped and stared, and brought his fist upon the table with such a crash that the salt cellar trembled on its gold scallop shell.

The hall was silent. The players froze in mid-motion.

'What treason is this?' Lord Herbert demanded.

Jack Morgan's smile remained but his black eyes were watchful.

'I had thought this a farce,' Lord Herbert cried. 'But now I see it is a heinous thing against our sovereign. Do you dare portray the queen as a grasping whore?' he shouted, pointing to the painted boy. 'And in my house, when her gracious sister is married to my son? I care not that the mad monk is Henry Lancaster – indeed that is well done! But who are these two fools that seek to ride with him? Are you Warwick, then? And is that sodden wretch Clarence?' To the abbot's friend and his drunken companion. 'Speak if you dare.'

They did not dare, glancing at each other, afraid. Then the leading player came forward, making obeisance.

'My lord, we humbly crave your lordship's pardon. We

66

meant no ill. The play is not of our making. We saw no treason in it, but thought it as your lordship said, a merry farce. We know nothing of the Earl of Warwick and the Duke of Clarence.'

'My lord,' Jack Morgan drawled, 'the play ends very well if you would but see it through.'

'Are you the playwright, then? Oh, Jack, you have stretched your wits too far and will stretch your neck also. Did you think I should not discover your meaning? I care not for your end unless it be on the gallows. Send these fellows forth.'

'My dear lord,' Lady Ann said softly, 'The players knew not what they did, I swear it. They have wives and babes with them and the weather is bitter. I pray you, for the goodwill you bear towards me, to let them stay. They will have other pieces for us, and must have learned this one unwittingly, for our pleasure. Punish Jack Morgan if you must, but do not send them forth unpaid and unfed.'

'Swear by the holy book that you knew nothing of this treachery!' Herbert commanded the leading player.

'My lord, they cannot swear by the holy book,' Jack interposed idly, 'for the Church does not look on them as Christian souls, nor permit them to be buried in holy ground.'

'We are all God's people,' Lady Ann cried very clearly, and the player took courage.

'My lord, we swear by our lives we meant no harm!'

His company followed his protestation sincerely.

'Then get you to the kitchen and find another play, one that I like well. And we shall hear you later.'

They bowed and the ass brayed, which was followed by a burst of frightened laughter, quickly hushed. Heads bent, they trooped from the hall, taking the donkey with them.

'You were quick to discern their meaning, my lady,' said Lord Herbert, ruffled that he had not.

'It was Harry that said he liked not to see the king mocked,' she answered, smiling, touching the boy's shoulder.

The jester turned his dark insolent face upon them.

'Aye, but which king, Lord Henry?' he asked maliciously.

The boy would have answered him straightway but paused, seeing the man's intention.

'Why, what king but the lawful one?' he said.

'Well spoken, Harry!' shouted Lord Herbert. 'And as for you, Jack, I see you are as great a knave as a fool, and shall have a taste of the whip. Twelfth Night shall be a sore back, bread, water and irons. Tell your jests to the rats for a while!'

He brooded over his wine long after the man had been hustled away, and finally called to his brother to join him while the rest of the company marvelled at a performer that ate hot coals.

'I like it not that the king's affairs are known by such as Jack Morgan,' he began, speaking quietly. 'By God, Dick, there is no peace for any of us. It is ill enough that Lancaster will not lie quiescent, but that Clarence should envy the king, and Warwick seek to become greater yet, is worse than all.'

'It was the king's marriage that turned Warwick against him, brother. And though the queen is proud and beautiful, and meet as any lady, it was not good policy for a monarch to take one from among his people.'

'And offend both France and Spain at a blow. He made a fool of Warwick, that was scouring on the doorsteps of the Infanta Isabella and the Lady Bona while his master courted elsewhere.'

'They say that the people cry "Warwick! Warwick!" as he rides through the streets, as though he were a god. And he strives to out-match the king always. But two years since King Edward gave a banquet of fifty courses for the knights of Bohemia, and shortly after Warwick dined them on sixty courses.'

'And have you heard the rumours of the archer of Blaybourgne?' Lord Herbert whispered. 'That is foul treason if ever I knew any. For they say he served the king's mother better than he did her father, and the king is base-born.'

'I believe it not.'

'Nor does any right-thinking man, and yet the people talk of it. And that comes from Warwick, who seeks to set Clarence in place of the king.'

'None would follow Clarence, brother.'

'They might if he had Warwick behind him, and Warwick has two daughters. He may yet try to make a queen as well as a king, Dick. And there is Queen Margaret in France, under Louis's protection, ready to listen to any that speak against King Edward.'

'She is said to hate Warwick.'

'She hates nothing so much as lack of power, and I would match her against Warwick for cunning, any day of the year.

She would embrace the devil himself if he gave her entry to England again.'

Sir Richard looked about him.

'Come, brother, we frown and sigh and conjure up black fancies out of nothing. Let us have those sorry players back again and make us merry.'

In June of the year of 1469 Warwick and Clarence slipped across the Channel to Calais. In July they were back with an army and an old old story. England, they said, was suffering from cruel misgovernment – this time through the queen's relatives. And in the north an agitator called Robin of Redesdale had roused a rabble of two thousand men. King Edward, though shrewd, was inclined to under-rate his enemies, and when the news reached him he was well away from London which he had left undefended. While Robin of Redesdale and his rebels, suddenly dropping their appearance of a merely local uprising, marched down to meet Warwick and Clarence.

Cut off himself, Edward sent an urgent summons to the Herberts and to Humphrey Stafford, Earl of Devon, to put the rebellion down.

Lord Herbert had been created Earl of Pembroke after his triumph at Harlech, and the prospect of further battle with further honours, though the honours were secondary to the battle, delighted him. At his castle of Raglan he ordered a splendid feast on the eve of the campaign, and called for Guto'r Glyn to compose a poem for the occasion. Henry waited on him at table, in that strange relationship of prisoner-son which he had known for eight years. And between washing his hands and receiving the linen towel Lord Herbert reminded him not to be late out of his bed.

'For we must march tomorrow, lad, and I would have you fresh. It is well for old soldiers to tell tales over their wine, but young squires must say their prayers and sleep!'

'Aye, my lord,' Henry said obediently.

'And you are fortunate to be my squire,' Lord Herbert reminded him. 'It should be two years hence ere you title yourself as such, but Harlech has given you those years in good measure. So, Squire Henry, look to my horse and armour – though I doubt not that others have looked to them already! – and if all is not to my liking then shall I set my boot on your backside!'

'Aye, my lord,' said Henry, faintly smiling.

'And afterwards you shall return to Pembroke. And – fetch my bread, Harry. And, Harry, come back when I speak with you, lad! Harry, the ladies shall receive you with the honour due to a seasoned warrior!'

The boy's pleasure at their future praise was so evident that Lord Herbert deplored it.

'You are a good lad, Harry,' he said in reproof, 'but the scent of a woman's bower draws you faster than the smell of gunpowder, and that will be your tragedy! Latin and sums, Harry. Books and learning. You'll be but a mole in the Royal Treasury while I sleep in a battle tent in my white hairs.'

That evening Guto'r Glyn drew inspiration from a deeper level than the feuds of two royal houses, and his song held foreboding even while it lauded his patron.

'You are the keeper of King Edward's peace,' he sang, bending over his harp. 'If the king be Charlemagne then you are Roland. In war you become a part of your sovereign lord. A limb of his, a hand, an elbow, a foot. You are called to every council. The name of Herbert rings in all men's ears. Mighty in battle, just and lawful in peace, honoured by the noble, loved by the lowly. Wisdom is on your tongue. Unsullied is your heart, great Herbert of Raglan, famous among Welshmen.'

Then his tone changed and the voice of the prophet spoke. 'Beware your enemies for they are many. The children of Rowenna are become as poisonous vipers. Murder is in the breasts of them that hate you, for you speak with two tongues. Beware the Saxons, Welsh Herbert of Raglan, lest they take you by the heels. Watch them by day and by night also. For the sword shines in its descent and the arrow flies secretly and the knife glitters in the shadows.'

Henry shivered and was cold, though the sun had soaked the castle walls all summer. The great hall was silent, not a soldier not a servitor moved as the bard finished and bowed his head. Then Lord Herbert called for more wine and praised Guto'r Glyn, and thanked him, only his extreme courtesy betraying that he too was disturbed by the prophecy.

It would have been wiser of Guto'r Glyn to warn his lord against a fiery temper and an overweaning nationalism – though the bard admired both qualities. William Herbert, at forty-six, was inclined to be cantankerous in his middle-age, and the Earl of Devon was not a Welshman. They met in Banbury town and quarrelled over their billets, which caused Sir Humphrey to move his company of West Country archers ten miles off, leaving the Herberts with their Welsh pikemen.

'Harry, lad,' said William Herbert, cooling down a little in reflection, 'never trust a Saxon!'

Before the breach could be healed the Redesdale rebels were upon them, and on 27 July 1469 the Welshmen under the two Herberts took the field at Edgcott alone.

It was Henry's first battle and he found that a siege held one advantage over it – the enemy were at a respectable distance. He had trotted behind his guardian on a little cob, taking no pleasure in the dazzle of Lord Herbert's armour, though it had cost him hours the night before to shine it with a bit of cloth. And he wished himself well away from the honour that had been thrust upon him. The noise as they joined battle was an unbelievable clamour of steel and shouts and neighing horses, and the rebels were rough. He could see, whenever he dared look, that chivalry was dead.

An arrow through the plate-armour of William Herbert's horse sent both man and beast to the ground, where Henry's foster-father rolled and clanked like some anchored fish in his heavy armour. In the scramble of steel and woollen legs, Henry jumped from his own cob and saw it butt its way to freedom. The dying horse threshed dreadfully, teeth bared, eyes rolling, and the boy endeavoured to set the knight on his feet without being kicked in the head.

'Thanks, lad!' William Herbert grunted. He seemed better-tempered in war than in peace, and gasped again, 'Good lad! Good Harry!' as the boy heaved and headed him upright. 'You are a sturdy fellow!'

His horse had cleared a little space around it, and Lord Herbert lifted his visor to sight the enemy.

'Stay behind me, lad, for your own safety!' he ordered, and clapped his visor shut again and clove one yelling rebel from head to gut.

Peeping ahead, glancing behind, Henry pressed after him into the thick of the fight. And then observed with alarm that whereas they had been followed by Welshmen they were now surrounded by strangers.

'Back to back, Harry!' his guardian shouted cheerfully. 'Hold your sword out at arms-length and keep a good grip on the hilt that it be not wrested from you. You'll spit a few traitors yet, lad!'

The boy shut his eyes and thrust out his sword, praying

71

that the enemy would be frightened enough by its glitter to pass it by. The movements of Lord Herbert's armoured back, the conversation he had with the fallen, gave him comfort.

'Ah, would you, you villain? There, traitor! What, you ploughshare, you stinking turd, you hussock, would you challenge a Herbert? There and there again! Now you know that you have guts for they spill upon the field! And you, you heinous carrion, fight on your stumps then if you can!'

Oh Jesus that died upon Good Friday, and Mary mild so full of mercy, send us safe home! Henry prayed. He opened his eyes to see a country lad no older than himself, armed only with a crude knife, try to close with him. His training was stronger than his fear. He lunged, and felt the blade run terribly through living flesh. The boy fell, shrieking for his mother, and Henry fell on top of him. As he scrambled, trembling and sweating, to his feet, he saw Lord Herbert thrown by a ring of men upon the ground.

'Who have we here?' one of the rebels asked, throwing back the visor.

William Herbert's eyes glared fierce and blue upon him. Then he caught sight of Henry, bloodied from wrist to shoulder, and shouted, 'Run, lad!' kicking their hands and faces with his rowelled spurs, laying open one man's cheek with his steel gauntlet. And to the knight who rode savagely into their midst, 'Leave me, Dick! Take Harry! Take Harry to Pembroke. We are lost.'

The knight paused only an instant, and seeing a great crowd of men upon them all, swung Henry up behind him; wielding his battle-axe to right and left as they passed across the field.

In his terror Henry had thought this was Sir Richard Herbert, but then saw that knight hurled from his horse and pinned to the earth by a dozen rough fellows.

'Sir, sir. Lord Herbert's brother is taken also!' Henry cried.

He twisted to see the man who had been kindly to him, and who had twice ridden through the rebels without sustaining a scratch. Less than a year ago at Harlech the boy had peeped fearfully at these two warriors and known them to be invincible. The sight of them helpless among their enemies drove everything but their courage and their charity from his mind.

'They were my friends, sir!' he cried, clasping the steel waist.

Above the uproar he heard Lord Herbert's great voice shouting, 'Masters, let me die! But spare my brother that is young and lusty, and meet to serve the greatest prince in Christendom!'

The boy began to weep silently, his cheek against the bloody jazerine, as the horse bore them further and further from Banbury Field.

CHAPTER SEVEN

King Henry: *My Lord of Somerset, what youth is that*
                    Of whom you seem to have so tender care?
Somerset: *My liege, it is young Henry, Earl of*
                    Richmond.
King Henry: *Come hither, England's hope.*

                    Henry VI, Part III, Act IV, Scene VI
                    William Shakespeare

Warwick and Clarence had won a temporary victory. They captured King Edward, who agreed amiably – for the moment – to their demands. They captured his seventeen-year-old brother, Richard of Gloucester, and the king's great friend and wenching companion the Lord Hastings. They beheaded the queen's father and the queen's brother, and both the Herberts, but they showed a spark of clemency in allowing Lord Herbert to write to Lady Ann before he was executed.

She had been white and calm when Sir Richard Corbet rode into Pembroke with the frightened boy behind him, and looked to their needs before Corbet mounted a fresh horse and departed secretly for his home in Shropshire. She had not moved nor wept, though the messenger wept bringing news of death, but when her husband's last letter was put into her hands she could not open it, and asked Henry to read it to her privately.

The writing was strong and firm, doughty even in the moments before oblivion, and he had sought to comfort her. Henry held his own tears in check for her sake until he reached the last lines.

Wife, pray for me, and take the said order of widowhood that ye promised me, as ye had in my life my heart and love . . .

Then she broke down, crying, 'He had no need to ask that of me. No need in all the world. For there was no man like him, nor shall be, and I am the less for his dying.'

And they mourned together, consoling each other as best

they might. Though over and over again Lady Ann cried, 'Not Warwick! Not Clarence! He had served with them faithfully for many years until this. They could have spared him, that was a goodly man and just.'

'Nay, madam,' said Henry, 'they are traitors both and will behave as traitors, showing neither justice nor mercy. For the Earl of Warwick would rule England, and the Duke of Clarence will do his bidding.'

Had the situation not been so tragic they could have thought it ludicrous, for no one wanted Clarence and could not take him seriously. So Warwick, finding he could not rule without Edward, and knowing that Edward would not long be ruled by him, fled the country with his ridiculous puppet of a son-in-law and sought the advice and support of Louis XI of France. And Louis, delighted to play one side against the other, counselled the earl to befriend Queen Margaret and pledge himself to the cause of Lancaster.

A year after Banbury Field, Warwick went down on his knees at Angers before the warrior queen – who kept him on them for a full half hour – and changed his allegiance. Neither of them had reason to like or trust each other. But Queen Margaret had a son she would see crowned eventually, and Warwick had another daughter, Ann, who he would see queen. And they were each other's only chance of restoration. So Anne Neville married Prince Edward, Warwick swore to be faithful to the house of Lancaster, and Clarence – sulky to find himself merely an ally – took the same oath.

A second expedition sailed for Devon in the summer of 1470, and marched for London before King Edward could reach his capital. The king, with his brother Richard of Gloucester, Lord Hastings, and some seven thousand men, escaped by ship and sought safety in Burgundy. Edward had not even enough money to pay the captain for their passage, but the style and courage of a monarch did not desert him. He took his own furred mantle from his shoulders as token payment, saying he would reward the man better in time to come. And the master bowed and was well content, though never had he seen such a poor company under so great a personage.

'So England once again returns to Lancaster,' Lady Ann observed, sitting in the sun with her embroidery, while Henry read a book. 'And my poor husband died for nothing.'

'Nay, Madam, he died for his king,' said Henry readily, 'and would have died for no other.'

A secret thought burned in him which he could in no way impart to the Lady Ann, which saddened and exalted him at once, which once again gave rise to fearful dreams. If Lancaster was back then King Henry would be released and Jasper would return and claim him, and so sure of this was Henry that he redoubled his efforts to be loving with the woman who had played mother to him for so long.

On 24 June 1470 Jasper Tudor landed in North Wales and recaptured Harlech. The news ran ahead of him like the fire with which he consumed Denbigh. Two thousand ardent Welshmen rose to his standard and marched down to Pembroke where no resistance awaited him. There, with a courtesy that matched his resolution, he begged Lady Ann to release his nephew into his custody. And she, poor woman, bereft of husband and power and counsel, entertained them both and then returned to her solar at Raglan, to embroider her widowhood away. That year of mournful peace, when Pembroke seemed untouched by royal tides, had subdued the boy : grateful to be chided by his tutors for a wrong declension, in place of the heartbreak of Harlech, the turbulence of Banbury. Jasper found him pale and quiet, and was wise not to trouble him with questions, cheering him with news of King Henry's release from the Tower.

Nightly the meek monarch rode through Henry's dreams. Now with his legs strapped beneath his horse, as he had been when the Yorkists captured him at Clitheroe five years before. Now as he was after his long incarceration : frail of body, weak of mind, and none too cleanly of person. Sometimes the boy confused him with the figure of Christ, and the dinner at Waddington Hall where the king was betrayed by a false monk, became the Last Supper with Judas lingering in the shadows. And the present cheers of the London populace were ominously blended into those of the crowd who hailed the Son of God with psalms as he rode upon an ass. And then the broken body hung from the cross, and the boy woke with a cry and prayed and slept uneasily again. For he knew King Henry was a good man, and saw his soul shine through his gentle face, and heard him say mildly he was very glad, and knew he would offer no resistance to friend or enemy but be crucified by both.

And though England welcomed its Lancastrian monarch with honest affection, though Warwick was a powerful warrior and a great man, though King Edward hid helpless in Burgundy, and Louis XI befriended the present regime, Queen Margaret still waited for the furore to died down. Herself she would have trusted in the vanguard of Warwick's army. Her beloved son she dared not risk. Her love stole her courage and kept her in France, and this was to prove her undoing. But in England her adherents were jubilant.

'Now to London,' said Jasper as autumn came upon them. 'And there we shall set your inheritance and mine in order.'

Adaptable though he tried to be and must be, Henry could not forget changing hands and sides four times in eight years.

'For how long, my lord?' he asked, with a formal bitterness that amazed his uncle.

'Why, Harry, my brother the king is on the throne. And if he make not old bones he has a son that shall rule after him. Aye, and a queen with the spirit of a man that shall help to keep him there.'

'Shall King Henry make you Earl of Pembroke again, now that the Lord Herbert is dead?'

'I dare hope so, Harry – and give me back my estate.'

'And shall King Henry make me Earl of Richmond?'

'That is more troublesome,' said Jasper slowly, 'for the Duke of Clarence bears that title, and he has sworn allegiance to Lancaster, and he and his heirs shall reign if the line fails.'

'My lord,' said Henry coldly, 'did not the Duke of Clarence betray King Edward, his own brother?'

'Aye, but he has helped King Henry, lad, and a king should not forget his friends.'

'So he who played traitor to his own blood shall be Earl of Richmond and heir to the throne, and have all honour beside?'

'Harry !' Jasper cautioned sharply. 'Beware lest you speak treason !'

'Nay, my lord, my lips are fast shut. I would only that you knew my mind. Treason is treason when it fails, and treason is great honour if it gain a crown. I mark you very well, my lord. I shall be silent.'

Jasper glanced at the boy, who stared straight before him in pale self-possession.

'Even I, a lowly person, remember my friends, my lord,' Henry continued obstinately, 'only they be both of York and

77

Lancaster, for it seems that men change sides which puzzles me sorely.'

Jasper was a plain soldier and unable to marshal his arguments to such excellent effect. But since he knew that the boy would rather be whipped than yield, in this mood, he turned to the affection that lay between them.

'It is even as you say lad; but that is war. And my allegiance has not altered by so much as a hair. King Henry's mother and mine were one great lady. I did not change and shall not, Harry. He showed me and your father much kindness, and raised us to a good estate when we had none.'

The boy looked at him quickly and quickly away again, too proud to succumb so easily.

'I do not care for war, my lord,' he said coolly, taking it into his uncle's camp.

'It is a harsh and bloody business,' Jasper replied, wandering this new maze. For he had never served, nor cared to serve, nor been trained to serve anything but with his sword.

'It is a foolish and a wasteful one.'

This point of view had never struck Jasper, except in a purely personal fashion when he saw a good friend fall or a good cause founder.

'Yet wars must be fought, lad, to gain a lasting peace.'

'My lord, England and Wales have known no peace for over a hundred years.'

Lord Herbert would have smacked his yellow head at the first sign of rebellion, but Jasper controlled himself and administered one rebuke.

'Watch your tongue, Harry! Remember that you ride to greet the king in seemly and honourable fashion.'

So they rode into London : the uncle bewildered, the nephew lacking his smile. Moreover, Henry thought the streets particularly dirty, and said so, ignoring the splendour of the capital city. And the thought of meeting the monarch who had haunted his dreams, infrequently but terribly, over the last nine years, made his limbs tremble.

King Henry was in meek and cheerful mood, washing his hands before he supped with his nobles.

'Rise, my brother,' he commanded Jasper, nodding and smiling. 'We thank you for your loyal services.'

And he dried his fingers carefully, pursing his lips over the task, and caught sight of Henry's grey eyes fixed on him in awe and uncertainty.

'Who is this pretty lad?'

78

'My nephew, Henry Tudor, sire. His mother was the Lady Margaret Beaufort, and once your ward.'

'Come hither, Harry Tudor, and speak to one that loves his country next to his God, and has been more sorrow to her than joy.'

The automatic chorus of reassurance passed over him unheard, for he knew the truth, and the boy knelt before him and no longer wondered at the tales of the hair shirt. There was great strength in the weak-chinned face, the strength of the saint, and great dignity without arrogance.

'Tell me, Harry Tudor,' said the king ruefully, for those he met were well-schooled in reply and he was weary of courtesies, 'do you learn the arts of war?'

The boy looked at him and found understanding in the mild blue eyes.

'Aye, sire. I learn them of necessity, and yet I do not love them so well as the arts of peace.'

The gentle smile became one triumphant smile.

'Why then, you and I are of one mind. For,' and he leaned forward and whispered, 'we do not like war, Harry Tudor! No, Harry, we do not. They make us go into battle in our armour, but we do not raise our hand against any Christian man – nor like to see their holy bodies quartered and their heads upon a pole. And you are so minded? Well, that is good. That is good. Grow quickly, Harry Tudor, and come you to court, and we shall talk of peace and godliness.'

He clapped his hands and laughed childishly, bringing forth Henry's smile which had been absent since he left Pembroke. Then he leaned forward again, wise with the wisdom of fools.

'Nay, Harry, come not to court, for it is full and rotten with corruption, lad!'

All Henry's breeding and compassion rose to the occasion.

'While your grace rules at court it cannot be corrupt, sire.'

The King's mouth dropped and hung open foolishly. He searched the boy's face for empty compliment and found only reverence.

'Now truly this is he who shall in time possess all!' he cried to those about him.

Few had heard the conversation. Most thought the king was rambling again. But some remembered, and later transformed the words into a prophecy.

'Pray to God,' he counselled the boy, 'not merely when they bid you but at all times. Care not over-greatly for dignity and honours, your state of life or the rich pomp of the world. But when aught offends God then must you care and mourn and grieve over that, Harry. For He created us and knows well what to do with us according to His most compassionate and pitiful will. He shall receive the prayers of His most unworthy servants and deal with them in mercy and truth. And pray for me, also, that needs prayers more than any man.'

They were restive, waiting to go in to the banquet, and he patted the boy's shoulder and went submissively to his meal.

Edward IV arrived from exile at the old port of Ravenspur in the mouth of the Humber on 15 March 1471, saying that he had returned only to claim his heritage of the Dukedom of York. So through York he trotted with a few gentlemen, crying allegiance to King Henry. But outside the city his army waited for him, ready to march to the Midlands where Edward would sound out Warwick and declare himself the annointed king. Warwick, saddled with the royal Lancasters, could hardly change sides again, but Clarence had no such inhibitions. The brothers met with smiles and professions of goodwill – though Clarence's treason would not be forgotten – and reached London two days ahead of Warwick and his troops. Had Queen Margaret been in England the situation would have turned out differently, but she was struggling against the Channel storms. And while she battled with nature, Warwick and Edward battled at Barnet on 14 April, between four and seven in the morning of Easter Sunday. Again the weather declared against the Lancastrians, this time with a fog, during which the Lancastrian Earl of Oxford's banner of a star with streams was mistaken for the Yorkist emblem of a blazing sun, and a volley of arrows came from their allies. Cries of 'Treachery!' broke the lines. Warwick fell, so did his brother the Marquess Montague, and when Queen Margaret and her son landed it was to hear news of a Yorkist victory.

She was not a woman to turn tail. Furthermore her seventeen-year-old Prince Edward was mettlesome, and ripe for revenge as well as power, like his mother. Together they conferred with the earls of Somerset and Devon and contacted Jasper Tudor, while young Henry was sent to his mother for safe-keeping. The Lady Margaret's husband, Henry Stafford, welcomed the boy amiably, but to Henry himself all living seemed to be a perpetual and painful reconstruction of broken pieces. He had remembered his mother as a pair of young arms, and a childish face. Now as he knelt before this handsome woman with her strong bones and long chin, saw her assured gestures and glimpsed a mind both learned and shrewd in politics, the girl was lost to him. And she on her part found a serious lad of fourteen years, scarred by war and insecurity.

It was Pembroke and Mortimer's Cross all over again: waiting for news that came late and dreadfully, piecing information together and consulting a map that hindered more than it helped. On paper Queen Margaret's intentions seemed sound enough. She planned to raise England from Dorset to Lancashire, to bring Wales to her side under Jasper, and then in one vast army to advance upon the capital. At first all was well. Bristol welcomed her with troops and guns and they marched smartly up the Vale of Berkeley, only to find the gates of Gloucester barred against them at ten o'clock at night. Unrested, unrefreshed, they marched again for the next possible crossing of the Severn at Tewkesbury, to join the Welsh army. But here, at four in the morning, the foot soldiers could not go on and they were forced to pitch a temporary camp.

'But King Edward was there, madam,' said the messenger, 'with his brother Duke Richard of Gloucester. Aye, and the Duke of Clarence, but it is Gloucester that is the warrior. God knows how hard and swiftly they must have marched to reach them! Queen Margaret took refuge in the abbey. Her son is slain, madam, and so are your kinsmen – Lord John of Somerset and the Duke of Somerset, Edmund Beaufort. And many other noble gentlemen. All slain most piteously. They say that Prince Edward cried on Clarence to save him. They say that Clarence slew him, others that Richard Gloucester slew him. I know not, only that he is dead and the queen like one that is dead – for very grief, poor lady.'

'And what of King Henry?'

'I know not, madam.'

'Then must we wait,' said Lady Margaret, and ordered him refreshment. She sat with her hands in her lap like some carved image, and Henry sat with her and sensed another dream from that Welsh one in which he had lived so long.

'My son,' she said at length, 'we are the heirs of Lancaster, you and I, if they should slay the king – and they will slay him.'

'Why, madam? He would not hurt them.'

'They will slay him because he is the king. His kingship hurts them. The cause of Lancaster hurts them. With King Henry dead they have nothing to fear from a woman and a boy, and so Lancaster dies and something dies here,' and she touched her breast. 'It is always so when a great house founders. Gaunt and Bolingbroke and Henry V, the proud Beauforts and all their line, reduced to the wife of Henry Stafford and a landless boy. Oh, they will slay him, and if they are so pitiless we must keep you safe, too.'

'I am but Harry Tudor, madam.'

'We must keep you safe,' she repeated.

The news came bitterly through May, and images marched in Henry's head and disturbed his sleep. King Edward taking his baby son in his arms and giving thanks for his delivery, while Queen Margaret rode captive through the streets of London, looking neither to right nor to left. King Henry, brought yet again from the Bishop's Palace to find his world reversed, holding out his arms in humble confidence to King Edward. Henry heard again that light and friendly voice, so unsuited to a monarch in its childishness and simplicity.

'My cousin of York, you are very welcome. I know that in your hands my life will not be in danger.'

'Madam, King Henry is dead!' said the messenger very low. 'I grieve to tell you, madam, but the king is dead. They say it is of melancholy, for the loss of his son.'

'They say what they would have us believe, and we do not. What else have you heard?'

'Madam, they say that between eleven and twelve o'clock of the night, on the twenty-first day of May, while London rejoiced with the Yorkist victory, he was dying peaceably in the Tower. But when they carried him through the city to show the populace, his body bled. It bled upon St Paul's pavement and upon the pavement at Blackfriars. So that they hurried it on to a boat and sailed it up the Thames for burial – at Chertsey. Some say, madam, that the back of his head was crushed as from a heavy blow.'

'God rest his soul. He was a gentle and a goodly prince,' said Lady Margaret, crossing herself. Then she rose and looked through the window, where England flowered. 'But mortals should fear God,' she continued, very pale and composed. 'He is a just avenger, and mindful of both good and evil deeds. And such a lord is God that with a little sparkle He can kindle a great fire. He will not prolong the days of tyrants,' she cried, and Henry saw that her eyes were full of tears. 'Now must we keep you safe,' she said, 'for you, through me, are all of Lancaster.'

'I would not leave you, madam,' Henry whispered.

'Nor I you, for you are all I have and all am like to have. Your birth came early and hard upon me. I shall bear no more children, but that is God's own will. And I have thought how we could keep you in Wales. But Harlech fell and Pembroke fell, and nothing will be too far from the king's reach nor strong enough to resist him. So I must lose you yet again, and yet I would not.'

'Madam,' Henry said, 'I remember how you held me in your arms, and how we rose and fell upon the see-saw, in Pembroke.'

'Aye, that was all they gave us, but on it we shall build, shall we not, Harry? For I cannot forget you, and I pray you will not forget me.'

The summer storm that blew in from the sea tossed the small ship cruelly. Thomas White, Mayor of Tenby, had behaved as a Welshman should. He had received Jasper Tudor and his nephew with respectful hospitality. He had hidden them in his house until the ship was ready to sail, and seen them safely aboard. As he watched the vessel slip from the harbour, with the last heir to the house of Lancaster aboard, he wished them well. He had done what must be done, and more than he safely could, out of loyalty to the red rose and the red dragon. He expected no return. But Jasper and Henry might have been pieces of bread cast on that dark water by his own hand. For in years to come Thomas White would be given the control and management of all the royal estates around Tenby. In the summer of 1471 he simply hoped that no one had noticed him, and went home to his supper.

The boy, sick at heart and stomach, retched over the ship's side and begged to be left alone. The last three years had seen too many reversals of fortune for him to take this one easily.

The little square-rigged vessel of some two hundred tons, carrying a master, a boatswain and sixteen hands, staggered from one mountainous wave to the next. Pitching, rolling, wallowing in each trough, righting herself briefly, and bucketing again. Water spewed from her blunt prow and battered her deck.

'Now is this a very storm of Lancaster!' said Jasper stoically. 'It is strange, Harry, how the weather fights for York and the mildest lamb of a sea becomes a wolf when Lancaster sets sail!'

'I care not, uncle, if it swallow me up.'

'You are sick, lad, and speak not from the heart but from the belly.'

'My lord,' said Henry, 'though a host of good friends greeted me upon the coast of France, and conferred all honour on me; though there was no more war and no more change; I should not rid myself of this sickness. For I have learned that there is no harbour safe enough to hold me, nor friend strong enough to save me. I go to nowhere, my lord, and possess nothing. Is that not night and storm enough?'

'Nay, Harry, Harry,' Jasper cried, embracing the boy. 'We'll rise again, lad.'

But Henry huddled below in the cabin and let the ship blow where she would. He heard the timbers groan on the sea's rack and counted his losses. Enemies who had been friends. Friends killed as enemies. Powys impaled upon an arrow in the green glade. The men of Harlech dying on the wet stones. Lord Herbert shouting '*Run*, lad!' as he rolled captive in the armour Henry had shone for him. Welshmen slain on Saxon fields for Saxon causes. His foster-mother Lady Ann threading her life away upon a tapestry. His mother Lady Margaret touching her breast and saying, 'So Lancaster dies, and something dies here.'

Dichotomy upon dichotomy. The civil war outwardly, and the tug of Wales and the Beauforts inwardly, divided him against himself. He remembered how, in his life, King Henry had been shuttled helplessly round the faithful strongholds of the north, offering no resistance : posted like some valuable packet between his foes and his followers for ten long years, and blessing all of them at the last. He heard the mild monarch say 'This is truly he who shall in time possess all!' And he felt the wonderment of being in one man's eyes someone who was whole and of importance, and clutched the memory to him as he was blown bitterly into exile.

PART TWO

KINGS' GAMES
1471–83

*So they said that these matters bee Kynges games, as it were
stage playes, and for the more part plaid upon scafoldes.
In which pore men be but ye lokers on. An thei yt wise be,
wil meddle no farther. For they that sometyme step up and
playe wt them when they cannot play their partes, they
disorder the play & do themself no good.*

> The History of King Richard III
> St Thomas More, c. 1510–18

CHAPTER EIGHT

Tout regarder, et faindre riens ne veoir;
Tout escouter, monstrant riens ne scavoir.
Look at everything, and pretend to see nothing;
Listen to everything, and do not show you understand it.

Philippe de Commines, fifteenth century

The duchy of Brittany was conscious of its personal dignity and independence. Its duke, François II, regarding himself as of the royal tradition, ruled his little realm by 'the grace of God' rather than the express permission of Louis XI – though he paid the French king taxes, and had received gifts from him in token of allegiance. And in this he was merely echoing the opinions of his predecessors, for the dukes of Brittany dreamed a regal dream and resisted both French and English interference. So Duke François II denied homage to the king of France, called himself sovereign seigneur, signed papers 'by our royal and ducal power and authority', bore a crown rather than a ducal chaplet on his coat-of-arms, minted his own coins, and obeyed the Pope's wishes even when Louis particularly advised him to ignore them. Bretons were excused from the duty of fighting outside the duchy, and no Breton could be tried in a French court; and though they could not evade Louis's taxes they contributed far less than any other small kingdom under his suzerainty.

Against the menace of Normandy, of Anjou, of Louis himself, Brittany had built a protective chain of fortresses. *Fougères, Vitré, Dol* and *Combourg* were the outer bastions against the Normans; backed by *Montmuran, Hédé, Dinan* and *Rhennes*. And against the ambition of France and Anjou stood *Châteaubriant, Ancenis, Nantes* and *Redon*.

From the spur of its coastline the Breton fishermen sailed out to garner the wealth of the sea, bringing back tunny to Concarneau and sardines to Douarnenée, collecting oysters from Cancale, setting lobster pots at Roscoff, and finding clams and cockles and mussels in abundance. From Nantes, at the mouth of the Loire, ships carried salt to England and Spain, and a brisk trade in sugar and spice developed.

Rhennes wine was known for its sweetness but the strong fragrant white Muscadet rivalled it in popularity.

Breton peasants spoke a dialect derived from the Celts, and understood the peasant tongues of Wales and Cornwall. And this little Britain had much in common with the greater Britain, being green and moist and pleasant, mild in climate and restful to heart and eye.

Certainly the duchy had its share of malcontents, its pro-English and pro-French factions and its independent party, but the general opinion of all good Bretons was that Brittany should remain their own private property and Duke François be served as lawful ruler. Nor did the friendship of Edward IV shake its neutrality. 'I should never *be* English, if it were not by force!' said the duke severely. 'I am not and do not wish to be *English*!'

The Hundred Years' War with England had robbed France of its prosperity, leaving a heritage of mercenaries roving the country and despoiling its castles and churches. In 1435 wolves had howled in the suburbs of Paris, and grass grew between the stones of its streets. The old order of religious chivalry was dying, and in the French renaissance the Age of Faith was becoming the Age of Reason. Between the nobles and the commoners a new middle class began to flourish, known as the *bourgeoisie*. Peasants left the land that their ancestors had tilled for centuries, and looked about them for better wages in other parts. The Church had lost much of its authority. Academic life suffered. Literature declined. Art, inspired originally by the suffering on the Cross and the humility of the Son of God, was giving way to a new ideal of man himself : man in his pride and beauty. In an attempt to establish law and order, a decree of 1439 gave only the king of France the power to raise an army. But more than thirty years later tales of rape and pillage were circulating among the people; and Thomas Basin, writing his history of Charles VII, wondered whether an army was not a menace to liberty rather than a protection. Moreover it cost a vast amount of money to maintain, and the people were taxed accordingly.

The court at Brittany, like the court at Paris, was obsessed by status and appearances, by the fine distinctions between one nobleman and another, by shades of magnificence in clothing and possessions, and by that most delicate and difficult of problems – seating at table. Above the court reigned François, nobler and prouder than any : living to the hilt of his wealth and dispensing charity with a free hand. A true renaissance prince, he played patron; and architects, artists, musicians, jewellers, gold- and silver-smiths, and humble monks illuminating divine manuscripts, thanked him on bended knee. While to all royal exiles he extended the hospitality and security of his protection.

So when Jasper of Pembroke and his young nephew Henry Tudor, Earl of Richmond, were washed up on his shores, he greeted them graciously. Jasper was no stranger to him, and besides he had de Valois blood in his veins and was acknow-ledged half-brother of the late King Henry. The duke did not entirely comprehend the lineage of Owen Tudor, but accepted it as ancient and honourable among the Welsh.

But on the lad who stood straight and tall before him in 1471, even after the terrors of flight and storm, he bent an even kindlier gaze. The blood of Edward the Confessor ran, though diluted, in those young veins. And Jasper was wily enough to remind him of the line of Lancaster – though seeming merely to explain the reason for their exile. The shadow of great John of Gaunt rose in the court of Brittany, and of the lovely Katharine Swynford, and of their children – named Beaufort because they were born at that Château. The Lady Margaret was drawn in, formerly a king's ward, now married into the house of Stafford, descendants of Edward III's youngest son, Thomas of Woodstock. Finally, lost in a hail of noble names, the duke waved his hand to ward off further revelations, and commanded the boy to come nearer, speaking in the French tongue.

And when Henry paid tribute to his coaching, in a speech as pretty and well-turned as it was pure and fluent, the duke smiled again, and nodded to Jasper that this was very well. But the gentility of his unexpected guests was not the only reason for harbouring them. They were valuable hostages, and he dared swear that Louis would love to use them in his own game against Edward IV of England. And though Edward had regained his throne and found a baby prince waiting for him, and could doubtless expect more sons from such a fertile wife, still England had hardly been a safe place for any king. And, if the fortunes of Lancaster should chance to rise again, it would have been politic to cherish this sprig of the great house. Even if it should not, the duke knew how to behave towards those of princely stock who had fallen on hard times. Jasper was a seasoned warrior, and the lad promised to be something more. Royally, he extended them his protection.

The boy had said his prayers and lay under the coverlet staring at the tapestry on the opposite wall, arms folded beneath his head. With the resilience of the young he was already savouring his new surroundings. As the door opened he sat up, ready for anything from a casual acquaintance to an assassin. But it was his uncle, smiling and at ease in fine clothes lent by his host. The contrast between Jasper's plain cropped head and the foppish velvets amused the boy, but his countenance remained grave and respectful. But, he wished some companion of his own age were with him, so that they could laugh together afterwards.

'Well, Harry?' said Jasper softly, sitting by the bed. 'Safe and sound, lad?'

'Aye, my lord. Thanks to your wit and the cunning of Master Thomas White of Tenby.' He thought back, anxious to forget no one. 'And many other good Welshmen that proved faithful.'

'Remember them, Harry. And reward them if it should ever lie in your power. Never forget your friends, for ill fortune shows who they may be. But fortunes change, lad. Fortunes change.' He looked about him. The duke had provided a chamber for the heir of Lancaster that was considerably finer than he could have expected at home. Indeed, at home he would still have been tumbled together with other boys of his age, and lucky to call a rough pallet his own. 'They live soft, here, lad!' said Jasper, accepting the fact.

He turned to more serious matters.

'Now the duke holds Brittany in a mailed fist, though he is courteous and smiling. He is a proud and noble man that rules royally and well. And he lives as a seigneur should; for if a man is king, Harry, he must show himself a king.' The vision of his half-brother came to mind. 'It is not well that a sovereign should behave as a monk, be his soul ever so pure. A king's virtues are between himself and God, but his people must see him as paramount. Now, Harry, the Court of Brittany is strict in etiquette. I have known a strange nobleman come unexpectedly to supper, and everyone save the duke rise and flutter and clack like pigeons – lest he be placed too high or too low! Dignity is all, here. And though a man be about to part with his head yet will they speak him fair, wrapping every word in a compliment so that one would think they knighted him! So watch all and say nothing, Harry. And listen well, and do not seem to show that you have heard. It behoves wanderers, and those who live on noble bounty, to give thanks kneeling for gifts both small and great. Remember that.'

'Aye, my lord!' The familiar sensation of being worthier than the position in which he found himself beset him. 'Uncle,' he said, 'what is to become of us now?'

'Nay lad, I know not. Watch and wait, and when opportunity comes – grasp it with both hands. The wheel of fortune turns always. Kings die. We shall see. And remember this also, we have not fled for nothing. Ours are powerful enemies, and no man with powerful enemies is without power. We shall see, Harry, we shall see.'

He saw the boy's eyes wander again to the tapestry on the wall, and walked over to discover the fascination.

The arras, nearly twelve feet long and nine feet broad, depicted six maidens in a field of flowers. Three were dancing, one combed another's head with a golden comb, but the sixth sat between the two groups, crowned by a chaplet of flowers. Her hair, as befitted a virgin, hung long and silver-fair. Her little dog sat by her, lolling a pink tongue. But as though she had been captured and disturbed in an instant of time, she was looking out : eyes wide and blue and gentle, mouth curved in a half-smile. Flowers covered every available inch of the tapestry, exquisitely wrought, minute and accurate in every detail : rose-red campions, pale wood anemones, ragged-robin and lady's slippers, pink clover, yellow and purple loose-strife, fool's parsley and ox-eye daisies, spear plume thistles and hare-bells. Birds pecked or sang. A harmless grass snake with jewelled eyes paused in the moment of uncoiling.

'So this is where your thoughts wander, Harry,' said Jasper wryly, 'while your poor uncle tries to make a politician of you! Well, well, your time will come, lad. You'll have maidens enough – but not in marriage yet. We must find a princess for you, Harry, that shall bring power and riches. Keep yourself for her.'

The boy hesitated, afraid to seem forward or frivolous, but the virgin with her crown of blossom had taken his heart.

'Will she be fair, uncle?' he asked hopefully.

'All princesses are fair, lad!' said Jasper, brushing the

question aside. 'But this one, I dare swear, reminds me of your lady mother when first I knew her. And your mother, Harry, is more than fair. She is able of wit and great of courage. A pity she has not the power she could wield right well.'

'Would you not have a princess also, uncle?' the boy dared ask.

Jasper laughed, and Henry loved the way he threw back his cropped head.

'Nay lad, I am a plain soldier. I was not fashioned for a lady's bower but for the field. War is my bride.' He understood the silent question between them. 'And you are son enough for me, Harry. And now a good night, and God bless you, lad.'

Long after he had gone the boy stared at the arras, until his eyes closed and her face glimmered white and sweet behind his lids.

The seasons unfolded and turned as he grew into young manhood. Brittany was mild and lovely after the grandeur of Wales. He held his own with his noble contemporaries, youngsters who hoped eventually for the honour of knighthood: fencing skilfully with the sword, practising with the lance, playing the rougher game of singlestick, perfecting his archery. And because he was nothing except in himself he tried harder than any. At seventeen, Duke François gave him the horse and hounds he longed for.

He called the horse Caprice. She courted him and coquetted with her hooves as he mounted her. His favourite mastiff was Roland, a splendid beast with great shoulder muscles and strong legs.

Galloping through the deep forests and green glades, past streams rich in reeds and irises, they hunted the hart, the grey wolf, and the ferocious boar, to the winding of horns.

'Eh, Roland! Hie away, lad!' Henry cried, flushed with pleasure as his boar-hound led all the others. 'On, on!'

The barking and yelping reached a crescendo, for this was no beast of flight with terrified eyes, but a quarry worthy of all their strength and bravery. Red-eyed, coarse-bristled, old and hoary in war, the wild boar plunged into a thicket and braced his back against a tree, ready to kill the mastiffs one by one.

'Roland!' Henry shouted, and the hound leaped forward before any of the others, the bells about his neck clamouring.

He was tossed aside, yelping, and paused to get breath and lick the wound in his flank. Relays of dogs, in a fury of howls and bells, were loosed. And the company circled round them, raising their stout ashen spears that were trimmed with crimson velvet and fringed with red silk, or graven or gilded, and leathered for a firm grip.

At bay, the beast snorted fearfully, tossing half a dozen bleeding dogs from him: some merely torn, some ripped from chest to belly, others disembowelled. The hounds drew back, momentarily daunted and were urged on again. And then Roland, recovered, arched his muscles for the leap and reached the target of the boar's throat. Together they rolled, the boar hunting vainly for the hound's under-belly. Then the boar came uppermost and Henry aimed his spear. It quivered in the plunging back, and twenty spears glittered after it. A porcupine now, the body reared in agony.

'Roland, away, lad!' Henry cried, and the hound dropped clear and crawled into the thicket.

The beast gazed balefully on his tormentors, shuddered, and keeled over, red eyes glazing.

A great shout went up, capped by the winding of horns, and each hunter came forward to snatch his weapon from the corpse and to examine his dogs. Henry passed his hands over Roland's sides and lifted his head.

'A scratch or two, my lord,' said a retainer comfortably. 'These are but flesh wounds. His muscles are not torn nor his bones broken.'

Others were not so fortunate. The euphoria of the hunt was ebbing as they took toll of their favourites; preparing to bury the dead and carry home the wounded for healing. Henry smoothed Roland's ears and spoke to him softly in encouragement, praising and condoling, then turned to his friends.

'The boar fought gallantly,' said Henry.

The code of chivalry to an enemy, even to a wild beast, spoke through him. He reflected that life was a strange business. For, though he had pity for this dead opponent, it was not the sort of pity that would have prevented his killing him.

To the love of venery he added the love of falconry, spending long hours listening to the falconer.

'For what could be more pleasing than a properly set up falcon?' asked Pierre Rigaud, and his little black eyes shone.

'See, my lord, I have a young one fresh from the nest. Stand away, my lord, for she is new to man and bates when any come near her!'

As he spoke, the falcon attempted to fly her perch, was frustrated by the jesses on her legs, and fluttered in a weird medley of bells and squawks : her yellow eyes fixed in outrage.

'Tonight, my lord, I begin her training,' said Rigaud, 'and that is the hardest part – though not the longest. For three days and three nights I shall carry her upon my wrist,' and he motioned the heavy leather gauntlet on his left hand. 'For three days and nights shall my will wrestle with hers, while I stroke her crop and breast with a feather, and speak lovingly unto her. Her looks will pierce me like arrows, but I shall not return her gaze. Only speak and stroke, and speak and stroke. We shall walk up and down, we shall sit, we shall stand, while she learns to trust her human perch. The wildness of nature is her weapon. Mine is patience. Soft words, sleeplessness, and patience. I shall woo her as one woos a beloved mistress, until out of very weariness she closes her eyes. And then, at last, I may close mine. So does she learn her first lesson.'

The falcon had settled again, striped breast quivering, striped feathers atremble on her legs, eyes alert.

'I train her through her belly, and always I love her, for a falcon mishandled will choose death rather than captivity. So I court her, and smooth her, until she learns to fly to my wrist from her perch, at a call. Then to fly a greater distance, and a greater still. Each time I lengthen her creance, until she may be loosed from it entirely. And in September, my lord, she shall be yours. Upright and still, her *maillolet* upon her head. What sight more beautiful?'

The falcon bated desperately.

'Come now, my love, my heart, my rose. Come my own,' said Rigaud, his voice changing as he spoke to her. 'A fine September morning shall be yours. You shall go forth from the château upon the earl's wrist, as lovely as any lady in the cavalcade. You shall be carried to green places, where the crane and the mallard hide, and the lapwing and the heron. The hood shall be loosed from your head and the joys of the hunt unfolded before you. You shall course like an arrow from the bow, in search of your prey. Shall swoop and sink your talons into feather and fur and flesh, and so crouch until the earl comes unto you, praising your prowess with sweet words. O, fairer than fair. O lady, whose price is above all the wages that this poor falconer shall earn all his days. Who speaks to you now? It is your Rigaud, is it not? O you who are lovelier than any.'

Many times that night and the following nights, Henry woke and thought of Rigaud in his sleepless quest. He imagined the falconer, deep-chested, heavy-limbed and swarthy; his face innocent of any water but the rain. He pictured the dark eyes, reddened for lack of rest, the coarse caressing fingers. He heard the rough voice soften as it addressed the bird, and marvelled at the terrible patience of his courtship.

The wet days of autumn drove him to the chess-board, where his good humour and smiling mouth disguised concentration and cunning. Once, playing with young Hubert – whose pride was greater than his commonsense – he narrowly missed serious injury. Hubert, finding himself unaccountably checkmated, aimed the massive board at Henry's head. Instantly, the young man guarded himself with his arm, and received a blow that pierced his velvet sleeve and cut the flesh beneath. Courtiers and servants surrounded them, in a chorus of alarm and reproach; and found Hubert red-cheeked and afraid, and Henry white and controlled. The duke came in person to make sure his hostage had suffered no harm.

'The earl will not die,' said the physician cheerfully, binding Henry's arm, 'but I dare swear he will carry the mark of this quarrel all his days! Had you not guarded yourself so swiftly, my lord, your head would have taken the force of the blow – then had it been another matter. Such a one, perchance, as when Charlot the son of Charlemagne broke Beaudonnet's skull!'

'Who and what is this villain?' cried the duke, outraged. 'Take him out and whip him soundly!'

'Nay, I pray your grace,' said Henry wearily. 'It was the work of a moment and shall not happen again.'

'Take him out and whip him!' the duke ordered, incensed. 'He shall learn better manners. What is his name? Whose son is he? I shall remember him. Wine for the Earl of Richmond! He looks palely.'

'Sit down, Harry,' said Jasper, as the court returned to its amusements. 'That lad's shoulders shall smart sharper than your arm!'

'And I have made an enemy, uncle,' said Henry ruefully, 'which is not well. An exile needs all the friends he can muster. I have enemies enough in England without one to plague me in Brittany!'

'Lad, if God be plagued by fools and villains why should you escape? Learn from him how an enemy can be contained and outwitted. It will keep you in fair practice. Besides, the lad has more of temper than of malice in him.'

'And is unwise,' said Henry, considering his uncle's statement. 'For if he lose his temper over a game how shall he fare in war? A hot head may end in a cold corpse, so Lord Herbert always said. And this is one like to run heedlessly into danger. Moreover he has angered the duke, and may be hindered at court. So take it for all in all,' Henry wound up philosophically, nursing his aching arm, 'I had rather he lost his temper than I lost mine!'

Jasper patted his shoulder.

'You were swift to defend yourself, Harry. Drink your wine and warm your blood, lad.'

'I learned swiftness at Banbury Field, my lord,' said Henry smiling. 'It takes but one battle to sharpen the wits wondrously. Squires must endure much to serve. I held Lord Herbert's horse before battle was joined, and shone his armour for him.'

'He was a goodly Welshman and a great warrior,' said Jasper generously, 'and ever mindful of you, Harry.'

'The Lady Ann was loving, also.'

They had not spoken of the Herberts since they left England : Henry out of delicacy, Jasper because he realized that the boy's loyalties tore both ways. But the shock of the blow had loosened Henry's tongue.

'I pray for the welfare of his soul, and for her contentment, each night,' he said quietly. 'I learned much from them both and they would have made me their son. I do not love my mother or my uncle the less for loving them.'

'I have ever counselled you to remember your friends, Harry. Nor would I bid you turn your heart from them that helped you.'

'And yet,' said Henry, gently ironical, 'had you met with Lord Herbert in battle you would have killed him!'

'Aye, lest he kill me.'

'I find life a puzzling business at best, my lord,' said Henry slowly. 'Passed between York and Lancaster. Shipped abroad from one country to another. And when a quarrel jars me my mind grows dark, my heart beats over-quickly. Then I see enemies behind every arras, mockery in friendship.'

Jasper was troubled, sensing old griefs and unable to help them. He reflected that the lad had known much adversity, but no more than he had suffered himself – and yet he could take each day as it came, and forget the black ones, and look forward to a lighter. And he wondered whether that old malady, carried by Queen Catherine of Valois from her father, had passed over him and blighted his nephew. For he recognized a withdrawal and a shrinking from vicissitudes that had characterized the onset of King Henry's illnesses.

'If I were king,' said Henry, 'I should see that I was rich, and that men thought me richer even than I was. I should trust few – but them with all my heart – and suspect many. I should not waste my land with war but keep a thrifty peace, and behind that peace I should watch secretly and patiently. I should have eyes and ears in every corner of my kingdom so that no man could over-reach me. And I should rule as I play chess, smiling and betraying nothing and keeping ever three and four moves ahead.'

'And take a crack on the head with the chess-board for your pains!' said Jasper, pushing him playfully.

The smile was coming slowly back.

'I pray you, my lord, remember that I took the crack not on my head but on my arm, and you did praise my swiftness!'

'Get to bed until supper, lad. The board has addled your wits, nonetheless! Secret and patient – you would make a dark prince, Harry!'

'I should not make one such as men love,' said Henry soberly, 'but any fool may be loved. And yet they should respect me, and be trustful in my keeping, and I should leave them richer than when I had come.'

Jasper was tickled by this fancy and laughed aloud.

'I'll teach you statesmanship, lad,' he cried. 'I tell you that it is well to be cunning when once upon the throne, yet no prince reaches that throne but by inheritance or love or force of arms. The common people, and nobles also, love to love their monarch. Shall they follow a penny-pinching chess-player through mud and blood? Cling to your dreams, Harry, but remember this – it is the heart that catches fire, not the head. Cold Lancaster spoke through you just now, let him not have the last word. When these dark calculating shadows crowd upon you send them flocking with the hosts of Llewelyn. Have you forgotten, lad? *There is a host in Rhosfair, there is drinking, there are golden bells . . .'*

'*. . . there is my Lord Llewelyn, and tall warriors follow him. A thousand, a host in green and white!'*

They were both smiling. Then Jasper pushed him gently towards the stairs.

At the foot the two young men met: Hubert subdued by the stripes on his back and Henry by the pain in his arm. They looked shamefacedly at each other, then clasped hands and ascended in amicable silence.

CHAPTER NINE

To trust in the world brings grief,
Life is a brief illusion.
I loved a slender young girl,
And she died, the fair maiden.

Lament for Gwen, Dafydd Nanmor, fifteenth century,
translated by Joseph P. Clancy

Only the written word connected him now with England,
and Wales was as silent as Lord Herbert's tomb in Tintern
Abbey. Subject to the vicissitudes of journeys over land and
sea, letters passed constantly between Henry and his mother;
the phrases of concern and esteem linking beloved strangers.

Madam, my most entirely well-beloved lady and mother,
I recommend me unto you in the most humble and lowly-
wise that I can, beseeching you of your continual and daily
blessings . . .

My own sweet and most dear son and all my worldly joy,
with my most hearty loving blessings I pray Almighty God
to give you long and good and prosperous life . . .

She had no hope of seeing him again, and he had been
reared in a country that was not her own, and now lived in
another just as foreign to her. But he was of her flesh and of
her heritage and she strove to keep those links alive; writing
now of little daily happenings, now of the broader field of
politics, and every letter breathed her trust in destiny and in
God. She was a woman who could have been a queen and
found herself the wife of a lesser nobleman; a woman far-
sighted and deep thinking, whose household cares were not
enough for her; a woman who happened to represent a
party which was no longer in power, and seemed to be in a
permanent eclipse. Above all she was a woman who loved
England and desired her son to love it also, though he had
never known it and was unlikely to discover it.

The pages came alive to Henry as he read them, descrip-
tions woven with personal stories and sharp vignettes of the

great men in King Edward's court. England was her passion and Europe her chess-board. Like the commander of a vast army she marshalled her facts, drew conclusions, often guessed cleverly ahead to the next move. And yet in none of this was a tutor who lectured him but a loving friend who counselled and took counsel with him. The political tidings he shared with Jasper, but the rest he kept to himself; never calling on his scrivener to write for him since he felt these matters lay between him and her alone. Much of what she said could be accounted treasonable, so they chose their messengers carefully and paid them well.

The storm that had blown them on the shores of Brittany was a fortuitous one : a landing in France might have been a different affair. Louis XI not only practised treachery but loved practising it; not only loved the treachery itself but the idea of himself as an arch-villain. So that the greatest praise in his ears was the suspicion and disquiet of other crowned and ducal rulers. Louis could have used the exiles as a weapon against England, as needles of discontent and possible rebellion, betraying them the moment they were no longer useful. But in the firm neutrality of Brittany they were a political something, to be watched and cared for judiciously.

The first feelers crossed the Channel when King Edward had had time to review the situation. He sent a courteous letter to the Duke of Brittany desiring him to release the former Earl of Richmond into his custody. He pointed out that though he had taken possession of the Richmond estate that was a mere formality, indeed a royal right since Henry Tudor had not come of age. He reminded the duke that Henry had lived honourably and safely under Yorkist rule for almost a decade, that he was not regarded as a traitor nor was his life in danger. He said that the Lady Margaret enjoyed security in England and the benefits of her high estate, undisturbed by him. And finally, to show his good faith, he was prepared to offer honourable reinstatement to Henry Tudor and the hand of one of his younger daughters in marriage. Would not this arrangement please both sides?

Henry's counsellors were divided. From his mother he received a plea to consider the offer, since the house of York had never been stronger and King Edward possessed two young sons, two brothers and two nephews – so securing the throne for his line. But Jasper, whose head was not worth the pole on which they would impale it, and whose life was dedicated to Lancaster, had doubts.

'Nay lad. I am too old in war and policy, and I tell you what I told your mother. No man would give a groat or an archer at this time for Harry Tudor, and yet he is in danger enough to raise a bidding even now. And though rebellion calls for armies and for gold, and though the people of England neither know you nor ask for you, yet are you safer here.'

'But if the king of England married me to his daughter I should be safe, uncle. For why should he kill his daughter's husband? And my mother says that he is subtle in policy and would rather bind those of Lancaster to him than risk them at his throat.'

'Your lady mother is a woman, Harry, and would have her son at home. I know not but the king means right well by you. It may be so. I know not but that his mercy and promises will play him false. An accident might befall you, lad – you would not be the first! King Henry met with such an accident. And as for marrying a princess . . . why, you might die of a melancholy fever the moment that your feet touched English soil. We should stay in Brittany.'

So the duke declined with equal courtesy, since his guests were unwilling to leave him. Edward expressed his regrets and seemed not unduly disturbed. He could raise the matter again, and again : concerned, amicable, persistent.

The confinement was not unpleasant but Henry felt his position keenly. His clothes, his education, his pastimes and his companions, were those that any young man of rank and quality might expect and enjoy. Yet he had the sensation of being discreetly watched, of being kept unobtrusively close. There was nothing he could do about it, except to take advantage of what was offered and try to forget what was being withheld. And so life continued until 1475 when he reached the age of eighteen.

With the lady of his tapestry he had conducted an affair of courtly love, keeping her in his mind at tournaments so that he charged as well as those who wore their living lady's favour. But Hubert and the others chaffed him and his pride was hurt, seeing first one and then another of them play the lover with older women or hunt the countryside for willing girls. And Jasper had warned him to avoid a prostitute for fear of disease, and then left him to his own devices. So between his shyness and his terror of the pox he remained chaste. Only once had he attempted to prove his manhood, when his hunting party met a group of milkmaids.

'There is one for each us!' said Hubert, flushed by the morning ride, and secured his choice.

The others bore off their giggling shrieking burdens, and Henry swept the last girl desperately up on to his saddle. But when they reached the privacy of a glade she wept so grievously and wrung her hands and wailed about her honour – which was all she had – that he let her go again. And indeed she was only a child, thanking him and bobbing a curtsey before she took to her heels. He asked a little kindness of her as she wiped her face with her skirt; and she agreed, round-eyed, not to betray the fact that she left him as pure as she had come to him. Then he sat moodily on the ground while his horse cropped peacefully nearby, and cursed and tore up a handful of grass.

He was quick to see that noble wives, tired of their husbands, were as much drawn by status as by lust. For unless one was a Hubert, with a flattering tongue and glint of eye which promised a host of pleasures, one must be of some consequence. Whereas he, a noble object of the duke's charity, was virginal and of slight consequence.

'You bring out the mother in them, Harry,' said Hubert, recounting his latest exploit, 'and though it is well to have a mother it is best that the mother be not your mistress! If women are not to your liking there are others.' And he indicated a pretty page lounging against the wall, who blushed and smiled at the attention.

'I am not one that loves boys!' said Henry, frowning.

'Then must you burn!'

Burn he did, playing the charmed spectator, envying even Jasper who took women as he took a meal – when needed – and was more attractive to them because they knew they were not paramount. So Henry made a show of hunting, at which he excelled, and while his friends pursued ladies he drove down the gentle hart and trembling hare.

Rigaud's dark shed had seemed so much a part of him, and the falcons so much his passion, that Henry was surprised to see a girl of fifteen unpacking her basket there at noon. And she, more startled than himself, made her curtsey and did not know where to look.

'Go you, go you to your mother!' Rigaud ordered gruffly, and when she had slipped past Henry, scarlet-cheeked, he said reluctantly, 'That is my youngest daughter, my lord, who fetches me food when I am not at home.'

Then he laid aside the black bread and milky cheese and spoke of other matters, and though Henry was curious he asked no questions, sensing that Rigaud's private life was sacred to him. And he watched the man courting his fierce birds and wondered whether he had courted his wife so subtly, and thinking of courtship remembered the shy girl agape at his fine clothes. He made enquiries as delicate as they were casual, and discovered Rigaud's other life, sad and complex and dark as the falconer himself.

'For he married a shrew, my lord,' said a groom, holding Henry's horse, 'though some say she was fair-tongued until she found he loved the falcons more. And the worse husband he made the better falconer he became. Yet was she fruitful for he has a hutful of children, though all are grown and most are gone. And they say he cared not for any but this last, and her he loves above all, watching her as he watches his hawks, and will not let any man come near her. So unless the maid takes a fancy to some fellow she will die unwed.'

Had he been Hubert he would have had to hunt the girl forthwith, but being Henry he dreamed of her instead, and came upon Rigaud frequently at noon without finding her there, and suspected that the falconer had altered the time of her coming – in which he was correct. And Rigaud smiled grimly to himself as the young earl looked covertly about the shed, and sighed and talked of anything but what truly brought him there. Once he called at Rigaud's hut when he was hunting, and asked for water, but a sour-faced woman served him and he could see nothing of the girl. As spring became summer and Brittany was abuzz with rumours of an English expedition, Henry began his first amorous campaign and planned it with as much care and cunning as King Edward devoted to his march on France.

His letters from Lady Margaret lay often half-read, and Jasper's groans at inactivity received as little attention as good manners demanded. Instead he made a study of peasant life from dawn to dark, amassing information from every source, from phrases and scraps of talk so scanty and diverse that no one except himself would have had use for them. And having drawn a picture of her day he drew conclusions, and was out on his horse alone just before first light on an August morning.

'Why, mushrooms are a poor man's meat, my lord,' a

servitor had said, 'and they spring up in the night like witch-craft, and belong to the one that picks them earliest.'

So he rode earlier than any, and prayed that she would be early too. And there she was with her basket, coming away from the field and singing to herself. He reined in beside her and the song stopped as she recognized him. She bent her head, gripped her rough basket, and said nothing to his courtesies, though he spoke first in French and then in the Breton dialect. And the dialect, springing from the same roots as the Welsh tongue, added a dimension of fantasy and made him feel at home again.

Henry had spent too much of his life among horses, hounds and hawks to spoil this quarry with a hasty victory. For the moment, as the sun rose, he contented himself by removing her fears. As though he had been on his way else-where he asked about the mushrooms, said he knew her father well, and then flicked the reins on his horse's neck and bade her a good morning. Looking back, twenty yards further on, he saw her staring after him, and smiled to himself.

He was as secret and as patient in this little matter as he had told Jasper he would be in a great estate, and sweeter even than the long conquest was the feeling that this was himself in his own world. Rigaud's protection had made her guileless, and though she knew that all their meetings could not be happy chances, yet she lacked the wit to see how they were planned. And he was always so mindful of her that she could not think he wished her harm. So he progressed, from the first moment that she told him her name was Berthe until that late summer evening when he slipped gold in the gate-keeper's hand and met her in the woods by appoint-ment.

She was late, since she slept with her mother and had to wait until the woman snored oblivion. And Rigaud, as Henry well knew, was keeping a long watch with a new hawk. So they were alone, and as safe in their grass and flower bed as those who lay within the château walls. Rigaud had taught him courtship, and the girl's innocence dis-guised the fact that he was as much a virgin as herself. Nor did she protest that he would think lightly of her, but went with him trustfully and was glad to please him, though once she cried out for her mother and wept a little.

They lay there until dawn and he looked down at her sleeping lids and thought of the tamed falcon, and was taken by a strange tenderness. His conscience gave him a sharp prick about Rigaud, but he stilled it by remembering that he was a lord and as such pursued his own code of honour. And though he never boasted of his victory there was an air about him, so that Hubert ceased to play the cockerel and shrugged his shoulders and said he was a secretive fellow.

'When you have done smiling to yourself,' said Jasper tartly, 'I'll speak of politics, but let me not disturb your inward thoughts for they must be weighty!'

'I crave your pardon, uncle.'

'The king of England has not forgotten Harry Tudor,' Jasper continued, mollified, 'and if you read your lady mother's letters you will find that we now perch upon the limb of a tree.'

And he picked up a twig and drew in the dust a triangle and a half-circle.

'For three years has King Edward milked England of her wealth and to some purpose,' and he prodded the triangle. 'He had no civil war to wage, with Lancaster gone, and yet his sword-arm itched for he is a great warrior. He should rust upon the wall as I do,' Jasper added crossly, 'then would he know what rusting was! But with this wealth he forged an army greater than any English monarch led, and sailed it out to France,' and he drew a line between the triangle and the half-circle, 'but three months ago, if you remember. For his brother-in-law Burgundy,' drawing a cross in France's centre, 'had promised him that if he fought from Calais Burgundy would prod Louis in the back. But when he got there he found the bold Charles skirmishing in another part and unmindful of his promise . . .'

'All this I know, uncle,' said Henry gently. 'And they have signed a treaty, for neither of them wanted war. And King Edward had the best of the bargain – having the best army – and so sailed home with 75,000 crowns in his pocket and 50,000 crowns a year to come, and his eldest daughter betrothed to the Dauphin Charles. And of them all she has the *worst* of the bargain for the Dauphin is an ugly creature and she a pretty child, so I have heard.'

'They are not married yet,' said Jasper sagely, 'and Louis has an old score to pay, for the king jilted his sister-in-law, Bona. So may the Dauphin yet insult the Princess Elizabeth of York and wipe her father's smile off his face. But it is not this of which I speak. Now here are we,' and he portioned off a little circle on the shore of France. 'And here is Edward,' and he shaded in England, 'and here is Louis, that has signed the Treaty of Pecquigni with him and a nine years' peace,' and he shaded a great part of France, 'and here is Charles of Burgundy that has signed the same treaty. So where is the Duke of Brittany now but surrounded by his enemies?'

Dragged from his summer nights in one brief moment, Henry stared at the little patch of dust, his smile vanishing.

'The duke has suffered a decline in power since he was forced to take an oath of allegiance to Louis last year,' Jasper continued, 'and Brittany was not then as independent as she has been. Now look at her, and look at us if Edward should decide you must go home!'

'The duke is proud and will not have us taken on a whim.'

'The duke is powerless and has no other choice. So pray that King Edward does not want a Tudor son-in-law – and watch yourself in the woods, Harry, at night. For there be eyes and ears in Brittany that could work for England.'

Henry flushed suddenly and Jasper chuckled.

'Nay lad, I am not your priest but your counsellor. Take what you want and pay for it.'

'Pay?' said Henry, jolted into speech.

Jasper looked at him lazily but with some compassion.

'I do not mean with gold,' he said, 'but your wench will cost you a falconer's friendship for a beginning, and maybe more before the end.'

'There are too many tongues in Brittany!' Henry cried, outraged.

'Now do you see what kings' crowns hang upon,' Jasper replied.

As the autumn drew in and nights were chilly Henry and his mistress sought the warmth of hay, and brought their love affair nearer to home. His nobility protected him to a great extent because no peasant would carry a tale about a lord unless it meant money, and no one in the château was interested enough to pay for such information. And the falconer's wife, hearing whispers and once finding the girl gone from her bed, was too fearful of Henry and her husband's wrath to say anything. So dank November came, and crisp December, before the falconer heard, and Henry found him there instead of Berthe.

'We'll have no play with words, my lord,' said Rigaud quietly. 'She is at home and shall not come again. I had not looked for this, my lord. I thought your courtesy too great to spoil her.'

He must have rehearsed his little speech over and over, for it came mechanically though his eyes were fierce. His arms hung at his sides, his shoulders drooped, about his person hung an air of lifelessness.

'She is with child!' he shouted suddenly.

The words came from Henry almost without his volition. A child in whose peasant veins ran a thin stream of royalty, and this rough falconer accused him of despoiling.

'Then does she bear a noble burden,' said Henry quietly.

The last atom of understanding had been destroyed, and Rigaud's hand went to the knife in his belt.

'Now hold your hand, good Rigaud,' Henry commanded. 'My death accomplishes nothing,' but his own hand moved to the hilt of his sword. 'Your daughter shall be well-provided. So shall the child. And the dowry I give her shall fetch her a husband. It is small hardship, then, for any of us.'

'Oh, my lord,' Rigaud whispered, 'you speak lightly of hardship that bears none. The falcon in my shed will fetch more gold than you can give my daughter. Where is her honour now, that was pure as any? I thought to give her to a goodly man. Oh you did tear my heart when you deflowered her, as no man will again. If there is justice in heaven I pray God to witness this. I pray you lose a child as I have done, then will you know grief. And I curse you, waking and sleeping, sitting or lying or standing, in youth and middle years and in old age, in company and solitude, to your life's end.'

Pale and proud they stared at one another, and then Henry turned on his heel and left him.

He bore the weight of Rigaud's curse as the news passed round the court: from the duke's smile as he gave Henry money for the girl and the bastard she carried, to Hubert's insensitive banter. Only Jasper said nothing, but must have told the Lady Margaret of it, for she wrote seeming to speak of King Edward and his brother Clarence.

The king has civil war within his family. First between the queen's relatives that are greedy for power, and his own brother Richard of Gloucester and his mother the Duchess Cecily that call them 'mongrel connections'. And then between Clarence and them all. For though Clarence is harm-

less unless he has a master such as Warwick was, he is an ambitious fool and cannot keep his fingers from the crown, and quarrels with every man.

The Duke of Gloucester keeps in the north, where they say he rules the border wisely and well, and the king has bestowed many honours upon him. But Clarence who does nothing says the king is partial, and ever seeks new friends that might help him. He even whispers plots with Louis of France, which is a perilous undertaking, for Louis only looks for mischief and would betray him if he took the whim. So though the house of York rules it is rifted with betrayal, and the house that is divided against itself cannot stand.

Yet must we ever look into our own hearts and learn from them, lest they betray our souls. The betrayer and the betrayed suffer separately and their suffering is different. Yet each can learn from the act of betrayal. Above all else must they put it behind them, when they have suffered, and go on apart. But Clarence is a foolish prince and returns again and again to the sins he has committed, and shall do until the king's patience fails, and so he learns nothing that should learn much.

On a fine morning in the early summer of 1476, as the court assembled for a hunting party, Henry heard news from his groom.

'They say that Rigaud's daughter is dead, my lord,' said the man, fumbling with Henry's stirrup and keeping his face averted.

'And what of the child?'

'Still-born, my lord.'

'The stirrup is well enough,' said Henry, after a chilled pause. 'How does poor Rigaud?'

'Why, he is in a maze of sorry thoughts, and sits like one that will not rise again. And though some go to comfort him he looks and says nothing.'

'I'll not hunt today,' said Henry slowly, beginning to dismount.

But Jasper rode beside him and halted him with a warning hand.

'You shall hunt, Harry, though you die for it,' he said in a low voice, and drew him away from the groom's busy ears. 'The wench is dead. Your mourning cannot give her life again and will cause talk at court. I told you, lad, to take and pay for it.'

'She paid for all!'

'She paid a princely price, now do you likewise. Your payment, Harry, shall be a smiling countenance. No nobleman sheds tears over a peasant mistress, but keeps them in his heart or for his private chamber. And if you love again, Harry, see that it be your wife – or else a woman that you cannot break. Life teaches cruelly, that is your lesson, lad. Now mount and ride, and see that you are foremost in the hunt. And, Harry, do not fall behind the rest – not only for your honour but for your safety. King Edward grows impatient, and he has friends in Brittany.'

So the little cavalcade rode out of the château : the gentlemen as fine as the ladies, and all merry at the prospect of the chase. And Henry was as gay as the rest and held his head high, but when he slipped the hood from the falcon's head his hand shook momentarily.

The bird looked about her with inhuman eyes, ruffling her striped feathers, and then soared high and true into the morning air. He watched her flight, and knowledge lay in him like a stone.

The embassy that arrived in Brittany, under the auspices of Bishop Stillington, brought protestations of friendship and kindness, and a pressing desire for Henry Tudor's welfare. Duke Francois was not deceived, but as he exchanged compliments he reflected on his position, of which he was presently reminded in the most delicate way.

'King Edward holds your love so dear, your grace,' said Bishop Stillington, 'that he would have proof of it. The king of France and the Duke of Burgundy have signed a treaty with him, and he has ever been a friend to Brittany. Wherefore he wonders why you will not let him have his subject, Henry Tudor. No harm shall come to him but all honour.'

'Inform the Earl of Richmond that I would speak to him,' said the duke, wavering.

Henry had lived so long with the prospect of betrayal that it haunted his dreams : from which he awoke thanking God for deliverance. Now the reality bore all the terrible aspects of a dream, and promised no awakening.

So they rode from the capital city of Nantes, at the mouth of the Loire, like a party of gentlemen taking delight in each other's company. But Henry rode in the midst of them, and their good manners did not prevent their watching him closely though the watching was covered by smiles. The great mass of the château grew smaller. First the sculptured arms of Brittany, flanking the drawbridge, became part of the stone. Then he could no longer distinguish the flowers that grew by the moat. And at last only the fair towers were visible.

Farewell, Nantes, Henry thought, and farewell, château – whose Tower of the Golden Crown I shall never see finished. And farewell, cathedral, for whom I held affection, since like Penelope's web its building never ends in completion. And farewell, port, from whose harbour sail all the sweet and sharp and savoury things of life.

Then he fell so silent that they spoke among themselves : courtly and adamant as sheathed swords.

'This is not well, your grace,' said Jean du Quelenc, Admiral of Brittany, gaining an audience of the duke. 'Since when has your duchy bowed her head to England?'

'Since England, Burgundy and France threatened her coast and borders !' said Duke François sternly.

The admiral stood his ground.

'We have been as a great church to the Earl of Richmond, giving him sanctuary. Is that sanctuary to be violated at the word of an English monarch? Shall not France and Burgundy smile and look sideways at us, and think secretly to themselves, "If the proud duke does thus and thus for England shall he not grant us like favours?" And what favours, your grace?'

'The duchy shall not stand in peril for one exiled nobleman.'

'Nay, your grace, it stands in greater peril for letting him go. It shows weakness and a want of mercy that does us much dishonour. Our enemies shall pounce upon the one, and our friends cry shame upon the other ! I do beseech your grace, out of the princely qualities and virtues that rule us, to find another answer in your heart. Send some man after them, one secret of counsel and cunning in policy, that he may steal the earl away and fetch him to safety.'

Pierre Landois, Treasurer of Brittany, smoothest of courtiers, sleek and wary as a cat, reached the Engish party at St Malo the evening before they prepared to embark. He had brought a very small company with him and some excellent

Rhennes wine, and he entreated them – out of the great friendship that Brittany bore England – to dine with him. Flattered, for the man's tongue surpassed even the wine in sweetness, they locked Henry in his chamber and settled to a night's carousal.

'The Earl of Richmond does not join us?' Landois asked, eyebrows raised.

'The earl has fallen into a sore ague, sir, and is better abed.'

'To England and King Edward!' Ladois cried, raising his silver cup.

'To England and King Edward!' they answered, tossing off the wine.

Two men from the treasurer's modest retinue searched from room to room as the embassy drank itself under the table. And Landois smiled, and toasted each of them, and their kindred, sipping his splendid wine. As the hardest English head lifted its final cup – to the swans that sail upon the Thames – a servant brought a message for Landois.

'I shall be with you presently,' he said aside. 'And now, my good lord, to the grass that grows green in the meadows!'

'Grass – green – meadows . . .'

The treasurer lifted the last man's head from a puddle of wine and saw that he was asleep. Then, cat-like, he left them to snore until morning.

There was nothing unprofessional about the way he conducted that difficult interview the following day. He had taken the precaution of placing Henry in sanctuary in St Malo, now he waited to hear what the English would say for themselves. Accusations of treachery, remonstrances about his conduct, found him unmoved.

'My good lords, I know nothing of this,' he said, elegant and sober in contrast to their rumpled finery and aching heads. 'If the earl slipped away while we drank it is the fault of the embassy! Yet this much may I promise, in the name of Brittany, if he is here we shall keep him here and keep him safely. He shall not move from Nantes once we have him.'

'And now, my lord bishop and my lords, I must return to the duke. He did but bid me grant you a fond-farewell, and that I have done.'

He paused, smiling, 'For your own sakes,' he added, 'I regret that the earl escaped. Ah me! *In vino veritas*, they say. And yet in too much wine may be found not the truth but a fuddled head!'

King Edward received the news with more philosophy than anyone had hoped, and came to an understanding with Duke François. He bade Brittany keep Henry very close, and so that all should remember that Henry Tudor was English property the English king would pay for his expenses out of the Richmond estates.

CHAPTER TEN

King Edward: Now am I seated as my soul delights,
*   Having my country's peace and brothers' loves*

Henry VI, Part III, Scene VII
William Shakespeare

Shortly before Jasper and Henry had sought refuge with him, the Duke of Brittany had married the daughter of Count Gaston IV of Foix, to give his duchy the heir she needed. In 1477, after six years of deferred hopes the child arrived, but was a daughter. Still, when one is born safely others may follow. The little duchess, magnificently robed, was christened with pomp and splendour – though not with that degree of rejoicing that would have attended a little duke. They named her Anne and found that she possessed a royal will of her own, and was healthy in spite of a lame foot. There were to be no more children.

In the meantime only Jasper, having nothing to lose, found possible good fortune in the child's sex. For when the girl came of age, and perhaps ruler of Brittany, she would need a strong husband – and here was Henry Tudor, lacking nothing but a rich wife with a rich estate.

'You could do worse, lad,' he observed, as they played backgammon.

Henry's smile was rueful.

'Aye, and I wait a dozen years or more, uncle!'

'Patience!' counselled Jasper, contemplating a move. 'Patience, Harry! The little duchess grows apace.'

'And has great purpose, uncle. Today I came upon her with her nurse in the gardens, and she used me as a horse for above an hour. "Come, my lady!" said the nurse, for she saw that the horse was weary. "Come, mistress, for you must rest!" The child has the will of a man and her noble father's frown. "Nay," she said, "I shall not!" Gently I strove to unwind her arms from about my neck. Less gently the nurse strove also. The Duchess Anne became a very limpet! In the end I galloped her to her chamber and said it was the stable and she should dismount. Whereupon she let me go and thanked me heartily, promising she should see me on another day. Uncle, I love her very well. I hope to love none better, save my own children. And yet I fear me I shall be too old when she is old enough to wed.'

'But she shall need a husband to defend her, and I have heard that the duke's physicians look for no more heirs. Consider the heiress of Burgundy, Harry. Between her father dying in the January of last year and her pretty Maximilian wedding her in the August, she lost Boulogne and the greater part of Picardy and Artois to Louis. And that flickering fellow Maximilian – a fool in the field if ever I knew of one! – promises to lose her more. You would do better by the little duchess, with this sword at your command also, than did the lovely Max by the Duchess Mary!'

'Well, we shall see, uncle. But I would not have a wife that ruled instead of me, and Brittany would be hers. Do you see me playing the meek husband at court? No, mark my words she will take some mincing lad that does as she says – or else some powerful prince that will bring lands as well as hands in wedlock. And I have nothing.'

'You have your life and youth, and much may be made of both. King Edward is content to forget you, for he has trouble enough at home. The queen breeds bravely – five daughters and three sons in fourteen years – but she has time to spare for her family, and the Woodvilles and Greys stand high at court, though not well-loved. And the treachery of Clarence hurt him besides. Nor has Louis forgotten him, though they say he is ill and fears death.'

Clarence's bids for power had been more of a nuisance than a danger, but they mounted, bursting out here and there in ill-considered plans and plots. He had attempted, through his sister Margaret of Burgundy, to win the hand of Duchess Mary; and confided in Louis what he would do when the Netherlands were in his grasp – which Louis obligingly passed on to Edward, thus ruining Clarence's chances. Then he had toyed with the notion of marrying the sister of James III of Scotland, and making a dash for the throne with the help of England's old enemy. He had long since lost his brother Richard's esteem by quarrelling over the Neville inheritance and trying to prevent his marriage with Ann Neville, widow of Prince Edward Lancaster. In a bout of sulky distrust he cried that he was in danger of being poisoned at court, and so stayed away from London. He had been implicated in the West Country rising, under the Lancastrian Earl of Oxford in 1474, urged on by Louis. He had hanged people privately, without proper trial, on the suspicion that they poisoned his wife Isabel Neville and her infant son – whereas she died in childbirth, and the infant died soon after.

Edward had borne with him as patiently as he could, but when Clarence spread rumours that the queen was practising witchcraft, and followed it by raising a minor rebellion in Huntingdon and Cambridge, the king brought him to trial for treason.

People say that the queen's family, remembering the execution of the queen's father and brother on Banbury Field, by order of Clarence and Warwick, would have him done away likewise. But the king sent the duke to the Tower and would do nothing, though no one spoke for his brother and all spoke against him. [Lady Margaret had written at the end of February 1478.] *And so Clarence, caught between brotherly love on the one side and queenly hatred on the other, met with an unlucky accident. On 18 February a cask of vintage wine from Malvasia, in the East of Morea, was brought into the Tower for the duke's pleasure. It is said that he drank himself into a stupor and so fell into the cask and was drowned. But others say that some waited until he snored and then held him by the heels with his face down in the wine.*

'Aye, there's your Yorkist!' Jasper cried. 'If they cannot kill Lancastrians they kill each other.'

The king is much grieved by this, [the letter ended] *and often says at court, 'O unhappy brother, for whose deliverance no man asked!' And though the Duke of Gloucester did not love him he swears he will avenge his death.*

'Well, that is one Yorkist the less,' said Jasper with some satisfaction. 'And whiten his memory though they will, he was a scurvy villain!'

Henry smiled to himself, reading through the letter yet again, finding his uncle's furious championship of Lancaster as comforting as his mother's more statesmanlike approach.

'So here we languish in this ducal backwater,' Jasper continued, 'and I grow older and the duke hangs back from war as though it was the pestilence. I keep my sword in practice,

Harry, and hope for better times. Harry, you know I wish you well, lad, and yet it was a breath of life when they tried to fetch you into England. I felt an old tide of blood rise in me that has not risen for seven long years.'

'Now it is my turn to counsel patience,' said Henry, putting away his letter, 'and if war beckons then I challenge you to a contest of archery, and we shall see who bends the best bow!'

'But it is not the same,' Jasper grumbled. 'And England and France stand still and nothing changes.'

The changes were subtle and slow, but they came nevertheless. In the March of 1481 Louis was stricken with apoplexy, a happy event which Duke François heard of during his supper. Immediately he gave a toast to the French king's health. His wording was courtly to the point of ambiguity, but they knew very well what he meant, and raised their cups with some satisfaction, hoping that even now the old tyrant was strangling on his last breath. And straightway the duke disregarded his oath of allegiance, since Louis was in no position to enforce it.

A little private sorrow the following year brought greater changes to Lady Margaret's life. Her husband Henry Stafford died, and though the marriage had never been one of passion and was childless she mourned him, for they had lived in mutual respect and affection for over twenty years and she was no longer young. Though Henry hardly knew his stepfather their relationship had been warm and courteous, and in his will Henry Stafford bequeathed him a trapper of four new horse harnesses of velvet. Politically-minded Jasper found opportunity even in this mild grief.

'The Lady Margaret must wed again,' he said, sending his condolences. 'Perchance a man in the king's favour this time. For he may rule many years yet, and we should do well to have a friend at court!'

In the November of 1482 Lady Margaret married Lord Thomas Stanley and her choice seemed as ambiguous as the man himself.

'Now is he for York or Lancaster?' Jasper mused. 'King Henry of sacred memory knighted him in 1460, but he was married to a Neville, and joined his brother-in-law Warwick at Banbury Field. And yet, though he fought against King Edward at that time, the king made him Steward of the Household the year after, where he is held in great esteem. And now he marries an heir of Lancaster.'

'A man of political ambition,' Henry offered. 'There are many such about the king. For Bishop Morton changed his allegiance, though he went into exile with Queen Margaret, and he has much power at court. And Chief Justice Fortescue, in the same case, did likewise – and so was able to write his book *De Laudibus Legum Anglie*, which my mother sent me. It has a Yorkist flavour to please the king, and yet it is a fine book that any monarch might read and profit by.'

'I should not like Lord Stanley on my side in battle, nonetheless,' said Jasper resolutely. 'For I should not know whether he was with or against me, and that is the truth!'

'I doubt not my mother's judgement, and Lord Stanley is close to the king. And in any case the thing is done and we must abide by it.'

'I tell you, Harry, this is a wily fox,' said Jasper, unconvinced, and he tapped the letter.

But his opinion had not been sought, and he turned his attention to other matters for Burgundy was in turmoil and this seemed closer to him than his sister-in-law's marriage.

The Duchess of Burgundy had fallen from her horse and was killed, leaving her feckless husband Maximilian to the attentions of the ailing Louis. Failing or not, the French king had a few cards to play before he left the table he had disrupted so lovingly and so long. He began by denying Maximilian the custody of his own children, and then contracted a match between his son, the Dauphin Charles, and Maximilian's daughter. Her stupendous dowry of the duchy and county of Burgundy, Artois, and a great deal else was to be administered meanwhile by the Dauphin. Louis had waited eighteen years to settle that ancient score of his wife's jilted sister, Bona of Savoy, and now he could strike at Edward through his eldest daughter. Regretfully, he cancelled the betrothal of Elizabeth of York to the Dauphin.

Edward, still heavy from the death of his second daughter Mary that same year, within weeks of her fifteenth birthday, now suffered for Elizabeth in a different way. His rage at the dishonour done to himself and her simmered down to a calculating coldness. He began secretly to prepare for war with France, stock-piling arms in various parts of England, while Louis made ready to attack him through Flanders.

Hidden in his château, and guarded as though death itself could be denied an entrance, Louis grasped at earthly trophies even yet. Queen Margaret, widow of Henry VI, had died in August, and the French king demanded that all her dogs be sent to him forthwith.

'For she has made me her heir,' he wrote, 'and this is all I shall get. I pray you not to keep any back, for you would cause me a terrible great displeasure!'

Gasping in his cushioned chair, watching the little animals gambol, eyes hooded and mouth pursed, he entered on the last months of his life.

On 9 April 1483 the ruined hulk which had been Edward IV lay on a hill of pillows. He who had been known as a goodly personage and princely to behold was now grotesque with fat, but his courage and political cunning were left him, and he sought to make a peace within his family that would ensure the peace of England for his son.

At one side of his bed stood his queen's relatives, on the other his friend Lord Hastings and the old nobility. And presiding over all was Bishop Morton preparing to send a royal soul to heaven and make sure of his own position on earth : a feat of dexterity at which he was an undoubted master.

The king gestured to the attendants to raise him higher, and to collect the assembled company at his right side so that he might see them. His heir Prince Edward, now at the Castle of Ludlow, was twelve years old; his second son Prince Richard hardly ten; a third son, George, had died in 1479. For these two young princes he begged a truce from both parties, warning them that if they split into factions during a child's reign all of them might perish. He wished that his brother Richard had been there, and prayed that Hastings and the queen might not quarrel before he came. And, rousing himself with difficulty to reach them through their grief, he spoke of ambition as a pestilent serpent, and the desire for vainglory and sovereignty as turning all things to mischief. He bade them, for the love that God bore to all men, to love each other; and trusted that they would for their own surety, and that of the boy who must be sheltered as he learned to rule them.

They wept bitterly and joined hands to show him that they heard and understood. But he feared for them, and for the boy, even as his eyes closed.

'King Edward is dead,' said Henry, in quiet disbelief, 'The Duke of Gloucester is Protector and has taken the young king in his custody, and the queen is in sanctuary with her son Dorset and Prince Richard and her daughters.'

'The wheel of fortune!' cried Jasper, and then with some irony, 'And is Lord Stanley, your new stepfather, with the queen or with the duke?'

'Why, with the Duke of Gloucester, for the late king made him an executor of his will in place of the queen.'

'Then my nose tells me that the wind lies in Gloucester's quarter.'

'My mother speaks of the Duke of Buckingham, that has supported Gloucester, and is a nephew of her late husband Henry Stafford. I know nothing of him.'

'Nor I, except that the queen made him wed her sister Catherine Woodville when he was but twelve years old, and that he hates her for it – aye, and hates his wife, for all that they have five children. I thought he lived at Brecon and was not much seen at court. His father died for Lancaster. What else says the Lady Margaret?'

'She waits and watches and knows not what will happen.'

'Then shall we do likewise, Harry, for now the scorpions are ringed with fire, and sting themselves to death. Mark me, lad. We shall see Yorkist against Yorkist until the last is slain, for they are proud and stately of stomach. And each one longs first to be next best to the king, then equal to the and at last chief and above the best. And when they have done slaughtering one another we may go home again! I pray that the Lord Stanley chooses his sides to some good purpose, and finds employment for us.'

'And the Duke of Gloucester has arrested the young king's uncle, Lord Rivers, and his half-brother Lord Richard Grey, and old Sir Thomas Vaughan, saying that they conspired against him and the nobility of the realm.'

'Aye, well,' said Jasper, enjoying himself, 'I dare swear they would have done the same to him had they moved faster!'

'And here is Buckingham again, that rode to meet the Protector, and is ever close to him in council, and like to supplant the Lord Hastings in favour.'

'He springs on every page, Harry. We must mark his progress! But then the Duke of Gloucester was never very merry with Lord Hastings, for the duke is a prudish man and Hastings always loved a trollop in his bed. What more?'

'They say that Dorset stole the treasure from the Tower, and that Sir Edward Woodville escaped with the royal fleet.'

'Now they are rightly matched,' said Jasper, growing more and more cheerful as the news unfolded. 'And we may watch them, Harry, as we watch a play. Seeing first one side act and then the other, and I am not sorry for any save the young king. And when they have done playing we can step forward, with Lord Stanley's help, and bowing to the ruined house of York, in humble-wise, commend our services. I like Lord Stanley better, Harry, he promises very well. And Bishop Morton is another that sniffs a change in the winds of state. Wise men both, after their fashion, that can turn their coats in a night, and come up smiling on the morrow.'

'My mother says the young king is nothing content, for he was reared among the queen's relatives and knows not Gloucester and his father's friends, but it boots him not – though Gloucester and Buckingham are kindly to him.'

'And when shall the young king be crowned?'

'The date set by the queen has been altered.'

'Aye, and shall be again. Mark me. Oh, Harry, this is the finest letter that ever your lady mother penned with her fair hand. And now I got to try my armour on, and see if I have grown too stout for it and must have a piece or two let in. And practise sword-play, horsed and armoured, in lieu of preferment at court.'

Henry put down the letter and laughed aloud.

'Set not your hopes too high,' he cautioned. 'And what is this of sword-play? I thought you peaceably prepared to take up some little post in government when England settled.'

'Why, so I am,' Jasper retorted, grinning, 'but when I sup with Yorkists, Harry, I take a sword to help me with my meat – and let another try the supper first, lest it be poisoned!'

CHAPTER ELEVEN

Buckingham: This noble isle doth want her proper limbs;
Her face defac'd with scars of infamy,
Her royal stock graft with ignoble plants.

Richard III, Act III, Scene VII
William Shakespeare

England was rich and beautiful : her rivers and streams abundant with fish, her trees heavy with fruit and foliage, her open fields gold with grain or white with sheep – the backbone of her prosperity. Monasteries kept their own fishponds and vineyards and dovecotes, and opened their doors to all who needed succour or shelter. The belly was considered as religiously as the soul, and the Abbot of St Alban's dined daily and well at his table in the middle of the hall. Fifteen steps high he sat above the rest, and his monks sang a hymn on every fifth step as they bore his food upwards. But he lodged and fed countless humble pilgrims, at no cost to themselves, for three days at a time. And each evening the poor came for the great baskets of broken bread and meats, and blessed him for his charity.

Bricks, which had first come into the country from Flanders a century before, were now manufactured of local clay, and a host of private and public buildings sprang up. Merchants and noblemen built fine houses and palaces that glowed russet and rose. Splendid guildhalls, intricate chantries, dignified colleges, magnificent churches, testified to England's prosperity. Grammar schools were now more frequently endowed than nunneries. Good churchmen urged the education of the sons and wards of yeomen, burghers and the lesser gentry, as well as the nobility. And boys were beaten or praised, according to their abilities, to speak and write and translate Latin as though it were their mothertongue. Without it no boy could hope to enter the Church, to practise medicine or the law or undertake civic duties. Eton and Winchester, the great public schools, drew pupils from the south to the north of England, to board and flog and instruct them into Oxford or Cambridge. Books were the perquisites of the rich; but a lighter education by word of mouth – the singing of ballads, the telling of stories – circulated among all classes. And William Caxton, setting up his printing press in Westminster in 1477, had the patronage of the court, and from his press poured translations of Cicero, of Aesop's *Fables*, and the popular works of Chaucer.

Suburbs spread from London, the flower of cities, and over fifty goldsmiths and silversmiths displayed wares worth a king's ransom, in the Strand leading to St Paul's. The wharves swarmed with ships of many nations. The Worshipful Companies of Mercers, Grocers, Drapers and Fishmongers conserved and extended their wealth – and supported each government as it came into power. On London bridge the houses rose tall and fine and crowded, and above the Tower rose the traitors' heads – rotting upon their poles.

The labourer, though his hours were long and his work hard, enjoyed good wages and full employment, due to the combination of war and plague. By command of the Church he could not be employed on Sundays and Saints' Days. He had his wakes and revels. Pageants trundled on wooden stages from place to place in the towns. The village procession to the butts for an archery competition was led by men disguised as Robin Hood and Little John. He laid wagers, wrestled, ran races, played hand-ball and foot-ball, threw the bar or the stone, and relished a little secret poaching in the woods and streams. The glut in land, and some thriftiness on his part, could buy him a few strips of his own to cultivate. Then, if a red-cheeked wench caught his fancy he courted her as he pleased; for the poor were richer than the rich in love, and having no material wealth to bargain for could indulge the wealth of the heart. Over him the landlord had power, and over the landlord the nobleman, and over him the king.

True, the roads were nothing more than muddy lanes, pitted with holes, water-logged in winter, reeking of dung and garbage in summer. But bushes were lopped for a distance of two hundred feet on either side of the main highways, so that no robbers could hide and spring out unnoticed by travellers. And yet, though Edward had enforced the public peace as his predecessor could not, every man rode warily, and every letter could not be sure of reaching its destination. The bridges were in no better state, and bishops granted indulgences and pardons to men who bequeathed money or materials for their repair. So each journey was a hazardous venture, to be alleviated only by fine weather and a local guide – who would know the driest ford and the safest road. In the best conditions a man reckoned to cover between thirty and forty miles a day; in poor conditions perhaps twenty to thirty. But a messenger on important business would ride fifty hard miles in that time, and a king's messenger could perform feats of horsemanship that verged on the impossible.

On humbler, domestic missions, the professional carriers gave good service from one part of England to another, though sometimes the winter rendered that service immobile. The long-distance carrier jogged from London to such distant places as Norfolk, Shrewsbury and Exeter, and back again, bearing money and valuables, letters and goods. The short-distance carrier would travel more frequently, but on a half-day circuit which enabled him to reach home the same night.

In spite of these conditions the government and daily round of England rolled inexorably on. Judges made their usual itineraries; merchants rode with their trains of laden pack-horses; pilgrims trudged to Canterbury, to Walsingham and other shrines; friars and pardoners exchanged the mercy of God for a groat; and armed retainers trotted to and fro on their lord's personal errands. Pausing and gaping as they passed, the peasant bent again to his endless tasks of hoeing and sowing, or licked his toiling oxen with a whip, turning the fruits of the earth to other men's profits. And in the green forests the hunting horn sounded and the falcon soared, and the wild boar and gentle hart turned at bay.

Above all this wealth and power loomed the pestilence, capricious and despotic, bred in the ports and cities, spreading to the countryside. Flea-bearing rats were its messengers, the gutters laden with refuse and running with sewage its good friends, the close dark houses its patrons. Democratic in aspect, it made no distinction between the mighty and the lowly, and all fell or fled before it. Then as suddenly as it had begun it ceased, passive but unconquered. And the people buried their dead and thanked God for their deliverance.

The messenger who galloped into Westminster from Stony Stratford had stopped only to change horses. He brought news that would set the palace in an uproar. For the Duke of Gloucester had arrested the young king's guardians, Lord Rivers and Sir Richard Grey, and taken the king into his personal custody.

Wailing and wringing her hands the queen gathered children and servants and baggage about her, and once more sought sanctuary. But this time there would be no warrior husband to fetch her out again, and no infant son to cheer her exile.

A different messenger reached Hastings, bearing Richard of Gloucester's letter to the Council, and Hastings sent another man to knock up the Lord Chancellor, Thomas Rotherham, Archbishop of York. At first the Archbishop's servants refused to wake him, but the man was so adamant that they finally conducted him to the bedside, where Rotherham heard the tale in astonished silence.

'Notwithstanding, my lord,' said the messenger, 'my Lord Hastings sends your lordship word that there is no need to fear. For he assures you that all shall be well.'

'*I* assure *him*,' the archbishop replied gravely, 'that be it as well as it may, it will never be so well as we have seen it!'

For a short time he sat up in bed, thinking things over, and then made up his mind. Calling his servants and bidding them arm themselves, he took the Great Seal that was in his keeping and personally delivered it before daybreak to the queen.

There she sat on the floor rushes, rocking to and fro with grief. She had not had time to dress properly or to cover her head, and the grey hair straggled over her shoulders, giving here and there a gilt-and-silver gleam of its former glory. Around her men jostled and argued and fetched and carried : a hive of bees bereft of their queen. Boxes and bundles and packs were hauled off carts, pulled out of carriages, spilling and tumbling their contents as they were thumped down. Rolls of cloth of gold and velvet and rich brocade. Carved chests, chairs covered in embroidered leather. Featherbeds, hangings, cushions and tapestries. Silver and gold cups and platters. Head-dresses sewn with pearls. Sumptuous pieces of armour. And still the queen moaned and hid her face in her hands, and did not know how to command her servants. So each man ordered the other, and countermanded orders, and sent one this way and the other that. While some sturdy fellows, who could find no means of moving the bulkier pieces of furniture, were knocking a hole in the wall to make a passage.

'Madam,' said Rotherham gently, stooping over her, 'be of good cheer. I trust the matter is nothing so sore as you take it to be. And the Lord Chamberlain, Lord Hastings, has sent me a message that puts me in hope and out of fear.'

He spoke more optimistically than he felt and she was not misled.

'Ah, may evil befall him!' she said, weeping, 'for he is one of them that labours to destroy me and my blood!'

'Madam, I assure you that if they crown any other king than your son, whom they now have with them, we shall on the morrow crown his *brother* – whom you have here with *you*!'

And he patted Prince Richard's shoulder as the boy stood watching his mother in bewilderment and terror.

'Madam, here is the Great Seal. That noble prince your husband delivered it unto me, so here I deliver it unto you – to the use and behalf of your son.'

She took the Seal and thanked him, and he kissed her hand. But even as he took his leave of her she crouched over the Seal, and wept aloud.

By first light the Thames was swarming with boats full of Gloucester's retainers: sent to search any who passed, and to prevent the queen going into sanctuary. And once more the citizens of London murmured among themselves, and no man left his house without a knife in his belt.

Hastings, endeavouring to improve the appearance of the situation, summoned the Council to St Paul's for conference, but the damage had been done. The royal family were under the protection of the Church, the queen's relatives under close guard at Pontefract, and Sir Edward Woodville had taken to the sea with the fleet. Still, Hastings lauded Richard, Duke of Gloucester's loyalty to the young king, and put out the news that the queen's brother and son had been arrested to prevent their assassinating Richard. This was further underlined by the duke's riding south, preceded by four carts and armour which had been stored for wars with the Scots, or possibly the French.

'Lo! Here be the barrels of harness seized from these traitors who planned to destroy the noble lords withal!' proclaimed the street criers, as the company passed.

Many wondered, but all had sense to hold their tongues, unless they went further and cried, 'Hang the traitors!'

On 2 May Rotherham received a letter signed by King Edward V, commanding him to see to the safeguard and sure keeping of the Great Seal of the realm, preparatory to the king's arrival in London. Uncertain now as to the wisdom of his action, and realizing that the queen's party was in eclipse, Rotherham retrieved the Seal from Elizabeth. Then he resigned his office and hoped that no one would punish his lapse of judgement. On 4 May Edmund Shaw, mayor of London, on horseback, with sheriffs and aldermen in scarlet, and five hundred citizens in violet, met the new king at Hornsea and conveyed him through the city to the Tower, to await his coronation.

Gloucester, gracious and soldierly and genial, officially took upon himself the role of Protector and added another title to it – Defender of the Realm. He undertook the charge and care of the young king's person, and gave himself permission to act for him. Then he set about the task of government.

Sir Edward Woodville escaped with his followers and two ships to the nearest safe foothold; Brittany, where Jasper and Henry welcomed him.

'Poor England is riven once again,' said Sir Edward over his wine.

'And this time you cannot blame Lancaster for it!' Jasper observed, finding it difficult to accept a former enemy as a present friend.

Sir Edward looked at him shrewdly, unprovoked.

'I would not quarrel with you, Pembroke,' he said courteously, out of good manners, giving Jasper the title that was not his. 'We are mewed up here as close as cats in a sack and must hope for better fortune. And when the young king comes to power he will not forget his mother's family, and I shall not forget that you befriended me.'

'Then here's my hand upon it, sir,' said Jasper, 'and my sword should you need one.'

'My uncle's sword itches to be free of the scabbard,' Henry observed, smiling, and they all laughed.

Lady Margaret's pen had never been busier, and they read Lord Stanley's opinions in every letter, though as usual they inclined to leave an opening for change. That May of 1483 was a turbulent one, with every man looking to his own protection, and praise of Gloucester's efficiency mingled with doubts as to the queen's future. For she had fled to sanctuary but one could not stay there for ever.

By the middle of June the picture had darkened, and now Henry scanned his mother's letters three and four times over, in an attempt to read more into them than she had written.

'What do you know of Buckingham?' Jasper asked Sir Edward, hearing the name linked with that of the Protector again and again.

'Only that he is proud and makes much of his descent from the youngest son of King Edward III, and mislikes our family. And he is comely and has a ready tongue, and keeps great state in his castle of Brecon. But he knew little of the Duke of Gloucester, I swear it, before King Edward died, and must have seized upon the opportunity to make himself an ally of the duke – nursing plans of his own.'

'Yet has he a long inheritance of Lancaster,' Henry broke in. 'Does he seek to be king?'

'I know not. I think not. Forigve me, my lords, but Lancaster's cause is long buried. Perchance Buckingham thought so, too, and so sought a high place at court by befriending Gloucester. But that other plotter Hastings will not like this, for he was always closest to the late king, and he and Buckingham may quarrel.'

'My mother's husband, Lord Stanley, is close to Lord Hastings,' said Henry, speculating on a rift in the ruling party and wondering as to its possible outcome.

'The Lord Stanley is not so close to any man that he cannot run away again!' said Jasper drily. 'And should Hastings fall he will not be there to watch it!'

But in this he was mistaken. For Stanley had spoken to Lord Hastings about the Duke of Gloucester's separate councils : one, of which they were a part, held in the Tower; the other, of which they knew nothing, held at the duke's house in Bishopsgate. And though Hastings had no doubts, Stanley worried and the evening before the Council in the Tower he dreamed a strange dream.

It seemed that he and Hastings hunted in a dark wood and were merry in the pursuit, when a wild boar charged from the undergrowth and tore them so grievously that the blood ran to their shoulders. As Stanley woke, shouting and sweating, an image of Gloucester's cognizance of the silver board came to his mind. Forthwith he sent a secret messenger, a man he could trust with such words in his mouth;

bidding Hastings ride with him that night, so they should be out of danger by daybreak.

The Lord Chamberlain rose reluctantly to hear the message. Then he yawned and laughed and scratched his head. For the queen's son Dorset had inherited the late king's mistress, Jane Shore; and when Dorset sought sanctuary Hastings had adopted her; and he wanted to creep back into the warmth of the bed and her white arms again.

'Why, sirrah!' said Hastings lazily, 'has your master such faith in dreams? Either his own fear fetches up such fantasies, or these things rise in the night by reason of his day's thoughts. Tell him it is plain witchcraft to believe in such visions.'

Seeing the man remained unconvinced, Hastings made his answer plainer still.

'If this were indeed a token of things to come should we not make them true by our flight? And if we were caught and brought back – for those who flee lack friends! – then would the boar have good cause to slash us with his tusks, thinking we fled from our own falsehood!'

The messenger glimpsed the white flesh of a woman's back, as Jane Shore stirred in her sleep and pulled the fine coverlet more firmly about her.

'Either there is no peril,' said Hastings kindly, 'or if there be peril then it is in the going rather than the biding. And if we should fall in peril, one way or the other, I had rather it were through other men's malice than our faint hearts.'

Jane Shore turned again, and her hand sought the empty place beside her as she called him. Hastings' face softened. Reassuringly he patted the messenger's shoulder as he dismissed him.

'Therefore go to your master, sirrah, and commend me to him. Pray him be merry and have no fear, for I am as sure of the boar he mentions as I am of mine own head!'

Day had turned to night, and night to day again, as the royal cooks soared into a fantasy of subtleties and sauces for the coming feast. Beasts were axed by the hundred and fowls by the thousand, and wine ordered by the cart-load. And every tailor in London plied his needle until his back ached and his fingers were raw. The air was light with pomp and pageantry when Richard of Gloucester joined his lords shortly after nine of the clock.

'I crave your several pardons for being so long away,' he said pleasantly. 'You must take my sleepiness to task for it!'

They all laughed and he turned to Bishop Morton, smiling.

'My lord, the strawberries grow ripe in your garden at Holborn. I require you to let us have a mess of them – as a token of your goodwill.'

'My lord,' Morton replied, showing all his blackened teeth as he matched courtesy with courtesy, 'I shall send my servant in all haste to fetch them.'

But his eyes were wary as he pondered the request. *A token of goodwill* he thought. Are we taking sides, then? And against whom?

'I beg you to excuse me a little while,' said Richard. 'I am scarcely awake! But I shall be with you presently to discuss many matters.'

Many matters, Morton pondered. He smelled a change in the wind and looked about him. Buckingham, smiling sourly, seemed to know more than he should. Richard Middleton, a known supporter of the Protector, was watching Lord Stanley narrowly; and Morton remembered that they had long been enemies, having quarrelled over some estates. But why should Middleton look so covertly, and with an air of being about to come into his own? He was not and could not be as powerful as Stanley. Hastings, on the other hand, had never been more jovial – nor more bawdy! They were roaring at his jokes. But Hastings was too concerned with women to observe politics. Rotherham seemed mistrustful, but then he had made a grievous error in taking the Great Seal to the queen. Had I possessed it, Morton thought, I should have held it longer, to see how matters lay. He wondered what excuse he might make to retire, because though he did not know what was afoot he sensed something amiss. Then his quick ears caught the sound of armed men moving into position outside the door, and he resolved not be be found running away. Better to see all through to the end, and trust to his wits and his good fortune.

Between ten and eleven o'clock Richard returned, and his new mood silenced them. Flinging himself down in his chair he frowned round him. Many a man there, with the question of what ailed him already on his lips, observed that lowering countenance and did not speak. There was a long silence.

'What are they worthy to have,' Richard asked with cold

ferocity, 'that compass and imagine the destruction of *me* –
that am so near of blood to the king, and Protector of his
royal person and his realm?'

No one dared answer, except Hastings who was feeling
genial after his night in Jane Shore's arms.

'They are worthy to be punished as heinous traitors,' he
declared roundly, 'whoever they be!'

Richard's eyes rested on him reflectively, but it was not
yet Hastings' turn.

'*I* mean,' he said, still more coldly, 'yonder sorceress – *my
brother's wife*! – the mother of the king!'

A murmuring in the room divided Richard's friends from
those lords who still hoped that all might be well with both
parties when the king was crowned. Morton moved unobtrusively away until he felt the comfort of a wall at his back.
Middleton took up a position behind Stanley. Buckingham
watched Hastings – who was clearly relieved that Richard
only nursed a grievance against the queen.

'You shall all see in what wise that sorceress, and that
other witch of her counsel – *Shore's wife*! – have by their
sorcery and witchcraft wasted my body!'

Holding Hastings' gaze he switched up a sleeve, and thrust
out that arm he was at other times careful to conceal, though
all men knew of it. For Cecily of York had suffered long and
terribly at his birth, labouring him feet first into the world,
and producing the runt of her great litter in consequence.
Tales circulated of his being born hunch-backed, with teeth
and hair, after two long years in the womb. A childhood illness had weakened the arm now quivering before them, so
that it was thinner and shorter than its fellow. But any man
there could have sworn to its efficiency on the field of battle.

So they stared at the wizened limb, which he presently
covered up again, and pondered on the discrepancies of his
accusation. No one hated Jane Shore more than the queen.
Indeed had the queen not been in sanctuary surely Jane
would have languished in prison. Still, strange circumstances
bred strange friends.

Hastings turned over the charms of Mistress Shore in his
mind and prayed no harm might come to her, but resolved
on loyalty to Richard, tempered with caution.

'Certainly my lord,' he spoke up sturdily, 'if they have
so heinously done this thing then they be worthy of heinous
punishment.'

'What?' cried Richard. 'Do you serve me with *ifs and*

buts? I tell you they *have* done so – and that will I make good on your body!'

Then he shouted, 'Traitor!' in a great voice, and crashed his fist upon the Council table.

A voice outside yelled '*Treason!*' and the room was filled with armed men.

'Arrest this traitor!' Richard cried, and two soldiers pinioned Hastings.

'What?' Hastings whispered, staring at him. '*Me*, my lord?'

Middleton lifted his sword and struck at Lord Stanley, who dodged aside before he was cleft to the teeth. Hastings, horror-stricken, saw him fall to the floor, clutching at the table's edge. The wound in his head poured blood on to his ears and shoulders, as in the dream.

'Lay not your hands upon a man of God!' said Bishop Morton sternly, as they attempted to seize him. 'I shall go with you peaceably – though I know not what I have done.'

Rotherham, his mistake with the Great Seal lying heavily upon him, made no resistance as he was hustled out.

'Now, my Lord Hastings,' said Richard quietly. 'Shrive yourself. Fetch a priest hither! No doubt you have other sins upon your conscience. It is not meet for a young king to be served by those who lie in sinful lust with a whore.'

The charges against Jane Shore and the queen might be trumped up, the arm be withered by something less than sorcery, but Richard's condemnation of lust came from his heart. Hastings looked at the bright justice of chastity and could comprehend nothing more. He stared imploringly at Buckingham, who smiled and turned away.

'By St Paul,' Richard said impatiently, 'I will not go to my dinner until I see your head off!'

The Lord Chamberlain held himself proudly as he walked on to the Tower Green. Since there was no block handy a workman brought a log of wood he had been using for repairs. Hastings drew one long last breath of the June air, and laid down his head.

CHAPTER TWELVE

*Farewell, my own sweet son. God send you good keeping.
Let me kiss you once more ere you go. For God knoweth
when we shall kiss together again.*

> Queen Elizabeth to Prince Richard of York
> *The History of King Richard III*
> St Thomas More

Queen Elizabeth, mother of the young king and widow of
King Edward IV, had dressed richly and with care for the
deputation that waited on her on 16 June. And by her side
stood Prince Richard, a small timid boy whose fair hair she
smoothed from time to time with fingers that were heavy
with rings.

Richard had sent Archbishop Bourchier to persuade her,
as a man old in years and great in goodness and wisdom
whom she might trust, to leave sanctuary. But her shrewd
eyes singled out others, whose services stood high in the
Protector's esteem, and they had come with armed retainers.

'The Duke of Gloucester commends himself to you,
madam,' Bourchier began, slightly ashamed of the role that
had been forced upon him, 'and desires that the young
prince be given into his protection. The tender youth of King
Edward takes no pleasure in ancient company, and with
whom should he prosper better than his brother? Should
you consider this a light matter, madam, I would say that
sometimes, without small things, greater ones cannot stand.'

'My lord,' the queen replied coldly, 'I doubt not that the
Protector finds it very convenient to have both princes, but I
trust this one in no keeping but my own!' And she kissed the
child's cheek.

'No man denies, good madam, that your grace of all folk is
necessary about her children. And if you would come from
sanctuary to a place more fitting for your state and theirs,
you should enjoy their company. For evil words walk far,
and mock the honour of the Duke of Gloucester and those
about him, and he would that the king were crowned in his
mother's presence and with her good grace.'

She had not been nineteen years at court and learned nothing of policy.

'I marvel greatly that my Lord Protector is so desirous to have this my second son in his keeping also,' she said lightly, 'for he has been sore diseased with illness and is but newly recovered. If nature miscarried him in his weakly condition the duke would run into a greater slander and suspicion. Nor do I intend, as yet, to come forth and jeopardize myself – as others of my family are jeopardized . . .'

John Howard broke in, crying angrily, 'Why madam, is there any reason that they should be in jeopardy?'

'Nay,' she returned, outraged by his interruption, 'nor why they be in prison, neither, as they are!'

'Harp not, my lady, upon that string,' Bourchier advised hastily. 'Madam, these noble lords, your kin, shall do well enough, I doubt not. As to your gracious person there never was nor could be any manner of jeopardy. Madam, the Protector desires to have Prince Richard in his keeping, lest in a moment of folly – or womanly tenderness – you should happen to send him abroad. Then our enemies will speak ill of England, and we shall all be at variance again.'

She made a show of relaxing in her splendid chair, of putting aside an unimportant request. Spreading out her hands and admiring her jewels, she said serenely, 'I purpose not to depart as yet. As for this gentleman, my son, I would that he should be where I am.'

She had not expected they would take this answer, and Bourchier gathered himself for the ultimatum.

'Truly, madam, there be many that think he cannot claim sanctuary, for he has neither the will to ask it nor the malice to deserve it. Therefore, madam,' though the words hurt him, diminishing his authority and that of the Holy Church, 'they reckon no sanctuary is broken if they take him from here by force.'

She sat very still, looking regally upon him, and her words were as brittle as her smile.

'Ah, sir, the Protector fears nothing but that this prince should escape him.' She turned to his argument, making savage play of it. 'So a child cannot ask for sanctuary?' she cried. 'Why, the law makes me his guardian! If I can ask the privilege for myself I may ask it for the child also. You may not take my *horse* from me, in sanctuary, may you take my *son* from me?'

They were silent, knowing her to be right, and yet right

133

was not enough. She knew this as well as they did, and her composure began to fall from her, piece by piece. An involuntary clasping of the jewelled hands, a brightening of the shrewd eyes, an unbending of that shrewish majesty.

'In this place was my other son, your present king, born and laid in his cradle,' she said hurriedly. 'This is not the first time I have sought sanctuary. For when the lord, my husband, was banished from his kingdom I fled here, being great with child. And when my lord returned safe again I went from here to greet him, and he took the babe in his arms and gave thanks to God.' Her voice almost betrayed her, but she stiffened herself. 'I pray God that my son, the king's, palace be as great a safeguard to him as this place was to me! Whoever breaks this sanctuary may God condemn!'

No one spoke, and then she began to rave against the Protector: a relentless outpouring of fact and fury, of truth and clever supposition.

'Madam,' cried Bourchier, terrified to listen, 'I will lay my body and soul for the security of this young duke, if you will deliver him. No man means him harm. Do you think, madam, that all save you lack loyalty and truth?'

The queen rose from her chair and paced slowly up and down, helpless. She searched their faces for friendship. Bourchier, she knew, was an honourable man. There were others. She found sympathy here, good faith there, some kindness. And above all else she had no choice. She took the child's hand in hers, though his fingers went to his eyes.

'My lord, and all my lords, I am not so unwise as to mistrust your honour. I purpose to give you such proof of it that, if you lack honour, you shall turn me to much sorrow, the realm to much heaviness, and yourselves to much reproach. For here is this gentleman,' and she pushed Prince Richard forward, bidding him keep up his head like a prince and not to look so woefully.

But she had still something to say that they should remember, and she spoke as a queen.

'We have had experience that the desire for a kingdom knows no kindred. The brother has been the brother's bane.' They digested this with some discomfort, remembering treacherous Clarence. 'Each one of these children is the other's defence, while they are asunder. For what wise merchant adventures all his goods in one ship? All this not withstanding, here I deliver him. Only one thing I beseech you. You think I fear too much. Be you well aware lest you fear too little!'

She took the child's face between her hands, and kissed his eyes and cheeks, that were wet with tears as her own.

'Farewell, my own sweet son. God send you good keeping.'

The boy stood there bewildered, his little velvet cap in his hands, staring up at the great lords who surrounded him with bows and smiles. Very slowly the queen turned her back and walked away, though he beseeched her not to leave him and every plea wrung her. So, attempting to comfort the child, and ashamed of causing so much grief, they escorted him to his uncle.

Richard of Gloucester awaited their coming in the Star Chamber, pale and grave, but when they presented the prince his demeanour changed. All his charm went out to this finely-dressed little fellow with the smeared and blubbered face.

'Now welcome, my lord,' said Richard, 'even with all my heart!'

And as the child stopped in mid-sob he swung him up into the air, crying, 'What, Dick? So sorry a countenance and about to see your brother? Edward awaits you, lad, and there is a new bow and arrows for you. See how well you can shoot against the king!'

Then he popped a comfit into the little mouth and kissed him heartily, and set him down again.

'You must smile in the streets, Dick,' he said, pushing him gently and playfully, 'for the people like a merry prince. First you shall ride to the Bishop's Palace where the king will greet you, and then both to the Tower to await the coronation. Then shall you be second gentleman in all the land.'

Caught between a hiccup and a bit of the comfit, Prince Richard said, 'But what of you, my lord duke? Are not you the second gentleman, being Protector?'

'Aye, Protector indeed – but only as these good fellows are, to keep you safe!' said Richard gaily, pointing to the mastiffs who were lying out of the heat of the sun.

Hearing themselves mentioned the great dogs came forward, one by one, to be fondled. And between the jokes and the sweet bulging in his cheek, and the loving muzzles, the prince found sorrow easier to bear.

'Leave us a little, my lords,' said Richard quietly, 'for I

would have him merrier ere he left us. We want no tears to cry slander on the king's counsellors.'

So for an hour he set aside his state, and became no more and no less than the indulgent uncle of a beloved nephew. And Prince Richard rode waving and smiling through the London streets, to join his brother who would soon be crowned king of England.

In the middle of St Paul's churchyard stood a timber cross and pulpit mounted on stone steps, from which sermons had been preached for almost three hundred years. The coronation should have fallen on this Sunday of 22 June, but had been postponed yet again, due it was said to treachery against the Protector. And instead, Dr Shaw, brother of the Mayor of London, climbed portentously a little nearer to heaven than his congregation, and asked God's blessing on them all. Then he raised his right hand as witness and proclaimed the words of Solomon.

'But the multiplying brood of the ungodly shall be of no profit, and with bastard slips they shall not strike deep root, nor shall they establish a sure hold!'

A bewildered but respectful silence greeted this beginning, and deepened as he gave them examples from the Old Testament and from ancient history, to prove that the sins of the fathers were visited on the children, and some that seemed rightful heirs were bastards born of bastards.

It was doubted, said Dr Shaw, getting to the meat of his argument, that the late King Edward was the lawfully conceived son of the late Duke of York. Even his late brother Clarence may not have been sired by his rightful father, and for this reason – they resembled other known men than him. But Richard the Protector, that noble prince, that pattern of knightly prowess, showed in his lineaments the very face of the noble duke his father.

A hum of disbelief, of suspicion, of fear, was stilled by the pastoral hand.

But not only were the late king's origins dubious, Dr Shaw continued, his marriage was also unlawful. A pretended marriage, made of great presumption and without the knowing and assent of the Lords of the Land – and by the sorcery and witchcraft of Dame Elizabeth Grey and her mother Jacquetta, Duchess of Luxembourg. A marriage made privily and secretly, without edition of banns, in a private chamber – a profane place – and not openly in the face of the

Church but contrary to its laws and customs. And at the time of the pretended marriage King Edward stood married and troth plight to one Dame Eleanor Butler, daughter of the Earl of Shrewsbury. So that the said king and queen lived together sinfully and damnably in adultery.

They waited quietly now, knowing what was to come.

Wherefore, said Dr Shaw logically, all the issue and children of this pretended marriage were bastards, and unable to inherit or to claim anything by inheritance, according to the law and custom of England.

There was a movement among the lords spiritual and temporal, not wholly due to unease. The Protector, his friend Buckingham, and a select group of followers had arrived a little late.

'This noble prince,' said Dr Shaw, retracing his steps, 'this pattern of knightly prowess, represents in his lineaments the very face of the noble duke his father! This is his father's own figure!' said Dr Shaw unluckily.

But it was not. Richard of York had been a well-made man, while the Protector was slight and wiry. That raised shoulder, that withered arm, the lines of suffering about the mouth were never York's private burden.

'The very print of his visage!' cried Dr Shaw, conscious of error. 'The plain express likeness of that noble duke!'

He left the pulpit eventually to a profound silence, and the people began to disperse in little groups, glancing at the royal party. And a rumour spread about London that the princes were in danger, and that the Princess Elizabeth of York should be smuggled abroad so that some member of the late King Edward's family might be saved. Dr Shaw, though he had preached on evidence given him in the name of the Protector, and later condoned by Parliament, kept out of public sight. Some said that Richard of Gloucester was enraged at the slander of his mother's honour, for it was enough that his late brother's marriage should be declared unlawful. And many noticed that though Buckingham pursued the Protector's cause relentlessly, the two men no longer seemed as friendly as they had been.

Still, it was Buckingham who called upon the attention of all good citizens from a platform at the east end of the Guildhall, two days later. Buckingham at his ease, richly dressed and savouring his present power, repeating the slanders of Dr Shaw, and bidding them search their hearts and find a good king to replace the bastard stock of King

Edward. He begged them plainly to show their minds.

The silence was embarrassing, and Buckingham whispered in the Mayor's ear asking him why they did not shout 'King Richard!'

'Sir, they comprehend you not,' said Sir Edward Shaw, softly and uncomfortably.

So Buckingham repeated that the realm needed not a child of bastard origin but an excellent soldierly prince – and whom did they choose to rule over them?

Still they did not answer, showing no more movement or understanding than a heap of stones.

'Sir, they are used to hearing the Recorder, for he is the mouth of the city,' whispered the mayor.

Buckingham's patience was not his strong suit, but he sat down as graciously as he could, and motioned Sir Thomas Fitzwilliam to repeat the command for the third time. They responded no better.

'Now this is a marvellous obstinate silence!' Buckingham cried out in an angry voice, and his hand moved automatically to the hilt of his sword.

A buzz of apprehension round the Guildhall was covered by Buckingham's curt motion to his own retainers, who started guiltily, aware of their fault, and shouted, 'King Richard! King Richard!' and threw up a little shoal of caps. Buckingham relaxed and smiled.

'Now is this a goodly cry and joyful!' he said heartily. 'And I shall accompany the mayor and aldermen to make your request of the Protector on the morrow.'

So they stood in Baynard's Castle, very fine in their violet clothes, and Buckingham played his part again, sending a loving message to the Duke of Gloucester – who expressed himself amazed at their coming, and wondered what they wished of him. The messenger was sent for a second time to beg him give them audience. But when he came from his chamber, not half as splendid in his dress as many that were present, and heard what they required, he said he could not – for the love he bore to the late king, and that which he now bore for his sons.

His face impassive, as he followed the next part of the ritual, Buckingham drew his friends round him and pretended to confer with them.

'My lord,' John Howard whispered to his neighbour, amused at the by-play, 'this puts me in mind of the consecration of a bishop. For the man has paid for his Bulls, and means well enough to be a bishop if he can. And yet they must ask him twice, and twice he must say nay. And at the third time he says yea – but always as though he were compelled against his will!'

'Aye, sir,' the man whispered back, looking straight ahead of him as though they were not in conversation, 'these matters be kings' games, and as if they were stage plays.'

'But for the most part played upon a scaffold,' whispered Howard, remembering Hastings.

'Well I shall not offer to step up and play with them,' said his neighbour, mindful of treason, 'for those that cannot play the right part disorder matters, and do themself no good!'

The conference was over.

'My lord,' cried Buckingham, bowing to Richard, 'we have gone so far that it is now no surety to retreat! Will you take the crown? And if you will not,' he continued, with more emphasis than the occasion warranted, 'then must we find one that shall!'

A few stared curiously at him. It was as though his pride and ambition had got the better of him, and certainly in figure and bearing he looked a more majestic figure than the pale-faced man in the gallery. The Protector had not missed his meaning either, but when he spoke his voice was even and gracious.

'Then here we take upon us the royal estate, pre-eminence and kingdom of the two noble realms, England and France. The one, from this day forward, by us and our heirs to rule, govern and defend . . .'

The words rolled over them, soothing, inspiring, protecting, exalting one nobleman above all the rest. There was no hesitation now in shouting what they must, 'King Richard! King Richard!' and Buckingham bowed lower than any of them. But the smile on his lips did not find an answer in his eyes. For they were now the two most powerful men in the kingdom, with the queen's family disbarred, and not even the late Duke of Clarence's son – poor Warwick – to put forward a claim. And Buckingham thought that if his daughter married Richard's only son, and Richard granted him the full inheritance of the de Bohun estates, that neither man could pull the other down. And if Richard's sickly son died, with or without issue, then Buckingham would see that his daughter lacked nothing : neither party nor fatherly counsel.

On this day also, the Lord Rivers, Sir Richard Grey and

old Sir Thomas Vaughan were led from their prison to the scaffold at Pontefract. Sir Richard Ratcliff, a man close to the Protector, travelling south for the coronation with his retainers, paused at Pontefract to order the executions. He intended to have no turbulent speeches, no pledges of innocence or cries of injustice, to disturb the populace. So the three noblemen took only their dignity with them into the silence.

In Brittany Henry sought out Sir Edward Woodville, and condoled with him on the loss of his two kinsmen, for Jasper said he could not bring himself to do more than nod his sympathy.

'I have no love for any of them, lad,' he said wryly, 'but you have got your mother's gracious policy, and a ready tongue, so go you to him – and say that I am sorry, though I am not.'

The ex-Admiral of the Fleet was in his chamber, and rose to clasp Henry's outstretched hands.

'Sir Richard Grey was young, and a gallant gentleman,' he said quietly, 'but it is the Lord Rivers' death that grieves me more. He was a knight both in body and soul, a staunch son of the Church with a most mystical piety. And yet the greatest jouster of his age – for he fought the Bastard of Burgundy at a famous tournament when he was but a stripling, sixteen long years since. And a man of the world, that travelled and loved Italy. And a man half out of touch with his times, for he was moved by the vision of the Holy Grail. And they say that when he rode from Ludlow with the young king he wore a hair shirt under his rich robes. We shall not see many such again, my lord. I thank you for your courtesy . . .'

'I cannot,' Henry cried passionately to Jasper, 'I cannot bear this difference between the public and the private face.'

'Then stab yourself, lad, and lie in the earth. For the difference will be there for all time. Should I let my enemy run me through with his sword because he has a wife and mother that will grieve for him? You are not six years old but six-and-twenty, Harry! Come, make me smile a little instead of scolding you. What of my good foul friend, the Lord Stanley. How does our lovely fox?'

Henry smiled in spite of himself, and answered, 'My lady mother says he is released from prison, and that he is to carry the mace at Duke Richard's coronation – and that she is to carry the queen's train.'

'Oh, how I love that man. Fox did I call him? He is a very serpent, for he slithers through their hands and waits to strike again! We shall be at court yet, Harry. What of my other pets? What of the Bishop Morton?'

'Imprisoned still, but under the care of Buckingham, at his castle of Brecon.'

Jasper's eyes glinted.

'I was about to ask you of our friend Buckingham, and now I have two answers in one. Now does that puzzle me, Harry. What can the great Buckingham want with the wily bishop?'

'Perchance he would seek the king's pardon for him, and so gain a friend?'

'I know this much,' said Jasper, ruminating. 'If I were King Richard I would not have the bishop in prison, for there his talents rust, and he is a man that loves to give them full play. And I would not have those talents working underground at Brecon, with Buckingham ready to listen to a bishop's silver tongue.'

Peter Curteys, the king's wardrober, had been put to a vast amount of worry and trouble, promising to furnish the robes for the coronation in nine days' time. The king alone must wear not one but two sets of robes : purple velvet furred with ermine, crimson velvet embroidered with gold and furred with miniver; doublet and stomacher of blue cloth of gold, and all most marvellously wrought with nets and pineapples. And two hats of estate, with round rolls behind them and beaks in front of them. Hose and shirt and coat and surcoat and mantle and hood of crimson satin. A tabard of white sarcenet and a coif of lawn. His shoes to be covered with crimson cloth of gold.

Among the stacks of rich materials Master Curteys held his head, and wondered whether his neck would be stretched if he failed to meet the royal requirements. At least he had the robes from the original coronation as a beginning. But Richard's son, Prince Edward, must have another gown. For one did not dress a royal heir in the same fashion as a duke's offspring.

The princes played in the Constable's garden at the Tower, and strove to understand their new state. Prince Richard's indisposition had been mild and short-lived, but Prince Edward's dental infection plagued him. Daily he rose, after an uneasy night, to the intolerable throb and ache of those troublesome gums and teeth. Dr Argentine of Strasbourg attended him, seeking to alleviate – by means of herbs and potions and poultices and an occasional bleeding – the prince's bane. The malady was beyond his skill, and a melancholy occasioned by the disease and by other matters assailed the boy.

Edward was afraid and alone. He had been trained to bear difficulties in silence, or to seek the advice of his elders, so he could not and would not share his fears with Richard. And when his brother asked how long they would be there, and when they should see their mother again, Edward comforted him with bright promises. So they shot at the butts, and walked in the sunshine with their arms about each other.

Edward made a daily confession, earnestly undertook the small penances that would cleanse his soul of sin, and bore himself graciously. All the friends and attendants he had known from babyhood had been gradually withdrawn from his service. So there were only the chaplain and Dr Argentine to lean on : the one for spiritual, the other for physical help. He told them at last that he believed he faced death. They rallied him, beseeching him to enjoy his brother's company and draw inspiration and guidance from his books. The Lord Rivers his uncle, patron of William Caxton and himself an elegant translator, had instilled a love of literature in the boy. He read aloud to Richard, who listened entranced to tales of chivalry and adventure. And they sat side by side, head to fair head, whiling away the time they had left.

In sanctuary still, with her five fair daughters, the queen-dowager gazed for a long moment on the priest who brought her the news of their death, then fell at his feet as he tried to comfort her. But she could not be comforted, and though the queen in her cried for vengeance on her enemies the mother wailed piteously.

'O my babes, my sweet babes. O my babes, my babes, my sweet babes.'

Over and over again.

CHAPTER THIRTEEN

When the lion had proclaimed that on pain
of death there should none horned beast abide
in that wood, one that had in his forehead a
bunch of flesh fled away at a great pace.

> *The History of King Richard III*
> St Thomas More

Morton's brief imprisonment had not sat hardly upon him, and even the four-day journey from London under close guard found him ready of tongue – though stiff in his bones. And Buckingham, coming forward to greet him, signalled that he was to be assisted from his horse with the courtesy due to his cloth.

'How now, my lord bishop?' he said. 'Find you the air somewhat sweeter in Brecon than in London?'

'Aye, my lord duke,' said Morton cheerfully, 'full sweet. Though not as sweet as freedom. But how should I complain that held of the king's good pleasure?'

'Well, we shall make your prison as comfortable as may be. I am told you play an excellent game of chess, my lord. Shall you and I pit our wits over kings of ivory, for our pleasure?'

Buckingham's tone and smile were no more than hospitality called for, but his eyes told another story. And Morton, analysing the scraps and dribbles of information he had garnered, and conjecturing still further, sensed a deeper meaning beneath the gracious phrases. So he assured him just as meaningfully.

'Why, my lord, I find this game more to my liking than the other! For then I may set up a king again on my own account – whereas this poor self has been set aside by one.'

Buckingham laughed and ushered him into the great hall at Brecon Castle, where a battery of odours promised a fine dinner.

'I am not such a one, my lord bishop, that would banish a good churchman to the dungeon, with bread and water to keep body and soul together, and rats for company,' said Buckingham lightly, though his smile indicated that he would do so if he desired, and might do so if he found Morton useless. 'So shall we dine right well, and I promise you that your chamber is meet for your needs.' Then he raised his voice, adding, 'But I pray you remember, my lord, that though I deal mercifully with you, you are my prisoner.'

Morton spread out his hands to bear witness that only God was his strength, and replied as clearly.

'These gentlemen will tell you, my lord, that my years are more powerful than my enemies. I shall abide here peaceably as long as it pleases the king and your lordship. I am no fiery youth to scale these mighty walls, but an old man that thanks you for small mercies – and hopes for greater ones.'

He looked Buckingham in the eyes, and saw that they understood each other.

'Then thrice welcome, my lord bishop. And though your earthly lord, King Richard, has bidden you to cease to meddle in earthly matters, you may yet serve your heavenly lord. When you have rested and refreshed yourself you shall give us a good grace upon our meat!'

Morton was an abstemious man, but even he could not resist the multiple seductions of Buckingham's cooks. Also his political nose smelled out a new drift in events, and added more relish to his food than a dozen spices. So he sat comfortably in his carved chair, next to his host; and blessed the boy that knelt before him with a silver basin of warm water, and dried his hands with some satisfaction on the spotless towel. Then settled to enjoy the long leisurely progress of a great dinner. The carver, sharp of knife and eye, remarked in private that the Bishop of Ely was a gracious gentleman, and applied himself to his craft diligently. And for two hours or more they worked their way through brawn and mustard, potage, beef and mutton and goose, vast crusty capon pies, venison and pheasant : and washed them down with cups of sweet wine.

'A *princely* spread, my lord,' said Morton mildly, as spoons, trenchers, crumbs and fragments were gathered in preparation for the second course.

Buckingham glanced at him quickly, but seeing only the humility of lowered eyelids, the folding of old hands, the bent white head, set the remark down to good manners. And smiled again.

'Yet indeed, my lord,' Morton continued idly, 'when your lordship comes into full possession of his inheritance, men shall say in truth that no subject has been so great since Warwick fell.'

A darkening of Buckingham's face told him what he had guessed : that Richard had no intention of giving so much power into another man's hands. So Morton remarked on the beauty of the gold salt cellar, fashioned like a ship in sail, and sent the conversation in a different direction.

Fresh table linen was set. The little boy proffered his basin of warm water again. And they bent their appetites to cheese scraped with sugar, to custards, and fruits seethed in half a dozen ways and twice as many spices, and more sweet wine.

'I shall attend you in your chamber myself, later, my lord,' said Buckingham, as he indicated that the meal was at an end. 'I would see that all is to your liking. And though the summer is with us I have ordered a fire to be lighted. The night air is often sharp in Brecon, and I would have you lie easy.'

'This old head shall lie easier tonight, my lord, than for many nights past – due to your lordship's gracious kindness,' said Morton quietly. 'For I may rather call your noble custody a liberal liberty more than a straight imprisonment.'

And once again they exchanged looks, and bowed.

Alone in his room, Morton felt the featherbed and pillows, and longed to creep between the sheets and sleep soundly. But he knew that the latter part of the evening must be dedicated to greater matters than slumber. He sat before the burning logs, and warmed his hands and feet thoughtfully at the flames, and waited.

'Kings' games !' he said to himself softly. 'Kings' games !'

And because he was sixty-three winters old, and had spent the last four days mostly on horseback, he dozed a little, waking with a start as a chamber door crashed open in the distance. And he saw Hastings' face as that other door was flung back, and Stanley falling under the table with blood about his ears, and the shouts of armed men crying treachery.

'I am too old for such matters,' he said wearily, but the sound of footsteps in the passage took the slump from his shoulders. 'Kings' games,' he whispered, and held his hands meditatively to the fire.

Buckingham had changed into a loose gown of emerald velvet, trimmed with miniver; and was followed by a page, tongue caught between his teeth, bearing an array of chess-men on an ivory board.

'Set it down, lad,' said Buckingham easily.

He looked round the chamber with the eye of a host, and the page waited with bowed head for his commands. Buckingham felt the bed and pillows, as Morton had done earlier, pulled the brocade hangings to see that they ran smoothly, stared at the tapestries – though he must have seen them a hundred times – and selected a little branch of cherries from the dish at the side-table.

'Bring us Rhennes wine, boy,' he ordered, 'and then leave us.'

'My Lord,' the page said inaudibly, and went swiftly out.

'Perchance you are too weary for a game, my lord?' Buckingham suggested out of courtesy.

'Your lordship's hospitality has taken my weariness from me,' said Morton automatically. 'And we shall all sleep long enough at the last !'

'And sleep peacefully, meanwhile, since our gracious King Richard rules England, and all loathsome traitors are rooted out,' said Buckingham seating himself, and he lifted the splendid monarch from the chess-board with a little smile. 'For England shall take profit from his reign, or am I much mistaken !' Then he replaced the piece as the page poured wine into two silver cups.

'To the king's good health and long life !' Buckingham cried. 'This heart and sword are his so long as he shall live !'

Morton waited until the boy had gone, and ventured to slip an embroidered cushion between himself and the chair. He was well awake now, watching Buckingham make the first move in both games.

'Surely, my lord,' Morton said slowly, bringing forth a humble pawn, 'it were folly for me to lie. For if I swear to the contrary your lordship, I wean, could not believe me.'

Buckingham's fingers closed round a mounted knight, and he hesitated.

'If the world had gone as I would have wished,' Morton continued, 'King Henry's son had had the crown, and not King Edward.'

He eyed Buckingham's battle-line of pawns with interest.

'But after God had ordered him to lose it, and King Edward to reign,' he went on mildly, 'I was never so foolish that I would strive for a dead man against the quick. So was I faithful chaplain to King Edward, and should have been

146

glad if his son had succeeded him. But then,' he added dryly, 'it was discovered that neither King Edward nor his children were legitimate heirs. And I have heard that the Duchess Cecily much disliked the king's imputations on her honour. It takes a cool man, my lord, to besmirch his mother while they reside under one roof, and this matter puzzled me sorely.'

Still Buckingham said nothing, seeming intent upon the one game.

'Young saplings grow into great trees, betimes, my lord,' Morton continued amiably. 'Then may King Richard find helpless children become noble warriors, and acquiescent boys defend their honour with the sword!'

Buckingham sent his knight on dangerous errantry, and reached for a comfit.

'Saplings may wither at the root, my lord bishop. The Prince Richard was but sickly when he joined his brother, and rumour says that Prince Edward suffers from a disease of the jaw that no physician can allay.'

It was Morton's turn to pause.

'Speak you of things past, or things to come, my lord?'

Buckingham said, 'King Richard need fear no treachery from his brother's bastards.'

A small sigh escaped Morton as he made his move. He played as he lived, cautiously, and risking nothing until the end was in sight.

'Now do you set your pawns against me in a fork, my lord,' and Buckingham interested, and surveyed the board shrewdly. 'You were saying that you would not be so foolish as to strive for a dead prince against a quick one.'

'If the secret judgement of God has otherwise provided,' said Morton heavily, for the news of the princes was grievous, 'I purpose not to spurn against a prick – nor labour to set up whom God pulls down,' and he crossed himself. 'As for the late Protector, our king . . . but you draw me out, my lord. Your wits are too sharp for mine, and I fear this old tongue will prove my undoing!'

He looked up and smiled.

'I have meddled too much with this world already, my lord. From this day forth I shall meddle with my books and my beads, and no further. Your move, my lord.'

'Be bold, good Morton!' said Buckingham, grinning, as he saw a way through the bishop's ranks. 'Say your thoughts and fear not. I promise you shall come to no hurt – and perchance to more good things than you guess. For I purpose to use your faithful secret counsel, and that is the cause for which I procured your custody from the king.'

He glanced triumphantly at Morton, who affected to conceal surprise.

'You should reckon yourself well at home here, my lord,' said Buckingham, unable to hide his pleasure. 'Else had you been in the hands of them with whom you would not have found like favour.'

Morton obligingly placed a pawn at risk, to allow Buckingham the full savour of his diplomacy, and spoke meekly.

'I thank you, but in good faith, my lord, I do not love to talk of princes – it is a dangerous pursuit. I think always on Aesop's tale. For when the lion had proclaimed that no horned beasts should abide in the wood, an ass – that had a bunch of flesh in his forehead – fled away at a great pace. Ah! I have put my pawn in peril, and your lordship shows no mercy!'

He set another one as bait, talking idly the while.

'A fox, seeing the ass run so fast, asked him whither he made such haste. And the ass answered him that he feared the proclamation of the horned beasts. Then the fox called him fool, saying that he had no horn in his head but a bunch of flesh, and the lion meant not him.'

Buckingham decided that Morton had brought out the pawn on purpose, was unable to see why, but steadfastly ignored it and sent his queen out at the head of his troops. Morton permitted himself a sigh, and saw a smile touch Buckingham's mouth as he interpreted it wrongly.

' "Why," said the ass, "I know that well enough. But what if the lion call it a horn? Where am I then?" '

Buckingham laughed, swaggered a knight into position, and cried, 'Check!' Then sat back and nibbled a piece of green ginger, and drank more wine.

'My lord bishop, I warrant you, neither lion nor boar shall pick a quarrel with anything spoken here. For it shall never reach their ears!'

'In faith, good sir,' said Morton, adroitly protecting his king, 'if it did it would turn me to little good – and to you, my lord, even less good!'

He sacrificed another pawn to Buckingham's vanity, having prepared a trap for the queen.

'Be bold, my lord,' said Buckingham impatiently. 'You

have my word, as one of the blood royal, that aught you say shall be secret between us.'

Morton was now as relaxed as Buckingham had been. Both games were going his way.

'Since King Richard is now in possession I do not propose to dispute his title. But for the weal of this great realm I wish that to those good abilities – of which he has many – he might have other virtues, such as Our Lord planted in the person of your grace.'

Buckingham flushed slightly, passed one hand over his mouth, and made no further pretence of chess. He began to pace up and down the chamber, thinking; while Morton prepared to follow him down whichever dark road he trod. At last the duke thrust back the curtains and drew counsel from the night.

'My lord bishop, I shall open my mind to you freely. More wine, my lord?'

'No, I thank your grace,' said Morton, closing the lid of his silver cup. 'My head is not so young and full of fire as your own, nor my stomach as hearty. The Plantagenets were ever good trenchermen,' he added, bringing Buckingham into that mighty host as if by chance.

'My lord bishop,' Buckingham cried, 'I have been most greviously wronged by the king. The lands of Humphrey de Bohun are mine by right since King Henry died, and King Richard promised them to me. He gave me a signed bill soon after his accession, and yet the letters patent have not been issued.'

'And never shall be, your grace – I know princes! They mislike overmuch power in others, and you cannot quarrel with the king's munificence. Why, what has he given you already? All royal lands in five western counties. The office of Chief Justice and Chamberlain of North and South Wales, and Constable of England — and a host of lesser offices, too numerous to count upon these fingers.'

But Buckingham was adrift, as Morton meant him to be, upon a royal tide.

'I have some goodly claim, lord bishop, being descended in the female line from King Edward III himself. I am as well-born as he, and yet he spurns me.'

'Tell me your grace, what said the king when you pressed him for your full inheritance?'

Buckingham repeated, sullenly, the words that had kept him company ever since.

' "What now, Duke Henry? Will you draw unto you the might of Henry Bolingbroke, whereby he wickedly usurped the crown? And so make you open for yourself the way thereunto?" '

'And had you thoughts of the crown, my lord?'

Buckingham laughed without humour, and said frankly, 'Aye, for two days at Tewkesbury, on the royal progress. I had thought myself a dead man there, for since the coronation the king and I are not as close as formerly. In great turmoil of mind, I feigned myself sick that I might not ride with him on the day he was crowned. But he sent a message saying that if I did not ride I should be carried. And so I rose and rode, and turned my head away when he was crowned, and feigned to be sick again on the morrow. And he said that all was done in hatred and despite of him, and so I came to Brecon that I might not be murdered – as others have been.'

'Truly, my lord,' said Morton, placing the tips of his fingers together judiciously, 'had I been King Richard I should have despatched you to heaven rather than Brecon. I wonder why he did not?'

'He yet may. But still, my lord, I have three sons to follow me. I have a brother. He cannot murder every one.'

'And so at Tewkesbury,' Morton reminded him gently, 'your mind reached for the crown?'

'For but two days. While I rode between Worcester and Bridgnorth, in a muse, I encountered with the Lady Margaret, now wife to the Lord Stanley. She had been as clean out of my mind as though I had never seen her, and she stayed me to ask a pardon for her son that was Henry, Earl of Richmond.'

Morton wondered why the duke was wandering up to Worcester when his road to Brecon lay to the south-east, and set it down as a pretext.

'She thought that now King Edward's daughters were cut off from succession he might marry one of them. And said that her son should take the lady even though she had no dowry, if he could but come safe home before she died. And then it came to me, my lord, that she and her son were both the bulwark and the portcullis between me and the gate to the crown. For they have the nearer claim. The fire grows low and I am cold,' he added hurriedly, and shouted for attendance. 'I keep you late and you are weary, and not so young as myself,' he said courteously. 'Yet must I beg your ear a little longer.'

'These ears shall not be stopped up, nor these eyes close, until your grace pleases,' said Morton, and his voice was strong and clear. 'I see your grace knows much of statesmanship, for he would not lay claim to the crown, when England would be as divided under him as under Richard. Now I commend your grace's wisdom, and see you have looked further than myself. But I interrupt your grace, and beg you to continue.'

'If such a one as Henry Tudor should marry Elizabeth of York,' said Buckingham slowly, 'then the two houses should be joined in one, and England prosper. But I know nothing of this man, and he has been abroad these many years.'

'Now I must think awhile, for your grace has over-reached me with this scheme,' said Morton, smiling. 'I know the Lady Margaret, and from time to time I have heard of her son – and always to his good. The late King Henry marvelled at his grace and breeding, and said he showed great wisdom for his years. And I have heard that he is well-learned and fair-spoken, keeping his own counsel but thinking all the more. Aye, and he knows adversity,' cried Morton, as though suddenly remembering, 'for was he not in the siege of Harlech? Adversity, your grace, teaches us more than twenty tutors. And while he is green to kingship you and I shall sow such seeds into that noble soil as shall grow into mighty trees, and you and I lie beneath their shade.'

'Is he a warrior, think you?'

'He must be, if he is to fight King Richard – for that is a very prince of warriors, like unto his father the Duke of York. Yet I have heard – it is strange how you quicken my thoughts, your grace, I remember much now you encourage me – I have heard that he will play his part, though he has little relish for war.'

Buckingham snorted.

'But why do we puzzle ourselves over his martial prowess, with such a one as the Duke of Buckingham to fight for him? Aye, and his uncle, that was Pembroke.'

'I do not want a king that hides behind me, and then comes forward to wrest the crown from my bloodied hand. I could do as much for myself!'

'My lord, is it not better to get ourselves a grateful

monarch, than have a haughty soldier with a proud stomach that will learn nothing from us? And he is affable and bold enough. Modest and upright, and devout. Youthful but grave. He has all the qualities of a king and but lacks the experience.'

'You speak as though you knew him well,' said Buckingham suspiciously.

'I do but picture him as I have heard of him, and the more I think on it the more I marvel at your grace's depth of thought and range of vision. Why, my lord, I think you mock me. For you brought me here only to wonder at your wisdom. I have given no counsel, only that of an old man that says yea and nay and knows himself to be out-matched.'

Buckingham warmed himself at the mended fire, and in this wealth of compliments.

'But if Elizabeth of York is queen, her mother will be plotting treason against me,' he said thoughtfully.

'My lord, a lady of forty-six years that has known the burden and perils of politics, that has had two goodly husbands and borne twelve children, and suffered much sorrow, shall be glad to look to her soul's health. You do most grievously misjudge the lady. I dare swear she will retire to some innocent pasture, within a twelve month of her daughter's marriage, and leave all worldly matters well behind her.'

'I mark your meaning,' said Buckingham, brightening.

'And now, your grace,' said Morton, refreshed, 'let us play queen with queen to get us a rightful king. The Lady Margaret and Queen Elizabeth shall make the match. There is a Reginald Bray of Lancashire, steward to Lady Margaret that would make a trusty messenger. Have I your leave to write to him, bidding him come to Brecon?'

'You have my leave, lord bishop, to do as you will!'

'Even to return to my own Isle of Ely, my lord?' Morton asked slyly.

'How can I let you go and keep this head on my shoulders, my lord?' Buckingham cried in desperation, for once more he had initiated a plot, only to find himself cast in a secondary role.

'Your head, your grace, is of no use except it be part of your living body. I shall lean upon your counsel and your mercy.'

'I hope I have done right,' Buckingham muttered, feeling

that he had been pledged somewhat faster and further than he intended.

Morton judged that he needed a little gracious bullying.

'You have this night made reparation to the house of Lancaster,' he said sternly. 'You have shown me how one of royal blood leaps to a king's solution, while we that build upon our little wits toil far behind. Speak not of right, your grace, when right is your inheritance.'

'Well, you have helped me to it,' said Buckingham, glad to patronize.

The blackened teeth showed in a grin, the venerable head wagged from side to side in protest.

'The tutor does not thank the pupil,' said Morton smoothly. 'Have I your leave to bid your grace good-night?'

CHAPTER FOURTEEN

And when King Richard of this hard tell
a mightye Ost he sent
against the duke of Buckingham,
his purpose to prevent.

Buckingham Betrayed by Banister
Bishop Percy's Folio MS.

Reginald Bray made all haste to Brecon, and though he was a brave gentleman he crossed himself several times as he rode back to Lancashire, knowing the message he carried was treason.

Dr Lewis, the Welsh physician who attended Lady Margaret, made the long journey from Lancashire to London, where he was received by the queen-dowager at Westminster with great cordiality. If anyone had wondered at the connection between the noble ladies it could have been explained away, since they were both of an age when women suffer strange humours, and Dr Lewis was well-known for his skills in these and other matters among people of rank. So he returned to Lord Stanley's household with a token of the queen-dowager's esteem upon his finger, and a gracious answer to Lady Margaret.

'The queen bids me tell you, my lady, that my visit has lightened her grace's burden. That you and she are in the same case with regard to this matter. And the knowledge that you share the same troubles, and seek to bring them to a right end, casts a light upon all that formerly seemed dark to her.'

'Did the queen obtain relief from the syrup you commended her?'

'Aye, my lady, and she pronounced it the true and proper medicine for such pains as she has suffered.'

Left to herself Lady Margaret knelt at her *prie-dieu* in gratitude. Having consulted God she then consulted her own fine mind, sorting and sifting until her part of the scheme was clear to her. Her husband, she judged, would help her provided he appeared to know nothing of the matter. If the outcome was good he would be there. If it were not then she would not be alive to see him wriggle out of it, and prosper. Buckingham could move nowhere but forward, and Morton could take care of himself. Jasper would give his life, and cost King Richard a high price for it. The Duke of Brittany had always been helpful and well-disposed to Henry. And in France their prospects were brighter, for Louis XI had died in the August and the court was in the same position as England had been under the young king. The former Dauphin, now Charles XIII, was too youthful to reign without advisers, and with the powerful Madame de Beaujeu as regent might look more favourably on the cause of Lancaster.

Lastly, and most fondly, she thought of her son, and prayed that she knew him better than he knew himself. For the difference between a landless exile and the king of England would demand a strength of purpose so far unasked of him. She knew he could endure stoically, that he valued moral rather than physical courage, that he was in all outward aspects fit to be a sovereign. She sensed that his ambition was greater than he realized, reading in all his letters a craving for power and freedom, a resentment that he had so far been denied the status that he felt was due to him. But she could not guess at his capacity for gambling. He would risk himself, of that she was sure, but had he the necessary fibre to risk a horde of others faithful to him? His devoutness would carry him a long way, if he could be made certain that the cause was godly. His mystical side would take him further, if it could be aroused. And she resolved to write to Jasper, too, and warn him that an open mind and fair dealing in such an enterprise must prove fatal. To gain a crown asked for more than a good heart and a steady purpose.

'There must be fire,' she said to herself, ruminating. 'There must be a great fire – and we shall light it in him.'

On 24 September 1483 the Duke of Buckingham composed a letter to Henry Tudor, formerly Earl of Richmond, in terms both respectful and firm, as became the commander of a rising. He bade Henry, in the name of England, to release the country of a grievous tyrant and take upon himself the crown. On St Luke's Day, 18 October, Buckingham wrote, the supporters of the red rose of Lancaster would take up arms all over the south and west in Henry's cause. In Kent and Surrey, in Wiltshire, Devon and Cornwall they would raise his standard. While in Wales Buckingham himself would march against the forces of York.

Lady Margaret, meanwhile, hesitating between a priest she had lately taken into her service – Christopher Urswick by name – and Hugh Conway, esquire chose the latter as a bearer of more dignity. And sent him with a letter to her son. But lest Conway be apprehended by Richard's men, yet another messenger, one Thomas Ramme, crossed the Channel from Dover to Calais while Conway sailed from Plymouth. Morton's instinct for political matters was sound. No one had thought seriously that Lancaster would invest its fortunes in an unknown exile, dependent upon the Duke François for his very existence. So the two messengers arrived at the court of Brittany quite safely, within a short time of each other, and asked to be taken into the presence of the Earl of Richmond.

Besides the importance of their tidings they bore a very natural curiosity as to the merits and appearance of this young man, in whom their own lives and futures rested. So, when they were told that the earl was at the butts, they followed with as much speed as decorum allowed. They permitted themselves a lift of the eyebrows, a covert closing of the lids, over the mincing lad who preceded them. For he tossed his long silken hair like a girl, and his tight little buttocks under the brief jerkin seemed to invite their attention.

'Pray God, sir, that the earl be not as this one, or he will fetch all England down – throne, crown, court and all!' said Thomas Ramme, with a grimace.

Hugh Conway nodded, but added that these were a decadent people, always at odds among themselves, and any Englishman was worth three foreigners. Which comforted them both immensely. They waited at a respectful distance for the summons.

The young man who turned to hear the page's request was of no great stature, a little above middle height, but straight-limbed and of noble bearing. Being heated by the sport he had removed his velvet doublet, unbuttoned the embroidered cuffs of his thin white shirt, and rolled the sleeves above the elbow. Now, as the page waited for his reply, he fitted another arrow into his bow, took careful aim, and shot. A small group of gentlemen about him applauded his accuracy.

'By the Lord,' said Thomas Ramme, 'he shoots in the

English fashion, for all that he has been twelve years at a Breton court. Do you mind how he presses the weight of his body into the horns of his bow?'

'Aye, and strikes the target fairly! Here comes Mistress Page, wagging his hips like a whore!'

The boy dropped his eyelids as he bade them follow him, then looked up through his thick fair lashes and smiled brilliantly. They thanked him, grinning broadly, and were conducted into the earl's presence with a sulky toss of the head.

He had laid aside his bow and was pulling on his dark-blue doublet.

'I ask your pardon, gentlemen,' he said easily, 'but I am not accustomed to *two* messengers from England! Else had I asked you to wait while I made myself more seemly. You come from my lady mother?'

They knelt, proffering the letters, and observed his face without seeming to watch, while he read them. It was a face young in age and old in policy, grave as a priest's as he digested the news. A long face with a strong nose, a fine mouth and clear grey eyes. A face neither plain nor handsome, framed by dark-gold hair. His expression did not change as he read, but he drew one quick short breath as he finished.

He detected a note of condescension in Buckingham's letter, for all that it promised aid and comfort and friends. But his mother had spoken from both heart and head: addressing him as her own sweet and most dear prince; charging him not to neglect so good an occasion offered, but with all speed to settle his mind how to return to England, and counselling him to land in Wales. Then she asked God to bless him.

'You will be weary, gentlemen,' said Henry. 'Rest and refresh yourselves for a space while I compose my answers. Then shall you summarily return to England that these matters may speedily be set afoot.'

They murmured their thanks and obedience, making low bows. But he could not contain his joy as coolly as he wished, and as they began to withdraw he stopped them.

Wales he knew, but England was a dream as foreign to him as Brittany had been a dozen years ago. He tried to remember the little he had seen of it, on his one journey to London, but it eluded him: as great a stranger as the bride they offered.

'I pray you, sirs,' he said, and a tremor in his voice touched them closely, 'how does the kingdom seem?'

It was Hugh Conway who surmised that he did not speak of politics.

'Why, my lord,' he replied gently, 'the realm is green and fair. The swans ride upon the Thames right royally, and the air is sweeter than wine.'

'I thank you, sir,' said Henry Tudor, 'for both that news and this.'

They glanced back once, seeing that his companions waited curiously for him to speak to them. Still he stood there, the blue doublet pulled carelessly over the fine shirt, that was bordered with lace and rich in blue needlework on high collar and narrow cuffs. The letters from England were grasped like fortune in both hands.

It was as though something long expected had happened, and yet as though the news were indeed wholly new and bewildering. The exile, the adventurer in him, who had answered the messengers at once and ordered their refreshment and an immediate return, was only one self. Beneath him lay a cautious, thinking man; and beneath that a superstitious one, who recognized an omen; and beneath him a mystical one, who followed an inner Holy Grail; and beneath that, darker and deeper waters which he could only commend to God. So Henry stood, with the letters in his hands, and could not speak.

The tableau was broken by Jasper, who touched his arm, alarmed by his stillness.

'How does the Lady Margaret?' he asked. 'For your face is as pale as her pages.'

Henry gave him the letters and walked a little way off, ashamed that he was trembling with excitement and fear, and stood with his back to all of them.

'The Earl of Richmond has had noble tidings,' he heard Jasper say, 'and he would be alone with me a while. You shall hear presently, my good lords, but for the moment I crave your courtesy and beg you take your leave.'

Then Jasper was beside him, grinning with triumph, stepping over a dozen years of exile.

'A kingdom, Harry!' cried Jasper, exultant. 'By God's Blessed Lady, lad, a kingdom for the asking! Why, by your countenance I thought your gracious mother lay dying. What, lad, no smiles? No shouts of joy? Have you lost at dice, then, or been thrown from your horse?'

'I find the news too deep for merriment,' said Henry with difficulty.

'You have accepted, though, Henry?' Jasper asked, his face falling lest some curious point of honour had caused his nephew to refuse.

His expression brought Henry's sense of humour back, and Jasper laughed and struck his hands together, relieved.

'I have not lost my wits, sir,' said Henry, smiling. 'You would think me a very fool and I said no! But I must sit down awhile. Where is that butt? It shall lend my back some strength.'

And he sat down with the comfort of the target behind him, and closed his eyes.

'Now would the dreamer in me like to die,' he said quietly to himself, 'for then he dies in sight of a fair promise.'

'Harry, Harry! I never dreamed a crown for you, Harry, and yet it is a princely dream, and the awakening shall be better,' Jasper cried. 'What poxy talk is this of dying? Die a dreamer? Nay, lad, die fighting if you must – or nobler still, fight to some purpose and win all!' He suddenly realized the full extent of the messages. 'Why, Harry, they even have a princess praying for you – on her fair knees this instant, I swear it, asking God for victory and two crowns. Could any man want more?'

'I know you too well, uncle, to believe that any princess weighs upon your thoughts. Had you been St George you would have fought the dragon valiantly – and forgot to untie the lady after!'

Jasper roared and slapped his thigh, then looked slyly at his nephew.

'Yet were you always sighing after that wench on the tapestry, Harry – and ever loved a light-haired lass above a dark one. Your present lady's husband must welcome her back into his arms, for you have no need of her! Elizabeth of York, they say, is like to silver for her beauty – as handsome as both father and mother put together.'

'The lady is a king's daughter, pure and pious and meet to be queen,' said Henry, embarrassed. 'I shall not quarrel with their choice of her.'

'Cold loins breed not hot princes!' Jasper cried, enjoying his joke.

'Nor love-sick lads win wars,' Henry answered, turning the conversation to his uncle's interests. 'I am no warrior, uncle, and love not war as you do. And King Richard is a noble soldier.'

'You hold your own right well,' said Jasper, jealous for his prowess, 'and will yield to no man.'

'I do as I am taught,' said Henry ruefully, 'and that is not enough. There was a man once, at Pembroke, Hugh Jenkins they called him, that said I did what I must and with a good heart – but that I had no stomach for it. Yet must I find a stomach, uncle. I cannot ask men's lives without I lead them bravely.'

He rose, and brushed the soil from his clothes abstractedly, while Jasper pondered.

'If Richard were a butt,' Henry continued, slapping the sturdy mound of earth, 'I should transfix him straight. But will he stand still while I aim? And were he a boar in truth as well as emblem, then should I hunt him. But will he not show more cunning than a beast? Nay, he is a man and thinks like a man, and is a goodly warrior. And so I am at loss to know how to conquer him.'

'Now shall I teach you kingship!' cried Jasper sternly, scrambling up beside him. 'Look well upon me, Henry Tudor. Do you see this scar?' And he pointed to the faint white line beneath his grey cropped hair. 'The man that marked me lies beneath the ground. He was a soldier, too, but did my thoughts betray my hand? Love is your weakness, Harry, and though heaven may welcome it the world will not. This is no game of chess, lad, where King Richard sits on one side of the board and you on the other, playing with smiles and courtesy. The crown is either yours or his, you may not share it. And know him well, he will not stay his hand for you. You see him over-sweetly. He does not see you likewise.

'*Usurper*, he will call you! And you call him *Murderer*, for that is what he is! *Bastard*, he will name you – and you name him *Tyrant*. He will not say *This is a better man*! – and serve you faithfully. He will reach for his sword! And by God he knows right well how to wield it, and has men in the Tower that will make you cry out if he captures you. And that head shall make grimaces on the pole, to frighten little children in their dreams, dying on a long shout for mercy!

'I'll teach you how I teach my men-at-arms. The truths of war are different from the truths of peace. Men are either for you or against you. Now will you live or die!'

He drew his sword from the scabbard so rapidly that it was no more than a flash, and drove it deep into the grass.

'There lies King Richard!' he shouted. 'Do not call him brother. Aye, though he holds his wife tenderly and loves his sickly son. Think not of him as a man. He is your mortal enemy!'

He withdrew the blade and plunged it again in the earth.

'He does not pray to God as you do. He is the devil's spawn!'

The blade glittered and was thrust again.

'He is no noble lord, but a foul traitor!'

Glittering and stabbing.

'His blood does not run red, but black with bile and hatred. His cause is not just. He is the murderer of his brother's children. He lay two years in his mother's womb, and came forth as other men go from this world – feet first. The midwives shrieked as they did fetch him out, for his hair grew to his shoulders and in his infant gums teeth bared at them. And he is hunch-backed, foul and deadly – and a heinous villain.' Driving deeper in the earth. 'Now do you mark your enemy, my lord?'

The colour was high in Henry's cheeks, but he made no answer. Breathing heavily from his exertions, Jasper paused and looked at him, and there was something like contempt on his face. He wrested his sword with difficulty from its target, and sheathed it.

'Tell them you have no stomach for the fight,' he said tiredly. 'Let England want for lack of one man's courage. Let York and Lancaster claw for the crown. Aye, and York fight York, and Lancaster tear Lancaster, turn and turn about in bloody tournament. Until all fail, and France divide the spoils. For here is no prince of valour, called by Almighty God to great estate, but a faint heart and a fickle gentleman – that would wait on charity until providence grew sick and spewed him forth like vomit!'

He was walking unsteadily away when a voice he had never heard called him by a name never used between them.

'Pembroke!'

He turned, and his heart leaped even as it misgave him. The red of shame had gone and left rage behind it.

'I would not slay you,' said Henry bitterly, 'although your tongue plays traitor well enough. Your love should deal more gently with my counsel, Pembroke, and thank me that I ask your good advice. For though my friends are few as yet, my lord, I shall have more than you dreamed of. God does not call a king to reckoning and leave him without soldiers. Take care, my lord, that you are not excluded from them!'

'I spoke not to a king but to a dreaming boy,' said Jasper, choosing his words carefully : fearful that too soft a tone might bring the dreamer back again.

'Then know, as of this moment, that the dream was ever royal, my lord,' cried Henry, and was astonished to find he spoke a deeper truth than he had reckoned. 'I am no hot-head prince to put my neck in foolish jeopardy, but one that thinks of dangers so he may combat them. I said, my lord, this was a perilous business. I did not say I spurned it. And, were your wits as ready as your sword and as your tongue, you would think better of me. I know my duty, Pembroke, I would you knew your own.'

For a few moments they faced each other in silence, and then a slow smile on Jasper's mouth was answered by Henry's laugh.

'Now let each crave the other's pardon, uncle,' he said, holding out his arms. 'We meant not what we spoke in anger.'

'And yet I liked what I heard – although I shall not stir your wrath again,' Jasper replied. 'My tongue has met its master, sire!'

The Duke of Brittany had begun a fresh game of diplomatic cunning with Richard III of England; and though he could not commend the manner in which the rightful heir to the throne had been supplanted, he had to admire Richard's thoroughness and speed. Within days of his coronation, Richard sent his Ambassador Hutton to the court of Brittany with special enquiries about the Earl of Richmond. Tact-fully, François II sent reply that the earl was safe in his keeping, and added that France was most interested in his person, too. Temporarily blocked, Richard replied that he would continue to pay for Henry's close custody.

'And now, Lord Henry,' said the duke, smiling. 'I see that our hospitality has furnished England with a new king – who will not, I am sure, forget his friends!'

He saw that the news had given Henry new purpose and dignity, and smiled again.

'Your welfare is as my own, my lord duke,' Henry replied,

'and I shall remember your grace's constant goodwill towards me and my uncle.'

'Then let us say fifteen ships and five thousand men. Should that not be enough, with the Duke of Buckingham's forces and those who rise with him along the coast?'

'This is *most* generous, your grace.'

Jasper, re-born, flung himself into the preparations.

'I had not thought so much was needed!' said Henry, astonished by the lists of supplies and their cost.

Maps and sea charts, food and water and candles, arms and powder : all that was necessary to keep a host of men alive and ready to land as a military force on the other side.

In the west and south of England Henry's supporters stood ready for the final word of command, but the men of Kent long-versed in rebellion, could not contain themselves. On 10 October, eight sorry days too soon, they struck the spark that should have united England and Wales, but, communications being so poor, the others could not follow them quickly enough. The Duke of Norfolk thrust his forces between ally and ally, and snapped up the spats and spurts of the rebellion as their standards rose.

Buckingham marched on the appointed day from Brecon, taking Bishop Morton with him. And on the following day King Richard, receiving the news at Grafton and piecing together the whole scheme, led his army across country towards Leicester and Coventry. His royal proclamation was overflowing with bitterness, as he commanded the sheriffs of Shropshire and other counties to come to his aid. He called Buckingham the most untrue creature living, and the falsest traitor. He denounced the damnable sins and vices of the rebels, crying that they acted to the great displeasure of God, and were an evil example to all Christian people. And he commanded a thousand pounds be paid in gold and silver to any man who discovered the whereabouts of that rebel and traitor the Duke of Buckingham, and promised a knighthood with it. But he pondered the identity of the usurper with bewilderment and incredulity, requiring some refreshment of his memory, since he knew the Lady Margaret but could not place the sire.

'An unknown *Welshman*!' he said at last, 'whose father I never *knew*, nor him personally *saw*!'

Officers of the Crown, alerted in Breconshire, were marching after Buckingham through the Forest of Dean. Sir Humphrey Stafford had broken down the bridge of the Severn ahead of him. He waited on one side, and the Vaughans waited on the other, promised the plunder of Brecon. And then nature herself, Yorkist as ever, took a hand in the duke's destruction. From the mountains poured a mighty deluge, known afterwards as Buckingham's Great Water. The devastation toppled houses, drowned honest folk in their beds, and cattle in the fields. Trapped, Buckingham turned back for Weobley. But his power had always been that of the autocrat rather than the father-protector, and the Welsh under his rule held no love for him. The violence of the king's proclamation, the terror of the waters which seemed to come from an outraged heaven, sent his forces scattering back to the hills from whence they had been raised. Alone, Buckingham sought out one man in Shropshire who owed him much, and begged a hiding-place.

Ralph Bannister had been in the duke's service from childhood : base by birth and nature. Constant gratitude can be a bitter bread to chew, and a master fallen from his high estate the cause for silent pleasure.

'Christ's curse on me and mine, my lord,' said Bannister obsequiously, looking out his oldest clothes, 'if ever I prove false to you. Your grace is welcome under my poor roof, and though it cost me my life I shall keep you safe.'

Helping him into the leather jacket, offering the leather breeches and coarse stockings, putting away the velvet and silk.

'This hat has twenty holes in it, my lord,' he said in pretended sorrow, 'but with this upon your grace's noble head and the hedging bill on your grace's back, no man would take you for a lord !'

It was meat and ale to him to see Buckingham's big body in these clumsy garments. It was payment to put the hedging bill in those well-kept hands, and picture them grown as rough and calloused as his own. But the sourer his thoughts the more gracious his tongue became. And while the duke was making the best of a poor supper Bannister sent word to Master Mitton, Bailiff of Shrewsbury town, that he had the rebel safe.

He was not man enough to stand there when the Herald at Arms arrived with a troop of soldiers. But he heard Buckingham's accusations of falseness and treachery, and heard the struggle as the duke set his pride and strength against too great odds. And he thought of the knighthood and the reward that awaited him. He was not destined to enjoy either. Richard, seeing what manner of man he dealt with, spoke bitterly of traitors who sought to rise by the misfortunes of those who had honoured them with their patronage. Cast into prison, Bannister reflected bitterly that there was one rule for the rich and another for the lowly. It was a thought which must have occurred to many a commoner in England and Wales, as they took up arms again and again.

Two courses were yet open to Buckingham and he tried them both. First he gave a full confession of the rebellion, with details of everyone involved and the plan of campaign, hoping for a pardon. The confession was accepted, the pardon was not offered. Then, thinking to stab Richard to the heart, he begged a private interview. This was refused.

On All Soul's Day, Sunday 2 November 1483, Henry Stafford, Duke of Buckingham, Constable of all England, and of all royal castles in five western counties, Chief Justice and Chamberlain of North and South Wales, was executed in Salisbury market place.

The storm that divided Buckingham from his supporters swept across the Channel, scattering Henry's ships like so many corks; driving all but two of them back upon the coasts of Normandy and Brittany.

They battled against the gale, ignorant of the failed rebellion. The risings in half a dozen counties were brutally put down, and when they sailed into the mouth of Poole Harbour armed soldiers were waiting for them to land. Something about them roused Henry's innate caution and Jasper's intuition. Hoisting sail again they turned and headed for Plymouth, where more armed men called greetings and bade them welcome.

'I know not why,' said Jasper, 'but I think it menacing. And we have but two ships and cannot fight them if they be enemies. I have slipped so often through those Yorkist fingers that I can smell them leagues away. We'll sail for home, lad, and fight again.'

'If any man will fight for us, uncle!'

'There is a time for battle,' Jasper observed philosophically, 'and a time to run away. So let us run, lad, before King Richard's fleet is after us!'

CHAPTER FIFTEEN

Twice have I promised you this,
A journey, a fair promise,
And man should not be backward
If he can, to keep his word.

The Court of Owain Glyndŵr at Sycarth
Iolo Goch, fourteenth century

But something had begun that could not be stayed by temporary misfortune. The Duke of Brittany had shown his hand, and Breton goods and ships were seized in English ports. Unable to play the friendly neutral any longer, he guarded his coasts and prepared to receive his guests again. And the French court, seeing an opportunity to flout Richard, gave Henry a passport from Normandy into Brittany, and intimated that they were willing to help him in other ways.

Buckingham and St Leger were dead, and many others – including poor Thomas Ramme, who had carried one of Henry's letters. But the Marquis of Dorset, the dowager-queen Elizabeth's son, had escaped; so had the Courtenays and Christopher Urswick and Lord Wells. They came across the Channel, singly or in little groups, to form a small court of Lancaster: Sir Giles Daubeney, Sir John Bourchier, Sir Robert Willoughby, Sir Thomas Arundel, Sir John Cheyney and his two brothers, Sir William Berkeley and his brother Thomas, Sir Richard Edgecombe, Edward Pynings, and a host of gentlemen: Lancastrians and former Yorkists. And awaiting them was Sir Edward Woodville, who had once commanded the English fleet.

By the end of November, Henry had borrowed a further ten thousand crowns from the Duke of Brittany at Paimpol, and given him a receipt for it. Whether either of them expected it to be honoured was uncertain, but both of them hoped, since they had now pushed too far forward to go back. The news of Buckingham's execution brought the refugees to a council in Rhennes, where Henry swore to make another invasion as soon as the time seemed propitious and the money available.

The failed rebellion, created out of wild enthusiasm and carried out with zest, had taught him calculation. He had accepted that the houses of York and Lancaster must be

166

cemented. Now he realized that England must be conquered through Wales, where Tudor roots lay deep. And he must be seen as the heir of Lancaster, however slender his connections were.

On Christmas Day 1483 his followers trooped into Rhennes Cathedral to pledge allegiance to each other and to the man who would reign over them, God willing. The snow lay thickly underfoot, and the flaring braziers and torches in the sombre building gave little warmth. The nobles wrapped their furred mantles about them, and their breath smoked on the icy air.

They had no circlet to put upon his head, but he seemed regal enough without one. And though his height was not great he stood with dignity, and committed himself wholly. He gave his oath to unite the white rose with the red, to marry Elizabeth of York and make her his queen as soon as the crown was his. He pledged himself to rule with justice and mercy, to bring peace to a torn realm and make it prosperous. He swore to lead them to victory or die upon the field.

His voice had lost its pleasant timbre and rang back, harsh and stern, from the stone walls and pillars. Without the smile his face seemed plain and pale and sombre, but strong too. And though he was no warrior, like John of Gaunt, like Richard of Gloucester, there was a stubborn courage in him that gave them confidence.

They have proclaimed him king, willed him to be king though they did not know him, hoped he could be king though they had no proof of his ability. Now in the moment of allegiance he became a king. One by one they paid homage, and knelt before a man who had taken upon himself the mystery of kingship. The earl was gone, resolved into a figurehead. Sure and safe as children under protection, they kissed the long jewelled hand, and bowed their heads before the long formal face. And Jasper of Pembroke, his nephew lost to him, acknowledged the image with them.

The huge candle in its silver sconce had burned four hours of the night away, and still Henry lay awake, watching the flame eat into the figure V scored in its wax. His transformation awed him, and was reflected in the finer chamber placed at his disposal. Carpets on the floor, white silk hangings on the walls, and a good bed of down beneath his body. Lawn sheets kept the faint roughness of fustian from his flesh, and the counterpane was furred with ermine. Curtains of white sarcenet and a canopy of cloth of gold shielded his bed from the winter draughts. Now a guard stood outside the heavy door. And if the log fire needed mending, or he fancied a last cup of mulled wine, some sleepy page would attend him. For he was king in name and had named a queen. And across the dark waters of the Channel a realm awaited him.

The pawns had all been played, and early in 1484 the pieces came forward. Richard's Act of Titulus Regius, pronouncing his brother's children to be bastards, was matched by the condemnation of the Chancellor of France, who deplored the princes' deaths. Bishop Morton, having escaped from Weobley to Ely, now slipped from the fastness of his Fens and arrived in Flanders : a busy spider in the web of cloaked riders and secret letters, with Christopher Urswick at his side. In England, Richard persuaded the queen-dowager and her daughters to leave sanctuary and put up a front of friendship at court. In France and Brittany, the death of Richard's only son and heir caused a buzz of speculation – one less to threaten Henry's claim. And still it was not time. News came slowly, anyway. Hampered by the perils of treason, watched at the ports and along the wretched bog-and-stone roads, Henry's messengers collected the loyalties of Wales and England, the seasoned calculations of Bishop Morton in Holland, and the rumours at all courts, little by little.

Henry Tudor had much to do and more to discover, but Richard III's greatest problem was centred in one man. If Henry died the rebellion died with him. Open communication was at an end between Brittany and England, so an underground approach was necessary. An offer to the Duke François, of the Richmond revenues in exchange for Henry Tudor's person, had been proudly rejected. But the duke now lay ill with a disorder of the mind, and his minister Pierre Landois held temporary power. Richard collected all the information he needed about Landois from Bishop Stillington, who had headed the tricked embassy in 1475. He formed a picture of a cunning politician who might well be bribed. But the roads and seas were no kinder to an English than to a French rider, and Bishop Morton had time to smell treachery in the wind.

At Vannes, the earlier capital of Brittany, Henry received Christopher Urswick at an unseasonable hour of the night: spattered with mud, from the first rains of September. The duchy was unsafe and Henry's life imperilled.

The fears that had sent him into an ague, nine years before, no longer beset him. Coolly, he ordered Urswick to beg a safe passport from Charles VIII and return with it as quickly as possible, while he made ready to depart. He dared tell no more but those closest to him, and he and Jasper pored over a map of byways between Brittany and France, planning a route and means of escape.

'Duke Françoise recovers from his sickness *here*,' said Jasper, pointing to a town on the confines of the duchy. 'So shall I ride, with our leading friends, to wish him well again. Then, two days after us, you follow another route with four attendants. We must leave the others of your court behind us, five hundred loyal gentlemen, so that Landois suspects nothing. He will be watching, but he must watch all of us. The rest you know, Harry. And we meet at Angers.'

In the two days that remained to him, Henry hunted; fighting his suspicions with his spear so that he might sleep soundly at night. Then a small cavalry of five set out: a humble thing that one might hardly notice, except that the earl was outstanding in his splendid clothes. They rode in a leisurely fashion past the washing-place in the town, where for centuries the linen had been cleansed and whitened on the smooth stones, and away from the grey walls and bastions of the castle, laughing and talking among themselves. Henry turned just once to see the cathedral, whose spire and dome shone like silver in the morning sun. They kept their easy pace for a few more miles, before entering a wood, and when they came out again the earl was still conspicuous among the others. But the face beneath the feathered cap was not Henry's, and one page seemed nobler than he had been.

Now they left the main road, studying a map at intervals, taking a maze of little lanes and bridle-paths that led circuitously to the border. They galloped when they could, trotted when they could not, never drawing rein until they crossed the frontier. An hour behind them, the horsemen of Pierre Landois rode and enquired and rode again.

The Duke of Brittany, recovering, raged at this slight upon his duchy's honour, and sent for Sir Edward Woodville — who knew rather less than he did.

'The Earl of Richmond is safe enough, sir!' said the duke testily, finding himself the enquired of rather than the enquirer. 'He is even now at Paris with the Earl of Pembroke and some of their retinue.'

'Then shall we give thanks to God, your grace. For we knew nothing – and without him we *are* nothing!'

'How many, sir?' asked the duke in his most royal manner.

'Five hundred, your grace.'

'Where is that cur, Landois? Give this nobleman money to convey himself and his friends to the court of Paris, while you are yet our treasurer! And mark you, Landois, we are much displeased! Nor do I think King Richard holds you so high in his favour. You have fallen between two masters.' Then turning to Sir Edward he said in a different tone, 'Convey our greetings to the Earl or Richmond. Tell him he has our friendship always, and that those who most heinously betrayed him shall be punished!'

Paris was nearer than Brittany and further allies flocked to join the Tudor cause. English students at the university swore their allegiance; among them Richard Fox, who left his studies to render service that was to last a lifetime. Nobles and gentry, even sheriffs, blew from England on this new wind to pledge themselves. And Bishop Morton, grave and shrewd and haughty, lifted a political nose to the air and found it good. But best and greatest of all who fled was John de Vere.

The grizzled Earl of Oxford had been imprisoned as far back as 1474 in Hammes Castle, near Calais, for capturing St Michael's Mount during one of Clarence's rebellions. And there he had lain, though not rusted, for a decade. This fresh turn of affairs had affected both the jailer and the jailed, and Oxford's warder, James Blount, not only set his charge free but came with him. The Earl, now forty-two years old, possessed the double benefit of high rank and superior military standing, and captivity had sharpened his appetite for both. He asked no more than to lay down his experience and his life for Lancaster. So he knelt before Henry, and Henry raised him to his feet: radiant with this noble prize.

'Now I begin to have good hope of success,' said Henry warmly.

There was, however, a slight blemish on his pleasure. The Marquis of Dorset seemed to have inherited his mother's changeable nature. He and Hastings had been King Edward's favourite companions in the lists of drinking and wenching – and all had enjoyed Jane Shore in their turn. With the king's death, he had fled into sanctuary, then slipped out to join Buckingham's rebellion and declare Henry king at Exeter, escaping across the Channel afterwards. But now his mother wrote, under Richard's influence, to persuade him to return home; where, she said, he would be pardoned and honoured. His attempted flight from Paris was checked, and Henry, fulfilling an old ambition to combine finance with politics, left Dorset as a guarantee against the money France had lent him; to be bought back if the second invasion was successful, and kept as bargaining power if it were not.

'Never trust a Grey or a Woodville, Harry!' said Jasper, too old in policy to be surprised. 'And give thanks to God that Richard has despatched so many of them. It shall save us a bloody reckoning. The daughters are well enough,' he added hastily, remembering that one of them would be Henry's queen, 'but the mother should be kept somewhere out of harm's way, for she was ever a fickle and a wayward woman!'

'The Stanleys, too, are cautious,' said Henry, pursuing a thought of his own. For Lord Thomas Stanley, Steward of the King's Household, had first held aloof and then hedged his promises with safeguards.

'*I* should be cautious, were I at the English court!' said Jasper.

In the November of 1484 the French council had lent three thousand livres towards the expedition, and the preparations for invasion were mounting steadily. They were at Rouen, negotiating for supplies when rumours reached them that Richard III, determined to cut his rival's chief comb, planned to marry Elizabeth of York.

'This nips me at the very stomach!' said Henry slowly, for her possession had been one of his strongest claims, and in a curious way he was fond of this pretty stranger.

'Nay, let your stomach be at ease,' said Jasper, thinking. 'For she is his niece, his brother's daughter, and such an incestuous union must be granted dispensation by the Pope himself. We know not that His Holiness will favour it – and if he does it will take time.'

'We *have* no time!' Henry cried, and was bitter at the thought of the little fleet, even now being assembled at Harfleur.

'Then let us cast about us for another queen, since this

one eludes us!' said Jasper shrewdly. 'A Welsh queen, that shall bring Wales to us twice over. Sir Walter Herbert has a sister.'

'I was once promised to a Herbert,' said Henry, weary of it all.

'And we shall be sure of him, if the cause is so close to home!'

'I know not, uncle. I wonder if I care not? We chop and change and go from this to that and the other, always.' Another piece of policy occurred to him. 'And though Wales love me twice over – once for myself and once for her – it is *England* that must love me, too. We need a broader view than Welsh king and queen, uncle.'

'And England needs a prince, Harry. There must be knowledge of the succession. They must have future princes in their heads before we land.' Jasper summoned his scrivener. 'Another of Sir Walter's sisters is married to a Northumberland,' he said. 'We may negotiate through him. And you may swear upon it,' he added, 'that the queen-dowager is hot with the notion of Richard and Elizabeth of York already! She cares not who her daughter marry, so long as she be a queen. And the girl can do nothing but what she is told.'

'And kings must do as subjects order them,' said Henry coldly, glancing at the scrivener, busy with his materials. 'Write if you must!'

He had made enquiries about Elizabeth, and though he knew it was their business to flatter and glorify, he cherished what he had heard. No one questioned her beauty, and he wanted her to be beatiful. But it was the little things that pleased him : her obedience and devotion, her kindnesses to servants, and above all her helplessness. For he knew what it meant to be helpless, and to feel imprisoned by circumstance.

The girl can do nothing but what she is told.

She had been promised to the present king of France, and jilted cruelly and publicly. She had fled to sanctuary and lived on charity. Even at the court Queen Ann had given her a gown because her others were so shabby. She had been promised to him, and he had failed to win her. And how did he seem to her? Better than King Richard, of that he was sure, but how much better? Had she enquired of him as he had enquired of her? Or did she sit and wait and watch and pray, past caring how they disposed of her?

The girl can do nothing but what she is told.

But, he had lived with the idea of her for almost eighteen months, and filled his head with dreams that a boy might be ashamed of in daylight. He had raised her to her feet, victorious from the field, and looked into her face. He had ordered her to be treated with all honour, lavishing clothes and jewels upon her. He had savoured the delight, the double delight, of holding a kingdom in his hand while they grew to know each other better. For even in the most ravishing visions he kept his head, and had no intention of being other than sole ruler of the realm and undisputed master of his household. He had imagined the pageantry of his wedding, the pageant of her crowning. He had entered on more domestic pleasures : their children playing about them, the royal progresses from which they retired in privacy to talk of lesser matters. He had bestowed her least desires upon her. He had ordered her chamber to be strewn with flowers, and his minstrels to play airs. He had, in short, made a fool of himself over someone whom he had never seen, and who must now be replaced. And, though he was sure that Sir Walter Herbert's sister would be both handsome and virtuous, he had not the heart to conjure her up.

Neither letter nor messenger ever reached their destination. Somewhere in the passage of time they were lost and remained untraced : suggestions for a match that was never intended to take place.

But more than ambition and the quest for a queen drove them. Delay promised to strengthen Richard's position and to weaken their own. Their stay at the French court was threatened by internal difficulties. Madame de Beaujeu, wife of the Duke of Bourbon, elder sister to Charles VIII, and present Regent of France, held sway only for the moment. The queen-mother and her younger daughter's husband, Duke Louis of Orleans, were forming a powerful opposition. The expedition hung between the two factions, frail as a thread.

'So it must be *soon* an' it be at all, sire !' Oxford advised him privately. 'We must move inch by inch, and what we grasp we must hold. Our safety lies in speedy preparation.'

'Yet must we seem at ease, and patient, as we press forward,' Jasper added, wise with long waiting.

'My lords,' said Henry simply. 'I am not merely *patient*. I have become patience *itself* – how could I live else?'

CHAPTER SIXTEEN

Shall I have the girl I love,
The grove of light, my truelove
With her silk top like a star
And her head's golden pillar?

A Girl's Hair,
        Dafydd ab Edmwnd, fifteenth century,
        translated by Anthony Conran

The Lord Thomas Stanley, furred against the cold of 1485,
rubbed his hands partly for comfort and partly out of habit,
as Humphrey Brereton delivered his lady's message in a low
voice.

'A matter of great secrecy, Master Brereton?' he said
softly, pondering, 'These are perilous times for secrets. You
must be close to the Lady Elizabeth to be entrusted with
secret messages.'

'Aye, my lord, and her true esquire.'

Stanley looked shrewdly at the fresh young face and steady
eyes, and leaned forward lest any of his secretaries should
overhear.

'Then tell the Lady Elizabeth to send away her servants
before the hour of nine tonight. And have a charcoal fire
burning, that our eyes might not smart from smoke. And
have divers spices and wine ready. For I find that counsel is
best given and taken at length and at ease. And bid your
lady listen well, for I shall knock but softly and have none
with me.' Aloud, he said in a dry voice, 'Commend me to
the Lady Elizabeth, and tell her that if she needs more
money she should apply to the king. I am but her host,
Master Brereton, not her purse! The king has been liberal
to her family, and will doubtless bend his mind to this matter
also.'

'I thank you, my lord.'

'And mark you well, Master Brereton, that the king's
patience be not tried further! I have suffered grievous
treachery in mine own household, and the knowledge lies
heavily upon my heart. I would not that the king were
troubled by any under my roof.'

The young man bowed in silence, one hand on his pleated doublet, and withdrew.

'And if there be any here that so much as approach the Lady Elizabeth's quarters, they shall seek their bread elsewhere !' he said coldly, looking round the chamber. 'I will have no plots hatched. Heads shall part from shoulders else, and necks be stretched. You have my word upon it.'

There was silence for fully half an hour.

Elizabeth of York had put on a furred mantle for warmth, and Stanley noted that the velvet was rubbed. But her beauty made nonsense of the shabby garment.

She was nervous, making sure that he sat well out of the draughts and within the heat of the fire. Then setting wine and spices before him, she said, 'Blend it, my lord, and drink to me !' and sat opposite.

'What are you reading in this ill light, my lady?' he asked, seeing that she did not know how to begin.

She looked at him steadfastly as she replied.

'It is a book of prophecy, my lord, that the king my father gave to me. Wherein it says I shall be queen of England.'

He laid down the book as though it burned him, was taken by a fit of coughing, and said he had mixed the spices too strong.

'Then shall I blend the wine myself, my lord, even as the king my father taught me.' A little pause ensued. 'My lord Stanley, I seek your counsel on a matter of some moment and great peril to us all.'

Her hands trembled as she gave him a fresh cup of wine.

'My lord, but half a year ago, my mother the queen and your wife the Lady Margaret would have had me marry the Earl of Richmond . . .'

'An ill-fated matter !' cried Stanley testily, 'and one in which I had no part.'

She was silent, perplexed how to find her way through this maze of politics. For she had heard that Stanley knew very well what the Lady Margaret was about, and would have welcomed Henry Tudor. But, as the rebellion failed, he had apologized to King Richard for his wife's conduct, and promised to keep her safely guarded so that she should plot no more.

'Ill-fated it was, my lord,' she began again, 'and now my lady mother turns this way and that. Not knowing, my lord,' she added hastily, out of duty, 'what best to do for my welfare.'

She shaded her eyes from the glare of the fire, and he wondered what strengths and what weaknesses lay behind that gentle face.

'I have heard rumours, my lord, that I fear to speak on.'

'Rumours, rumours!' said Stanley uneasily, moving in his chair. 'Only the king holds the key to these riddles, and even he – it is said – is not privy to all matters!'

'My lord, I have heard that Queen Ann is sick unto death,' the girl said hurriedly, afraid of her own words. 'I have heard that should she die King Richard may twine a white rose with a white, to secure the house of York.' She turned her face from him, and he saw that she was crying silently. 'My lord, I have learned much of the affairs of state since my father died. I have learned that a prince may be taken from sanctuary, and him and his brother never seen after. I have learned that a proud queen must accept charity from one she mistrusts, and outwardly mend a quarrel that should be healed with blood. Yet she is but a woman,' she added, 'and lacks powerful friends. And the king has promised that we shall be found husbands and portions, and she be granted seven hundred marks a year.'

'A royal sum,' said Stanley, who had paid that for two pairs of falcons. But he took pity on the girl, whose wit and experience were no match for his own. 'I will speak plainly, Lady Bessie,' he said kindly. 'The king may not take his niece in marriage – neither the Pope nor the people would so let him. Neither do I know he so purposes,' he added, covering himself. 'Indeed, *I have not* heard so! So diverse are these rumours that none may trust in them.'

'And yet the book of reason says I shall be queen of England. And you, my lord, believe in prophecy.'

He stared for a long time into the heart of the fire, thinking of past and present perils.

'I had a dream once,' he said to himself. And then, on a sigh, 'Poor Hastings!'

She was at his side, a little breathless with her daring, laying one long pale hand on his sleeve.

'Father Stanley, since you comfort me truly on this rumoured marriage, there is another way to make me queen. They tell me nothing, my lord, and yet surely the Earl of Richmond has not forgotten the crown?'

Ambition, ambition, always ambition, Stanley thought.

Though he had a fair share of it, and was not the head of a powerful family solely by good fortune.

'Tell me what is in your mind, Lady Bessie, and I will answer you truly.'

'The Earl of Richmond is in the same case as myself. How should our fortunes change unless we risk all? Oh, my lord, Father Stanley, fetch him to England, raise friends and money for Lancaster, and unite the white rose and the red under one crown!'

Stanley had hardly been idle, but did not intend to say so.

'Why, my lady, has your lady mother changed weather-cock fashion for Henry Tudor again?' he asked, and his voice was harder.

'Nay, my lord,' she whispered, suddenly afraid of him. 'I have had no converse with my mother. This I thought on by myself. I have little wit, my lord, for politics. Yet it seemed to me that I was a king's daughter and no bastard, and might take my brothers' places. For so the king my father would have wished.'

He took her by the chin and looked intently at her face, but there was no guile in those blue eyes. She was just a girl who, by the dint of a book of prophecy, a clutch of broken promises, and an earl with yellow hair, had thought she should be queen of England.

'Mark you well, my lady,' said Stanley, releasing her. 'I'll have no Woodville meddling! Too many good gentlemen lie in the earth – aye, and *shall* lie yet – but not for the queen-dowager.'

'You would not speak so, sir, if she were queen, and my father at her side!' she said, soft and chilled.

'I speak as all men speak that do not wish their heads risked at a whim, madam. Your lady mother shall command respect of any Stanley. But it is well to remember that she blows as the wind blows – and no wind blows crowns.'

'You shall not be betrayed by me, my lord,' said the girl, and returned with dignity to her chair. 'Indeed,' she added, trying to match him in policy, 'had you a servant hidden that would bear you witness, you could despatch me to the block, my lord. So have I trusted *you*!'

He smiled, amused by her innocence.

'And what of a clerk to write these treasonable letters, madam? For I dare trust no one here. Twice I have offended the king, and twice have my connections saved me. But I find strange faces about me and must be cautious. Nor have

I a messenger that would not run to the king straightway!'

'Then shall I find both clerk and messenger!' she said triumphantly. 'For *I* shall write the letters, my lord, and my squire Humphrey Brereton will bear them safely.'

'Well, well!' He pondered, for the girl had given him the opening he sought. 'Take your pen, madam!' he said, his mind made up. 'And write this. *To my brother, Sir William Stanley, at Holt Castle. Mine own heartily beloved brother, I recommend me unto you . . .*'

Under her diligent fingers the letters took shape, brief and strange. Sir William was to ride to an old tavern on the outskirts of London, upon the third day of May. For his retinue he must bring no more than seven honest and sober yeomen, dressed in green. For his safety he must stay in hostels where he was not recognized. The purpose of the meeting was ambiguously worded, but a postscript bade him burn the letter the moment it was read. Similar instructions were addressed to Stanley's son George, Lord Strange; to his younger sons, Edmund and James; to Sir John Savage and Sir Gilbert Talbot.

When they were signed and sealed Stanley weighed them thoughtfully in his hand.

'Here lie our fortunes or our heads!' he observed, and was even now thinking of ways to explain them if they were found by the wrong readers.

'Shall I summon Master Brereton, my lord?' Elizabeth asked, putting away her writing materials.

'Not at this hour of the night, madam! Else we shall have a hornet's nest of gossip about our ears. Tomorrow, before daybreak, will be soon enough. Bring the gentleman to me yourself. I do amaze myself, madam,' he said quizzically, 'to trust to such a scheme and such a messenger! Yet the king will not look for treason in such a quarter. And those that are hunted dare not stay overlong in one place. So I shall move outside London, near the inn where we shall meet. And, meanwhile, madam, we shall cause King Richard no discontent.'

He bowed, and kissed the hand extended to him, and saw that in her mind she was already queen. And he smiled a little sourly to himself, because he had lived nearly fifty years and knew the cost of queenship. She knew so little as to imagine that she had set the scheme in his head. Yet had not he and the Lady Margaret, with a network of messengers and good friends, cast about them these last months? Had not Sir Richard ap Howell of Mostyn Hall in Flintshire turned his house into a meeting-place for the Welsh lords who favoured Lancaster? And were they not already decided that Wales should be attempted at the second try, and the banner of Cadwaladr raised to bring all Welshmen under it? Only, this time, they had kept the weathervane Woodvilles out of it.

But King Richard had made him keep the Lady Margaret under close watch in a different part of the country, and set another close watch on Stanley himself. So they had been puzzled how to move, with every move doubly checked on both sides. It had not occurred to him that the girl had a head and mind of her own, though she was trusting to a green lad and a green dream.

Well, thought Stanley comfortably, if Humphrey Brereton falls into the wrong hands those letters were written by the princess. It will go hard with both her and her esquire, but such a wild attempt may be set down to youthful folly. They must look to themselves if I am to keep my place at court.

Humphrey Brereton was as innocent of guile as the princess, and the sight of her standing by his pallet before dawn brought only a determination to die in her service.

'Madam?' he stammered, clutching the fustian blankets to his chest.

'Arise and dress and come with me to the Lord Stanley, Master Brereton. We have need of you,' she whispered.

Even the sight of Lord Stanley's unshaven face could not blemish his happiness.

'My life, my trust and my land – all this lies in your keeping, Master Brereton,' said Stanley gravely. 'You may make and you may mar. You may undo me.' He saw that Humphrey did not give a groat for him, except as an accessory, and touched on something that would. 'You may undo this lady!' he said sternly, and the lad's smile disappeared. 'So take these six letters in your hand and bring them unto the north country. It is written on the back of each where they should be delivered. And if any man waylay you, for God's sake destroy them. And keep a sharp knife about you, Master Brereton, for it is better to die quickly by your own hand than slowly by rack and fire!'

The boy was as pale as the girl now, and Stanley smiled grimly. For if they played at queen's games they must know the price of losing.

179

'My lord,' said Humphrey, bowing, 'I shall die sooner than betray the Lady Elizabeth – or you,' he added, out of good manners.

Outside the chamber the princess beckoned that he should follow her to her own quarters. They crept through the silent house, whispering to the dogs who rose and growled softly from their places by doors and hearths.

'Master Brereton,' said Elizabeth, shaken by the prospect of torture, 'I would speak with you a moment. God has sent me a little wit. When you ride into the north I beg you to seek no company but such as is the best. And – sit not too long over your wine, lest in heart you be too merry and say words that shall be thought on.'

She untied the thong from a leather pouch and shook it open on the bed. The sudden flush in her cheeks hurt him, for he knew there was less than she wanted or needed.

'A poor reward I shall give you,' she said beseechingly. 'It is but three pounds. But if I am queen you shall be better rewarded.'

'I want nothing, madam. Nothing, I beg.'

But she put the coins in his hands, folding his fingers over them and smiling. They would be with him, honoured and unspent until the day he died.

'And now, sir, a cup of wine – for you have not broken your fast. And I pray you hasten, and stop for nothing until you are beyond the city !'

He drank to her health, kissed the outstretched hand worshipfully, and was clattering over the cobbles before another winter day could begin.

Sir William Stanley was inspecting a fish-pond when Humphrey Brereton arrived, and he greeted him somewhat abstractedly.

'Why ride so hastily?' he asked, looking at the spattered clothes and exhausted face.

'Break that letter, sir, and you shall see !' cried Humphrey, annoyed at such a reception of the future queen's messenger.

Sir William read the letter, tore it in three and threw the pieces into the pond. As the last tatter sank he said, suddenly brisk, 'I'll give you a hundred shillings to ride to Latham *now* !'

'Sir, I *cannot* ride now. My horse is tired, and I came from London with the sleep in mine eyes !'

Sir William looked at him closely, to make sure that it

was fatigue and not a faint heart, and satisfied himself.

'Then lie down, Master Brereton, and sleep well for the space of three hours. I'll get a fresh horse to bring you to Latham. And I'll give you a hundred shillings besides.'

Humphrey was too tired to know what he ate or drank, and fell upon the pallet in his muddied clothes to seek a brief oblivion. Within four hours he was heading for Latham and Stanley's son, Lord Strange. By nightfall he had hammered the porter awake – who came grumbling and sorting his keys – and two stout servants who lifted their torches high to see the messenger's face, and then preceded him. Up stone stairs they trod, and down echoing passages and past heavy doors. A regiment of flames burned from iron holders along the walls. A guard of dogs rose and whined and padded to inspect them. Then draughts and damp and echoes became comfort and candle-light, and the warmth of a log fire.

'How fares my father, Master Brereton?' George Strange asked courteously, and called for mulled wine as he opened his letter. Then looked gravely at him. 'This world is not as it should be,' he observed, and thought for so long that Humphrey had drunk his first cup and was beginning on the second. 'Commend me unto my father,' said Lord Strange at last, 'and ask his blessing. For if I live I shall keep this appointment. How weary are you, Master Brereton?'

And he held the paper to the candle-flame until it was consumed.

'Weary enough, my lord. Yet strong enough to do your lordship's bidding.'

'Will you rest and eat for a space, and then ride on to Manchester? You could be there by daylight.'

'Aye, my lord,' said Humphrey as willingly as he could, though his bones begged for sleep.

They had spiced the pork well and it warmed and wakened him a little. Then off into the dark to another house and another place; across this wild country of rock and hussock, whose trees were bent by the wind in arthritic prayer. He tumbled rather than dismounted, from his horse, and was led into the presence of Edmund and James Stanley.

Two at a blow! thought Humphrey wearily, delivering both letters.

Now James was a priest and had been saying matins with his brother before Brereton arrived, but when he read his letter he slapped his thigh and laughed aloud. And Edmund joined him, throwing one arm round his brother's shoulders.

They were young, and the prospect of war pleased them. Humphrey even had to remind them to destroy the letters.

'May good befall our father, that noble lord,' said Edward. 'The old eagle as he is called, begins to stir and rise!'

'Buckingham's blood shall be avenged! That which was spilled at Salisbury,' said James, his face radiant above the black cassock.

'And good befall the Lady Elizabeth,' said Edward, admiring the elegant handwriting.

'We trust in God to bring her lord over the sea,' James added, smiling.

'Here are forty shillings, Master Brereton, in gold. What may we do for you?'

He was swaying on his feet, unable to answer, so they put him to bed.

Sir John Savage took a different view, and saw a fresher Humphrey.

'Woman's wit is wonderful,' he said, raising his eyebrows, 'and so is woman! I think my uncle Stanley's head has been turned by the Lady Elizabeth. But whether it comes to weal or woe I am at my uncle's bidding. Now, good Master Brereton, here are forty shillings for you. Are you weary?' – putting the letter on the fire and watching it burn.

But by this time Humphrey knew the right answer, and was almost at the end of his mission.

'No, my lord. Grant me three hours' sleep and a fresh horse and I'll to Sheffield Castle in all haste.'

To Sir Gilbert Talbot he gave the last of the letters, and Talbot smiled first at the message and then at the messenger.

'Commend me, I pray you, to the Lady Elizabeth – who has no peer in all the land. Tell her she chose her esquire well. And give my greetings to the Lord Stanley. He may count on me.'

Humphrey sighed, and the sigh turned into a yawn.

'Here are three pounds,' said Sir Gilbert, 'though a soft bed and a long sleep will serve you better! Do you return to London at once?'

'No, my lord, for the Lord Stanley counselled me to stay away some little time, and to visit my family at Malpas in Cheshire. So that it would seem I sported among my friends.'

'Then God go with you, Master Brereton. You have earned your sport.'

King Richard was strolling with Lord Stanley in the garden

as Brereton approached, and Stanley turned to Humphrey and closed one eye meaningfully.

Then aloud, in a surprised voice, he cried, 'Welcome, Humphrey! But where have you been? For I have missed you these three weeks.'

The messenger knelt before them both and gave his answer.

'I have been in Cheshire, sire and my lord, visiting my old friends.'

'Master Brereton was born in Malpas, your grace, in the county of Cheshire – from whence come the finest of your grace's bowmen,' said Stanley. 'Tell King Richard, Humphrey, how fare all in that county? How fare King Richard's faithful commons?'

'They will be trusty with their bows, when the king commands them, sire and my lord.'

'We thank you, Master Humphrey,' said Richard gravely, 'and you also, Lord Stanley, that are chief of these commons. If we have Yorkshire, and you Lancashire and Cheshire, we divide the north of England between us, my lord, and yet unite them for we are friends.'

'Your grace is kind enough to say so,' Stanley murmured.

'We swear by Mary that we know no such good friends beneath the sky,' said the king, lifting his dark face to the sunlight.

A fair May wind blew Master Brereton and his retinue to France, and he was glad to get there, for all that Lord Stanley's eagle flew from the top mast. He had spent one half of the voyage vomiting over the side, and the other half guarding the mules' saddle-bags which were sewn full of gold.

'No man in France durst come near that ship,' Stanley had assured him. 'And if any man ask whose ship it be then say it be the Lord Stanley's vessel.'

'*This is the Lord Stanley's vessel!*' Humphrey rehearsed to a black vision of pirates. They would all fall back amazed. He only hoped they did. He had tried to excuse himself from the trip, but the Lady Elizabeth begged so sweetly that he was unmanned.

Neither robbed, scuttled nor drowned, they led their three mules ashore peaceably enough – though the animals tended to hold ideas of their own as to pace and distance – and made their way by degrees to Bigeram Abbey. Thundering upon the gate, Humphrey demanded in his best French a speedy entrance, and the promise of gold for a fee. A shrewd eye peered through the peep-hole, and a broad English voice replied to him.

'I'll none of thy gold nor none of thy fee. But I'll open't gates for *thee*, Master Brereton, for I was born but three miles from Malpas and knew thy father!'

Somewhat dashed, Humphrey rode in and accepted a cup of rough red wine in memory of old times.

'I have a message of great import from England, for the Lord Henry,' he said, as though he and the Earl of Richmond were old acquaintances.

'The earl is at the butts, sir, yonder.'

Humphrey approached, humble and curious, and dropped upon one knee.

'My lord,' he said, to the grass and two scarlet linen legs, 'my name is Humphrey Brereton, and I bring you a letter from the Lady Elizabeth, King Edward's daughter, and three mules that bear good gold in their saddle-flaps, and,' he felt in his doublet, and his fingers closed in farewell upon her token, 'this rich ring set with a precious stone.'

'I thank you, Master Brereton,' said Henry pleasantly, and Humphrey dared to look up.

The earl stood quite still with the ring in his hand, then lifted it three times to his lips. Then he read the letter, pondering, and Humphrey's opinion of him fell.

What manner of man was this that did not cry out with joy, and leap straightway upon his horse, shouting 'God for Elizabeth!' Why did he not pale or flush up or tremble? Were his knees shaking? No, steady as his countenance. The paltry fellow! Did he breathe fast? No, he breathed like the unfeeling bastard that he was. Bastard on both sides, let it be well remembered! And now he was folding it as though it were an ordinary letter.

Humphrey could bear no more, and the grass was wetting the knee of his best hose.

'My lord,' he cried, leaping up, 'why stand you so still and give me no answer? I am come from the Stanleys to make you king of England! To give you a fair princess, a king's daughter, such as there is none other in Christendom!'

Henry looked at him, startled, then repressed a smile.

'Her name is Elizabeth,' cried Humphrey, very red, and did not care if they brought him down with their damned arrows. 'A lovely lady to look upon – and well can she mark by prophecy.'

The comprehension in Henry's eyes nearly stopped him, but he floundered on manfully.

'I may be called a poor messenger if I get no answer of you, my lord. Must I sail from here with a heavy heart? What shall I say when I come home?'

'One moment, sir,' said Henry kindly. 'This matter needs some counsel.'

He drew aside with the Earl of Oxford, Lord Ferrers and Lord Lisle, and came back smiling.

'Master Brereton, I can give no answer for the space of three weeks. But when three weeks are come and gone I'll answer you right well. You shall be a welcome guest, sir. And now let us look at your mules.'

Humphrey could have run him through with his sword. Silent, he led the awkward beasts into the privacy of the stables, and cut open the saddle-bags. Gold ran into the straw. Gold from the Stanleys, from Savage, from Talbot, from the Lady Margaret, from a hundred sources small and great. The four lords smiled on one another.

'We can set out at daybreak, my lord,' said Oxford, 'and buy arms from Paris. But we shall need more than this.'

Brereton stood by the slashed saddle-flaps, his dreams tumbled into the straw with the money. The story he had composed in his head for the Lady Elizabeth would not now be told. Certainly, he had exaggerated a little here and there. A man rarely swooned with love, but one expected something more than a smile and a few thanks. Three weeks to wait! Good God, the fellow was hewn from stone!

So he sulked, and kicked his heels, oblivious of the details that must be settled before a date was given. Of ships to be fitted, of men collected and fed and armed, and paid to stand idle or fight. Of holds to be packed and clothes and horses purchased. And of ten thousand things attendant upon an invasion so momentous that failure meant death and success the throne of England.

The earl that returned was another man, open and smiling, sweet in his apologies.

'Master Brereton,' said Henry, walking with him in the garden, 'commend me most humbly to the Lady Elizabeth and speak to her loving-wise on my behalf. Tell her that I shall come, and that I trust in the might of God to make her my queen. And give her this letter, I pray you. Commend me also to my lady mother, and to my father Lord Stanley, and to these other gentlemen. Here are their letters also. I have conferred with my commanders, Master Brereton, and we shall land at Milford Haven in August, God willing. They may expect us then. We shall bring the Welsh to our standards along the coast, and meet our friends on the road from Shrewsbury.'

Humphrey bowed and took the letters, seeing them as so many hours' sleep lost and horses wearied; but proud, nevertheless, to be so trusted.

'And Master Brereton,' said Henry smiling, 'I fear I seemed too deep in thought to show the honour that I felt when I received the lady's letter – and that you judged me tardy in reply!'

'Nay, my lord,' said Humphrey, reddening. 'I know nothing of princes' hearts.'

'A prince is a man, Master Brereton, and has a heart like any other. Yet must a prince's affairs command him first. The Lady Elizabeth is the daughter of a king and knows this well. She will not blame me that I made sure of the means ere I sought the end. Yet tell her that of all the riches that she sent *these* are the richest.'

From the breast of his doublet he took the letter and the ring, and set them to his lips.

PART THREE

THE LONG YELLOW SUMMER
August, 1485

In what seas are thy anchors, and where art thou thyself?
When wilt thou, Black Bull, come to land;
how long shall we wait?
On the Feast of the Virgin, fair Gwynedd in her singing,
watched the seas.

Lewis Glyn Cothi,
fifteenth century

CHAPTER SEVENTEEN

*There will be fire in Manaw and a proud
progress through Anglesey . . . and Denbigh
awaits us, and flames in Rhuddlan and Rhos.*

Dafydd Llwyd, fifteenth century

1 August 1485

Six ships with fretted prows and nets of rigging rode at
anchor in the harbour of Harfleur. Pennants flew from their
masts. Shields, bearing the arms of the nobles who sailed in
them, ornamented their gunwales and fighting tops.

All morning they had been crammed with the accoutre-
ments of war and the sustenance of their passengers : salt-
fish, salt-meat, bread and beer, and wine and fruit for
prouder stomachs; bows and arrows, halberds, hand-guns,
knives, swords and battle-axes. Each squire saw his master's
armour stowed away : helmet, war-shield, jazerine and
placard, arm and leg and knee and elbow-pieces, and the
steel shoes with their long rowelled spurs. Chests of fine
raiment followed : shirts of lawn and holland; sumptuous
gowns embossed with gold and furred with vair or budge,
miniver or pampilion; satin and velvet doublets lined in
damask, with slashed and padded sleeves; caps bravely
jewelled and spangle-feathered; stout leather buskins; boots
soft as gloves; shoes covered with tissue cloth of gold; a
rainbow of hose. Then those personal possessions, without
which no gentleman – let alone one who might be king –
could travel : jewelled collars and daggers, rich chains and
rings, gold cups, illuminated prayer-books, embroidered
cushions, carved chairs, branched velvet hangings, ivory
chess-sets, fine wax candles and silver sconces, and a legion
of small rare treasures. Then the baggage animals, who must
bear all this, herded through side-doors into the hold; and
the broad-chested war-horses that could gallop with an
armoured knight upon their backs; and the lighter swifter
steeds for messengers and scouts; and the squires' sturdy
little cobs. And last of all the eighteen hundred mercenaries,
under their leader Philibert de Shaundé of Brittany.

'A motley! A rabble!' said the Earl of Oxford distastefully, watching them straggle aboard. 'The French king gives with a closed fist!'

'No matter!' Henry replied, smiling.

For they would fight for him, and he had sixty thousand francs beside. His face was radiant as he stood in the leading ship. He sniffed the salt air, watched the sails belly out, and felt the timbers stir and give as the vessel got underway. The blunt prow breasted a steel sea, on which small white waves scudded and peaked and fell, spraying a fine rain of drops on those in the bows. The helmsman stared ahead of him, hands on the wheel, legs braced well apart, and took the first roll and plunge of the ship as though he were a barnacle on her deck. One by one the other vessels raised anchor and cast off, sails filling, followed by a chorus of cheers from the harbour. A flock of sea-birds called and wheeled above their masts. Before them glittered the broad waters of the Channel. And they were out of Harfleur and running before a prosperous wind for England.

For six days, while horses and soldiers grew cramped and weary, while water staled and bread hardened and salt-meat and fish burdened queasy stomachs, they pursued their goal. Warily, they hugged the coasts of Normandy and Brittany, while the English fleet patrolled Hampshire, and Richard's squadrons waited in Dorset and Devon and Cornwall. Cunningly they skirted Land's End and slipped well outside the Bristol Channel, with the wind following all the way. And on the morning of the seventh day the ship's master sent word to the Earl of Richmond that land was sighted.

He left his bunk without reluctance, shivering in the early cold. And he saw the black mounds of the Prescelly Hills rising from the water, and stood smiling, until the sea took them over again.

'We shall see naught else for close on twelve hours, my lord,' said the master, 'for the coast here lies low. Then must we use our cunning, for we shall be upon the islands seaward of Milford Haven. Do you know the saying, my lord, *Dangers in Milford there is none, save the Crow, the Carre and the Cattlestone?*'

'I had not heard. These waters are strange to me.'

'The Crow is far seaward,' the master said, delighted to instruct a nobleman, 'in the common tideway, and one of the chiefest dangers. It lies south-east of the mouth near Linney Point. The Carre be a ridge of rocks on the Pembroke side against Paterchurch, overflowed at half-flood, so

that unwary mariners might think themselves well enough –
until their vessel is holed. And the Cattlestone be a great
rock in the harbour near Burton, that shall not trouble *us* so
far up in the haven.'

'I had thought it a calm and gentle harbour, sir.'

'Aye, calm and gentle and hospitable, sixteen fathoms or
more at the entrance, even at low ebb. And offering good
landing points in bays and creeks, like a great tree that
forks its branches, and it takes ships of two and three hundred tonnage. At Pembroke Ferry eight to ten fathoms, and
good riding up the channel.

'Sixteen miles long, or more, my lord,' the master continued, seeing that the earl showed no inclination to go
below, and had nothing to say for himself either. 'At full
sea the spring tide rises four fathoms high, and at neap tide
two fathoms. And yet the harbour has teeth, my lord, and
no man desires to find himself a morsel between them! The
Smale and the Skutwell be two such, four leagues west by
north of St Anne's Head: the one above the sea always, the
other covered at half-flood. The three Oyster Stones be
others, at the mouth of Nangle Bay. And no place in the
mouth may a ship ride easy or weigh anchor – for jagged
rock – until it comes to Ratte Island (a musket shot from the
mainland!) or Dale Rode or St Mary Well.'

'You are master of the seas as well as of your ship,' said
Henry courteously, 'And so twelve hours must pass? They
might be twelve days, for all the patience that I lack!'

'Nay, my lord, we shall not hold you so long in check! I'll
send you word when we sight the seaward islands, and
show how we cheat the rocks of their prey and fetch us safe
to port.'

The sturdy way he ruled the vessel, and watched the tricks
and turns of current, keeping the dangers ahead of him and
yet undeterred by their prospect, fascinated Henry.

'What land lies there?' he asked, pointing due west.

'Nay, my lord, I know not and care not. For I have heard
that if a man sail too far west he shall reach the end of the
earth and fall down, ship and company and all!'

'So no man ventures?'

'No, my lord, unless he has an addled pate!'

'And yet cargo ships sail from the east for many weeks,
and reach England and France, and do not fall down. And
at some time a mariner of stout heart, such as your own,
must have found his way uncharted in strange seas.'

'Aye, my lord, some hare-brained wild fellow! But my good wife has eight children, and I must find bread and meat for all.' He added in mild reproach, 'And you know well, good my lord, that the earth be flat. We must not try God's patience!'

He consulted his sea-chart, which was minutely drawn on vellum. Lines radiated from a centre to all parts of the compass, enabling him to lay his course from harbour to harbour. Here was the coast of France, and there the coast of England and Wales: neatly punched with bays and inlets. Dots and crosses indicated reefs and hazards, and the estuaries were marked with a double line. The name of each port, written very small and black, stood at right angles to the coast, so that he had to turn it this and that way to read it.

Henry thought of the tales he had heard from his tutor and at court, of travels and pilgrimages and crusades and expeditions, of trading routes opened and new markets discovered. Pepper from Malabar and ginger from Surat. Saffron from Balsara and Persia, cloves from Maluco and nutmegs from Banda. He was not a man to hazard good money on foolish schemes, and yet these voyagers had his admiration. And he knew that he was not made of the mettle that steered a little ship due west and sailed until it reached – what? Yet, if such a one should come to him when he was king he would give him gold, and watch for his return.

So he mused, his pleasant face intent upon the sea that washed and rolled without ceasing against the timbers of the ship. But the master kept his eyes upon his compass-box and quadrant. He must check the time of full tide at Milford Haven, to know when they best could enter, and this took all of a man's mind; being the age of the moon multiplied by forty-eight, and divided by the number of minutes in one hour, which add six and then deduct twelve.

They sighted the seaward islands late that afternoon, and changed course.

'Do you see, my lord, that finger of stone pointing to heaven? That be St Anne's Chapel, having a tower like a pigeon-house full twenty feet high. Without it we should not find the entrance to the harbour. Watch how the helmsman keeps it within his sight, and so comes to the headland.'

And now the ships were alive with men, swarming to the gunwales to cheer the rocky coast. Gravely the small vessels swung round St Anne's Head and into Milford Haven: blue

sails blown by a soft south wind, the *fleur-de-lis* shimmering
in the evening sun. A nook of ground stretched out into a
gentle bay, and they let down anchor at Dale Point, where
the intricate and lengthy process of getting everybody and
everything on to dry land would begin.

But Henry was first ashore, and drawing apart from the
rest, knelt for the first time in fourteen long years on Welsh
soil, and kissed it and crossed himself.

'*Judica me, Deus, et decerne causam meam,*' he began.

'Judge me, O Lord and plead my cause against an ungodly
nation . . . For thou art the God of my strength . . . O send
out thy thought and thy truth; let them lead me; let them
bring me unto thy holy hill . . . Hope thou in God, for I shall
yet praise Him, Who is the health of my countenance . . .'

For the adventure had been none of his seeking and he
did not know what would become of him.

Sir Rhys ap Thomas, Lord of West Wales, was he of whom
the people said *All the kingdom is the king's, save where
Rhys doth spread his wings*. Reared in the court of Burgundy, that jewel of renaissance France, he combined
elegance with military prowess and a passionate Welsh
nationalism. So that his fortress, Carew Castle, massive and
ponderous without, became a palace within. And here he
held jousts and tournaments, and hung his stone walls with
tapestries from Arras, and filled his cellars with the wines
of Gascony and Rochelle and Bordeaux, and set a princely
table, and kept a string of harpists, and a gaggle of tumblers
and fools. He also housed and fed the family prophet, Robert
of the Dale – a shrewd soothsayer with a weakness for strong
drink. After he had made all preparations for Henry's coming, and sent his scouts to the Dale to watch for ships, he
called for Robert and demanded what the future held.

'Ah, noble lord,' said Robert, who did not mind being a
Delphic oracle but declined to be a specific one, 'the ways of
princes are too perilous for prophecy!' Then correctly divin-
ing Sir Rhys' expression, he added, 'Yet shall I dream on
this matter for a day and a night, and speak with you again.'

The result was not as precise as his lord could have wished.

'Full well I wend, that in the end, Richmond sprung from
British race, from out this land the boar shall chase!'

Sir Rhys turned over the vagaries of this doggerel and
decided that it lacked detail.

'Will my lord permit me to return to my tankard of ale?'

Robert asked hopefully – for the malt liquor was freshly brewed, and did not keep well.

'Nay!' said his patron. 'I must know more than this, good Robert. *In the end*, you say? When shall that be? In twenty years, perchance, when I shall be too old and you too drink-sodden to care?'

Robert had been at the ale already, but he was not too fuddled to miss the reprimand.

Stretching one arm before him, and striking an heroic attitude, he cried, 'Hie thee to the Dale, my lord! And have a care of us all, I pray thee.'

It was fortunate that a messenger should have returned at that moment, to announce that six French ships had been sighted from St Anne's Head. In the noise and flurry of trumpets and drums and horses and men Robert slipped away unnoticed. He was the kind of prophet who discovers his best visions in the bottom of an empty cup.

So Henry saw them approaching by the light of ten score torches: a vast train of two thousand horsemen and retainers, with the great Rhys at their head on his courser, *Grey Fetterlocks*.

'Fetch that rabble from the fires!' Oxford ordered his captains, 'and see that they stand upright, and come not with gnawed bones in their hands! For Sir Rhys knows a soldier when he sees one – and these look like whores!'

'My dear cousin,' Henry cried, coming forward to greet his first supporter in Wales. 'I thank you for this goodly welcome.'

Then, with Rhys at his side, he mounted a hillock and looked round upon the host.

'Beloved countrymen!' he cried. 'Fellow-soldiers! It is upward of fourteen years since I was escaped out of these parts with my uncle, the Earl of Pembroke, and at length are we returned again.'

He paused, seeing that men craned and twisted to define him in the dusk.

'Fetch me a ring of torches,' he ordered, 'so they may know for whom they fight.'

'I fled for my life,' he shouted, radiant in the torchlight. 'I now return for my crown.'

A murmur ran through the ranks. They had heard him.

'My life and my crown are inseparable. I must either enjoy both or lose both. But I am come, fellow-soldiers and my countrymen, more in your right than in mine own.'

He hesitated; the gold collar of Lancaster glittered upon his breast.

'Here I stand before you,' he said more quietly, but every word carried in the stillness, and between his pauses he heard the night wind in the coarse grass. 'But what name to give myself I am altogether to seek. A private man I will not be called, since I am of the noblest in this kingdom. And yet a prince you cannot well call me while another professes my right. Yet let us show all men that the Lord of Hosts is with us. Let us by living procure this realm, or by dying conclude our miseries.'

There was a moment's hush as he finished speaking, and then such a beating of drums and a blaring of trumpets that he started. And above the clamour rang the name he would not give himself. 'King Henry! King Henry!'

It seemed that they would never stop, and Rhys waited a long time to speak in his turn. He spoke for them, to Henry, taking care that every word was loud and clear for the benefit of all.

'My lord and master, take us to your protection. Our hearts are as well-furnished as our bodies. God gives you command of both.' And on a great shout, 'God prosper our proceedings!'

'King Henry!' they roared, above the blare of trumpets, the thunder of drums. 'King Henry!'

Then the Bishop of St David's held out his hands, and they called for silence so that he could set the seal of the Church upon their venture. For each man knew what this would cost, and that the full price might be exacted from him and his. So they stood patiently while the bishop wished Henry the strength of Jacob and Israel. And they stiffened to attention as he called aloud upon the Lord of Hosts to show His vengeance upon the enemy and His blessing upon the deliverers. And again they cried 'King Henry! King Henry!' until their throats were hoarse.

'And now, your grace,' said Rhys privately, 'let us offer your French army ease and refreshment. We have provisions with us, and a voyage makes the hardiest weary.'

'He has noted them!' said Oxford to Jasper, in disgust. 'I commend his courtesy.'

Indeed, Rhys was as disappointed in Henry's mercenaries as Oxford himself. Smiling, he walked along their slovenly lines; speaking to one or two in their own tongue and finding them ignorant; inspecting their arms and finding them inadequate; allowing no criticism to escape him and wishing them back at home.

'I think, my lord,' said Oxford drily, as he walked with him, 'that King Charles emptied his prisons to furnish us with this motley!'

'My lord,' Rhys replied urbanely, 'I have found that the sorriest rascal will fight fiercely for his own skin. Give them food and arms and they will serve us well enough!'

Both armies, the French under Henry's command, the Welsh with Rhys, were up by daybreak; breakfasting on bread and ale, stamping out the fires, forming into columns. They were to travel by different routes to Shrewsbury. Scouts and messengers rode out first : the ones to spy out the land, the others carrying letters to Lady Margaret, the Stanleys and English supporters, and to the chieftains along the Welsh coast.

To these trusty and well-beloved high men of the tribes Henry sent a command in the name of the king. He desired and prayed them that in all haste they should array themselves for war against that odious tyrant Richard. He abjured them to fail not as they should answer to their peril. And beneath the signet he wrote *Henricus Rex*.

His tone was royal, but the campaign was in the balance and he dared not fail for lack of them. Rumour had already hinted that Sir Walter Herbert, that pillar of Yorkist loyalty, would declare for Richard; even that Rhys himself planned treachery. But as they reached Haverford West the first news came in. Pembroke town was prepared to support Jasper as its rightful earl, and Henry as its natural and immediate lord. And Herbert would join Rhys to march through Carmarthenshire. The people ran from their doors and lined the streets to cheer the soldiers as they tramped in.

'Now must this be our slowest journey!' Jasper warned Henry that evening. 'Ten miles in one day is no distance, my lord nephew.'

'It is those scurvy Frenchmen,' said Oxford predictably. 'They fear blisters on their sorry feet.'

'Their feet will blister fast enough tomorrow,' said Jasper, tracing their route through the Prescelly Hills. 'Thirty hard miles on mountain tracks lie between us and Nefern before nightfall.'

'The greater an army the slower it moves,' said Rhys, and Oxford nodded. 'So, sire, if you reckon twenty miles a day it shall be near enough. And we should all meet at Cefn Digoll by the thirteenth day of August, which is the eve of Saturday.'

'We should have fetched slave-drivers with us,' said Oxford, half-serious. 'A whip cracked about those French heels would send them forth speedily!'

'We shall have Welsh heels with us, too, my lord,' said Henry lightly. 'We would not have *them* whipped! Every man must fare the same, else shall we war among ourselves. My lords,' he said firmly, as they seemed prepared to dispute his authority, 'we slept not at all last night, and tomorrow shall be a long day.'

They knelt and kissed the formal hand, and bade him sleep well and soundly.

Oxford was up before any of them cuffing his squire awake, roaring among the French tents and shouting for ale.

'Wales lies before you, now, sire,' said Rhys, as they prepared to go their separate ways. 'Unfurl your banners that all men know who comes. I wish you God speed and a safe keeping.'

Then he mounted Grey Fetterlocks and ordered his captains to see that every man was ready. Oxford raised one rueful arm in salute, and glared down the lines of subdued French faces. The trumpeters stood forth, and the drummers flexed their wrists, preparatory to the long march.

'Now Christ Jesu keep them!' said Rhys to himself, and gave the order to advance on Carmarthenshire.

As the day grew older the sun climbed higher, and the tracks became rougher and steeper. Their steady tramp now ragged, they pressed and sweated on; scrambling over rocks, stumbling on heather and hussocks, treading down forests of bracken, dragging the leaden cannons and clumsy signals after them, hauling the awkward carts full of arms and provisions – whose wheels threatened to break and cascade their loads down every slope they negotiated. Philibert de Shaundé had long since given up his little leadership, and lapsed into cold courtesy while Oxford urged them mercilessly on. After fifteen cruel miles they halted.

'Fall out!' Oxford commanded his captains, and could not resist adding of the Frenchmen, 'and fall out they will. Look how that carrion rolls upon the grass. No ale, or they will sleep like swine. God's water is good enough for men upon a march.'

Baskets of bread were carried round. The soldiers seized their chunks and tore them with their teeth; lay on their bellies over the dripping bunches of grass and drank the mountain water; wet their heads and faces against the heat of the day; soaked strips of cloth and bound their swollen feet. Squires grazed and watered the horses and looked to their master's needs.

All about them lay hills and sun and silence. Sheep cropped, and stared incuriously at the invaders. Birds swooped and called. From a crag an eagle dropped, talons outstretched, taking a prey too small and far away for them to see or hear.

Then on again with the vast equipage jolting behind them. And at last downhill, in the cool of the evening, to Nefern, where they camped at Ragwr-llwyd and soothed their burns and blisters.

'Now are they broken in,' said Oxford, enjoying his wine, 'and may know what to look for. Thirty miles is no mean feat, your grace.'

'My lord, we think you covered *sixty* miles,' said Henry, amused. 'For we saw you riding here and there among the troops.'

'Aye, sire, they know my face,' said Oxford grimly. 'And shall know it better ere we join battle.'

The beacons on the hills had hailed their coming, and the gates of Cardigan were open when they approached it at noon of the following day, to be given a rapturous reception. At the tavern of *The Three Mariners* the landlord brought out every cask of ale and would take no payment for any. And here they were joined by Richard Griffith and John Morgan with their men. Greetings and ale-drinking had taken up the time. It was Oxford's pleasure to inform everyone that they must cover the next fourteen miles before dark – and he personally kicked three Frenchmen sober. But the winds along the coast were fresh, after the cauldron of the hills. The fumes in their heads vanished as they tramped or rode on. And in the rough carts lay new provisions of oats and hay and salt-fish, jolting from side to side and sometimes mingling their contents.

At Llwyn Dafydd, on their fourth night in Wales, the army camped in their usual fashion. But Henry and his noblemen were entertained by Dafydd ab Ifan in his house, and ate hens boiled with bacon, yellow as cowslips, from a tablecloth, and slept between good linen sheets.

On the Thursday they marched twenty-six sweating miles to Machynlleth, and again the commanders enjoyed civil hospitality at Mathafarn, while their soldiers compared the state of their feet. They were in milder country now : a place of woods and waterfalls, of flowering valleys and rush-clad streams and green hills. And it was pleasant to sit by the camp-fires and sing nostalgic songs, and roast a newly-captured rabbit or a poached fish. Oxford still haunted the French, but his curses were becoming fewer as they strove not to displease him. His crest of the Blue Boar had caught their ribald fancy, and they coined a coarser nickname. By their own fires, the little Welsh contingent produced harpists, and prepared to celebrate in a more poetic fashion. The Bretons, comprehending and translating to their fellow mercenaries, were tickled by portentous references to wizards and prophecies.

'For,' as one of them said, 'what is life, my friends, but food and wine and women and war?'

Practical to the core of their Gallic hearts, they agreed with him. But the sounds swelled into the summer evening with a peculiar ecstasy.

'A highway was made to the northy in dignity – Earl with the golden cuirass, of handsome bearing ... A conqueror like Dyfn thou shalt win. Bendigedfran, the warrior, was less than thou ... Great ruler of land and sea.'

Silent, the French listened, captured in spite of themselves.

'Iorweth is in thy goodly arms – offspring of Princes, thou of the many feasts. Thy wine to the minstrels, and the green gowns, and bread in stacks before the brave ... Peacock of Tudor ... Bull of Anglesey ...'

The rapt dark faces brooded over the flames, pondering the legend, finding in the heart of the fire an answer to a savage past.

On Friday they followed the River Dovey as far as Mallwyd, and struck across Montgomeryshire by Pen-y-bont and Neuadd to Dolardoun in the parish of Castle Caerinion.

The march had taken its toll, and Henry borrowed a fresh horse and gave a receipt for payment.

The beacons fired in Pembroke spread their message like fire itself. To the north and east and west of Wales the hills flared news of the coming. And from the chieftain in his stronghold to the shepherd on the mountains, Wales rose to his standard. Men who had been taught to wield no other weapon could carry a pitchfork, or take an axe from the wall or a scythe from the shed, or pick up a bill-hook. They came from the valleys, the fields, the mines : with a little money in their belts if they had some, and a little food if they had not. Old men who would be left behind in the long march, young men following a dream, boys with their fathers, middle-aged farmers seeking a last adventure. He who had been promised would lead them.

As far as Henry could see on the Long Mountain stood rank upon rank of Welshmen, with the *uchelwyr*, their chieftains, at their head. Richard ap Howell of Mostyn with sixteen hundred Flintshire colliers. The men of Arfon under their High Sheriff. William ap Gruffydd of Penrhyn. Rhys of Bodychan. Ap Meredith of Yspytty. They had driven cattle enough to feed the entire army, and the beasts grazed quietly after their trek, watched by lads of eleven and twelve who would taste war for the first time. Here was Sir Walter Herbert, striding forward to bend the knee and renew an old acquaintance. There were the Vaughans and the Gams, and Arnold Butler and Sir Thomas Perrot of Haroldson and Sir John Wogan of Wistern Castle. And, nobler than any present, Rhys ap Thomas leading his two thousand : as fresh and disciplined now as they had been at the Dale.

And something which had been growing in him since he kissed the Welsh soil, casting out calculation and suspicion and that darkness which was his shadow, came to flower. The legend wrapped him, raised him, bore him far out and beyond himself. In its sun he rode before them, catching their throats into a shout of joy and homage. He did not care that the tears stood in his eyes, seeing that they, too, wept for exaltation.

But Oxford, cast in a sterner mould, looked somewhat askance upon the scythes and pitchforks, though there were bows too, and spears enough to comfort any warrior with their bronze and burnished heads.

'Well, Pembroke !' he said drily. 'If they cannot fight I dare swear they may kick and strangle !'

'I had sooner face an armoured knight in his pride than a bill-hook in the hands of an ardent Welshman!' said Jasper soberly. 'You misjudge us sorely, my lord. These are here to give their lives if need be. No man may offer more.'

Not a quarter of those present either saw or heard their king address them, but the myth had run ahead of him. They did not need the man when his praises could be sung over the camp-fires. He was among them, and that was enough. Whole oxen were roasted that night on Cefn Digoll, and the glow was seen for miles about as though night were broad day.

CHAPTER EIGHTEEN

A worthy sight it was to see,
How the Welshmen rose wholly with him
And shogged him to Shrewsbury.

The Rose of England
Bishop Percy's Folio MS.

Fair Shrewsbury, like all other towns, had enough to do to take care of itself without being troubled by the quarrels of princes. Or so it thought, on a hot August Monday of 1485, when the morning sun promised to become an afternoon's torment, and its bridge was down, its gates open like a mouth taking a breath of air. The watchman on the stout tower looking towards the blue mountains of Wales must have been asleep already. The people jostled and chattered and bought and sold within, and the labourers toiled without. And all were going about their rightful business, asking no more than that they might be left in peace.

Only those near the Welsh gate noted the herald in white and green, who rode into their midst and demanded to speak to Master Mitton the bailiff. And fewer still saw the bailiff read the letter and lose some of his colour as he pondered its contents.

'Where is this – noble gentleman – sir?' he said at last, as the messenger accepted a draught of ale with thanks.

'King Henry has camped with his forces on Bicton Heath, sir, where he awaits your answer.'

Master Mitton thought of all that might happen to Shrewsbury if he let the invader in, and all that might happen if he did not. He decided on the latter.

'Sir, inform your lord that I know no king but him that sits upon the throne. And by *his* command do I guard this town.'

The messenger finished his ale, made his bow, leaped upon his horse and spurred across the bridge : as cheerful in his departure as at his arrival. Master Mitton turned from white to red as the need for haste possessed him. An army, by Our Lady, and camped but three miles off !

In minutes the bells were ringing all over Shrewsbury,

followed by the watchman on the tower winding his horn for dear life. The hustle of a Monday morning became bedlam. Burghers drew wadded coats of mail from the chests where they lay in safe-keeping; reached for their bows and swords and knives. A dozen temporary watchmen ran for the walls, furnished with more brass horns on leather baldrics, which they wound as they sprinted. People hurried for safety; women and children seeking the sanctity of the church. The town cannons were drawn into position and enthusiastic but amateur gunners appointed to supervise their firing. Meat and drink and chattels and armour were crammed into the town hall. A hubbub of peasants and cattle from the suburbs poured, panic-stricken, into the market square. Two felons were released from the stocks. And even as they were about to draw up the bridge a little fellow, who had been letting the sheep look after themselves, scuttled across driving his woolly charges before him, the collie barking at his heels.

'Sir!' he shouted to Master Mitton, breathless with excitement and terror, 'Sir, there is a great host marching from Bicton Heath!'

'Then why did no man see them sooner?' the bailiff demanded of heaven.

'Sir, sir, I thought it was the sun shining on the heath,' said the boy, 'and then I saw it was the light of their spears!'

'How many, boy? How many?'

'Sir,' said the child, making the most of a glorious moment in a dull life, attempting a good round sum to impress everybody, 'close on twenty thousand!'

The bailiff was in no mood to haggle over numbers. He fetched the lad a cuff that sent him into the sheep, who received him with perplexity.

'And sir,' said the boy, heaving two fat wethers away from him, 'knights in armour, sir! And tents like daisies in a field! And marching for Shrewsbury, sir!' he shouted, and ran for safety.

'Now must this have been the light we saw on Saturday!' groaned Master Mitton. 'And the priest telling us it was the Angels of God watching over Shrewsbury since we had mended the church roof! Christ have mercy upon us all!' He saw that his citizens lacked his leadership, and caught at one or two of them as they ran past, crying, 'Have no fear good people! We shall withstand the tyrant. Pull up that drawbridge in heaven's name!' he roared, as they strained at the iron wheel. 'Let down the portcullis! Make fast the gates!'

Since none but himself knew the identity of the army, which might well have been that of some Welsh chieftain making a swift bid for market-day, they continued to screech and shout and arm and provision themselves in ignorance. But Master Mitton remembered that this was the usurper whom King Richard had denounced but two months since. Comforted to think that he had made the right answer, he called a general meeting in the market-place and stood on the top step of the market-cross.

'Good people of Shrewsbury!' he cried, 'In zeal and hearty favour of King Richard we are called upon to resist a heinous traitor! An unknown Welshman of bastard stock, with his band of cut-throats and outrageous damnable villains. One that purposes to overthrow our lawful sovereign, and bring the realm to bloody strife!'

They understood this and shouted, throwing up their caps.

'This captain, Henry Tudor, with a mighty army, is camped on Bicton Heath. Good folk, stand firm. We are provisioned and well-armed. King Richard will deliver us! God will watch over us – did we not mend the church roof? And Shrewsbury yields to none!'

The host was moving purposefully forward: soldiers, supporters and boys now numbered some six thousand. And the lads of the town pointed out different pennants and standards, the archers with bows the height of themselves, the shimmering armour from which the sun struck lightning.

'And cannons, Dick,' whispered one boy, nudging his younger brother. 'They have *cannons*!' Trundling on sleds, black mouths gaping.

'And *hand-guns*!' Sophisticated weapons, with a hole in one end of the iron tube through which the powder was fired, a touch-hole at one side with a small pan beneath to hold the powder, and a cover for the pan to turn it off and on by means of a pivot.

They marvelled at the spangled feathers on the helmets, at the knee and elbow pieces intricately wrought into fan-shapes, at the elaborate war-shields.

Master Mitton had recovered his dignity, and now waited until the intruders should be within hailing distance. Cowering below him, the people heard the tread of many feet, the steady trot and plod of hooves, the jingle of harnesses, the rumble of carts. Then all sounds ceased, and Shrewsbury was bathed in sunlight and silence.

The bailiff stood up where all could see him : a stout and rosy man of simple heart. He did not like his duty at the moment, but knew it must be done.

The same herald rode forward, enjoying his task.

'Sir, King Henry bids you unbar the gates !'

'I know no king but Richard, the third of that name !' called Mitton sturdily, looking round for the pretender. 'And at these gates shall no man enter !'

A little flurry in the vanguard caught his attention. The herald bowed and backed his horse unobtrusively away, where it cropped the grass peaceably. And a slim knight in silver-blue armour, with a gold cuirass, cantered forward, visor lifted so that the bailiff glimpsed a pair of grey eyes and a strong nose and mouth.

'Sir !' Henry cried across the water, 'we bid the good folk of Shrewsbury to have no fear of us ! We mean them no hurt. We march to meet the Duke of Gloucester, whose hand has spilled the blood of his dear nephews.'

His faith in himself and his self-appointed title was absolute. The royal 'we' came naturally from his lips.

'Wherefore we pray you, sir bailiff, to let us in, to provision our army, and to give us troops in token of your good faith. Which service shall be remembered in King Henry's name !'

'My lord,' said Master Mitton, impressed, but following his line of duty, 'King Richard has our allegiance, and though you blast our walls you shall not enter !'

A tall, dark-visaged nobleman bearing the crest of the Blue Boar rode forward, and from his gestures the bailiff guessed that he commended violence. But the young knight shook his head until the plumes swayed, and then spoke again, holding his restless horse in check.

'Sir, the town of Shrewsbury is under our protection. We shall not harm her nor her people. And, since you do not take our word, Sir William Stanley, Chamberlain of North Wales, shall persuade you otherwise. Await his messenger, therefore, while we return to camp.'

He signalled the host to withdraw, and the unwieldy mass re-formed and marched away in good order. A sense of anti-climax settled on the town as they watched the cannons trundle off. They had been ready and valiant, and must remain so for a day and a night. At the moment nothing else could be done. So Master Mitton ordered the offenders to be put back in the stocks; the stall-holders began to assemble their wares and heave the wooden booths upright; and the boys – bitterly disappointed – scrambled down from the walls to have their heads smacked.

In his tent Henry conferred with his commanders. They had doffed their little ovens of armour and sat, by his express courtesy, in the coolness of their shirts. So far they had advanced unchecked, but this would not continue for much longer, and Richard's movements could only be calculated roughly by means of supposition and the scraps of news brought by their scouts. Oxford's long forefinger rested on the city of Nottingham.

'The Duke of Gloucester lies here, sire – or did when we landed seven days since. Yet has he eyes and ears in every place, and must know of our landing even now.'

'Not from any in my territory, my lord,' said Rhys ap Thomas proudly.

'Sir Rhys,' said Henry politely, 'we know you to be the Lord of West Wales. Yet let us suppose that even one pair of eyes saw our meeting in the Dale, or one pair of ears heard on it. How long would it take a man, riding hard in fine weather, and having his way to make through your territory, to reach Nottingham?'

'Four days.'

'Then does the Duke of Gloucester know of our coming.'

'Norfolk holds the south coast,' said Oxford, 'and must be summoned from there before the duke can move to meet us. And he has London to raise. Take it that, even now, they march to Nottingham, they cannot intercept us ere – Friday.'

'How long before a pair of Shrewsbury legs mounts a horse and clacks news of our presence here?' Henry enquired.

'No time at all, sire, for we have soldiers posted at all points about the town. And our coming surprised them or they had been more ready!'

'With letters from Sir William Stanley,' said Jasper, 'Shrewsbury should be ours, and then no tongues will tell tales!'

Henry sat back in the carved chair, which travelled on a cart until he needed it.

'If I were Richard of Gloucester,' he said slowly, taking on that role, 'what should I do?'

They waited respectfully.

'I should judge,' said Henry, thinking matters out, 'that the force that landed, being but a small one, was not of great account in its present state. Therefore it must needs collect more troops, which would slow its progress. Then should I discount the Welsh support. No, good Sir Rhys, I speak not of yourself but of Wales as Richard sees it : a barren country peopled by poor barbarians. As Richard of Gloucester, I look upon the Welsh as hinds to be herded at will. As Richard I know nothing of their hearts, and have long forgotten that their cries for freedom rise not from petty ills but from their roots. So would I reckon that this little force of Henry Tudor's, this motley troop of French and exiled English, might pluck a few wild natives here, a sack of oats there, and slowly cover little distances.

'As Richard, I should summon all my forces, select the flower of my army, send messages to all my followers – with bribes and threats and sweet words – and sit at Nottingham until the axe was great enough to crush the nutshell. Perhaps I would hunt a little, so that my people see I think but poorly of this intruder. My lords, we have marched more than a hundred miles and thirty, and marched hard with good guides to lead us. For all that Richard knows we are even yet wandering in the wilds of Wales.'

'Sire,' said Jasper, and the title sounded oddly on his tongue, for he had called Henry 'lad' and 'Harry' as long as both could remember, 'the Duke of Gloucester is valiant and cunning in war. The troops he marshals are mighty in number and great in prowess. Well-armed, well-fed, and fighting on their native soil. Do not discount him easily.'

'I do not discount his cunning nor his might, good uncle,' said Henry quietly, 'but I say that some of his men have divided hearts and may hang back, or may join us. The heart is much, my lord. Take away the hot hearts of my Welshmen and what have you? The sawdust figures that swing at quintain !'

Rhys and Jasper and the Welsh chieftains were with him, but Oxford never dabbled in mysteries and saw the campaign with a soldier's eye.

'By your leave I shall speak out, sire,' he said firmly. Henry inclined his head. 'The Duke of Gloucester has ten thousand men at least. The Yorkshire men are with him to the end. There is Norfolk, the White Lion both in badge and spirit, and his son Surrey, with their East Anglian contingents. Then Northumberland will bring his borderers – wild men and hardy. There will be others, too, but on these he can count. Now we have but four thousand seasoned troops – I say nothing of the peasants with their pitchforks, they will fight as best they may, but that best is no match for Richard's soldiers. Sir Walter Hungerford and Sir Thomas Bourchier should join us – captains of consequence. But they bring only hundreds, your grace. Richard commands thousands.'

He hesitated, and Henry flushed.

'You reckon poorly, my lord,' he said stiffly. 'What of Lord Stanley, my mother's husband, and his brother, Sir William?'

'The Cheshire bowmen are renowned, sire, and their skill and numbers would turn the scale. I do not say they will not, but the Lord Stanley was ever a cautious man and will wait to see how we fare. We must look for signs of favour from them. The first will be the letters to Shrewsbury. If they should not come then we may sit like fowls in the pot, to be taken.'

'Sir William has not hindered our advance, my lord.'

'He has not helped it neither,' said Oxford frankly. Continuing, 'The second sign, your grace, will be your meeting with both Stanleys at Stafford or Lichfield. The third and last, and one of greatest import – upon the field, wherever that may be. Until then all is mere sawing of the air!'

They pondered in silence on the Stanleys. But Henry, though his anxiety was as sharp as theirs, was the first to smile.

'Then, my lords,' he said, 'we may be certain of London, in any event. For if we win we march to it in triumph, and if we do not our heads shall decorate its Tower!'

'Some hundreds will lie upon the field first, your grace,' said Rhys, smiling in his turn.

Their thoughts had taken another and a happier direction.

'We have all England to gain,' said Oxford, 'and I shall see that not a single Frenchman lays his bones upon the field without he takes two Yorkists with him.'

There was a chorus then. 'And my men, sire!' 'And mine, sir!' 'And mine!'

'And mine, my liege lord,' cried a voice from the tent flap.

'Good Shropshire men and true, to the number of eight hundred!'

Sir Richard Corbet knelt before him, his helm beneath his arm, his face streaked with sweat and dust from the march.

'Welcome, good Sir Richard,' cried Henry, holding out both hands. 'We have not seen you in some sixteen years, and we swear you have not altered by so much as a hair!'

'There are grey ones , here and there, sire,' said Sir Richard, 'but I pray that both grey and brown may grow white in your service.'

'Wine for Sir Richard! Come, sit by us, sire. You shall see a change in *us*. For we were not thirteen, and a frightened boy, when you swung us upon your horse and rode from Banbury Field.'

'I should have known you anywhere, your grace. True, you were shorter by a foot, but resolute and hardy withal – and with a smile, even as now, that would win a friend or shame an enemy. I rejoice to see you, sire. And now,' returning to his business, 'how stand we, my liege lord? Shrewsbury town is locked and barred like a box of frightened geese. They wound their horns as we passed, and fired a cannon. Though I fear they harmed themselves more than us, for the shot flew wide and the gun seemed to smoke on their side of the wall more than ours. They had best stick to marketing.'

'Nay, my lord, we would not have them hurt,' said Henry kindly. 'We await letters from Sir William. Until then, sir, we may rest ourselves. Your supper will be a splendid one. Are we to have shields of brawn in armour, uncle?' he asked Jasper seriously.

'I fear not, sire, like the pike in Latimer sauce they have all been eaten!'

'And the mutton royal, richly garnished? And the perch in jelly dipped? And the tart poleyn?'

Oxford looked bewildered from uncle to nephew, but though their faces were as solemn as priests their eyes twinkled.

'Likewise, your grace. Also the roast peacock, and the castles of jelly in temple-wise made, and the baked quinces, and the sturgeon with fresh fennel.'

'Not even a single subtlety, with writing of ballads?' Henry asked with a frown.

'I regret, sire, not even one miserable subtlety. The butler is fled, and the panterers have lost their knives and spoons!'

Sir Richard Corbet roared with laughter and slapped his thigh, and Oxford's face relaxed.

'The only dancing girls may be found in the French tents, your grace!' he growled, and was rewarded by a shout of merriment from them all.

'Then, Sir Richard, we must partake of a fowl roast over an open fire,' cried Henry, smiling, 'and old bread and a hard piece of cheese! But we have noble wine enough to drown it.'

'And friends and loyal subjects to share it, sire. And your realm beneath your feet.'

'Aye, and that is best of all. Now would I speak with your men, so that they may know whom they serve.'

He made his rounds conscientiously in different parts of the camp, each evening, and a cheer rose from every company as he walked among them. His smile and words brought warmth to each group over the fires, and left warmth behind it. His assumption of kingship made them the surer of his cause. His ease made him one of them. His dignity set him apart. And greater than he, his legend passed ahead of him. He heard it in the songs that were sung like litanies. Star of Owen. Peacock of Tudor. Bull of Anglesey.

With the close of evening came the letters from Sir William Stanley, bidding Shrewsbury open its gates, and their relief was further lightened by the messenger's tale of their delivery.

'An' we live all, sire!' said Rowland Warburton, grinning. 'They *would* not let me in – though I cried out from whom I came, and pointed to my livery. And there would I be yet, but that I was fain to thrust the papers on an arrow head and fire it over the wall. Where it was greeted first by cries of treason, and then in silence, and at last with hearty good will. And Shrewsbury awaits your grace.'

At dawn they dressed themselves in full array, struck camp, and marched again to the town – where Master Mitton met them, surrounded by his municipal officers and important burghers. One small point troubled the bailiff, even as he made his deepest obeisance, and Rhys ap Thomas smiled grimly as he heard it. For Master Mitton, like Sir Rhys, had given King Richard his solemn oath that only over his body would any usurper pass.

'Then must the bailiff stretch himself upon the ground, or stand beneath a bridge as I did at the Dale,' said Rhys, 'and let your horse ride over him, sire. When he is fully and most honourably absolved from his oath.'

Somewhat gingerly the stout man lay in the dust, regretting his best clothes.

'Fear not, Master Mitton, 'said Henry kindly. 'She will never so much as graze you with an hoof!'

Nor did the mare touch him: ears pricked, eyes starting, as she stepped delicately over the mound of the bailiff's belly.

'Now, Master Mitton,' said Henry amiably, as the man dusted himself down, 'what offence have we made you that you kept us out of our town?'

'My lord, I knew no king but Richard that was crowned in London.'

'And what will you say when we have put King Richard down?'

'Why then, I'll be as true to you, my lord, after I am sworn. I am not a man to take an oath lightly, as you have seen. I'll hold Shrewsbury in safe keeping for you thereafter.'

'Were it not a great pity that such a man as this should die, my lord?' Henry asked, turning to Oxford whose hand was on his sword. 'He shall not be harmed in any case. We freely pardon you, Master Mitton. And now let us see how Shrewsbury receives us!'

It received them with homely pageantry: decorating its doors with green boughs, strewing flowers and sweet herbs beneath their feet. Many of the sheep that had been driven into the town for safety now rotated slowly on spits for the feast. And Henry worshipped at mass, giving thanks to God for his present triumph, before he marched to England.

CHAPTER NINETEEN

When Yorke and Lancaster made warre
within this ffamous land,
the liues of all our Noble men
did in great danger stand.

White Rose & Red
Bishop Percy's Folio MS.

Freshly provisioned, their horses fed and rested, and a contingent of Shrewsbury men swelling their ranks, they set off for Newport on the Wednesday morning. They made the twenty-mile march at a swinging pace, seasoned by the Welsh trek, rested by their recent delay, and camped on Forton Heath. The tide was beginning to rise higher, come in faster, now, and their spirits rose with it. Moreover they stood on English soil, and the Welsh in particular took heart from this.

'*You* are fighting Richard of Gloucester, sire,' said Oxford, grinning, 'but these wild chieftains of yours have come to fight the *Saxons*!'

'Aye, my lord, but if we fight beneath one standard what matter?'

'I shall feel easier, nonetheless, for a few hundred English soldiers.'

'We shall have them shortly, by God's good grace. And tonight we sleep at Fortune House, by the express desire of Hugh Forton — now does this seem a splendid omen!'

That same day Humphrey Cotes swore allegiance to King Henry; and here, too, they were joined by Sir Gilbert Talbot and five hundred tall men, dependants of the Earl of Shrewsbury — which delighted Oxford. On the Thursday they marched for Stafford, where Sir William Stanley waited with a small retinue, having left his soldiers a little way behind. Henry greeted him graciously, showing none of the anxiety he felt, though Oxford listened to every word distrustfully. Sir William, new to the myth and the man, addressed Henry courteously, but as the Earl of Richmond.

'King Richard had news of your landing some days since, my lord,' he said gravely, 'and his messengers live in their saddles. He has them posted at intervals of twenty miles along the roads, so that they may travel fresh and speedily. And he made much ado that your progress, even upon these borders I guard for him, was so swift. He fears treachery, and has feared it for some time past. And shortly before you landed, my lord, he ordered my brother the Lord Stanley to return to court or send his son Lord Strange. Since my brother judged it meet to stay he sent his son in his stead. And now King Richard demands that my brother attend him, on the instant.'

'What answer did my father Lord Stanley make, sir?' Henry asked, disturbed.

'He replied that he was sick, my lord. But he fears for the life of the Lord Strange.'

'And so might I, even now, fear for the life of *my* son!' said Rhys ap Thomas contemptuously. 'Had I sent him as the Duke of Gloucester bade me. But I made him answer "No!" and so it rested.'

Sir William Stanley turned a distressed, irresolute face upon the Welshman.

'In the fastness of your strongholds, Sir Rhys, you might play fox as long as it please you. Those close to the king's person and high in the realm of England have little choice!'

'*Fox*, say you?' cried Rhys ap Thomas in deeper contempt. 'I have declared myself even at the Dale for King Henry! I wait not, sirrah, until the game is *won* ere I swivel forth my allegiance. Nor do I call a bloody tyrant "king" and name the rightful monarch "my lord", Sir William!'

'I crave your grace's pardon, I had forgot myself,' said Sir William hurriedly, turning an angry face on Rhys as he spoke. 'Welcome, my sovereign King Henry!' the formula came readily from his tongue, though its grace could not surmount his evident uneasiness. 'Challenge your heritage and the land that is your own, and shall be yours. And remember, when you are king, those that are for you now. Our swords are yours, sire.'

'We are full glad of you,' said Henry simply. 'Through the help of my father Lord Stanley, and you, we trust in England to continue king.' Then seeing his commanders' stormy expressions he added lightly, 'Peace, my lords, we know that all your hearts are brave and your swords loyal to us. Pray put a rein upon your tongues also. The house divided against itself shall never stand – and that England has learned most cruelly, with bloody civil strife. All shall be well.'

But the news gnawed him. He was uncertain of the Stanleys, whose support had been of the passive variety, with much spoken and little done. Nevertheless they conferred together, using all the knowledge Sir William could give them.

'The Lord Stanley will meet you at Lichfield, sire,' said Sir William, finding it on the map. 'Some sixteen miles hence. He has prepared the town for your coming and waits there with his men. The king – the Duke of Gloucester – lies at Nottingham, drawing his forces into one great army. There he will stay until those from London join him, and he judges the time ripe for assault.'

'Have I your grace's leave to speak?' Oxford asked. 'Sir William, think you that the Duke of Gloucester, so wise in war, may let us march well into the Midlands down Watling Street – and catch us between London and himself?'

'Nay, that I know not. Had you come as you were, with little forces, he could have snapped you up, even as you say. But with such as Sir Gilbert Talbot joining you, and other good gentlemen, and rumours of yet more, I think he dare not. For if you gather on the way to London as you have gathered thus far, he risks those coming to your standards that might have come to his.'

'It will take him but a day to march from Nottingham to Leicester,' said Oxford judiciously. 'The Lord Stanley lies at Lichfield, which we shall reach tomorrow. Now if the Duke of Gloucester marches at the same time he may strike down through Leicester and intercept us – here!'

He drew a wide circle round Atherstone with his finger.

'The Lord Stanley and your good self, Sir William,' Oxford continued, feeling his way, 'with three thousand archers and three thousand cavalry, and our good soldiers and our good rabble, shall be there in force to meet him.'

'My brother and I must stay our hands a while,' said Sir William, embarrassed. 'I do not think that we should march together – before the day of battle.' He hurried to explain to their sudden silence. 'The Duke of Gloucester knows not whether we be for him or against him. We think it best that he should be surprised, and for the sake of the Lord Strange – who is his hostage – we must bide our time. I swear, your grace, we shall not disappoint you. No treachery, sire, but cautious counsel.'

Henry frowned down the words on Oxford's lips, the disgust on Rhys's face.

'We know we have your allegiance, sir,' he said. 'You also have our trust.'

'As Chamberlain of North Wales,' Sir William replied, bowing, 'I turned a blind eye on your grace's progress there. Did I not serve your grace right well?'

'You have our trust,' Henry repeated, while his commanders exchanged glances, 'and we are kinsmen by my mother's marriage. Wine for these nobles!' he ordered, and was gracious with each of them.

'This gnaws my bowels!' said Oxford, when they were alone again. '*The Duke of Gloucester knows not whether we be for him or against him,*' he mimicked bitterly. Aye, and no more do we! *For the sake of the Lord Strange we must abide our time!* Why, sire, when has the life of one gentleman counted for so much? Had I seven sons, and every one of them in Richard's hands, I should not stay my course.'

'Know this of me also, sire,' said Jasper slowly. 'I would condemn no man wholly that perjured himself for wife or child, though I should judge him the less for it. But it is not the life of Stanley's son that frets him and his brother, it is their own skins. And the man that will not declare himself – him I condemn.'

Henry sighed and shifted.

'We can do naught but wait, uncle. We cannot force them.'

'Aye, sire, and make a showing on the field good enough to persuade the Stanleys that – for the sake of their skins – it were best to choose our side,' said Oxford grimly.

'Both heart and right are with us,' Jasper added. 'We but need the Lord of Hosts, and the Stanleys may sink in their own muck.'

'You speak too hardly of them,' said Henry. 'We have no cause to fear them – and must take their word.'

'But a fox is a fox,' said Rhys ap Thomas, 'and if he cannot discover one safe hole will find another. I fear that if we die on the field the Stanleys will yet keep their place at court, and cry "King Richard! King Richard!" But we must hope.'

They found Lichfield as hospitable as Sir William had promised them: rode through the town, firing their guns into the air, and camped on the Friday outside its walls. But Lord Stanley was not there to greet them. He had left a message of goodwill behind him, saying that he proposed to set up camp at Atherstone.

'*Between* Richard and ourselves,' said Oxford, very red. 'Aye, that I see full well. Sire, let us provision ourselves, with the help of these good people, so that we ask nothing of any Stanley, and proceed to Tamworth on the morrow. We shall not fight at Atherstone, on that we may count. But now must we move warily, for Richard's men are in every place, and he is poised to strike us. We are close, your grace, full close.'

'Then is this joyful news!' said Henry. 'For we shall meet in battle!'

But there was no joy behind the words, and the old feeling of emptiness beset him. Had they marched from Lichfield with the Stanleys he would have known a light heart, now on the road to Tamworth without them he rode more and more slowly. Until, feeling no pressure on her sides, the mare took her own pace and walked as she would. Some twenty gentlemen of Henry's retinue, not daring to break into his thoughts, slowed their own mounts to keep him company. But the army under its military leaders kept up a brisk pace which drew them far ahead. They had not broken camp before the afternoon, waiting for news; leaving receipts for oats and hay and bread and beer and meat; and re-stocking the carts; and making sure that every man had a good meal in his belly, for this might be the last before battle. So Henry came to himself when he could no longer see the last baggage animals in that violet dusk.

'My friends,' he said, reining in his desultory mare, 'we fear that we have lost our army! Why did you not rouse us sooner?'

'Sire, we feared to disturb your grace.'

'Then do our thoughts beg your several pardons!' he said frankly. 'for they were far away from what should most concern them. We must go softly now, for the enemy is near, and may be closer than we suspect.'

'Sire, were it not best that we stayed circumspectly at the next village? Not with pomp, or proclamation of what you are, but as a party of gentlemen that have lost their way?'

'Then am I Henry Tudor once again,' said Henry rue- fully. 'Use me as one of you, speak in a familiar fashion – and talk of hunting that they might think we pursue nothing richer than game.'

They attracted no more attention than fine clothes usually

did, and wrapping themselves in their cloaks they dozed on the floor of *The Three Tuns*. But Henry, closing his eyes so they might think he slept, spent the early hours of Saturday morning marshalling and dismissing arguments.

Once the Stanleys were persuaded to Richard's side they would betray all and any that had assisted Henry. Besides the nobles with him, or coming to him, the Welsh nation as a whole would probably suffer a punishment similar to that inflicted on them after the fall of Owain Glyndŵr. And then there was his mother Lady Margaret, excused once but never twice, and with her Beaufort inheritance already willed by Richard to his heir John de la Pole, Earl of Suffolk. He bore no affection for the Woodvilles and Greys, who had flickered this way and that, but he minded that Elizabeth of York would be affected. For Stanley could put her up as an instigator of rebellion. And what would become of her he could not guess – at best the humiliation of a husband far inferior in station, and close to Richard's heart. In setting her at his side as future queen he had offered her all or nothing.

Surprised by the misery of this purely personal consideration, when thousands of lives and the Welsh nation demanded his first thoughts, he reviewed what he knew of Elizabeth. Her courage and dignity were great, but he cared that she mended her dresses frugally; that she had put her trust in him, and sent him a letter and a rich ring and what money she could. He hoped that her loyal gentleman, Humphrey Brereton, had excused Henry's necessary delay in replying to her, with splendid words. It seemed hard that a girl should wait for weeks, when she gave a cry from the heart that should have been answered straightway. But he was longer and better versed in adversity than she, and knew that love and chivalry must wait on gold and equipment.

She shall have all honour when I am king, he thought.

He had been told many times that she was beautiful, and wished he might see how near report came to reality. Then he remembered Humphrey Brereton's outburst, and the long tale of his perilous ride from house to house; bearing news that could have racked and hanged and disembowelled him, and set his body in quarters on the city walls. And he knew that no man risks his life, for no more than a sweet thanks and a little money, without good cause. So she was beautiful.

He thought of the lady on the tapestry in his bedchamber at Nantes, and her image formed in his mind. The pale gentle face and flower eyes, the tongues of silver-gilt hair. Silver-gilt hair. Every sweet thought brought a sour one in its wake. The queen-dowager had had silver-gilt hair, and was even now consolidating her position at court; while her slipper son Dorset lay in custody in France. Well, she too must be treated with all honour – and good sense. As a king he could not afford to let Dame Elizabeth make mischief. As a man he could hardly hope to win the affection of his wife by imprisoning her mother. So he must make her welcome, treat her as a former queen, and in good time persuade her to a pleasant monastery with a generous pension, from which place of retirement she should join the court on state occasions. He would see that her daughters got good portions and noble husbands. He would ransom Dorset and watch him closely – now there was another waverer, bent only on his own preferment. Which brought him back to the Stanleys. Could he trust them? And if not, then how should he win the field? And if he won the field despite them, how should he deal with them afterward? Could one treat one's mother's husband and his brother as heinous traitors? Oh, one could – but at what cost? Lancashire and Cheshire brewing fresh treachery out of revenge, his subjects crying that he was no better than Richard?

So the night passed slowly and in much heaviness, and as soon as the first grey light appeared they paid their reckoning and were galloping for Tamworth. But with daylight came new counsel.

'My friends,' said Henry, 'it would seem ill to tell our army that we lost them in the train of our thoughts. What trust shall they have in us, who lose them when we should lead them? Let us rather say that we left them not by grievous error but by wise design – to seek a message from our secret allies. Which lie I shall make truth this very day, and ride with your good selves as escort to Atherstone, where the Lord Stanley abides.'

A chorus of approval greeted this suggestion and they rode on in better spirits, seeing that he looked always two moves ahead.

His return to his army was hailed with relief. His explanation soothed them. But he had eaten and was upon his horse again before the army began to collect itself for departure. To his commanders alone he entrusted the reason for his going, though Oxford was fearful for him – thinking he might be captured on the way, or taken there with treachery.

'My lord Oxford,' said Henry in quiet rebuke, 'do you snatch every brave deed for yourself? What king are we that starts at every shadow and will not risk ourself? We tell you we shall fetch good news from Atherstone, and so we pray you lead our army north of there and we shall meet at Orton on the hill.'

Then he was off, taking comfort in action, and greater comfort still in his reception. For both Stanleys came forward and bent the knee and greeted him loyally; but Henry, with a gesture even more gracious, then knelt to the Lord Stanley and called him father and asked his blessing.

'Stand up, my dear son,' said Lord Stanley, touched. 'You have my blessing, and your mother's blessing by me. Thrice welcome, gentle prince!'

'What news of the Lord Strange, our brother, whose welfare is at our heart always?' Henry asked.

'My son attempted to make his escape,' said Stanley slowly, 'but was recaptured by Duke Richard's men.' He hesitated, and spoke heavily. 'And I am told, by those that watch and listen for me, that my son – in fear of his life – confessed that Sir John Savage and ourselves had made treasonable compact with your grace. My son is a brave and honourable gentleman,' he added with difficulty, 'but the Duke Richard has means to persuade even the bravest.'

'This is ill news indeed, both for ourself and you,' said Henry gravely.

'It changes nothing,' said Stanley, though he was troubled. 'And yet must we dissimulate a little longer, sire. Duke Richard will hope to the last that we may be persuaded to his side. In our turn, we would not endanger Lord Strange's life sooner than we must.'

Henry's heart misgave him. For who could tell which was the foxer, and which the foxed? And all hung upon the Stanleys.

Still, he smiled and seemed confident, riding out to meet the famous bowmen of England in their white and scarlet livery.

Then he swept off his fine cap, crying, 'Cheshire and Lancashire, welcome unto us!'

Their shouts rang strong and true. And as evening began to fall two Yorkist captains rode into Atherstone with their men tramping behind them. Sir Walter Hungerford and Sir Thomas Bourchier, summoned from London by Richard, had parted from Sir Robert Brackenbury at Stony Stratford, leaving him to carry news of their treachery. There were more to come. On the Sunday morning Sir John Savage, Sir Brian Sanford and Sir Simon Digby joined them; and all escorted Henry back to his army.

'This is no rabble, either, sire!' said Oxford appreciatively, still sore at the recollection of Henry's motley from Harfleur. 'For these are proper soldiers and well-armed.'

'Good Oxford,' said Henry pleasantly, 'I pray you let my Frenchmen be. Their leader is a noble gentleman. They will fight when they must. As to their manner – it is the custom to pay many sweet compliments in France, but they can be as hot as any in a quarrel.'

Then he walked among them, and wherever he went he was received gladly.

Their 'eyes and ears' as Jasper called them, rode in with messages : solitary men in the fire of youth or the seasoned caution of middle-age. Richard had left Nottingham on the Friday, and since then the news had mounted steadily.

'The duke's army can be seen for miles along the road, and the duke himself rides proudly, with frowning countenance, upon a marvellous white courser. And he wears a crown upon his helm that all might know him.'

'Norfolk and Surrey are with him, and the East Anglian men.'

'Northumberland is coming with his wild borderers, and York is sending a stout troop.'

'The army took fully an hour, from first man to last, to leave the city of Nottingham, and another hour to enter Leicester. They march four abreast, in two divisions, and wings of horsemen range on every side, and the force numbers six thousand even without Northumberland's troops.'

'Leicester greeted the duke with a loud salute from the city guns. His own bed was carried into their finest hostelry – *The Blue Boar*. Some say there are three hundred gold crowns hidden in the mattress.'

'I discount the crowns,' said Oxford drily, 'unless they are for his funeral, and much do I resent *The Blue Boar*'s hospitality. For that is *my* crest.'

Now, on this Sunday afternoon, 21 August 1485, they waited until a messenger galloped in on his lathered horse.

'The Duke of Gloucester led his army over Bow Bridge to Elmesthorpe, nine miles out of Leicester, this morning. And the greater part of his forces is encamped at Stapleton, in some fields known as the Bradshaws.'

They consulted the map for the last time.

'So he tarries at Stapleton,' said Oxford, 'in an excellent position either to fall upon us, if we attempt to march down Watling Street, or to block a possible advance on Leicester. What says your grace? Do we meet him or flee him?'

The answer was implicit in his tone. Oxford had run long and far enough.

'Where should we meet him?' Henry asked, for the map seemed more hindrance than help.

'Now let us ask our good John Hardwick, that knows this country well, sire, and he can lead us there.'

'Your grace,' said Hardwick, bowing, 'north-east of Atherstone is an old trackway called Fenn Lane, that runs through Fenny Drayton to a nook of the river near Shenton Mill – by the name of White Moors.'

'And what is the best vantage point?' Oxford interposed. 'Where may we survey the Duke's army?'

'From Ambien Hill, my lord – so called from the old English *ana beame*, meaning one tree...'

'A pox on your tree!' said Oxford testily. 'May Duke Richard hang from it! Where is this hill?'

'One mile from White Moors, my lord, rising some four hundred feet. This is barren country, my lord, and there is a treacherous marsh on the banks of the Sence stream – which it were best to avoid.'

'We must use it for our defence, your grace,' said Oxford, 'at least it lies between ourselves and Stapleton,' as Hardwick drew a little map of his own to make matters clear. 'And if Duke Richard hears, as he must, that we advance to White Moors, he will march north to Sutton Cheney.'

Henry looked round on his commanders. One by one they nodded their heads.

'Strike camp!' Henry ordered.

They doused the fires, folded up the mushroom field of tents, made ready themselves and their arms, harnessed the horses to the heavy carts and guns, and marched.

Henry's smile was absent, his long face grave. Unanimated, it bore the stamp of exile, older than his twenty-eight years, plain as a priest's. The lines between nose and mouth were strongly marked now, the mouth set and sad, the eyes without light. He was in the grip of an old melancholy, born of deferred hope. But Jasper's grey cropped head was erect, Rhys's dark eyes brilliant with the prospect of battle, and Oxford smiled grimly as he rode, mailed fist doubled arrogantly on one hip.

Then the northern Welsh, out of the bowels of captivity, struck up *Gwyr Harlech*, at first very softly so that it was no more than a rumble in their throats; and then, as words and feelings mounted, louder and louder still.

'Seventeen years since,' said Jasper, 'and newer than yesterday!'

A faint flush on Henry's cheeks, a sheen in his eyes, betrayed him. He was there with them again; hearing the challenge of David ap Einion; shrinking at the cannonade; darting between tooth and stone tooth of the battlements. He straightened in his saddle and held up his head and smiled at Jasper.

More than half the army did not comprehend the words, but the spirit could be in no doubt. The song ended in a great shout, and then cheer upon cheer rose from every rank.

'The Welsh are ready to fight!' Henry observed with pride.

'They should save their breath for marching, your grace,' Oxford grumbled.

They camped for the night on the plain of White Moors; somewhat dashed to find the Stanleys between themselves and Ambien Hill, and the royal army near enough on its far side to take advantage of it before they could. But that was one of the hazards of war.

'Well, it will be a fine day, sire,' Oxford said cheerfully, 'and that is better than cutting a man into the mud with the rain streaming from your helm. Or fighting with hands so cold that you know not whether it is your fingers or the hilt – and snow in the eyes, and a black light that knows not friend from foe. There lie the Stanleys, your grace, betwixt the two armies that it may be seen they fight for either side, or neither, as the case may be. Christ save us! They make me out a very babe for strategy. I shall not lose my sleep for them, yet I should rest easier, sire, if I could read their minds, for good or ill. And there, your grace, beyond us, the Duke of Gloucester lies on Harper's Hill.' His regret for their position was obvious, but he added, 'And yet the marsh protects us, and a wood beyond that – or had he cut us down on Fenn Lane.'

The tents glimmered fitfully in the half-light, and brighter still shone the fires, so that hill and plain seemed to harbour an army of glow-worms.

'He has a good number,' said Oxford quietly, 'and good men, and the hill. Yet one cannot have all things, your grace, for the sun will be in their eyes.'

'If you were the Lord of Hosts, good Oxford, what outcome would you prophesy?'

Oxford brooded, smoothing his cheeks and chin. For they were outnumbered two to one in any case, and Richard could count every man as a master of his craft. Moreover, Richard was a warrior, while Henry must lean upon the counsel of his commanders. Oxford had not seen a happier set of circumstances for the enemy in many years.

'Your grace,' he said, 'I think not on prophecies but on a bright sword. And if every man wield his well on the morrow we need fear nothing.'

For a long time Henry stood in silence, knowing what Oxford meant beneath the bold words and steadfast face.

CHAPTER TWENTY

God that shope both sea and land,
& ffor all creatures dyed ont tree,
saue & keep the realme of England
to liue in peace & tranquillitye.

Bosworth Feilde
Bishop Percy's Folio MS.

King Richard sat in his pavilion on Harper's Hill, having no more appetite for company than for the food they set before him. Presently he ordered both away, and sat in silence in his sombre finery, with the gold chain of York upon his breast heavy in alternate suns and white roses, and the white boar pendant gleaming as he shifted.

Throughout the year of 1484 he had been ready for invasion, setting men he could trust in important strongholds, piling arms in the Tower of London, prohibiting village games that they might practise archery instead. And none of his professional soldiers lacked a helmet, and those who could not afford armour had tunics stuffed with tow, and stout leather jackets, and every man was well-armed and used to battle.

He had ordered a trial mobilization of forces in Middlesex and Surrey and Hertfordshire, called upon all Sheriffs in England and Wales to resist the insatiable covetousness of the usurper, commanded the Commissioners of Array throughout the country to muster men, and sent Richard Williams to act as castellan of Pembroke, Tenby, Haverford West, Ciegarran and Tenby. What had become of Williams? The coasts were watched, beacons stacked with wood in readiness to be lit, a system of signalling lights set up on the hills. How had it come about that they heralded Henry Tudor and were not used against him? He guessed that Rhys ap Thomas had played him false, and Walter Herbert turned an old Yorkist coat, and many, many others besides. Except Madoc of Coetmor.

'Here's to you, Madoc!' said Richard drily, raising his cup of wine. 'The only true Welshman we have found!'

But one Welshman against such a multitude was no great

comfort. Nor were those damned Welsh bards, that had said the Tudor would land at Milford. And since Milford-on-sea in Hampshire faced the French coast he had sent the royal fleet to guard it, and flung a wide embrace of squadrons round the south. And it was Milford Haven, after all. Still, had the invasion remained a motley force of eighteen hundred scurvy Frenchmen, and a matter of ragged Welsh with home-made spears, pottering and pillaging their way along the coast until their courage and supplies ran out, he would have feared nothing. But there was treachery at home. He had thought the Stanleys understood him, and needed him as much as he needed them, but Stanley's Beaufort wife, and those captains who had already deserted to the other side, had weighed the scale sadly. And though he knew that Norfolk was for him he was not so sure of Northumberland, a surly fellow, jealous and dissatisfied. For the house of Percy had wielded supreme power in Yorkshire before Richard ruled it, and blamed him that the county gave its love and service elsewhere.

But still the royal summons to arms read like a very book of heraldry : sonorous, noble, ancient.

The Earls Norfolk, Surrey, Kent, Shrewsbury, Lincoln, Northumberland, Westmoreland. The Lords Zouch, Maltravers, Arundel, Wells, Grey of Condor, Bowes, Audley, Berkeley, Ferrers of Chartley, Ferrers of Groby, Fitzhugh, Scrope of Upsal, Scrope of Bolton, Dacres, Lumley, Greystocke. The Knights Spencer, Harbottle, Ward, Ridley, Moberly, Clutton, Horsley, Percy, Manners, Conway, Akerston, Gray, Sanfort, Thomas Brackenbury, Bowdrye, Robbye, Constable, Conyers, Wardley, Rosse, Sturley, Clyfton, North Stafford, Ryder, Utridge, Huntingdon, Willmarley, Swayley, Bryan, Stapleton, Ratcliffe, Mallinere, Dacres, Thoresby, Musgrave, Murkenfield, Broughton, Owen, Tempest, Ashton, Macklefield, Ward, Middleton, Coleburn, Neville, Hurlstean, Herne, and the Harringtons – James, Robert and Thomas.

And when he had ridden from Nottingham his army had stretched out for three miles along the road, with the royal banner of England fluttering in the hands of Triball the standard-bearer : three gold lions on crimson, three gold *fleur-de-lis* on azure, quartered. A singular of boars shining silver on the badges of his retainers; a pride of lions on Norfolk's jackets; a forest of pennons flying swallow-tailed in the breeze. And they had marched and ridden in excellent order, being in no haste, knowing their strength and quality.

'There are too many overmighty subjects!' he said to himself.

Buckingham, clad in a blue velvet gown blazing with gold cartwheels at the coronation, turning his treacherous head aside as the crown was placed. Buckingham, boasting that he would have as many Stafford knots as ever did Warwick have ragged staves. Well, Buckingham had died like a traitor, and others would follow him.

'But have we not sought to heal old wounds?' he cried, bitter that they could turn against him.

The royal progress through the Midlands and the North, in the July and August of 1483, had been rich in benefices. He had excused the town of Oxford from its crown fee, and Worcester from its benevolences. He had restored the forests of Woodstock to their people, and bestowed money on Tewkesbury Abbey. Had made Gloucester a county in its own right, had rewarded his friends and been merciful enough with his enemies. And he had striven to attain a new standard of morality, urging England to be pure in mind and body, ordering his judges to be impartial as well as firm. He had always stood apart from the joyful fornication regarded as a nobleman's right. He had beheaded the adulterous Hastings, and set his strumpet Jane Shore to open penance in the streets.

'And benefices to Queen's College,' he murmured, 'and seven hundred pounds to King's College, and the bones of King Henry removed from Chertsey and buried right honourably. And Dame Elizabeth and her daughters brought out of sanctuary, and granted pensions.'

Which reminded him of the rumours concerning his marriage to Elizabeth of York, and that shameful public denial in the hall of the Knights of St John at Clerkenwell.

'They slandered us,' he said. 'It was Rotherham that rumoured it!'

And the Chancellor of France at the opening of the States-General in Tours, crying that King Edward's sons, already full-grown and noble, were put to death with impunity – and the royal crown transferred by the favour of the people to their murderer.

'They slandered us!' he cried, and the soldier on guard outside his tent started.

Enemies had noted, too, that his son had died a year

almost to the day of King Edward's death. They said that it was the will of God.

He saw again the sickly boy in his splendid clothes, too weak to ride a horse, borne through the loyal city of York in loud rejoicing. And out of gratitude Richard had remitted a large portion of their yearly taxes, though the Treasury could ill afford it. And when the boy died, and his two sturdy bastards flourished like two reproaches, he had grieved : signing the funeral expenses, and writing by the lad's name in his own hand, *whom God pardon* – though the child needed none. And his wife died also, on a day when there was a great eclipse of the sun, and they had whispered about that too, and said he poisoned her.

'They slandered us !'

But what of Rivers and Grey and Vaughan? What of Hastings? What of his own brother-in-law, Sir Thomas St Leger?

'They were traitors.'

The tide that he and Buckingham had turned was running wilfully now in its own strength, carrying him and all before it.

And those he had called open murderers, adventurers, adulterers and extortioners; those who had daily sown seed of noise and slander against his person; led by a bastard captain, an unknown Welshman; now camped in White Moors and setting their greedy hands and eyes upon his crown.

He reached for the gold circlet and smoothed it, as he thought. He had considered every move. He had entrenched himself at Nottingham, whose town held the approach over the Trent, and commanded the main road to north and south, and a waterway of connections, whose castle on its sandstone cliff stood like a host of cares, in the middle of his realm.

We have been loyal to England, he thought. She should have shown like loyalty to us. We have been ever active on her behalf. More than two thousand documents we signed, to heal and to protect her.

The documents and the protection resolved itself into one document. And in his mind he saw three signatures. The hand of his nephew, Edward V, royally large and stiff – to show them that he knew his duty and his station; then his own neat italic script, with the motto, *Loyaulté me lie* – Loyalty bindeth me; and lastly Buckingham's careless sprawl with his motto, *Souvente me souvene* – Remember me often.

'Sire,' said a timid voice, breaking into his thoughts, 'the Bishop of Dunkeld would speak with your grace.'

He rose to greet him courteously, glancing at the ugly fellow who shambled behind.

'We see you have a bodyguard, my lord bishop! Do you fear treachery against your cloth?'

The Bishop of Dunkeld, an ambassador of Scotland, had but come to pay his respects, and intended to be well out of the way of battle. He smiled and shook his head.

'Nay, your grace, this is an ignorant fellow of poor parentage that I have raised up in my household. He follows me like a dog and has a good heart. He knows his place, sire, none better. His ears and mouth are stopped.'

'But not his eyes,' Richard observed, seeing that the man was captivated by the beauty of the gold crown. 'What is he called?'

'His name is of no import, sire, but since you are gracious enough to ask it is McGregor.'

'This is the crown of England, McGregor,' said Richard loudly, to the fellow's evident rapture. 'And we purpose to wear it in battle, that live or die we shall be king of England.'

McGregor stared from the royal circlet to the royal face and back again, fascinated. This was the nearest he would ever get to glory, and his lips moved as he mentally re-told the tale and magnified it.

'I had not thought to stay, sire,' said the bishop hesitating, 'but I am told you have no chaplains with you. Your grace is welcome to my poor services of intercession for the morrow.'

'My lord bishop,' said Richard impatiently, 'if we have no chaplains that is our intention, not our fault. Should our quarrel be godly we need no supplication. And if it is not then prayers were a dire blasphemy.'

The bishop bowed, exchanged a few courtesies, and called McGregor to heel. The fellow was refining and shaping his imaginary story to the point where it became a personal confidence between himself and the monarch, and he jumped at the command.

'Make your bow to the king, you stupid dog,' whispered the bishop, irritated by the man's gaping.

'Why he bows to the crown,' cried Richard, grimly

228

amused, setting it on the table at his side, and then his hand moved to his sword.

Shouts and scuffles outside the tent brought both king and bishop out to ascertain the cause, pushing the rough fellow aside in their haste. And yet the tumult was nothing : a matter of two soldiers finding they shared the same sweetheart, and over-ready with their knives.

The crown gleamed from the shadows of the tent, where Richard had set it down, and McGregor put forward a coarse finger to stroke it. Its radiance bemused his small eyes. Its touch was magnetic, persuading him to lift it in both hands and place it momentarily upon his shaggy head. Bewitched, he thrust it in his shirt and ran. Ran like a madman and felt like a king, with the treasure cool and heavy against his dirty flesh. He possessed it for almost three minutes before they flung him down, and dragged him unrepentant before Richard.

'My father was hangit,' said McGregor stoutly, in explanation, 'and his father before him. The one for stealing sheep, the other for stealing cattle. And so shall I be hangit in my turn – not for a mangy sheep or a wee bit cattle, but for a thing of great price. Aye, sire – and my lord bishop – I stole the *Crown of England*. And I'm *proud* on it !'

He had condemned himself out of his own mouth and pronounced his own sentence, so they took him away to see that justice was roughly done.

And the crown shone in the dark tent, while the king groaned in his dreams, and started up, teeth clenched; and sought rest that would not come, and cried down phantoms that rose again; on the eye of Bosworth Field.

CHAPTER TWENTY-ONE

... after the conflict the blood of stallions
and a bewildering fear among the folk:
And the sweat upon the shirts and blows on the body,
and the water in the jerkins, and Deira in pain,
and joy upon joy with the innocent.

> Ode to St David
> on the eve of Bosworth
> Dafydd Llwyd, fifteenth century

Others had slept no better, and the herald from Henry Tudor, at dawn on St Bartholomew's Eve, 22 August, found an unshaven and ill-tempered Lord Stanley growling in his tent. He hovered over the courteous request that he should join forces and array for battle, looking like some ancient bloodhound, with his long jowls and drooping lids.

'Commend me unto King Henry,' said Stanley drily, 'and inform him to set his own folks in order. I shall come to him in good time.'

Slowly he accepted the armour from his bearer, and slowly donned it piece by plated piece : sabatons and greaves, cuisses and poleyns, breast-plate and fauld, gorget and pauldrons, vambraces and couters; lined and padded for comfort, hinged with steel, dimpled on the inner side from the blows of the hammer that wrought it.

And his thoughts moved distractedly from York to Lancaster and back again. On Harper's Hill his son lay in perilous custody. Outside, his cavalry put on their proud scarlet and looked to their horses, and a quarter of a mile away his brother's bowmen gathered under the banner of the White Hart. Between them they had close on six thousand troops, all symbols of their power. But more than these, though involving all of them, the future of the Stanleys lay in the balance.

'Now how should I choose aright?' he asked himself, and shook his head.

The herald from Richard was less gracious than the Tudor courier. Blanch Sanglier bowed as curtly as a man could, almost on the verge of ill manners, and delivered a royal ultimatum. The king commanded the Lord Stanley to join with him against the enemy forthwith, and his disobedience should cost him his son's head.

The command did not make up Stanley's mind for him, but it did arouse his pride. He was not, after all, hesitating from cowardice but from caution. Holding his noble helm in both his hands, the old eagle stared at the herald doughtily.

'Tell the king I have other sons,' he said.

And now he completed the ritual of dressing with greater satisfaction, though his heart was heavy. He tested the gleaming curve-edged blade of his pole-axe and ran his fingers lovingly over its flukes, twirling the shaft as a preliminary warming-up. In the left side of his waist-belt he thrust the long dagger. On the right side hung his great sword in its leather straps, and the bearer fastened the scabbard to his thigh. Lastly he set the helm upon his head and drew on his steel gauntlets, and accepted the round shield whose centre bore a golden eagle.

'Well, Tom,' he said to his armourer, who stood by to see that all was in good order, 'you have done your alterations fairly. I am somewhat easier since these rivets were loosened, for though I am thin enough in the face my belly increases with the years!'

'The Lord Stanley's girth is not yet as great as his might,' the armourer murmured. 'Your lordship looks very well – though I regret that you may not wear your crested helm in battle, for that is noblest of all.'

'You make a coxcomb of me, Tom,' said Stanley good-humouredly. 'But though an eagle on a chapeau in fine gold, that hovers over an infant in its nest swaddled in azure, be princely for a tournament – it would serve me ill for less courtly purposes. Why, some rough fellow might shoot it off.'

Then he strode out to meet his brother.

'How goes the field, Will?'

'The king is on Ambien Hill with close on ten thousand men, and he looks to be adopting the Swiss formation. First a long screen of archers, spread out to seem more than they truly are, in the shape of a bent bow – with Surrey and Brackenbury on the left of them, and Norfolk on the right. Their flanks protected by two squadrons of two hundred cavalry each, and they in their turn protected by a thousand bowmen and artillerymen – and some with hand-guns, and they in turn backed by two thousand pikemen with spears nigh on three times their own height. Then the main ward, where the king himself commands, of some two thousand foot and fifteen hundred cavalry.'

'Now Christ have mercy on us all,' muttered Stanley, veering towards the Yorkists in his mind. 'And what of my son, what of Henry Tudor?'

'Oxford leads the van and has taken the major part of their forces with him. They look to be four thousand, with a skirmisher line of French and Welsh and English bowmen. Behind them, the Shropshire levies at the right under Talbot, Savage and his men on the left, with Sanford and Digby as his captains. Then Henry Tudor, Pembroke and Rhys ap Thomas lead the main ward of Welshmen, backed by their field pieces, which are not many.'

'The Welsh are not so many, neither,' Stanley observed gloomily, 'if you discount lads with catapults and farmers with bill-hooks! Will, we shall stay where we are. You at the head, myself at the rear, with the men between us. Move not until they are in full combat, that we might deal the grace blow. And watch Northumberland. If he holds back then we may take it that the king has been betrayed.'

'They say,' said Sir William hesitantly, 'that Norfolk found a note pinned to his tent door at daybreak, which said, *Jockey of Norfolk, be not too bold, for Dickon thy master is bought and sold.*'

'Truly? Still, wait and see, Will. It may be but some miserable jest.'

'And they say that when King Richard rode over Bow Bridge yesterday he struck his foot upon the side, and an old beldame cried that he should strike his head upon the same stone before two days were out.'

'Say you so?' cried Stanley, more impressed by the prophecy than the note on Norfolk's tent.

'Aye, and a blind wheelwright in Leicester, one that has the gift of foretelling to a great degree, said that if the moon changed twice that day the king was lost. And so it did change, from the first to second quarter.'

'It is not that I wish for King Richard's victory,' said Stanley, veering now to the Tudor side, 'but that I would not you and I chose amiss!'

'Well, brother, I am with you. So shall we watch close and move swiftly.' He hesitated. 'But what of Lord Strange?'

Stanley said uncomfortably, 'My son must take his

chance. He is a brave and goodly gentleman and would not that I bent the knee in shame.'

So having brought honour and policy into an unlikely marriage they arrayed their men in battle formation.

Richard presented a face paler and more drawn than usual to his commanders, but he was ready, though he would eat no breakfast and could celebrate no mass.

'There will be time enough for both,' he said, knowing that only action could refresh his body and soul. 'We must be done with the Welshman first.'

The news from Lord Stanley increased his pallor, but it was the white of rage not fear.

'Execute Lord Strange!' he said briefly.

'Your grace,' Sir William Harrington ventured, 'should we not wait until the battle is won, and so have *all* the Stanleys?'

'Aye, if you will,' said Richard wearily. 'We care not if he die now or later.'

A lad was proud to hold White Surrey's bridle : the horse armoured from crupper to chamfron over a white cloth emblazoned in red and gold and blue.

'Now, my beauty,' Richard said softly to his courser, 'you and we shall be one warrior.'

The charger tossed his head, ready for war.

The first rays of the morning sun flushed the countryside with a grace it did not normally possess, and which full light would expose as a barren place of open marsh and scrub and twisted thorn. Rough and uneven, the lumpy ground was made treacherous by little streams, nourishing the thirsty alders whose red roots, part-submerged, promised to trap or trip unwary feet.

To the west, on the horse-shoe curve of Ambien Hill, King Richard fanned out his ten thousand men. The rising sun dazzled the tips of their standards, glancing off weapons and transforming their armour to fire coals. And before them stood the heralds in their coats of arms, and the trumpeters whose instruments were hung with silk, embroidered with leopards and lilies and silver boars.

To the north, the Cheshire bowmen in white and red stood rank on ready rank. Each man's bow was as tall as himself : the staves fashioned from yew, and the strings of hemp or flax. At their sides they carried a little forest of arrows, whose wands of oak or ash or hard-beam were plumed with grey goose-feathers : and the feathers chosen from different parts of the wing so that they might fly truly, as a bird flies. Each arrow was a cloth-yard long, notched deep and narrow for the bow-string, and bound at the notching with white silk. Their burnished heads, round and pointed like a bodkin – rather than forked or broad – were formed to plunge needle-wise into their living target. Upon his left arm every bowman wore a laced close-sleeve and a leather glove. He could hit any mark at two hundred and twenty yards and many at twice that length : judging distance, side-winds and the arrow's compass even as he let fly. And every man bent with the strength of his whole body, firing from the right side of the bow, and could pierce an oak door four inches thick.

To the east, with the sun already warming their backs, the Tudor army seemed smaller and less splendid than the other two. But Oxford's banner of star and streams dominated his vanguard of archers : Talbot and his 'mastiffs' were on the right wing; Savage and his 'unicorns' on the left. The nobility of Rhys ap Thomas's troops hid the humbler ranks behind them, and Rhys's three black ravens appeared to peck savagely above the head of his standard.

Then, in azure and silver and green and gold and red the pennants unfurled, swallow-tailed or pointed at the fly : charged with armorial devices and richly fringed in gold; exotic birds on the morning wind. Henry Tudor's banners unfolded : St George for England, a red cross on white sarcenet; the dun cow on yellow; borderings of red roses for Lancaster and *fleur-de-lys* for France. And above the field, for Wales, a scarlet velvet dragon with horny head and forked tongue, with scaly back and rolls like armour on its breast and belly, winged and taloned and pointed of tail : on white and green silk.

And here and there among the troops were placed men armoured like Henry himself, so that treachery did not know where to look. True, they were not so splendid, and had a man peered hard enough he would have seen that they were only poor facsimiles. But who, in the heat of the fight, would take mere gilding for other than gold? Or stop to notice that their pieces were not beautifully wrought but painted to seem so? And they held themselves in kingly fashion, honoured to be pawns.

A Milanese armourer at the French court had fashioned

Henry's suit, and since his craft was at his finger-tips he had allowed his art a supreme flight of fancy, turning to the antique style which simulated an heroic body. A border of Tudor roses flowered about the heart, over a lion's head. On the waist two dragons were rampant. And all embossed in gold on blue steel, with a fantasy of figures and flowers and scallops and fan-shapes wrought on helm and pauldrons and couters and poleyns, and upon the fauld.

So he rode from rank to rank on his bay horse, that all might see him, and stood upon a hillock. In the hands of Sir William Brandon the dragon of Cadwaladr writhed and forked its scarlet tongue.

Suspicion and fear had left him now that the moment was come. A radiance richer than any sunlight could bestow was on his face. He held himself easily in the saddle and looked all about him, grey eyes bright, dark-gold hair falling to his shoulders, the magnificent helm beneath his arm. The chasm between himself and circumstance had closed, and the image was made whole. A great silence fell so that he could hear the silk of the banners slapping and slithering on their poles. He raised one arm in greeting, palm outwards, and lifted his head and called upon the Lord of Hosts.

'If this cause be not just – and the quarrel godly – let God the giver of victory judge and determine!

'For long we have sought the furious boar, and now we have found him. Wherefore let us not fear to enter into the bout where we may slay him.'

The field was arrayed for battle, to north and east and west.

'Backward we cannot flee, so that here we stand like sheep in a fold, encompassed by our enemies!'

The boys holding the horses were fresh-faced and subdued, as he had been at Banbury.

'Therefore let all fear be set aside, and like sworn brethren let us join in one! Remember that victory is not got with a multitude of men, but with the courage of hearts and the valiantness of minds. The smaller that our number be the more glory to us if we vanquish. You shall find me this day rather dead carrion than a living prisoner.'

The sun illuminated the plain, gilding the royal host on Ambien Hill; making a rosy blush of Stanley's columns; dancing on the stream that protected their left wing, glimmering among the reeds and hummocks of the marsh on their right. It flung the shadow of his army to Henry's feet, and behind him stretched his own shadow now grown great.

He seemed to stand outside himself and watch this other man upon his armoured horse. So that, marvelling, he thought 'This is the king!' and spoke through the mask.

'Now advance forward!' he cried, possessed. 'True men against traitors. The scourges of God against tyrants. True inheritors against usurpers. Display my banner with good courage. March forth like strong rumbustious champions. And in the name of God and St George let every man courageously advance forth his standard!'

The shout shook every fibre of his being as he stood apart. But the king sat gloriously upon his horse, and smiled into the cauldron of the sun.

The knights buckled their helms. The archers smoothed their arrow feathers true and flexed their bows. The infantry raised their hedge of pikes. The artillery looked to their powder and shot. Cannons and slingals were wheeled into place. Battle-axes and swords brandished. And in the rear, hundreds of Welsh peasants spat on their hands and took a firm grip upon whatever homely weapon they had carried with them on the march into Leicestershire.

For a long moment marsh, field and hill seemed to hang motionless on the summer air : the armies a splendid pattern, woven into a drab ground, formal and beautiful and still as a tapestry. Then, high and clear, a trumpet sounded the attack.

'Battle is joined!' Oxford yelled.

He raised his hand in final salute, and clapped his visor shut. Ten years of imprisonment lay behind him, possibly death on the field or the block before him. But this bright morning he was the Blue Boar, and they should find him mighty in war. As the Tudor army passed the marshland Norfolk raised his standard on Ambien Hill, and poured down the slopes with the river of his vanguard.

Battle commenced with the graceful ritual of the archers, who stood forth as one man : left foot a convenient distance before the right, left arm tense, holding the bow by the middle. The bowstring between the first and second fingers of the right hand; the shaft of the arrow resting on the knuckles of the left hand. Then the string was drawn back to the right ear, and sang as it discharged its messenger.

The tableau, suspended for a fraction of time longer, shattered as the arrows found their mark. Men fell, clutching breasts and heads, and the lines reformed, shooting again, and again, and again.

To the north, the Stanley bowmen watched with the judicious eyes of masters gazing upon promising pupils, and remained where they were.

It was the turn of the artillery, and horses shifted and whinnied nervously as heavy cannons discharged fragments of stone or iron into the opposing side. After each exchange little clouds of smoke hung meditatively on the air. So that, but for the casualties, one would have thought it a play with every man taking his part in good order.

Then the opening scene was lost in clamorous disarray as the two battalions met and fought hand to hand : the White Lion and the Blue Boar wielding axe and sword with democratic fervour, upon noble and lowly alike. Oxford shouted to his men to close ranks and keep no more than ten feet from the standard. They formed an arrow-head of infantry, with Talbot and Savage as the broad base. Three and four deep, the pikemen thrust their twenty-foot weapons of ash and steel forward through their own ranks : becoming an impenetrable barrier. As men from the outer triangle fell others took their places, and in this stubborn back-to-back fighting Norfolk was toppled from his horse.

'Leave him to me, you dogs,' yelled Oxford, and risked dismounting in order to engage with him.

His squire, praying fervently that everyone would understand the nature of this personal encounter, and let him and them be, took Oxford's horse and battle-axe in his keeping.

Norfolk got to his feet with some difficulty and wielded his sword.

'Now, White Lion !' cried Oxford, grinning behind his helm. 'The Blue Boar would contend with you. Ah, would you, would you?' As the sword nearly severed his hand. And he struck at Norfolk's head. 'That's for Lancaster !' he shouted.

The beaver fell from Norfolk's helmet, exposing his face.

'Now do I see you !' Oxford shouted, exultant.

But in the moment that his blade glittered his enemy fell, with an arrow in his head.

'Who did that?' Oxford roared, unmindful of the crush. 'What scurvy archer shot Norfolk?'

'I pray you, my lord,' quavered his squire. 'Mount you in good haste. This is no tournament, my lord. They do not fight courtly-wise.'

Oxford hewed a couple of foot soldiers and mounted, grumbling.

'If I should find that bowman,' he muttered, sheathing his sword and making swift use of his axe, 'I'll hang him. Aye, upon the first tree. Even upon that one tree by which Ambien Hill is called. Aye, and hang him – what, would you? Would you, sir? You are too mighty for your estate! Why, a better knight than Norfolk could not die! And by the hand of a common turd such as my horse would be ashamed to discharge. What, would you, would you? Though he might die in a better cause, say I. Watch my back, lad! Oh, you are ambitious, you lowly hind of York, and must fall. What, you sir, in likewise? Well, you die right nobly – and better than poor Norfolk! What, would you? Would you? . . .'

Take away the head and the body is lost. A pride of white lions faltered, looking for orders that were now silent. While unicorns and mastiffs savaged their hesitation : fanning out in fresh confidence as the enemy paused.

Now Sir Gilbert Talbot endeavoured to unhorse Norfolk's son Surrey, and though Sir William Conyers and Sir Richard Clarendon came to Surrey's rescue they were struck down by a group of unicorns. Talbot, riding into their midst to claim his quarry, saw one of his soldiers engage the knight and call for his surrender.

'Nay, not to such as you!' cried Surrey, severing his arm.

Then seeing that all was lost, hearing them say that his father was slain, he proffered his sword to Talbot and let them lead him from the field.

From his vantage point Richard observed the tide turning a little in the Tudor favour, and rightly judged it time to intervene. He sent word to Northumberland, the Lord Percy, to ride in and reinforce them. But more than the Stanleys were gauging which side to support in the final event. Courteously Northumberland replied that he felt it his duty to watch the Cheshire and Lancashire cavalry and bowmen, and thus fall upon them if they showed signs of joining the enemy. With the treacherously idle both before and beside him, Richard took action himself.

He feared nothing that the field might offer, and until now he had thought it offered very little in the way of opposition. Had Norfolk not fallen, had Surrey not been captured, Henry's first and best battalion could have been despatched in reasonable comfort.

'Where is Henry Tudor?' he demanded.

'There, sire, at the far end of the field. Under the Welsh banner near White Moors.'

Richard stood in his stirrups and shaded his eyes against the glare. Beyond the bloody chaos in the valley a little patch of red and white and green fluttered upon a hillock.

'Fetch us a cup of water, lad,' he said coolly to the boy who had held his horse.

He took the silver cup and drank deeply, for though he could not have swallowed a morsel of bread his throat was dry. And while he drank he kept his eyes on that fleck of colour.

'Then is it time he joined us in battle,' said Richard. 'Order our captains to cut a path for us through the field!'

'Sire,' said Catesby, fearing the risk and cost of such a venture, 'the Stanleys may fall upon us as we pass them. I beg your grace to fly! I fear treachery. We shall fight another day.'

But the king's ears were stopped, his eyes on that distant standard. He buckled on his helmet purposefully, his mind made up.

'Give our battle-axe into our hand,' he said, 'and set the crown of England on our head.' And he put his lips to the golden circlet as it was given him. 'For by Him that shaped both land and sea, king of England this day we shall live or die.' Then he cried in a great voice 'Advance our standards!' and clapped his spurs to White Surrey's sides.

The onslaught of the royal force was terrible. Men fell or were felled, scattering and dying beneath the hammering hooves and swinging axe, as Richard drove possessed for the Welsh banner.

The Stanley bowmen saw him pass like a scythe across the field. Saw Oxford's battalion shiver into confusion, while behind him Norfolk's men rallied and pressed forward again. The cries of Savage and Talbot collecting their scattered hedge together, the roars of Oxford as he cantered this way and that, cursing, praising, cutting down in one breath, sounded faintly above the tumult. Knights, unhorsed, fought on foot until axe and sword splintered, and then reached for their daggers; and when those were gone they laid open faces with their mailed gauntlets.

In the streams men seemed to lie and drink who could

239

drink no more. Hands outflung that would not grip. Legs smashed and splayed that would not stand again.

And in the mêlée Richard rode on, axe swinging from left to right, yelling the battle-cry of the Plantagenets, and moving, man by fallen man, nearer to White Moors.

Other eyes had seen the tide turn and turn again, though they did not know who pressed to meet them.

'Advance our standards!' Henry shouted, and clapped down his visor.

Scraps of poetry flickered up and out in his mind as he hewed and slashed; as though that mind sought to lift itself above the cruelty man wrought on man, and make a morning of dark chaos.

> *The lord of bright Llwyfenydd, where is his peer?*
> *Red their swords – may the blades not be cleaned!*

Over their heads, high in the heavens, a flock of crows wheeled and cried harshly, waiting for the silence that would herald their coming.

> *Quicker his blood to earth than to his wedding.*
> *Quicker the crows were fed than we could bury him!*

And faster and faster, as his training took him over and his heart grew sick, did the wheels of memory throw off their sparks of beauty and terror, as if the soul itself were threatened in its stronghold. And were arrested in a supreme moment by shouts of *Treachery! Treachery!* and the long and terrible cry *A Plantagenet! A Plantagenet!*

The company fell away before him, leaving him confronted by the God of War himself, a golden circlet upon his helm. And in the instant of the bright sword being held at arms-length, in the instant of the fell axe being wielded, the two men knew each other.

Richard's splendid armour was dented and smeared by encounters. White Surrey's lordly trappings, torn and splattered, clung to his flanks. His mouth was bloody from a cruel bridle. And both man and stallion, beside themsides, had become one awful weapon of war.

To Richard's amazement, so that for a brief space he could have laughed aloud, the unknown Welshman seemed small and of no great import.

'I have slain five of you today, already,' he gasped, as

White Surrey wheeled and he strained him round again. 'I have struck giants down' – Sir John Cheney, half as big again as Richard, unhorsed like a child in that mad charge – 'And now I have you!'

He raised his axe, whose flukes ran with Lancastrian blood, in both mailed hands, and brought it down with all his strength.

Sir William Brandon, moving to shield Henry with his body, took the full force of the blow and fell with the Welsh banner beneath him. As though that fall had brought them to themselves again, the Welshmen poured in from all sides, seeing the White Boar in their midst. It was a Welshman who pulled the standard free and held it high once more.

'King Henry! King Henry!' cried Rhys Fawr ap Meredydd.

The dragon, released, flew scarlet on its white and green, forked of tongue and tail. Triball, Richard's own standard-bearer, his legs hacked from under him, saw the gold lions and *fleur-de-lys* lie trampled on the mud in which he died.

Demented, fighting on foot and yelling for a fresh horse – the loss of White Surrey thick in his throat – Richard went down. They hewed his noble armour piece by princely piece, tore his fine clothes, and fought among themselves to be the man that killed him.

At last the Stanleys had given orders to attack. Their cavalry poured forward, and the Cheshire bowmen sent a superb arc of arrows into the air.

The battle had lasted two hours and was nearly over, though they were still chasing the Yorkists into Cadeby and Stoke Golding. The Tudor losses were not great, perhaps a hundred men : but the toll of Richard's friends was greater: gentle Brackenbury, Ratcliffe, brave Norfolk, the Lord Ferrers, John Kendall his secretary, and a host of good gentlemen faithful to him. The Wars of the Roses had been won, all but a single thorn which would be plucked out later. They had cost England thirteen battles, three kings, one Prince of Wales, twelve dukes, one marquis, eighteen earls, one viscount, twenty-three barons, knights and gentlemen unnumbered, and a hundred thousand men.

Henry's hands shook as he removed his helm and looked about him. The dust of victory lay already in his mouth. In the quietest corner of the field the first crows were sailing in to feed.

Someone had strapped the naked body of Richard Plantagenet upon a horse. The white limbs dangled: one shoulder a little higher than the other, one arm a little thinner and shorter than its fellow. The dark hair, streaked and tangled with blood and sweat, hung in strips over the white face. They had not even cared to close his eyes, which dimmed above the clenched teeth in final resolution. Then one rough fellow slapped the horse's rump and sent it into a stumbling trot along the road to Leicester, the corpse upon its back jerking at every step. And the head was grazed on the stones of Bow Bridge.

Now Henry issued his first royal proclamation, commanding his people on pain of death, that no manner of man rob or spoil no manner of commons coming from the field, but suffer them to pass home to their dwelling-places with their horse and harness.

'Henry, by the grace of God, king of England and of France, Prince of Wales and Lord of Ireland . . .'

Then he knelt to pray that he might rule in peace and justice those people whom God now committed and assigned to his governance.

Lord Stanley, riding down a few stray rebels, saw a gleam of gold under a hawthorn bush, and hooked up the battered crown upon his lance.

PART FOUR

WHITE ROSE AND RED
1485–86

Renowned yorke the white rose gaue;
braue Lancaster the redd;
by wedlocke both inoyned were
to lye in one princely bed.

White Rose & Red
Bishop Percy's Folio *MS*

CHAPTER TWENTY-TWO

*It was conceived not to be an epidemic disease,
but to proceed from a malignity in the constitution
of the air, gathered by the predispositions of the
seasons.*

> *Sir Francis Bacon, on the sweating sickness.*
> History of King Henry VII

He had done all that should be done : knighting eleven of his
followers upon the field; ordering lists to be made of all those
who had ever shown themselves to be true and loyal friends,
that he might reward them. Now he permitted himself a joyful service, speeding Sir Robert Willoughby with an escort
to Sheriff Hutton to tell a princess she should be queen. And
he sent good tidings to his mother and to the queen dowager
Elizabeth. Then rode like an emperor into Leicester, where
for two days he rested; and where for two days the despoiled
body of Richard was exposed at the church of Grey Friars,
so that all should see he was dead.

Refreshed and jubilant, they moved at a leisurely pace
down Watling Street, and ahead of them rode the trumpeters
to proclaim their coming. People ran out of houses, lined the
dusty roads, crowded behind their mayor and chief citizens.
And every town produced laden tables and flowing cups,
until – as Jasper said at St Alban's – a man longed for silence
and a peaceful crust.

'You shall have silence and peaceful crusts in plenty, good
uncle,' said Henry, accepting a posy from a small girl. 'We
beg you, sir, to give this child a groat in our name. The royal
treasury shall reimburse you. Aye, uncle, you have had your
turn at war and now must join us in tranquillity. For we shall
set down sedition, and your sword must rust in a good cause.
There shall be no wars in England under our rule, we
promise you.'

He was grinning with pleasure, but Jasper lifted his eyebrows.

'Say you so?' he remarked, with the air of one who knows
better. 'I'll lay you a hundred gold crowns that this sword is
out again in a twelvemonth for some scurvy Yorkist.'

245

'We beg you do not call our new relations scurvy, uncle. They will be so much at court. Could you not beat them at cards or dice, and so settle your account that way?'

'What say you, Oxford?' Jasper asked, as that doughty nobleman rode up. 'The king will have no war in his realm.'

'Well, if you have, sire, we are ready for it. And I tell you now that I thought but little of our chances on Bosworth Field, against that host of Richard Plantagenet. Aye, precious little. So if we sent him running we can send others after him. But that is not why I am come. Those Frenchmen, sire . . .'

'Oh, not our poor Frenchmen again, good Oxford, we beseech you. They fought as hard as any.'

'It is not their prowess that troubles me but their health, sire. Last night a man was taken sick, and this morning he is dead. Just now two more fell, even as they marched, as though a hand had struck them down. And there are others here and there among the ranks.'

'The pestilence,' said Jasper, crossing himself.

'Nay, not the pestilence, Pembroke. For that comes with a swelling in the groin or purple spots upon the body, or chokes a man as he sleeps. But this has neither swellings nor patches nor chokings. It is a sweating sickness, with much fever and griping of the bowels and a cruel malaise of the head – and it is deadly.'

'What say the physicians?' Henry asked, concerned.

Oxford's opinion of the medical profession was as low as his opinion of the French troops.

'They pluck their lips and shake their heads and say all manner of wise things in Latin. But the outcome, in honest English, is that they do not know – except that the dead should be buried. They say they need to observe the sickness more closely before a remedy may be found and tried.'

'Then are we all at risk?'

'Sire, the physicians say this is a disease that the French brought with them, and therefore no Englishman may die of it. And so I say, sire, that we march for London and let them die if they will – or fall behind.'

'Good Oxford,' said Henry, smiling in spite of the gravity of the situation, 'we think Almighty God forgot sweet mercy when He made you.'

'Well, if He did,' growled Oxford, 'He gave me a double measure of sound sense. And I would they had stayed in France with their sweating sickness. At any rate they need no nursing, only burying.' He grinned suddenly. 'When I heard that they were sick,' he said, 'I thought it was jail fever!'

And rode off, delighted by his wit.

'It may abate,' said Henry, disturbed. 'I would not that we entered London with it.'

Within the walls of London the palaces of the lords spiritual and the lords temporal stood among their gardens and orchards. Upon the waters of the Thames, fresh for twenty miles below the port, ships of many nations rode at anchor. Westminster, home of Parliament and the Law Courts, was still a separate town, though linked to its capital by a noble line of houses along the Strand. But the city was spreading beyond its square mile, branching out as far as Holborn and Charing Cross, to Old Street and Bishopsgate and Aldgate, and creeping along the riverbank into the open country beyond. And in all ways London thrived.

If you sought luxury then the goldsmiths and silversmiths were famed as far as Venice. Established companies of Vintners, Grocers, Mercers, Skinners, Haberdashers, Fishmongers, Cloth-makers and Merchant Tailors made sure that all bodily needs were supplied – and the supplies of a required standard. There was a granary in Leadenhall, woollen cloths in Bakewell Hall, and a Stocks Market in the city centre. And the parish of St. Martin-le-grand was busy with shoe-makers and pouch-makers.

If you were sick or aged or beggarly the ancient hospitals of St Thomas in Southwark, or St Bartholomew in West Smithfield, or St Mary Spital beyond Bishopsgate, or St Thomas of Cheapside, or St. Katharine by Thames-side, or St Anthony in Threadneedle Street would take you in.

White Friars, Blackfriars, Greyfriars, Austin friars, nuns of the Order of St Clare and St Benedictine would pray for your soul. And, lest you thought too little upon the last end, frescoes of the Dance of Death adorned the cloisters of St Paul's.

The mayor and aldermen of London had long since charged and commanded every freeman of the city, who had a house in the open streets, to hang out a lantern from his door or window at the hour of seven of the bell at night. (The candle therein to be made of a certain weight, that it might burn and consume the night away.) Also, they strictly charged and commanded that for the honesty of their city, no manner of person should lay or suffer to be laid any dung, rubbish or other noisome thing in the open streets and lanes – upon a fine of fourpence. Scold's bridles, ducking stools, stocks, blocks and gallows took care of other offenders; and above all of them loomed the Tower. No leper had been allowed within the gates for fully fifteen years. And still London stank and was riddled with diseases, and badly lit, and acquainted with all evils of mind and body.

But the heads of the merchants were abuzz with future profit, for a monarch and his retinue must be royally clad, and there was a coronation and a wedding to come. Crimson and purple cloth of gold at eight pounds a yard for the king, and white cloth of gold at thirty three shillings and fourpence for his henchmen. The purple velvet lining for the royal robe would be forty shillings, and from Oxford's crimson velvet at thirty shillings and his crimson satin at sixteen shillings to the robes of the king confessor (humble in russet cloth for thirteen shillings and fourpence) they worked the prices out. And then, God save us, there were trimmings of ermine and miniver; a river of sarcenet and woollen cloth; fringes and tassles of gold silk; ostrich feathers for caps. And ceremonial swords – each a marvel of crafts-manship, engraving, scrolling and embossing – and rich saddles and richer horse trappings. Velvet for red roses and red dragons. The orders flowed in, scratched upon parch-ment with quills, spelled in any way that happened to suit their fancy.

Henry rode into his capital on the third day of September, and the heat made odours rise that were best buried in a pomander. His bay horse picked its way delicately through the filthy streets and the stinking press of loyal crowds. Gar-bage rotted in heaps, courted by flies and blue-bottles, rooted by dogs and cats. Frogs squatted and croaked in cess pools. Rich and poor alike harboured three types of body louse, and nightly endured the torment of bed bugs. Each time the rushes were scraped from the floor, matted with spittle and relics of past suppers, someone caught a fever.

So Henry inhaled his pomander as often as good manners allowed, and was received into his splendid and malodorous city with thanksgiving. They had been expecting to greet King Richard in triumph, so the basis of the reception was already laid. Mayor and aldermen met him at Shoreditch clad in scarlet, with the dignity of an accompanying sword-bearer and sergeants, and all their servants dressed in tawny medley. Prominent citizens wore bright murrey, and four hundred and thirty-five persons escorted Henry to St Paul's where he would present his three standards. The blind poet Bernard André sang his Latin sapphics in honour of the occasion, a heartfelt *Te Deum* was chanted, and when all was over the king retired to his temporary lodgings in the bishop of London's house.

From Sheriff Hutton came Elizabeth of York, to be united with her mother and delivered into her care until the wedding. And with her travelled poor Edward Warwick, Clarence's son, to be taken to the Tower for the duration of his life. His sweet and vacant smile, his mild countenance and timid good manners commanded mercy. But his claim to the throne commanded vigilance, and though Henry's conscience troubled him he signed the order of imprisonment – bidding them look after him kindly and well.

And now, from having no property but his clothes and no friend but his uncle, Henry Tudor had been raised to a kingdom full of subjects, a host of noble companions, and three women who depended on his loving kindness.

He received his mother first, lifting her to her feet and kissing her with reverence. The years of his absence had changed her from a handsome woman to an ascetic one; glancing from her pale, strong-boned face to the crafty eyes of Lord Stanley he wondered again at that marriage.

Then in a mixture of graciousness and curiosity – with the curiosity well-masked – he received the queen dowager Elizabeth. She looked proudly all about her, as though she would live down her uncertain past in that moment. And to her, since it appeared she needed kindness most, he spoke with smiling consideration, promising reparation for her sufferings. She thanked him in a gentler tone than she had meant to, and presented her eldest daughter.

The movement through the crowd told him how much the marriage meant to England. Someone with a simple heart or a politic head had decreed Elizabeth of York wear no jewels but her gold cross, and be dressed in white as became a virgin. So unreal did she seem, an emblem of beauty and purity, that he kissed her cold fingers without a tremor. Then he noticed the pleasant anguish on Humphrey Brereton's face, the kindness of his mother's smile, Jasper's covert grin of admiration, and looked at her again.

One silver-gilt lock strayed over her shoulder as she curt-seyed, and the dowager queen leaned forward and stroked it into place, anxious that he should find no blemish in her daughter.

'This lady is the chiefest jewel in our crown,' said Henry warmly, 'and all our troubles but a little matter that led us to her.'

The girl murmured her obedience and glanced in shy recognition at the rich ring on his finger.

'We bear this token of our love, madam, as proudly as ever knight bore his lady's favour,' said Henry, and the murmur of those round him was appreciative.

The courtly phrases brought both smile and colour to Elizabeth's face. She retreated on another curtsey, to join her mother.

'You spoke the lady very fair, sire,' Jasper observed, as everyone departed.

'It was no hardship, uncle.'

'Why, so I thought. I have no love for Yorkists,' as though this were a revelation to them both, 'and yet that lady may command my services, if she be so minded. Why do you smile, sire?'

'That a brave Lancastrian, after thirty grievous years of strife, should proffer his sword to York without a protest.'

Kingship was a chest of treasure and of toys in one. Henry delved into it, fascinated, and the harder he worked the more he found to do. By his side, studious, abstemious, devoted, the Lady Margaret employed herself in the over-seeing of his establishments. There was a palace at Westminster, at Greenwich and at Sheen, and a castle at Windsor to be ordered. Stables of horses, leashes of greyhounds, flights of falcons. The repairs of barges and payments of bargemen, who ferried the royal party to and fro upon the Thomas. There were chairs and litters and chariots and their rich furnishings. There was every household article, from a cauldron to a carpet, and every article of wardrobe to be checked. Physicians, surgeons, apothecaries, minstrels, priests, fools, ladies and gentlemen in waiting, cooks and scullions, servitors and retainers must be paid. There were offerings to be made, annuities to be awarded, gifts to be bestowed. From the royal cellars full of fine wines, to the royal roofs that should be mended, he and she sifted every item.

Shoes for the footmen at sixpence the pair, wages for

workmen at sixpence a day, two shillings a month for the board wages of a jester, sixpence for the messenger who carried letters between London and Greenwich, beer for the staff at two shillings and eight pence the barrel. They laboured happily, immersed in their various tasks, and Lady Margaret noted that when he was tired or in need of privacy he came to her chamber and sat and watched her sew.

She looked at him with some indulgence that evening and bent to her needlework as she spoke, so that she might not seem to advise him but to converse naturally.

'We women have more power for good than you would grant us, sire, and it is as needful for the greatest prince in Christendom to have a loving wife as for the lowliest of all his subjects. Men speak and women listen. Men rule and women serve. Men make war and women make children. That is our rightful function. And in return for their lives and loves they ask for nothing but a man's protection, and a little kindness.'

'Well, madam, have we been unkind to any lady?'

'I think you are unkind to one – and that is not your mother who is grateful to you – but one that is like I was once. Aye, very like, except that life sharpened my eyes and wits, and sorrow moulded me.'

'We have been most attentive to the Lady Elizabeth,' said Henry guiltily. 'She is much at court and joins our revels. Last night she won a sum of money from me at cards.'

Lady Margaret selected a fresh thread of colour.

'You have played the skilful courtier right well, your grace, but nothing more. The affairs of state are cold, my lord. You must have tenderness to solace you. And though no king may wed where he chooses, yet you should show the lady more than courtesy. Fine phrases spoken in public, my lord, sound empty if there be neither friendship nor understanding behind them.'

'Do you lecture us, madam?'

'I should not dare, sire,' she said, mocking him gently, 'but I have ever said what I think is right, and shall do now – by your leave. I would see the lady content, and you content with her. A monarch stands as one upon a tower, who looks at what is passing in the plain. But he is a man, after all, and should be able to shut his chamber door and sweeten his eminence with love.'

She had damaged his vanity.

'I was ever a good and loving friend to all my husbands,'

251

Lady Margaret continued, as he remained in hurt silence. 'The Lady Elizabeth will be so to you, and you shall draw more comfort from a wife than from a mother.'

Henry remembered Lord Herbert striding into his wife's solar, striving to say the right things about her embroidery, his blunt head wagging in admiration. He set vanity by the heels.

'What would you have us do, madam, since compliments and courtesy are not to your liking? The lady is fair, and we have said so. We are bound by oath to wed, and we shall wed her.'

'I think that I should speak to her, sire, as a man does to a woman, and privately. The evenings are warm and the gardens lovely still, and you may walk and talk together out of the noise of court.'

It was a minute or so before he replied, but the reply was gracious.

'We thank you for your counsel, madam, which is both wise and good.'

She caught his hand and kissed it.

'What manner of man was my father?' Henry asked.

She paused, looking a long way back.

'I knew him such a little while,' she answered slowly, 'that I remember but two things about him. He had a voice such as your own, and yellow hair.'

'So passes memory with time, and makes poor shadows of us all.'

She flushed slightly.

'One matter troubles me, my son, and I would speak of it. You are my earthly joy. I have none other. What I do for you I do with a glad heart. That set aside, I desire only to prepare myself for God.'

He was ahead of her, knowing she spoke of Lord Stanley.

'I am no longer young, my lord. I can bear no more children, and my good husband has sons to his name. For my soul's health – although I would not hurt him – I would we separated, that I might end my days in prayer. How does this seem to you?'

Unspoken, the thought of Stanley lay between them: found wanting in all but the ability to survive.

'It seems both meet and right, madam. Would you that we spoke with him?'

She inclined her head.

'The Lord Stanley is a noble gentleman,' said Henry

252

firmly, 'and will see that this is good. We have rewarded and exalted him, and shall do. He shall serve us faithfully with no repining.'

He rose and stretched, turning to the window, looking out on his realm.

'As for that other matter that we spoke of, we shall befriend the Lady Elizabeth. For we have learned much of you – and of women through you. By the Cross, madam, we are right glad we are a man.'

CHAPTER TWENTY-THREE

Long I've loved a tall young maid
But never have we trysted.
And when I, who've known distress,
Was hoping for her gladness,
She that I courted, whispered
To me, to cut short my word –
'I'll not love a wandering man's
Ungentle lack of substance!'

Building for Love
Anonymous, fifteenth century

Well, this should not be hard upon me, Henry reflected, as they strolled in the September evening. The long hand he clasped lightly felt cold, but the girl was shy and needed only his encouragement. Their attendants were a good distance behind, and any guard had withdrawn himself from their notice, so they were as much alone as they would be until they married.

'Our delight in your company is so great,' he began, 'that we would be alone with you awhile, lady. For the court and state eats up our time more than we wish, and we would know you better.'

'Your grace is pleased to say so, and I am glad of it.'

Her reply, though sweet, was as cold as her hand. He tried again.

'And though the night is beautiful, yet when we look upon your face we see a greater beauty – and rejoice in it. You are fair, madam,' he added sincerely, and a little interest stirred him.

'On such a night as this, long since,' she said with difficulty, 'the king, my father, entertained the Lord of Gruthuyse – the Duke of Burgundy's ambassador. And they walked in the gardens and in the vineyard of pleasure, and after we had supped we danced and played games . . .'

She stopped, and begged his pardon for her chatter.

'But this was long ago,' she said, subdued, 'and of no interest to your grace.'

'All that has pleased you pleases us, madam,' he replied

gently, for there was a sadness about her that moved him: a suggestion that once she had been happy and the happiness had gone. 'How old were you, lady, when you delighted in these things? Did you play ninepins? Did you dance yourself?'

'My father danced with me, my lord, and made me merry. And the Duke of Buckingham danced with me also, and I wore a bright blue gown. I was but six years old.' His attentiveness warmed her. 'We played with closheys of ivory, and my mother played at morteaulx – and she could bowl the ball finely. And the ambassador, that was a handsome gentleman, had three chambers of pleasance allotted him – all hung with white silk. There were comfits and syrups . . .'

Her tale was finished. Uneasily, she smiled at him and looked away again.

'Now will this be our great good fortune to set aright. For we shall keep a splendid court together, lady. When shall you marry us?'

'When your grace pleases,' she replied, almost inaudibly.

'And does that please you, madam?'

'I am your grace's humble servant.'

A rare gust of temper took him, who was always calm and deliberate.

'What empty phrase is this?' he cried, adopting his mother's words unconsciously. 'Come, madam, we are king and queen in truth, but shall that stand between us? May we not be man and woman – aye, and husband and wife – also? We have sought to know you, that this marriage may be more than a convenience of state. And you answer us with *yeas* and *nays* and speak of humble servants, when we would have a loving helpmeet by us. Do not talk of duty,' he cautioned, as she opened her mouth submissively, 'we have enough of duties at court. We ask you for your friendship, madam, if we have not your love. Why, am I crooked? Does my face displease you?' He had lapsed into the first person in his disturbance, and her expression changed. 'I am a man, as other men. And I tell you, madam, that other ladies have found me comely enough!'

She was scarlet with fear and embarrassment.

'And now you weep, like any woman that has not her own way. Well, that is better than nothing. I thought I had a very tapestry beside me, that could not change its countenance. Speak up! Do I displease you? You wrote a loving letter to me once, and sent a ring. But now I see you did as you were bidden – and I am sick of courtesy.'

She put both hands before her face and sobbed for wretchedness.

'We shall be answered,' Henry said inexorably. 'Was your letter nothing but good policy, madam?'

'God help and save me, sire, I wrote it all myself. But that was to a prince I did not know, and he seemed fine and fair – a silver knight to rescue a sad lady. And then you won the field and came to London, and you are real, your grace – and I know not how to speak with you. For how can dreams live and walk? I beg your grace's understanding.'

'Come, stand with me beneath this tree. They must not see you weep, Elizabeth. England has had sorrow enough and expects us to be merry. So I was a dream once?' he added, and smiled to himself. 'Here, lady, dry your eyes for you will spoil them. Now tell me more of this.'

'There were some at court that laughed behind their hands when the Dauphin did not marry me. And then King Richard smiled upon me, and they whispered slander. Oh, my lord, you would have pitied me then. Miserable creature that I was, and passed from king to king as it pleased them. I said I would rather endure the torments that St Catherine bore for love of Christ, than be joined to a man that was the enemy of my family. But though I spoke bravely it brooked me not, for if he had so desired he would have married me. Princesses do as they are bidden, sire. They are not asked.'

'Then Henry Tudor asks you, humbly, will you wed him?'

She dried her face and fingers, beginning to find her way in this new set of circumstances.

'Would your grace give me leave to understand him better?' she said timidly. 'I know that they would have us wed tomorrow if they could, but will you wait a little? And talk with me, as you have done this evening?'

'Most gladly, lady. Will three months suffice you? I doubt that I can hold them off much longer. For my parliament are as anxious for the wedding as though they wedded you themselves – I blame them not for that!' he added lightly.

She moved a little closer in the shadow of the tree, and he let her stand by him, not even offering to take her hand lest he frighten her off again.

'What will you say to them, my lord?'

'Now let me think,' said Henry, enjoying himself in a new game of subtlety. 'I shall say that I desire to make my own position safe. Aye, that is very sound. They will believe me. I shall say that I won the crown in battle, and not by right of your inheritance – which is something purer than my own, madam. And Morton will smile and smooth his hands, and my gallant gentlemen will call me a churl for keeping a lady waiting, and England will name me a laggard lover. But you shall have your three months, Elizabeth.'

She sensed his strength and began to lean upon it.

'How will you bear this, my lord?'

'Oh, very well,' said Henry cheerfully. 'We know the truth, so what matters? If they say nothing harder I shall have a joyful reign.'

She smiled for the first time in his company, and ventured a confidence.

'I like you truly, my lord.'

'Then that is a good beginning,' and he bowed over her hand. 'Come, lady, let us lighten the court with our presence. And I shall be your friend, but you have one that is as true as any could be.'

'And who is that, my lord?'

'My mother, Lady Margaret.'

They paced through the gardens, their attendants walking respectfully behind them, and the hand that Henry held in his was warm and confident.

CHAPTER TWENTY-FOUR

*... be it ordained ... that the inheritance of the crown
of the realm of England and France ... be rest and
remain and abide in the most royal person of our new
Sovereign-Lord, King Henry the VIIth, and in the
heirs of his body lawfully comen perpetually ... and
in noon other.*

Rotuli Parliamentorum, 1485

Behind the scenes of rejoicing, the savouring of coming
pomp and a new reign and a new peace, Henry set quietly
and forcefully to work with his Council. As he looked round
the long table that morning he felt he had chosen well.

Here was Bishop Morton in the flesh, who had so long
been an intelligence upon paper : haughty and astute. Stanley the cautious, wholly won to his service since there was
nowhere else to go, and welcome for his cunning; and his
brother William and his son Lord Strange, both dedicated,
both useful. Richard Fox, who had joined him in Paris, son
of a Lincolnshire yeoman : as watchful and shrewd as Henry
himself. Busy Sir Robert Willoughby, who was driving hard
bargains with the merchants for coronation purchases. Giles
Daubeney, who had served both Edward IV and Richard
III, and thrown in his lot with Lancaster when the princes
were murdered. Oxford, frank of tongue and staunch of
service. John Alcock, who had been tutor to the young king,
Edward V. Jasper of the ready sword. Reginald Bray, trusted
with so much and failing in nothing. Sir Edward Pynings,
Lord Dynham, Edgecombe, Guildford and others. All men
whose virtues lay in their minds rather than their escut-
cheons. For Henry did not intend to be ruled by barons, but
to be served by able politicians.

So his smile rose from satisfaction as well as amiability as
he welcomed them, and set about the business of the coronation. And while he read the details they waited in respectful
silence.

'My lords,' said Henry briskly, setting down the papers,
'we purpose, as we have promised, to wed the Princess Elizabeth of York, and that is understood. Moreover, this mar-

riage is our delight as well as our bounden duty.'

They liked this very well.

'But we see that our excellent advisers have assumed that the princess will be crowned at the same time as ourself, which purposes a speedy marriage, and neither our marriage nor her coronation is our wish at the moment.'

A little silence followed, though Morton smiled to himself and admired the sacred ring upon his hand, unsurprised.

'This is no dishonour or discourtesy to the lady, who is as meet to be queen as she is noble and beautiful. We are king by right of conquest rather than dynastic claim. For though our line is royal many have said we are of bastard blood. And truly,' he added, with gentle humour, 'our ancestors indulged their fancies rather than their families or the state. But the Princess Elizabeth has no such shadow sinister upon her escutcheon, being daughter of a rightful king and lawfully descended on both sides. If we are not seen to rule by virtue of our own strength then shall people say, "This is no king, but the queen's husband".'

The silence was broken by Morton, whose blackened teeth were in full display.

'You speak with the wisdom of the prophets, sire, and with much humility. For no man here would doubt your royal blood. And yet, as you say, people clack among themselves. So you would be crowned first, and alone, sire – is that your wish?'

'Aye, for we must look facts in the face, as the Holy Bible says. We are king in fact. Let us be crowned in fact, and govern in fact. That goodly man King Henry had the crown by right – was that enough for him and England?'

'One little matter, sire,' said Morton, as one by one they nodded their agreement. 'I should not wait too long to marry the Lady Elizabeth, or it may seem you are unwilling. Then would you lose half England, and we be back where we began.'

'You have our solemn promise, my lord bishop. I say more. It is our wish to wed the lady. But we are king first and husband after, for we rule through no woman nor are governed by any.'

'Do the plans please you, otherwise, sire?' asked Robert Willoughby, after a pause.

'They please us very well, good Willoughby. Let the writs be issued on the fifteenth of this month, to summon the lords spiritual and temporal, and those high in our commons, to our crowning. And good Sir Robert, though the people must see us in our splendour, avoid all damnable pomp and outrageous superfluities. We shall be looking to your accounts.'

Willoughby bowed, reading this command rightly as the best possible goods for the least possible expenditure.

'And speaking of accounts,' said Henry, taking up another sheaf of papers, 'we see our royal treasury is much depleted. Duke Richard bought his friends to no good purpose and at a high cost to our realm. We shall be watching both private and public moneys. Let no paper pass you by that has not our initials on it. We propose to sever our household revenues from those of the state, and set a limit on them, so that our people shall see we take their welfare to our heart.'

'The traitors who fought for York,' Morton observed, putting his fingers judiciously in an arch, 'should be attaindered, sire. There is some goodly revenue in their lands and possessions.'

'And if, by an Act of Resumption, you restored to yourself all the lands appertaining to the late King Henry, sire,' said Fox quietly, 'you would find much property your own that is not so now.'

'We thank you, and we shall note these things. What shall our good merchants lend us for our coronation?'

'Ten thousand pounds, sire?' Robert Willoughby suggested.

'We shall entreat them for this sum. And we must ransom the Marquis Dorset and Lord Feneway from France, which will cost us two thousand more. Shall they be pleased to lend this also?'

'They should be pleased to invest in their own futures, sire!' Oxford said bluntly. 'We risked our lives that they might trade in peace, not long since.'

Henry, signing state papers, smiled at his tone.

'And now, my lords,' he said briskly, 'we have dealt with our title and our finance. Our coronation shall be on 30 October, and we shall call Parliament eight days after that. Let us deal with kindlier matters. Our mother, the Lady Margaret, whose lands were attaindered by Duke Richard, should have some part of our private and public revenue.'

They inclined their heads.

'And that other lady, the queen dowager – stripped of her estates, her honour and virtue slandered, her children bastardized, her kinsmen slain – shall be restored to her rightful dignity.'

A little rustle round the table indicated that they were unsure, but too good-mannered to speak of it.

'We shall welcome the lady at our court for state occasions,' Henry continued, answering their uncertainty, 'and grant her various lordships for life. The income from these may be spent at her pleasure, but on her death both lands and income shall revert to the crown.'

Smiles of varying degrees showed Henry that they were with him, as he bestowed dignity and money, but not power, upon a woman who might misuse such a commodity.

'But why do we speak of death?' said Henry idly, busy with his papers. 'The lady is not old and should enjoy a long and godly life – perhaps re-marriage.'

'With whom should the queen marry, sire?' Oxford asked, lost in these hints and subtleties,

'We had not thought,' Henry replied, looking up, 'but now you question us we think of Scotland. King James wants a wife. We might approach him in good time, my lords. We must have peace with Scotland. We cannot spend time and money in these border squabbles. And King James has two sons, and the late King Edward has daughters. We shall see, my lords.'

Morton pursed his lips and narrowed his eyes, seeing the moves ahead.

'We shall not keep you much longer, my lords,' said Henry, 'but we propose to honour each of our Council, and others who have proved our friends, upon the eve of our coronation.'

Jasper, Duke of Bedford. Oxford, High Admiral of England and Constable of the Tower. Sir William Stanley, Lord Chamberlain. Stanley, Earl of Derby and master forester of all game north of the Trent. Morton, Chancellor of England. Earldoms and knighthoods for the rest.

A little flush of pleasure and gratitude warmed the Council Chamber.

'And last of all,' said Henry easily, 'we shall have a bodyguard about us, as in the court of France. Some fifty soldiers – though there may be more if we think fit. And we shall name them the Yeomen of the Guard. Ah, there is one more matter, and a weighty one. We shall repeal the Act of Titulus Regius – that false and slanderous document of Duke Richard's making – by which King Edward's children were

261

bastardized. The Act shall be removed from the Rolls and burned. And any man that has a copy of it must deliver it up to the Chancellor before the coming of next Easter. And if he do not, then shall be subject to fines and imprisonments at our pleasure.'

He had spoken sternly and colourlessly, springing it upon them even as they congratulated themselves on their coming honours, and they agreed hastily. A sly humour lightened his next words.

'We have been thinking, my lords,' he said amiably, 'what a damnable want of mercy it shows to kill or maim a rich man, or throw him into a dark dungeon – except his fault be treasonable.'

He looked round his Council to find those who could think with him.

Morton smiled first.

'So have I often felt, sire,' he observed. 'For what does it profit him or the realm? But if he pay for his fault with his purse, rather than with his body, then would the people commend your gracious mercy.'

'A fine, sire, is more merciful,' said Fox demurely.

'We thank you for your good advice,' Henry replied, serene. 'You have our leave to go.'

Bemused, admiring, they bowed and left him, one by one. Only Jasper lingered, reaching for a wistful moment at the intimacy they had known.

'I said you would make a dark prince, sire,' he whispered, 'and so you do.'

In the bustle of preparation for Henry's crowning the sweating sickness struck London, and its citizens fell in the streets even as they talked; or burned with fever in the morning and were cold by night. Thomas Hill, the mayor who had greeted Henry at Shoreditch, was one of the first to die. Before another mayor could be elected four aldermen died. The assembly chose Sir William Stocker, John's brother, as mayor – and he lived no more than seven days after. But on 8 October, at the Guildhall, John Wade took his place, and survived.

The sickness raged from the third week in September to the end of October, in stinking sweats and high fevers, in agonized heads and tortured bowels. In the beginning it killed outright. But then it was observed that if a man took to his bed straightway – with not so much as a hand outside the covers – and kept warm, and drank temperate cordials, he would live. For once, the poor suffered less than the rich, though no one knew why. Nor did they know why it abated as suddenly as it had come. But every man took it as an omen, and said that the king would rule only with the sweat of his brow, and that his reign would be troublesome.

At one minute after noon, on the eve of the coronation, the Mayor of London, aldermen, heralds of arms, sergeants at arms, trumpeters and minstrels and officers, assembled at the Tower. And from there they escorted the king to be, through Cheapside and Fleet Street and down into the Great Hall in the Palace of Westminster.

He rode bare-headed beneath his canopy of gold baudekin, the web of which was gold and the woof silk and all gloriously embroidered : resplendent in purple and ermine with the collar of Lancaster upon his breast, and his horse rich in trappings. At certain places along the route the four knights who bore the canopy changed with four others, so that many noblemen might be honoured. London flocked to cheer him as the cavalcade jingled through the dirty streets : shouting themselves dry for Henry, and hoarse for Elizabeth in her open litter : and then dispersed reluctantly, to soothe their throats.

On the Sunday morning, Sir Giles Daubeney, Chamberlain for the day, brought his royal burden of robes into Henry's chamber, and began the leisurely dressing of a monarch in crimson and gold. Even the splendour of the eve was outmatched as Daubeney tied gilt and silver tags, laced the stockings with satin bands, and settled the surcoat of miniver and the mantle of crimson that was garnished with gold ribbon, and smoothed the hood of estate bordered in ermine.

'You look but palely, sire,' he observed, and signalled a page to bring mulled wine. 'The day is cold and fine, sire.'

'And so are we,' said Henry ruefully, mocking his own discomfiture. 'For this is very well, sir, but we are not. We would sooner fight Bosworth over again. And today, good Daubeney, we remember King Henry VI that once told us to fear nothing and care for nothing but God. We shall build a tomb for that gentle prince, and ask the Pope to have him canonized. For if ever sad saint was made unhappy monarch that saint was Henry Lancaster. We shall not be as good a man, sir.'

'But a better king, sire – craving your pardon.'

The populace had to content themselves with the scenes outside the Abbey, and the sounds that came from within it. They pushed and pressed and shivered in the autumn air, and held their ragged children aloft and jostled their neighbours unmercifully.

From Westminster Hall to the Abbey the ground had been laid with striped cloth by the almoner. And now came the aged Bourchier, who had crowned two kings and lived through six reigns. A little behind him walked Rotherham of York and John Esteney, Abbot of Westminster, bearing the gold chalice. Then Henry, bare of head and feet, supported by the Bishop of Exeter and Bishop Morton of Ely. Then Jasper, Duke of Bedford, carrying the crown of England; Suffolk with the dove-headed sceptre and Arundel with the rod of gold; Stanley holding the sword of state in its scabbard; the Earls of Shrewsbury, Devonshire and Nottingham with naked swords; Essex with the king's gold spurs; and the newly created Knights of Bath in livery.

Henry acted as he had on Bosworth Field, losing himself in his state, as the orison *Omnipotens Sempiterne Deus* rose into the vaulted roof; and heard the congregation cry, 'Yea, yea, yea. So be it. King Henry! King Henry!' as he was presented to them.

With the cold jewelled hands that were his and yet not his, he presented the king's offerings : the pall, the pound of gold, the coins of the realm. He prostrated that body on the carpeted and cushioned pavement before the high altar as they sang *Deus Humilium*. His voice took the oaths upon the sacrament. And then Bourchier loosed the splendid clothes and anointed head and breast and back and shoulders and elbows with holy oil, in the form of a cross. *Ungantur caput . . . ungantur scapule. . . .* He dried the king with a linen cloth and drew on the linen gloves and the tabard and coif, and blessed the sword, and blessed the stole that was woven in gold and set with precious stones. *Accipe gladium, accipe armillam . . .*

St Edward's crown, first raised towards heaven, was lowered on his head. The ruby ring blessed and threaded onto the fourth finger of his right hand. *Accipe regie dignitatis. . . .* And chanting and solemn mass, and the toothless mouth of old Bourchier set in aged resolution. The royal gloves over the linen ones – stiff with embroidery – and the sceptre in one hand and the rod of gold in the other, sandals and spurs. Weight upon crushing weight over the crimson velvet and satin, over the miniver and ermine, his lawn shirt sweat-soaked already; and crawling from his forehead little beads of moisture which the archbishop wiped away.

One by one they paid homage and swore fealty, kneeling before an image that might have been marble or stone but for the grey eyes in the pale face. Then the crowned king kissed the book of the Gospel, and took the sacred wafer in his mouth and drank from the chalice of holy wine. And the chanting merged from solemnity and rose to jubilation as they led him out. He moved languidly in the heaviness and heat of his robes, and the bishops supported him and matched their pace to his own.

They spoke little, and only of what immediately concerned them, as they divested and re-arrayed him for the populace. The ritual had hushed their tongues and channelled their emotions, so that they laid aside even the wet lawn shirt with reverence; and dried his body and dressed him in purple and miniver, and gave him to his people.

The usual ritual of a royal banquet was superimposed by the greater ritual of the coronation. While everyone recovered from the glut and glory of the first course the king's champion rode into the hall, and cried that whoever said King Henry was not their rightful king should fight him at utterance.

'King Henry! King Henry!' they shouted obediently, joyfully.

So the knight rode into three parts of the hall, demanding the king's allegiance, and was rewarded each time by a great shout. Then he commanded a gold cup of wine to be brought; and drank, and flung the dregs to the floor, and departed with the cup.

Now the royal heralds called thrice for their allegiance, and they answered them likewise.

'King Henry! King Henry!'

Until the night darkened and the torches were lit, and the long day was done.

The Parliament that met on 7 November found the king in full command of himself and them. Just once did his sense of mischief break through, and that was privately, so only Jasper enjoyed the comment. For the Chancellor, John Alcock, bishop of Worcester, preached the opening sermon which was long and eulogistic. He likened Henry to Agrippa who had put down sedition in Rome, and spoke of the mutual duties of king and subjects, who between them provided the wax and honey of the realm's hive. He said that the ages of silver, bronze and iron were past, and now the golden age was come.

'God has sent us a second Joshua!' he cried.

'We pray you, uncle,' said Henry, speaking softly and keeping his face attentively towards his Parliament, 'what thought you of that sermon?'

Jasper replied with twinkling solemnity, 'No fault in it, sire – except he praised your grace too much!'

Henry's smile broadened, 'Truly, we were of that opinion ourself, my lord!'

CHAPTER TWENTY-FIVE

Thus let one blood be made of two,
and hereafter let one house seek the rule.

> *Pietro Carmeliano of Brescia*
> *at the court of King Henry VII*

So for the third time in four months the citizens of London prepared to celebrate a royal spectacle, and this time it was Elizabeth's day. Though snow lay on the ground they turned out in their thousands to greet her. Fires burned in the streets to roast sheep and oxen for the poorer populace, and hogsheads of wine and barrels of beer were set in divers places for their enjoyment.

A winter bride, she came in white cloth of gold, and a white mantle fastened across the breast in a rich knot of silk. Smooth and fair her hair hung down her back, imprisoned by a glittering net.

All the pomp and power of London bowed before her, from Oxford to the last herald. All the pomp and power of the house of York was paraded in her servants' liveries of murrey and blue, and her own white rose embroidered on the horses' trappings. The people exchanged remarks on her beauty, shouted rough compliments, and called that they loved her and wished her well. One vast fellow in a sheepskin jacket held his urchin high above his head, crying, 'I have six such sons, my lady. May you have twice as many.' So that she laughed and bowed her gleaming head in token of his goodwill, and he grinned round on his neighbours, delighted by her courtesy.

The first half of the service was in English, and as leisurely as the second which was in Latin. Two symbols of two houses, they made their responses; kneeling in prayer, taking the sacrament, leading by way of Psalm 68 and the Kyrie and the Lord's Prayer, through a series of six collects and blessings, and into the nuptial mass. Henry crowned her thumb and first and second fingers lightly with the ring, and slipped it into place on the third. They were cold and stiff, even in the warmth of their robes, by the end, as Henry raised his bride to her feet and kissed her formally on both cheeks.

Then bells clamoured from steeple to steeple, surging and retreating like the sea. Guns exclaimed upon the air, marking the cacophony in measured booms, so that the citizens — between the sight of the royal pair, and the noise of celebration, and the promise of free meat and drink to come — threatened to suffocate themselves with excitement.

The tailors could now rest content, but the cooks reached a meridian. The kitchen fires had not been let out for a week, and the scullions had run to and fro in a frenzy of mincing, chopping, plucking, turning, stirring, skimming and carrying. A mountain of white napery had been drawn, couched and spread upon the tables; gold and silver salt cellars set; cups, spoons and fair carving knives placed. Tapestries covered the rough white bands of mortar in the hall, candelabra hung ready to be lit. Twelve torch bearers stood behind the royal table, to hold the winter evening at bay.

Grace was said, the royal hands washed and dried, the covers removed from the bread, and the domestic campaign was underway with the first subtlety. Fashioned from sugar in a marvel of skill and artistry, it was put on the high table to be admired, before the guests broke off a turret here or a flag there and popped the fragment into their mouths. The dishes followed in indigestible magnificence : brawn, venison, hart, pheasant, swan, capon, lampreys, crane, pike, heron, carp, kid, perch, mutton, custards, tarts and fruit. Another subtlety, with the writing of ballads on its base, ended the first course; another brought in the second course when they had finished washing, and the tables were re-laid.

Sturdily the company worked through peacock, partridge, plovers, sturgeon, rabbit, lark, quail, baked quinces, marchpane royal, cold baked meats, cakes and dried fruits and gingerbread, and little temples of jelly. They washed down the orgy with draughts of wine, crumbling their bread, eating more slowly as the hours passed : unwilling to leave a single dish untasted.

But at the high table Henry and Elizabeth ate sparingly, nibbling hot moist almonds before their meat to prevent the fumes of the wine from fuddling their heads. Fifty dishes were prepared and served for the marriage feast at Whitehall, a multitude of stomachs wildly disordered, and the cooks complimented on a meet and fitting banquet.

It had been a day of ceremony, and one last ceremony was to come. In the royal bedchamber the groom porter entered; bringing wood for the fire and tall wax candles for the table. A second groom carried a tray of syrups, green ginger and junkets. A third bore wines: Tyre, Hippocras and Muscadel. Yet another set out wooden bowls of soft Bristol toilet soap, scented with herbs; silver basins and ewers and thick towels. A fifth rolled solemnly up and down the bedstead to make it even, and then took his place with three other grooms, one at each corner of the huge bed. Faces intent, they laid the canvas, beat the feather bed with abandon, slipped a blanket over it, tucked in the fine white sheet, pummelled the bolster and pillows: moving in silent unison. They smoothed the top sheet, stroked the wrinkles from the blankets, set the head-sheet of Rhennes cloth, and covered the whole with a counterpane of ermine and cloth of gold. Standing on stools they fixed the gold tester over the bed, hung curtains of white sarcenet about it, and then curtains of heavy arras. And stepped down in quiet satisfaction.

The gentleman usher inspected their arrangements, nipped up a thread of wool from the carpet, and indicated that they might withdraw.

Tired patient dolls, in their separate dressing-rooms, Elizabeth and Henry were divested of their robes by half a dozen attendants. Each garment, as it was removed, was brushed busily and put away or set aside for laundering. Automatically now, the bridal couple held out obedient arms and legs, and ducked obedient heads through the necks of their nightgowns. Their hair was combed with combs of ivory, embroidered mantles put ceremoniously upon their shoulders – that in another few minutes would be as ceremoniously removed.

Elizabeth's procession entered the royal bedchamber. A waiting woman turned back the covers and scattered rose petals over the sheets. Then Henry's procession, with rather less noise than was usual on such occasions – since he had forbidden even the mildest connubial jest – escorted him to bed. Side by side they sat against the high pillows, while the priest blessed them and wished them fruitful union of the flesh. The last head bowed, the last pair of legs paced discreetly backwards, the last strains of the minstrels faded, the door closed, and a numb silence descended.

Henry was the first to break it.

'Madam,' he said, 'we do not purpose to spend this night in discomfort. The roses are very well but not, I think, in our bed!'

She looked at him startled, and seeing he was in earnest she slipped out and helped him to roll back the covers. In amicable silence they brushed the fragrant dried scraps to the floor, and climbed back again.

'You have eaten little and drunk less today,' said Henry, reaching for the wine and comfits. 'Does it please you to join us?'

She was uncertain of her stomach, by reason of exhaustion and prolonged formality, and hesitated.

'Elizabeth,' said Henry kindly, 'I am king of England and you are my wife, and shall shortly be queen. We have done all that our people required of us for one day. The time is now our own, and you and we may do as we please. This chamber is our private place and we shall rest and take joy in it. The ginger will aid your digestion and the wine make you merry.'

'I will have Hippocras, my lord,' she said softly, 'and a piece of green ginger.'

'And call me not your lord or your grace, while we are together, I beg of you. I am but Henry now, or Harry if that pleases you better.'

'My father called me Bessie, even in company, my lord – Harry.'

She remembered that her father had been his enemy, and sipped her wine embarrassed. But he smiled and said the name was both pretty and plain in one.

'You wear my ring always,' she observed, heartened by the smile. 'I am rejoiced it pleases you. And I shall embroider a mantle for you, and garnish your helmet with jewels, and embroider a cushion for your chair.'

'And I shall give you all that you desire. A nightingale,' he said, remembering his daydreams in France, 'and a pair of clavichords, and a pomander box if you so wish.'

She clasped her hands round the gold cup, then a shadow passed over her mood.

'Harry, they tell me you will let no paper pass without you sign it. And that – unlike my father, though I loved him too – you spend no more than is needful. I do commend you for it,' she added hastily, 'but what if, through no fault of my own, I spend more than you allow my household?'

'Why then, Bessie, I must order you to the dungeon and

feed you upon bread and water, until you mend your ways.'

Her open mouth made him laugh. His laugh made her smile.

'But truly, my lord – Harry – what shall I do?'

He could see her, forehead puckered over accounts which would not balance, and kissed her hand affectionately.

'I should help you from my privy purse, Bessie, and so make all well.'

'I have been poor since my father died,' she explained. 'It is a fearful matter, Harry, to open a purse and find so little in it.'

'And I have been poor since I was a child,' he replied, 'and lived on charity – and that is fearful too. So, Bessie, let us be happy while we may in this splendid chamber, and forget ill fortune. We shall be king and queen, and man and wife, together. So ruling one great family and one lesser one.'

She remembered the rough fellow in his sheepskin jacket, and laughed aloud.

'There was a man in Cheapside today,' she said, 'that held a little urchin up and cried he had six sons, and wished me twice as many. And this I hope, my lord,' she added earnestly, 'to bear you many sons and so make safe your throne. For I am not wise in politics as is your lady mother. I cannot speak with you on the affairs of state as she does. So would I be your loving wife, and loving mother to our children, and pray God to give us long life and good health and a devout death.'

'God grant all these things,' he replied, touching her cup with his. Her guilelessness shamed him, who was devious and knew it. 'I think that I shall love you for the virtue that I lack,' he said humbly. 'And think not that I want a queen to advise me. Betwixt the two of us, Bessie, though I listen to my mother's counsel, I do as I think best. Only it were a sad lack of courtesy to tell her so – and once she gave me counsel better than I deserved.'

They were easy with each other now, on the comfort of the pillows, with the comfort of spiced wine in their stomachs, and the comfort of fire and candle-light, under the dull sheen of the tester.

'We have waited for each other, madam, and been kept waiting, long enough. I think we know ourselves a little better than we did. We'll warm cold policy with gentle hearts – and you shall be crowned queen, Bessie, as soon as England seems at rest.'

'Your will is mine, my lord, and ever shall be.'

He kissed the long fingers and soft cheeks, and stroked the silver fall of hair.

'If you would bear twelve princes, lady,' he said, smiling, 'we should wait no longer.'